Pilgrim's Inn

DATE DUE

GAYLORD · PRINTED IN U.S.A.

Servant Publications
Ann Arbor, Michigan

Originally published as *The Herb of Grace*.

This edition published in 1993 by Servant Publications
P.O. Box 8617
Ann Arbor, Michigan 48107

Cover design by Michael Andaloro
Cover illustration by Jeffrey Terreson

93 94 95 96 97 10 9 8 7 6 5 4 3 2 1

Printed in the United States of America
ISBN 0-89283-830-2

Library of Congress Cataloging-in-Publication Data

Goudge, Elizabeth, 1900–
  [Herb of Grace]
  Pilgrim's Inn / Elizabeth Goudge.
    335p. cm
  ISBN 0-89283-830-2
  1. Family—England—Fiction. I. Title.
PR6013.074H47 1993
823'.912—dc20   93-9191

There's rue for you: and here's some for me:
we may call it herb of grace o' Sundays:
O, you must wear your rue with a difference.

—Hamlet

CHAPTER

– 1 –

$\mathcal{C}$HE SUN, shining through the uncurtained east window, woke Sally to a new day. It spread a long cloak of gold over her body as it lay upon the bed, and the loving warmth reached through to the very soul of her, and she woke up smiling, stirred a little, rubbed her knuckles childishly in her eyes, then stretched out her long body beneath the cloak of gold and lay still again, happy and completely unafraid. She always woke up happy, because she had been born happy and didn't seem able to help it. And she was not afraid because nothing had yet happened to her to make her afraid, and in body, mind and spirit she was equally healthy and well-balanced and saw those things that hadn't yet happened in their true proportions. But the thrill of tranquil happiness with which she awoke was followed always by a slight sensation of guilt. Other people were not born happy. Other people were afraid. Her immunity seemed very wrong, and she was ashamed of it. "I'm sorry, I'm sorry," she whispered now, and she spoke to all those people who hadn't her transcendent luck. Her arms, lying stretched out beside her, moved a little. She would, if she could, have taken them all into her arms and rocked them as a mother her child. But it couldn't be done, and knowing it couldn't she suddenly abandoned herself to joy like a bird to the wind, leaped from bed, her tall body in its yellow pyjamas like a sword of gold in the sun, flashed into the adjoining bathroom, banged the door, stripped, sprang into the bath, turned on the shower and broke into loud, uproarious song.

7

Her father had gone away yesterday to spend a night at Winchester and then two nights at Bournemouth, visiting Important Personages who wanted their portraits painted, and she was alone in the flat for two days. She whole-heartedly loved her father, but he was quite extraordinarily untidy, and she enjoyed a few days on her own getting the flat straight, for she had an innate love of order that made its production from chaos one of the chief joys of her existence. The fact that everything would become immediately disordered again upon his return did not worry her. She took things as they came and knew that everything must be paid for: her father's presence by cigarette ash on the carpet, and order by possessing nothing of him but his old coat hanging behind the door. She would miss him today, but she would be gloriously tidy. And she liked being alone sometimes; one discovered things. And of course she wasn't really alone, for Mrs. Rutherford in the flat above kept an eye on her; as she was reminded by a faint remonstrance of tapping on the floor overhead. She remembered suddenly that Mrs. Rutherford's bedroom was just above and that she made a good deal of noise when she let herself go in the early mornings, switched her glorious contralto from "Gloria in Excelsis Deo" to a southern gospel song and turned off the shower. Back in her bedroom she remembered that Mr. Rutherford, this time, was just above, and suffered from headaches, and she tried to shut her drawers very quietly and not to fall over anything. For though she was orderly she was also a bit clumsy. She was twenty-one years old, but she had not yet outgrown the colt-like stage. Like all only children, she was in some ways too old for her age, and in other ways too young; she still fell over material things as though she were fifteen, but immaterial things, such as friendships, the griefs of little children, the desires of men and the jealousies of women, she handled with an instinctive sensitiveness that a woman of thirty-five could not have bettered.

There were those who thought Sally Adair beautiful and those who thought her the reverse. She was tall and straight, big-boned and muscular, and perhaps when she was forty she would have to take steps if she did not want to grow fat. But there was no danger of that yet. She played games hard whenever she got the chance and was at her happiest on a horse or rowing a boat, and there was not a scrap of laziness in her. With her big bones and her tendency to fall over things she could hardly be called graceful, but yet she had a sort of grace, born of her complete unself-consciousness and the perfect balance of her strong young body. She had a glorious mop of unruly red-brown curls, the white skin that goes with such hair, and golden eyes like a lion's that looked you straight in the face with a lion's courage. Her voice was deep and beautiful, and the Scotch Nannie who had looked after her through her childhood had imparted to it a Scotch lilt that increased its beauty. But she had no beauty of feature. Her face was too broad across the cheekbones, her mouth was too large; though mercifully the teeth within it were small and white and even. Her nose turned up and had freckles on it. Though her hands were big they were beautifully shaped, with long fingers, but to her shame she took sevens in shoes. Those who did not think her beautiful had a clear case, but those who thought otherwise had not only the hair and the eyes to back their opinion, for there was in Sally an indefinable quality that affected them as the hearing of a perfect piece of music affected them, or the sight of a perfect picture. It was not a quality that could be analysed, but her father came closest to it when he said that in Sally there was no distortion. Neither heredity, environment, accident nor disease had played any tricks with her. She came nearer to being what she had been meant to be than anyone he had known.

Sally's mother had died at her birth, but that had not been the tragedy it might have been, for the fatherhood of John Adair was the best thing in him—as fine a thing as the deep, innate maternity of Sally herself—and any tendency to indulgence in him had been counteracted by the stern discipline of Janet Gillespie, the Scotch Nannie who had stayed with Sally until she had been packed off to boarding-school at the age of fourteen. At eighteen Sally had left school and, turning her back upon all tempting offers of privileged war-work, had unhesitatingly gone on the land, where she had worked cheerfully and uncomplainingly at all sorts of back-breaking tasks until her extraordinary gift for handling living creatures had been discovered and she had become a shepherdess in the Cumberland hills. Sally at the lambing season had been Sally in her element. Motherless lambs brought up on the bottle by her had not known that they were motherless.

Sally, demobbed, had been offered by her father Somerville, the Slade, the R.A.D.A.—anything she liked to mention—but insisting that she had no more intellect than one of her own sheep, she had installed herself in his flat as companion-housekeeper, to the infinite delight and contentment of the two of them. For Sally maligned herself when she said that she had no intellect. It was true that at school she had never passed any examination by anything except the skin of her teeth, but when it came to the business of living she was a clever woman. She liked everyone she met, she enjoyed everything she did, so intensely that her relationship and her activities were touched with that spark of light that men call genius. She was not an artist in the accepted sense of the word, but when she cooked a meal or tidied a room she was yet unmistakably her father's daughter. A room arranged by Sally, a meal she had cooked, were as unforgettable as her father's pictures. Imaginative, deft touches here and there were like the glimmer of light on water that without it would have been opaque and dull.

An upbringing by a father who had been middle-aged when she was born, and by a stern Presbyterian Scotswoman, a sojourn at school for four years only and then a complete concentration upon lambs, had made of Sally a curiously individual person, neither of her father's generation nor her own, and so in some ways a little lonely. She did not speak the idiom of her own contemporaries, or share their disillusionments. She had worked hard in the war, but she had not suffered other than vicariously. In the presence of young men who had faced death day after day, night after night, for years, and of girls who had worked in the war hospitals and known the meaning of human agony, she was ashamed. The men sensed her shame and loved her for it; and they loved, too, the ignorance of which she was ashamed; it rested them. But the girls misjudged her humility, her unself-consciousness, her rather devastating truthfulness; it was a pose, they thought. And so her closest friends in her own generation were men rather than girls.... And for this, again, the girls disliked her.... But none of the men were very close friends, for her shame made her inwardly withdraw herself a little.

In appearance, as well as in speech and manner, Sally was individual. A dusting of powder over her distressing freckles was her only concession to make-up, her father having impressed upon her very forcibly that a mouth the size of hers did not require the emphasis of lipstick. She gave her copper curls a hard brushing every day, and washed them every week, but that was all she did about them. Most of her clothes she made herself, and though she was enough her father's daughter to make her sense of colour and line unerring, their simplicity was child-like. She seldom wore jewels, and when she did they were mother's old-fashioned ones, that lived in the old cedarwood box in her bottom drawer. Her fastidiousness was such that it had in itself almost the quality of a dual garment; body and spirit she clothed herself in it. Yet there was nothing aloof about it. She did not mind what dirty work she did if the result was likely to be a patch of cleanliness.

– 2 –

Dressed in a clean, green overall, with her hair brushed to flame, and singing snatches of a hymn tune alternately with snatches of the latest musical comedy, Sally moved about her shining kitchen preparing her breakfast. The spring sun glinting on the fittings of her electric stove, lighting up the scarlet geraniums on the window-sill, made her utterly happy. The smell of the coffee made her feel happy, too, and the smell of toast. She laid her breakfast tray daintily and sat down to the kitchen table to eat and to review the coming day. After breakfast Mrs. Baker would come, and they would start the housework, and then while Mrs. Baker was having her elevenses she would go to the greengrocer's, and perhaps she would meet the five children there and talk to them. They were usually there about eleven in the holidays, buying lettuce for their mother, and sometimes they brought their mother's pekinese with them. She loved those children, and she loved their pekinese, and she wished they were hers. And then she would come back and finish the housework, have lunch, go for a walk by the river, and watch the sun on the water and hear the seagulls crying. After that she would come home and have a read, put on her new frock and go to Jan Carruthers' cocktail party. That would be fun. Parties were always fun. Then she would come home and bake some cakes, and after supper she would listen to the wireless and go on with the sweater she was knitting for her father, and then go upstairs and help Mrs. Rutherford with her patchwork quilt for a while, and say good night to her. She hoped that not too many people would come in to see her, thinking she was lonely. She was never lonely.

The morning worked out according to plan. Leaving Mrs. Baker to wield the broom in the rest of the flat, Sally tackled her father's studio. Their Chelsea flat was a lovely, luxurious place, the home of a rich and famous man who loved beauty. To Sally's mind it was a bit too full of things; but, then, it was not John Adair who had given to Sally her love of order, simplicity and space. Providing everything he ate out of, trod on or sat on was a thing of beauty, he did not mind how jumbled up everything was. His studio was so jumbled up that Mrs. Baker, when first required by him to clean it up a bit, but not on any account to move anything, had been taken with the palpitations and had gone home. So now Sally dealt with it. It took her a good two hours, but clumsy though she was she had never yet smashed anything, and had never yet failed to restore everything she moved to the exact place where it had been before. She passed through the studio like light, making new without commotion, her long fingers touching bottles and tubes, canvases, palettes and rags with the reverence of a sacristan at work in a holy place.

She did indeed reverence her father's art. Fame and the perfecting of his technique had not dimmed his discernment. In every beautiful woman, in every famous man, who came to him, he could still see and portray what Sally called the Patient Angel. For a long time she had been at a loss as to how to describe the invisible presence that in some miraculous way her father's genius could present to one's consciousness as one's eyes looked upon the visible form. Then one day she had found a battered old volume of "Sonnets from the Portuguese" fallen down behind a bookshelf, opened it at random and found the words she wanted leaping up at her from the page.

"Because thou hast the power and own'st the grace
To look through and behind this mask of me,
(Against which years have beat thus blanchingly
With their rains,) and behold my soul's true face,
The dim and weary witness of life's race,—
Because thou hast the faith and love to see,
Through that same soul's distracting lethargy,
The patient angel waiting for a place
In the new heavens...."

Angel seemed the right word. Yet now and then, very occasionally, Sally had seen something in a portrait that had made her turn cold with horror.... It was as though the angel had two faces, and only one of them of light.

She never questioned her father about his work. Aware of her abysmal ignorance, she was afraid to hurt him by clumsy misunderstanding. But she thought she knew how it was that consciously or unconsciously he came to see the Patient Angel. He was not content merely to observe his sitters in the studio. Whenever he could he strolled unobtrusively into their lives and watched them entertaining, being entertained, working, eating, reading, perhaps even sleeping. They were for the most part unaware of his scrutiny, for his entrances and exits were very cleverly contrived. There was a big portfolio in the studio full of lightning sketches that he had made, sometimes upon a scrap of paper, sometimes upon the back of a menu or a concert programme, sometimes of the men and women whose portraits he was painting, but often just of some stranger's face that had caught his fancy. They were so nakedly revealing that the first time she had opened the portfolio Sally had immediately shut it up again, as one shuts the door of a private room opened inadvertently. Then, longing to look again, she had gone to her father and asked his permission.

"Certainly," he had replied, his clever, ugly face creased with delight at the honesty of this young daughter of his. "There is nothing in the studio that you may not examine to your heart's content... provided you leave everything exactly as it was before."

And so now, when she had finished cleaning the studio, she always rewarded herself by sitting down with the portfolio and looking for the latest sketches.

There were quite a batch of them today, and she chuckled with delight at the audacity and insight of the hasty scribbles. But there was one that was not so hasty, and at sight of it Sally had the oddest feeling, as though someone had given her a violent shove in the back, so that the world turned upside down for a moment. It was larger than usual and had obviously been drawn at leisure. At the bottom of the sheet of paper John Adair had scribbled "D. E. at Rehearsal." Evidently he had sat unobserved in the auditorium of a theatre or concert hall and drawn this man as he worked upon the stage. Sally put the other sketches back in the portfolio, and taking just this one went to the window-seat and sat down there, laying it on her lap and studying it intently. She had never seen this face before, she was quite certain, and yet she knew it, and would always know it. If she were to meet this man twenty years hence in the street she would know him. It was ridiculous, but it was true.

The sketch had been faintly coloured, probably from memory, when John Adair had been in his studio again, and gave to this man smooth, pale-gold hair, blue eyes, a fine, tanned skin, a finely shaped head and perfect features. John Adair, to whom conventional beauty was an exasperation, had conceded this much grudgingly, as though he regretted it, and then had drawn with vigour and pleasure all that was individual in the face: the hard bones showing almost savagely through the taut skin, the hollowed temples, the dark stains beneath the eyes with their curious look of vacancy, contrasting so oddly with the keenness of the rest of the face, the obstinate line of the jaw, the suggestion of bitterness about the mouth with its lines of endurance. It was a young face, with the youth of it crossed out, as it were, by the lines slashed mercilessly by John Adair's pencil across the broad, low forehead and from the nose to the bitter mouth, and the beauty of it marred by the stains beneath the eyes and the tautness of the skin. The head stood out in startling fairness against a strange background—the background of a wood, with the shapes of queer beasts and birds just discernible among the trees. It was like the landscape of a dream, and it had the vagueness of a dream that is half forgotten upon waking. At first Sally had scarcely noticed this background, but when she did notice it she looked at it long and attentively, with an odd feeling of familiarity.

Then she looked again at the portrait, and a sudden rage took possession of her. She was sure her father had not been fair. He must dislike this man, for he had cruelly accentuated the obstinacy, the bitterness, the—how was she to put it?—threadbare look of the face. And then, looking again, she was not so sure about the cruelty. This was not only a portrait of D. E., whoever he might be, it was a portrait of many men whom she knew. That was how countless men had gone through the war—men of thought and sensitiveness to whom the whole damnable business was almost unendurable—with just that almost savage obstinacy that a little dog shows when he is getting the worst of it in a senseless dog-fight but means to hold on till the end: men so tired that their eyes looked at you as though they were sleep-walkers who did not see you at all; men who were bitter and sick of heart because now that the thing was over it did not seem to have accomplished much. So there was a Patient Angel waiting not only behind each person but behind each type of person, thought Sally, and so behind each of us two angels, and the beating of the years hammered out the future not only of oneself but of something more than oneself. You suffered not only for yourself but for all the people who shared your kind of temperament and your courage redeemed them as their courage redeemed you.... And perhaps old houses had their Angel, created through the years by the people who lived there... and nations... and...

"Fool!" said Sally suddenly and ferociously to herself, and flushed scarlet to the roots of her copper-coloured hair. It was wonderful what high-faluting theories about suffering one could formulate when one did not happen to be suffering oneself.

Far away in the flat—miles away it sounded—the door of the cupboard where the Hoover was kept slammed meaningly and then the kitchen door slammed. Mrs. Baker's elevenses were long overdue. Without looking at it again, Sally put the drawing back in the portfolio, and the portfolio in its accustomed place, and returned to her duties.

– 3 –

Mrs. Baker comfortably established with a pot of steaming hot tea and a rock bun, Sally put on her white woolly blanket coat, took her shopping-basket, got into the lift, sailed down to the street and sallied forth to the greengrocer's. The heavenly beauty of the spring day sent her mercurial spirits soaring upwards, and she sang softly as she walked along the street, swinging her basket. The beautiful old houses about her seemed lovely as the houses in a fairytale, their windows and brass knockers winking in the sun, their roofs and weather-worn stones revealing unexpected colours in the bright, clear light. Fragile clouds like puffs of white smoke fled across the blue sky before the wind, and she could hear the crying of the gulls down by the river. There was something to be said for London on a day like this. At first, after her open-air life on the hills, she had found it hard to be cooped up in London, but she was getting acclimatized now. Yet she wished they had a cottage in the country, especially now that the lease of their flat had only a few more months to run and they could not renew it. It might not be easy to find another home, and they might, as her father suggested, have to "take a good long holiday somewhere," and the holidays in the exceedingly expensive hotels which her father preferred were not much to her taste. John Adair had little liking for the simple life; he said it was not simple, but the most damnably complicated method of wasting time that had ever existed. He liked a constant supply of hot water, a refrigerator, a lift, an electric toaster, a telephone beside his bed, central heating and electric fires, and anything whatever that reduced the time spent upon the practical side of living to a minimum and left him free to paint.

But Sally did not want to be set free for anything, for it was living itself that she enjoyed. She liked lighting a real fire of logs and fir-cones and toasting bread on an old-fashioned toaster. And she liked the lovely curve of an old staircase and the fun of running up and down it. And she vastly preferred writing a letter and walking with it to the post to using the telephone and hearing with horror her voice committing itself to things she would never have dreamed of doing if she'd had the time to think. "It's my stupid brain," she said to herself. "I like the leisurely things, and taking my time about them. That's partly, I think, why I like children so much. They're never in a hurry to get on to something else." But in spite of her dislike of hurry she quickened her pace. It was always round about eleven that the five children and the pekinese were in the greengrocer's shop, and she was late this morning, and if she did not hurry she would miss them.

Her luck was good today, and she did not miss them. They were not in the shop when she arrived, and she took as long as she could buying lettuce and rhubarb for lunch, and a glorious bunch of flame-coloured tulips for the dining-room, and a bundle of asparagus as a gift for Mrs. Rutherford because she had selfishly made too much noise in the bathroom this morning, and because they looked so lovely a bunch of violets for she did not know whom—a mass of them all together in a great basket, and she could not resist them. She bought everything at the most exorbitant price and with a pang of shame, because so few people nowadays could afford to buy asparagus and tulips and violets. She spent a long time stowing it all away in her basket, still hopefully waiting, and then just as she turned to go they arrived.

The pekinese, as always, arrived first—a little, roundabout, assertive young thing with exquisite snow-white fur, wearing a scarlet harness attached to a scarlet lead, upon which she panted and strained in a state of bustle and hurry that seemed chronic with her. Attached to the other end of the lead were the twins, aged round about five. They were beautiful children, and Sally, whose acquaintance with five-year-olds was not as yet intimate, would have given all she possessed to have them for her own. They both had dark, softly curling hair, the little girl's cut as short as her brother's, dark eyes and small yet strong bodies. The boy was the sturdier of the two, with red cheeks, eyes flashing with extreme wickedness and an impudent grin. The little girl had only a faint rose-colour in her cheeks, but her eyes were just as wicked. They always wore the most enchanting clothes—smocks or jerseys of honey colour, jade or cherry, kilted skirts or knickerbockers of nutbrown or turquoise-blue—and some loving and careful person had always seemed to look them over very carefully before starting out, for there was never a button undone or a hint of anything showing that should not show.

Sally guessed that this loving and careful person was their older sister. She always came just behind them, her small face a trifle anxious, her grey-green eyes squinting a little in an effort to keep the twins and the pekinese all in focus together. Once, when Sally had asked her age, she had whispered that she was twelve, but she did not look as much. She was small, thin and freckled, with straight, fair, bobbed hair cut in an old-fashioned fringe across her forehead. She was not pretty, but she had a delicate precision and charm that were very captivating. In her pale, pastel-coloured frocks she was like some fragile flower—a sweet pea or a wild anemone. Sally had the feeling that she was beset by many fears but was not in the habit of mentioning them.... At least, not in the presence of the brother next to her in age, who would certainly have laughed at them.... Of all the children, Sally liked this brother least. He was in his middle teens, tall and dark and amazingly handsome, rosy cheeked and bright-eyed as his little brother, so brimful of laughter and vitality that his presence struck one like a blow in the face. Sally was sure that what he wanted in life, that he would get. He would be jolly and kind to those who did not oppose him, but ruthless to those who did. But he would not know that he was being ruthless. He would never know enough about other people to guess what would hurt them and what would not. He was brave and honest, generous and affectionate, but he had very few sensitivities.

The same could not be said of the elder brother; he looked a bundle of them. He was tall, thin and bony, with a sallow skin and lustreless, dark hair. At first sight one thought the younger brother had stolen all the beauty and left him none at all, but when one looked again one was not so sure. Movement transformed him. When he stood still his angular body appeared to have little grace, yet when he walked it had an almost fluid loveliness. And when his quick, sudden smile touched his thin lips, and his shy, fawn's eyes lit up with delight, his face was alive as very few faces ever are, almost shining with that deep-welling life that is tapped by so very few.... Sally hoped almost with desperation that things would not be too hard for him.... John Adair had an amusing habit of planting people in their appropriate centuries, and Sally had caught it from him. She had no difficulty with these three. The girl had strayed from a page of Kate Greenaway, the handsome boy had sailed with Drake upon his piratical expeditions and firmly refused to be browbeaten by him, but the elder had come to this place and this time from a much earlier age, from the age of chivalry. The very first moment Sally had set eyes on this boy she had been reminded of some picture she had seen somewhere—the picture of a young Chevalier attired in silk and fur, with a hunting-horn slung over his shoulder, riding a white horse through a dark wood. It was a strange wood, full of mysterious shapes of beasts—bears and dogs and deer. Up at the top of the picture, with a glorious disregard of perspective, was a lake or river, with swans upon it. The young knight had pulled his beautiful horse to a standstill and was gazing with rapt and reverent attention at something which he saw.... With a sudden sense of shock Sally realized today that the background of the remembered but unidentified picture, that she always set behind the figure of this boy, was much the same as the one her father had set behind the head of the young man in the sketch in the portfolio.... They must both of them have been remembering the same picture.

Her purchases completed, she stood now watching the children make theirs, smiling at them and receiving their answering smiles. Though she saw them almost daily in the holidays she had never yet asked them where they lived or what their name was. In spite of her friendliness her innate humility made Sally reticent, and particularly so with those who most attracted her. She could not ask them questions or force herself upon them; it would have been a sort of sacrilege. Before loveliness that called forth her love she was reverent and shy, not taking, but asking wordlessly that she might be taken. The children, naturally, were unaware of her inhibitions. And they regarded her as a hoary grown-up. Not as old as Mother, of course, but getting on.

That they loved, even worshipped, their mother was obvious. It was always "for Mother" that they seemed to be shopping. They chose with care the crispest lettuce for her, and they asked repeatedly, and generally in vain, if there wasn't just *one* grape-fruit for her. The elder boy, whenever he had any money, seemed to spend it all on flowers for her, and he would look longingly at the grapes that only millionaires could buy. Today they bought lettuce, received with sorrow the customary information that grape-fruit was said to be on its way but wasn't in yet, and then, as they were about to go, their eyes were caught by the great basket of violets. They turned out their pockets, but there was nothing worth mentioning in them. The dead mouse in the little boy's pocket and the skeleton of a rabbit's head in the Pirate's pocket were doubtless interesting relics, but of no commercial value. Even the eldest boy, who possessed a handsome hogskin purse, searched it in vain.

"You shouldn't have got Mother that book on the ballet," said the Pirate. "She wasn't in the least interested."

His tone was unconsciously brutal, and the Chevalier flushed; not so much at his brother's tone, Sally thought, as at the memory it evoked of his mother's lack of interest in what possibly interested him intensely. She dived into her basket and came forward quickly, the violets in her hand.

"Please will you take them to your mother?" she said. "I think I just bought them for the sake of buying them, because they were so lovely. I'd no reason to buy them."

The quick delight of a fellow feeling rippled over the Chevalier's face.... That was exactly what he was always doing himself—buying something just because it was beautiful and then not knowing quite what to do with it when he'd got it.... Then he flushed again and gave her a stiff, awkward little bow.

"I couldn't take them," he said gently. "You could wear them yourself. You could wear them on your coat."

And his eyes went appreciatively from the violets to her white coat and copper hair. He thought the copper and violet and white would be good together.

But at this point a long-legged child exploded suddenly from the back of the shop with great news,

"The bananas have come," she said. "Dad's unpacking 'em."

"Then you'd better take yours along now," said the lady of the shop to the children. "Two to each blue ration book, by rights, but never enough to go round really, so if you don't they'll all be gone in no time. Fetch 'em along, Vi. Tell Dad to give you ten for the young Eliots. They've not their books with them, but it don't matter."

The Chevalier looked eagerly at Sally and flushed again, a tentative question forming itself upon his lips. It was one which he found it difficult to put with sufficient delicacy to a lady, but the Pirate crashed in with it like a breaker pounding a bottle on the beach.

"Are you over age for bananas? If you are, have some of ours."

Sally's remembrance of bananas was a far-away memory of rather nauseating scented soap, but she knew they would like her to accept.

"Thank you," she said. "Yes, I *am* over age for bananas and I haven't tasted one for seven years. I'd like one very much."

"Oh, more than one," pleaded the Chevalier.

"Three," decided the Pirate. "One from each of us, not counting the twins. Better not dock the twins of bananas or there'll be the hell of a row."

"I'd rather just have one," said Sally.

"Two," said the Pirate, a master of compromise, and the bananas at this point appearing, he took them from Vi and dealt them around, one each to the Chevalier and Kate Greenaway, two each for Sally, himself and the twins.

"Thank you *very* much," said the Chevalier, as he took the violets. "Thank you—Mother will—Mary! Mary, stop it! Hi, Mary!"

Mary the pekinese had perceived a mongrel over three times her size outside in the gutter. With a sudden wrench she jerked her lead out of the hands of the smaller twin, and hot with that hatred which the intolerant type of canine aristocrat feels for all lack of breeding, she dashed outside to make an end of it. The mongrel fled, squealing, Mary after it and the children after Mary, and Sally was deserted.

Well, anyway, she thought, as she walked home, she knew their name now.... Eliot.... And their mother, perhaps, would wear her violets. She wondered about their mother. She must be a very lovely woman to have such lovely children. And queenly, for it seemed natural to them to bring her gifts. And perhaps hard to please, or they would not have been so careful over the choosing of her lettuces. But she could not be really motherly, or she would not have hurt her eldest son by not being interested in the book he had given her.... Unreasonably, acting upon surmise only, Sally felt that she did not like Mrs. Eliot.

– 4 –

The rest of the day continued to work out according to plan, and at six o'clock Sally found herself starting out for Jan Carruthers' cocktail party in her new frock. She was much preoccupied with it as she walked along. To save coupons she had made it herself out of a very fine grey wool material, soft and thin. It had a flared skirt that floated around her as she walked and a soft cross-over bodice that she hoped disguised the sturdy chest development which was the price she paid for her contralto singing voice. With it she wore a little, short, loose-swinging, grey squirrel coat, and she had spent her very last coupons on grey silk stockings and grey suede shoes to match. Squinting from side to side she noted that the skirt flared out just as she had hoped it would, and glancing at herself in shop windows she was obliged to note that she looked very nice indeed. Yet she noted it with that familiar sinking of shame.... For the fur coat had cost a pretty penny.

She had been a little late in starting out, owing to finding at the last moment that she had forgotten to take the tacking threads out of the pleats of her skirt, and she arrived in Jan's beautiful sea-green drawing-room a little flushed, with her curls tossed by the spring wind. Jan's husband was very nearly, but not quite, as distinguished a portrait-painter as John Adair, and the room was seething with the kind of people whom the drawing-rooms of distinguished people do seeth with. Sally, not quite accustomed yet to the extraordinarily sustained noise which the well-bred make when eating and drinking together, felt suddenly scared. She had thought this party was going to be fun, but just for the moment it seemed as though she did not know anybody.... And no other woman in the room was wearing a home-made frock.

Jan, ten years older than she was, dark and lacquered and ten years smarter and more sophisticated, descended upon her.

"Darling!" cried Jan passionately, though they scarcely knew each other. "Lovely to see you. What a sweet frock! Did you make it?"

Sally was at a loss to understand the edge to her voice. She did not know that Roger Carruthers was not quite as distinguished as her father.

"Yes," she said truthfully, and did not seem able to find anything else to say.

"Have a drink," was Jan's advice. "Though it's none of it worth drinking these days. And if there's anything left to eat, darling, you'll have to look at it through a magnifying glass. Roger, get Sally a drink. Where is the man? Must have bolted to the studio. He's hopeless. Charles! Get Sally a drink."

And, her duty done by Sally, she was gone. Charles, however, an elegant young man of tender years but immense self-confidence, was immediately appreciative of Sally's charm. He got her a cool amber drink, a sausage on a stick and half a cheese-straw, and engaged her in deeply intellectual conversation. He found her, however, distressingly lacking in intellect, though upon this discovery he did not leave her, for, looking at her from the front, from which position he could not observe how distressingly her nose turned up at the tip, he thought her pretty... and warm and glowing and somehow comforting.... Not that he exactly needed comfort, for being of tender years, he hadn't been in the war, and the world had treated him all right so far; but there was no harm in it when allied with copper-coloured hair and tawny eyes. Gracefully adjusting himself to her lower mentality, he observed that there were quite a number of Big Noises in the room.

"Eliot's here," he added.

Eliot? Sally had been interested before—even though she had not been quite able to follow her companion into the deep waters of surrealist art—because she was always interested; but now she was thrilled. Could he possibly be the father of her five children? Eliot was not an unusual name, but there was just a chance.

"Who is he?" she asked eagerly.

"Eliot? Why, David Eliot. You know. He's back on the stage again after years as a bomber pilot."

"I don't think I know about him," said Sally humbly. "I don't really know anything about anybody yet. You see, for the last three years I've been looking after sheep in the Cumberland hills."

"My God!" murmured Charles with horror, pity and complete understanding.... No wonder the poor girl knew nothing whatever.... He cupped her elbow very gently in his hand. "I'll show him to you," he promised kindly. "I might even be able to introduce him to you. I know him. My brother understudied for him once."

He piloted her through the throng and planted her near the fireplace, beside a small white magnolia tree growing in a purple pot.

"There!" he said, as to a child set down before a Punch-and-Judy show. "Good view. Coming this way."

"Which?" asked Sally, her eyes passing from one middle-aged gentleman to another and rejecting them all as quite unworthy of the twins.

"He's seen me," murmured Charles triumphantly.

An impartial observer might have been a little doubtful as to whether the man edging towards them through the crowd had seen Charles, or the space on the mantelpiece beside Charles where he could put an empty glass that was getting in his way, but he came to them, put down his glass and replied courteously, if a little vaguely, to Charles' greeting. He was much too young to be the father of those children. Sally stood very straight and still, looking at the face that she had felt she had always known when she had seen it in her father's drawing. Only this face was not quite like the face of the drawing. That had been an unmasked face. This was the same face, but masked. She didn't feel anything very particular; only rather odd and tired. She wondered vaguely if this was falling in love. They said in books that one felt so wonderful when one fell in love. She wasn't feeling wonderful at all; just odd and a bit sick. Books were very misleading. And Charles seemed to have forgotten about the introduction. Another girl would have recalled herself to his mind by moving forward a little. But not Sally. Why should Charles remember, she thought? She felt in the way, and made a gentle movement of withdrawal.

Something in the sweet humility of the movement caught David Eliot's eye, and he turned round.

Charles remembered his manners.

"This is Sally," he said, with kind patronage. "I don't know her other name.... She used to keep sheep in Cumberland," he added warningly, so that David should know that if it was intelligence he wanted it was no good applying here.

David smiled charmingly at Sally and gave her a little half-mocking bow.

"A shepherdess," he said. "As far as I know, the first shepherdess I've ever met," and the pose of his graceful body, the bending of his fair, shining head, were quite unconsciously those of a Dresden figure on a mantelpiece, bowing to a maiden in Arcady.

It was sweetly spoken, charmingly done, yet somehow it made Sally feel wretched. It didn't mean anything. She knew that he said the right thing, performed the appropriate action, so unceasingly day after day, night after night, that it had become simply automatic.

She could not force a reply. She just stood there dumbly, the colour draining from her face. Her silence, her stillness, tugged at David's attention. A minute before she had been just another pretty girl at this confounded party who would ask him for his autograph, delaying yet again his effort to get away before his aching head split open. He couldn't imagine what he'd come here for, except that Roger Carruthers (who had disappeared) was a friend of his, and somehow these days it really seemed easier just to go on keeping on than to make the effort of wrenching oneself off the treadmill. But now her unexpected stillness did the wrenching for him. The noise, the crowd, the heat, melted into a sort of dark blur against which he saw with strange vividness the straight, sturdy figure in the soft grey dress, the mop of rumpled curls, the tawny lion's eyes with their straight, clear glance, and a rosy face from which the colour drained, leaving it white as the magnolia flowers.

"Come this way," he said quickly, and taking her arm he opened a door half hidden behind the magnolia tree.

He knew his way about the house. Beyond was a dim, cool passage, with a window and a cushioned window-seat. He shut the door behind them, and the noise and the heat and the fumes of smoke vanished with such suddenness that it seemed to Sally that a sword had come down, completely separating all that had been before in her life from all that was to come. He took her to the window-seat and opened the window.

"Better?" he asked.

"I wasn't feeling faint," said Sally.

"Weren't you? You looked as though you were. Sorry. Like to go back?"

"No," said Sally with her usual abrupt truthfulness.

He laughed and sat down beside her.

"Nor would I. Infernal din in there. Why must human beings always make such a noise? They're at it from the very beginning. The first thing a baby does is yell. After that I suppose it's just habit."

He went on talking nonsense in his clear, rapid, beautiful voice, charmingly, automatically, as though he were wound up. Sally, making quiet, appropriate answers, wished they could pay proper attention to each other. Talk such as this was like a nebulous mist between them, like the spray that some insects fling out in self-preservation. Perhaps that was the reason why people did talk like this; they wanted to isolate themselves.... She remembered that it is always the sick animal who wants isolation.... And suddenly she did not blame her father that in his drawing he had torn away the mask. When her old sheep-dog had been sick, and hidden himself away in a dark corner, she had had to bring him out into the light and give him a dose.

"You're rather a silent shepherdess. What are you thinking of?"

"My sheep-dog," said the accurate Sally.

He laughed suddenly, delightedly, and the transformation of his face by natural laughter reminded her of someone.

"Tell me about your life with the sheep," he commanded her.

She clasped her hands in her lap and tried to obey. She told him about the old farm where she had lived, about the loveliness of summer mornings on the fells, looking down at the enclosed, enchanted valleys below, about the gales and the snowstorms, and how hard it had been sometimes to get up early in the pitch dark and bitter cold of winter mornings. She told him about the lambing season and the fight to save the lives of motherless lambs, about the heroism of fell shepherds and the wisdom of their dogs, and about the shaggy, little pony she had been allowed to ride. She found it very hard to tell it to a bomber pilot; it all sounded so tame; and she was hot with the old familiar shame, because she had suffered nothing at all in this war except cold and fatigue and the stiffness of chilblained fingers and toes.

David Eliot meanwhile leaned back in the window-seat, relieved for what felt like the first time in weeks from the sound of his own voice going on and on inanely and intolerably, and listened with the queerest sensation of relief. It was extraordinary how restful it was to be with someone who knew nothing whatever about war, who had not, it seemed, even heard a bomb exploding; someone who was not nerve-wracked or tired to death, who had taken no part in the torture and death of the innocent, who was not trying to forget, or alternatively taking a ghoulish or vain-glorious delight in remembering. He was sick of the war, he never wanted to think of it again, he wanted to thrust the whole damnable business out of his mind for ever; and yet he couldn't, because in every face he looked into, except the face of the crass young like that fool Charles, he saw the memory of it as a tightness about the mouth and a shadow in the eyes.... Or he thought he did.... He knew he was in an idiotically morbid state.... But this girl's mouth was like a happy child's, and her steady eyes were full of light. And yet she was no crass young fool shut up within herself. Young though she was, there was that about her face that told him that somehow, through the loveliness of the hills or her love and care for sheep and dogs and ponies, she had been already set free.

She had no more to say, and so was silent, and to his horror he heard his voice running on again in the usual banalities.

"That was a queer sort of life for a girl like you. What does it feel like to come back to civilization again?"

She looked at him wonderingly, as though she questioned his apparent conception of civilization. Then she smiled.

"I'm happy in London," she said. "But I miss Cumberland. When I'm just waking up in the mornings, before I'm quite awake, I hear the sheep-bells ringing in the hills, and the sound of the streams. You know how they sound, coming down from the heights. And how one remembers it."

"All the water-sounds are unforgettable," he said gently. "The best sound of all, I think, is the sound of ripples slapping against the hull of a boat. I've got an old grandmother who lives down in the sea-marshes in Hampshire. I go there sometimes and mess about in a boat."

"You go often?" she asked.

"I used to, before the war. Not so often now. There isn't time. Re-starting the old job after the war takes a lot of doing."

"It can't be easy," she said. "It must be like going back to some place where you were very happy when you were a child, and you think it will be the same again, and then it just isn't. I suppose one would need to be reborn and be a child again to have it the same."

Her understanding delighted him. It had been hell to return to work he had loved and find that the savour had gone out. Reborn? That wasn't so easy. "How can a man enter a second time into his mother's womb and be born?" And the answer to that question seemed to him a signpost one could not read because of the scales over one's eyes, pointing along a road through a dark wood that one could not follow anyway because one's limbs had turned to lead. He believed firmly that the road existed, and that it led somewhere— that at least was something—but there was no way that he knew of to recapture the vision and strength of a child.

Sally suddenly remembered of whom David had reminded her

when he laughed. There was no likeness of feature between him and the young Chevalier, but in a moment of delight their faces came alive in just the same way.... And behind them both was that wood.

"You're the seventh Eliot I've met today," she said. "No, the sixth—one was a dog."

"In our family the dogs are counted in," said David. "Don't tell me you've met my young cousins, and their wretched little pekinese?"

She described the Chevalier, the Pirate and Kate Greenaway, the twins and Mary, and he laughed again.

"They are my young cousins all right. Their father is my uncle.... Were they on their own?"

There was a hunger in his question that Sally did not understand.

"They're always on their own," she said. "I've never seen their mother, though I've made a sort of picture of her in my mind. I imagine her very lovely. Is she?"

"Yes," said David. "She is very lovely."

And again she did not understand the tone of his voice, though it chilled her to the bone. She got up, feeling desolate.

"I think I ought to be going now," she said childishly.

They went back to the smoke-filled room, and there was such a noise that they could say good-bye only wordlessly. David's gesture of farewell, in the brief moment before the crowd absorbed him, was memorable for its grace, but so mechanical that Sally felt he had pushed her straight out of his mind and slammed the door. She went at once, and all the way home, though the sun was shining, she hugged herself in her fur coat because she still felt cold. She made no plans for seeing David Eliot again, though with such a famous father that would have been easy. She did not even mean to question her father about him, or about the portrait in the studio. Sally had too much pride to batter against a door that had been shut.

CHAPTER

2

– 1 –

HE WOMAN WHO SAT IN THE CORNER of the railway carriage with her eyes shut was attracting a good deal of attention. She was vaguely aware of it, even as she was vaguely aware of the sun on her face, but she was as used to the one as to the other, for she had attracted attention in the cradle. She was that kind of woman. And the man who was sitting opposite to her liked that kind of woman. Settling himself more comfortably into his corner, he yielded luxuriously to the attraction.

He had been studying her for not more than a bare twenty minutes, since he had got into her train at Winchester, and yet already the picture of her outward seeming was stamped so deeply upon his memory that he knew he could never forget it. Were she to get out at the next station (which heaven forbid), he believed he would yet be able, should he desire, to paint her with complete accuracy. And he believed he would so desire. He'd add her portrait to the ones he kept in his old portfolio—those he drew as studies for his commissioned portraits, or simply because he wanted to draw them, because a face interested him, as this woman's face interested him; as David Eliot's face had interested him when, all unknown to the victim, he had dropped in at rehearsal, watched him at work and set down what he had seen.

Yes, she was highly paintable. Most people, regarding beauty as the perquisite of youth, would have said, "How lovely she must have been!" but to his eye she had not yet attained to the beauty of which she was capable. And she never would, unless she stopped stewing in her own juice and made up her mind one way or the other, for her mouth in repose was the strained, bitter mouth of a self-pitying woman with divided allegiance, and was a great imperfection. But otherwise the pure oval of her face was flawless, and to his artist's eye the clear ivory pallor of her skin unmarred by the fine network of lines traced about eyes and mouth, or by the shadows upon the eyelids and beneath the closed eyes; for the delicacy of the lines was a thing to marvel at, and those shadows—they were the colour of the underneath of a wild violet petal, a colour most exquisitely lovely, but abominably difficult to paint. The thick bow of the lips was vividly reddened, and though the colour accentuated their hardness it did not irritate him, as women's make-up so frequently did, by too strong an emphasis, for the contrast between the ivory of the skin and the darkness of the hair was already so striking that the red lips could not provide a stronger. Her features were clear-cut, her neck long and slender, her figure slim and boyish; yet he guessed that when she moved it would be with the most excellent feminine grace. He admired her clothes: the absurd little black hat adroitly poised like a bird in flight upon the shining dark hair, faintly streaked with grey at the temples, the worn yet perfectly cut black dress and coat, the beautiful silver-fox fur, the immaculate black gloves and shoes, the string of pearls. He wondered if she was a widow, for the only touches of colour about her were her lipstick and the bunch of violets she wore in her coat. If she was, he decided, she would not be one for long, for she was wholly desirable, and if and when she condescended to open her eyes he expected to find them the eyes of a woman who desired to be desired.

Ten minutes later the train jolted to a standstill, she opened her eyes and their glances met. As he expected, they were dark and full of ardour, and they did not fall before the interest in his. For a long moment he held her eyes with his own; for he, too, for most of his life had been accustomed to attract to himself whom he would, and could do it still when he cared to take the trouble. Silently, with his look, he paid respectful tribute to her beauty. Silently, with her answering look, she accepted the tribute as her right, yet thanked him for it. Then, dismissing him from her mind, she took off her gloves, opened her bag, took a letter out of it and settled back in her corner to read it. It interested him to see that the letter was written on cheap notepaper in uneducated handwriting, and that the beautiful slim hands now revealed to him were ringless except for a wedding ring. He decided, upon the evidence of her obvious weariness, of the hands (women with much washing-up to do seldom bothered with their rings nowadays) and the letter, that she was worn out with chores to which she was unsuited and unused and was going down into the country to interview some woman who had answered her frantic advertisement for a servant. He decided that in that case she was not a widow, but the wife of some hungry boar of a man who insisted upon a good dinner every day no matter how uncongenial pots and pans might be to his wife. She wore black not as a sign of grief but because it suited her. He decided that she had at any rate escaped the burden of children, for there was nothing maternal about that exquisite boyish figure.

But here he was wrong, for Nadine Eliot had borne five children, and she was going down into the country to interview not a servant, but a prospective Nannie for the twins. If she could get hold of a Nannie for the twins, she thought, then she could go on living; but if she couldn't, then her dearest wish would be for extinction. She doubted if she even wanted life after death; not if it meant having baby angels underfoot all day. People whose acquaintance with the twins was not intimate sometimes told her that they were little angels, and upon those occasions she smiled her charming smile, but made no verbal reply. She was not an unloving mother, but she was not naturally a child-lover, and she was so desperately tired. The birth of the twins had been a harrowing experience, and she had never fully recovered from it. She ought not to have had them, of course, for after the birth of her third child the doctor had told her she should not have another. But just before the war she had been reunited with her husband, from whom she had been separated for some time, and then had come the war, and George had fought hard and gallantly before the wound which had returned him to England and a safe appointment at the War Office, and she had admired and pitied him, and so—well—the twins had come. She could yet make a success of them, she thought, and of her difficult married life, and of her motherhood of her three older children, if she could find a really good Nannie. Her whole salvation depended upon a really good Nannie. If, when one reached exhaustion point one could say to one's children: "Go to the nursery, darlings," then one could be a good mother; if not, no.... At least she couldn't.

She looked down at the letter in her hands. Usually one couldn't tell much about the writer from the letter of a not very well educated woman; they all seemed to have the same handwriting and to express themselves in the same stilted sort of way. But this letter was different. One could tell quite a lot about the writer from it. She read it again.

"Dear Madam,

I saw your advertisement for a nurse for your children. Before the war, when your three elder children lived at Damerosehay, I was nursemaid to them. You may not remember me, for you did not come to Damerosehay often. I was Jill Baker, and I married Alf Watson, who helped in the garden at Damerosehay. He was killed at Dunkirk. I have no children. I have been working in day nurseries for children, having none of my own, but now I am living with my Auntie Rose at the Herb of Grace, the old inn at the Hard. I have not seen your twins, Madam, but if they are anything like Master Ben and Master Tommy and Miss Caroline in the old days I shall love them.

"Yours faithfully,

"Jill Watson."

It was both a revealing and a rather startling letter. To begin with, Jill did not even mention the matter of wages, and such an omission at this moment of national history, when noble behaviour sustained through a long war had caused a violent swing of the pendulum and returned everybody to the acquisitive manners of the jungle, was enough to take one's breath away. Then the patient understatement in the two sentences, "He was killed at Dunkirk. I have no children," was oddly touching. And then there was the obvious love of children. (Imagine any women, thought Nadine, *choosing* to work in a day nursery.) Unworldly, patient, loving—could one ask for finer qualities in a Nannie? There was, of course, the hint of disapproval contained in the sentence, "You did not come to Damerosehay very often." But, then a Nannie was always disapproving of the mother. You couldn't have a Nannie and not be disapproved of. And she was, after all, used to being disapproved of, just as she was used to being the centre of interest.

It was true that in the days when she had been separated from

George, and the children had lived with his mother at Damerosehay, she had not gone there very often, but she did vaguely remember Jill—a thin, pasty-faced little creature, hardly more than a child, whom the wicked Tommy had teased unmercifully. Yet she had apparently forgiven Tommy, and would doubtless forgive Jeremy, the elder of the twins if he did the same. As he undoubtedly would, for Jerry was very like Tommy.... Only worse.... Josephine, the younger twin, was not so wicked, but the fertility of her imagination was a thing to make one tremble.

Jill's letter had arrived only two days ago, and Nadine had not wasted time. The Hard, as far as she remembered, was not very far from Damerosehay, so she had rung up her mother-in-law and asked for a bed for three nights. Lucilla Eliot's instant eager request that George and the children should come, too, she had refused with the information that George could not leave the War Office.... She simply *must* have a rest from George and the children.... Then she had written to Jill and said that she would come and see her at the Herb of Grace. Then she had summoned a long-suffering elderly cousin to look after her husband and children in her absence, shut the door of her elegant, but servantless, Chelsea house behind her, and caught the train for Hampshire. For three whole nights and two whole days she would be free of domesticity. For three whole nights and two whole days she would be at Damerosehay; and what that meant only an Eliot could fully understand. To an Eliot, even for an Eliot who was one only by marriage, Damerosehay was not only the home of Lucilla Eliot, Grandmother, their best-beloved, it was the shrine of their particular tradition. The family, regarded as a unity, had its roots in the place and drew its life from it.

Nadine put the letter down on her lap for a moment, and the draught from the window blew it to the floor. John Adair stooped politely and picked it up, and the words at the top caught his eye.... Herb of Grace.... Carefully he memorized the unusual address, then handed the letter to the woman opposite, who put it back in her bag, snapped it shut and drew on her gloves again, for they were approaching the station where she must get out. Then with a small, tired sigh she gazed up at the dressing-case in the rack above her head. It was a beautiful one, but abominably heavy. It had been given her in the days of lady's maids and a plethora of porters. But the sigh had the effect she intended.

"Allow me," said the man opposite, and lifted it down for her.

"Oh, thank you!" she cried, with a delightful surprise that did not in the least deceive him.

"Got anything anywhere else?" he enquired.

He knew she hadn't, but he wanted to hear her speak again, for she had a beautiful voice, and her smile was enchanting.

"Nothing else, thank you."

"Lovely day."

"Lovely."

And now she, too, looked at him with real attention. For his voice also was arresting. "Nice old thing," she had thought before, when he had got in at Winchester. But now she saw that she had been deceived by the baldness of his head, and by his tawny, greying beard, for he was not old. Only sixtyish. He had a good figure, tall, strong and upright. His face looked as though the features had been shaken up and then assembled anyhow. The large mouth was crooked, the nose had apparently been broken in the shaking process, one of his enquiring, bushy eyebrows mounted higher in enquiry than the other. Yet it was an attractive face, redeemed from ugliness by the humour and expressiveness of the mouth, the breadth of the forehead, the kindliness and penetration of the tawny lion's eyes. His shabby, loose-fitting tweeds had been expensive once, and he wore them with a careless grace that was almost regal. Sixty-ish though he might be, he was still exceedingly attractive and immensely vigorous. Tired to death as she was, Nadine was seized with a sudden ridiculous desire not to get out at her station at all, but to cast herself upon his chest and ask him to take her wherever it was that he was going.... For she had a feeling that he was going to an exceedingly expensive hotel somewhere—the sort of hotel where you lie in a deck-chair in the sun and do nothing at all, and where delicious food is set before you without any volition of your own, where the bath-water is always piping hot (again without any volition of your own) and you are called in the morning with a cup of tea.... Only of course such hotels did not exist these days.... The sight of this man, so obviously not of this present age, had taken her back to the age where he belonged, the pre-Hitler age. "Grandmother would like him," she thought. "He's a gentleman."

"Good-bye," he said, opening the carriage door for her.

"Good-bye," she answered, and suppressing the desire to fall on his chest she stepped out of the carriage and moved gracefully down the platform, to where her brother-in-law Hilary was blinking short-sightedly through his spectacles at every part of the train except the right one.

– 2 –

"I'm here, Hilary," she said.

He swung round, smiled at her, took her case in his left hand and seized her right hand in a grasp that made her wince. Yet she returned the grip and gave him the very sweetest smile she could possibly conjure up. Nadine and Hilary had little in common and they were, in addition, slightly scared of each other. Hilary, a bachelor country parson, was not lacking in that courage which distinguished all the Eliots, but he was definitely scared of three things—women of the type of Nadine, whom he described to himself as "women of the world," the percolation of luxury into his personal life, and pride. Nadine shied like a startled thoroughbred from that something in Hilary, she did not quite know what, which seemed always to challenge her to some action that she did not want to take.

"It's sweet of you to meet me, Hilary," she said.

"I had to," said Hilary, with his usual devastating truthfulness. "The village taxi has broken down again and mine was the only car available."

"I am afraid I am a great nuisance, taking up your time like this," murmured Nadine, as they left the station and approached the battered old Ford.

"Not at all," said Hilary cheerfully. "I had to come in to the bank, anyhow. Get in, will you? The self-starter is out of order. I'll have to wind her up. How's George?"

"Not too bad," said Nadine. "He's never been the same since that lung wound, you know. He's wretched always with this miserable asthma."

"Ought to live in the country," said Hilary, levering the handle.

"He has this War Office appointment," said Nadine, mentally thanking God for it.... How she would hate to live permanently in the country!

"Ought to leave the army now," said Hilary. "He's getting on. We're all getting on. Especially my old Ford. There! She's off!"

The Ford coughed twice, bounced spasmodically and stopped

again just as Hilary settled himself in the driver's seat. He gave no exclamation of impatience. He just smiled, got out, and wound her up again. At the third trial they really were off.

"Wonderful old car," said Hilary, with deep affection. "Thirteen years old and still serviceable. Don't know what I'd do if I hadn't got her. Mine's a scattered parish, you know. I'd never get through all the visiting without her."

Hilary had been badly wounded and gassed as a Chaplain in the First World War and had permanently impaired health and a permanently lamed and painful leg. Because of this he had been appointed to a small country parish, and had now been Vicar of Fairhaven for twenty-seven years. He was sixty-six years old, the eldest of Lucilla Eliot's five children, and so the nominal head of the Eliot family. But only nominal. It was Lucilla who ruled. In looks all the Eliots were either very beautiful or very plain, according as they took after Grandmother or Grandfather Eliot. There were no half measures. They were either one thing or the other. Hilary was the other. He was bald and stout and looked already an old man. Yet he had the Eliot charm, inherited from Lucilla: a complete lack of affectation, a simplicity that was wholly disarming and yet a little misleading, because it was combined with considerable astuteness.... Nadine was always uncomfortably aware that Hilary's kind brown eyes saw a very great deal more than most people realized.... And he had, too, a charm that was all of his own, an indefinable air of aristocracy that was the outcome of his own secret spiritual victories. In Hilary that something in a man that is independent of inheritance, training or tradition, though it has its roots in them like a plant in the soil, had grown to unusual height and strength. No one took much notice of Hilary when they first met him, but they found that he grew upon them.

Fairhaven had no station and, being of a conservative turn of mind, hoped it never would, and very few shops. Visitors had to be met, and anything very ambitious in the way of a purchase had to be made at Radford, down whose main street Hilary's Ford was now chugging. It was a second-rate modern sea-coast town of which Fairhaven, boasting ancient history, always expected the worst.

"They're putting up a holiday camp here now," said Hilary.

"One would expect that," said Nadine.

But they both spoke placidly, for four good lengthy English miles divided Radford and Fairhaven, and the one and only good thing to be said about this lean post-war period was that its shortages put a brake upon so-called progress. It would be a very long time before the vulgarity of Radford engulfed Fairhaven.

Fairhaven consisted of two hamlets, Big Village and Little Village. Big Village, a few miles inland, had one of the loveliest and most ancient churches in all Hampshire and its cob cottages, with their thatched roofs and whitewashed walls, squatted around it like white chickens round a grey old hen. The whole place, deeply embedded in orchards and gardens and haystacks and cupped in a small, sheltered green valley, was now so much a part of its native earth that it seemed a thing not built upon that earth, but grown out of it; as Little Village had grown out of the mysterious sea-marshes that linked the peaceful beauty of the green inland pastures to the terror of the sea. Little Village, consisting of the old house of Damerosehay sheltering behind its wind-twisted oakwood, the shop and Coastguard Station, the "Eel and Lobster," a few fishermen's cottages and the Harbour, boasted no white and gold gleaming in the sun. Its fuchsias and tamarisk trees clustered about solid walls of grey stone, and the shadows of the wheeling gulls touched with dim blue roofs of slate that were the colour of a sunless sea. Little Village had elbowed its way through the exquisite shifting colours of the marshes with the knowledge that they could at any time be swept away like a rainbow by the incoming storm of the sea, and had armoured itself accordingly like some crustacean of the deep. It was a matter of temperament which of the two hamlets one considered the more beautiful. Adventurous hearts preferred Little Village, and of these was Nadine. She was a little surprised at her own preference, for she was no country lover, and Big Village possessed more of the amenities of civilization than Little Village. But there was something about Little Village and the marshes that allied itself with what was best in one and resolved confusions. She seldom paid a visit to Damerosehay without going away again strengthened and subtly changed. As they chugged along the main road she watched eagerly for the narrow, rutted lane that led down to the marshes and gave one one's first breath of the sea.

"How's Grandmother?" she asked.

"Eighty-five years old," said Hilary.

"Not failing?" she asked anxiously.

Grandmother was to the Eliot family what the hub of a wheel is to the spokes. She kept them together. She was the heart of Damerosehay. In a sense she was Damerosehay. None of her children or grandchildren dared to think what life would be without her.

"Not in herself," said Hilary cheerfully. "Mentally and spiritually she's as alert as ever she was. We're all tied to her apron-strings more firmly than ever, I think. But physically she's very tired. And she misses Ellen."

Ellen, Grandmother's maid, who had been with her since her marriage, had died suddenly just before the war.

"Poor Grandmother!" said Nadine. "Losing Ellen must have been like losing an arm or a leg."

"Worse," said Hilary briefly.

The car swung to the right into the rutted lane, and the cool tang of the sea came to meet them. They were silent while Nadine watched for what to returning Eliots was the first sight of home—the two cornfields that marked the place where the lane swung east towards Little Village; the cultivated one upon the landward side of the lane and the wild one in the marsh that had sprung up year by year ever since a grain-ship had been wrecked there, bearing a strange stunted harvest that could not be reaped, but only reverenced for the mystery of renewal. The real cornfield was being harrowed, and Hilary drove slowly, that Nadine might feast her eyes upon the sight of the two old horses passing back and forth, with a cloud of gleaming gulls following after.

"Lovely," murmured Nadine.

"One of the best sights in the world," said Hilary. "Remember how the children used to hang over the gate to watch!"

"It always seems a little odd," she said, "to come home to Damerosehay and not be welcomed by the children."

In the pre-war days, when Nadine had been separated from George and had been managing an antique furniture shop in London, and her three elder children, Ben, Tommy and Caroline, had lived with Grandmother at Damerosehay, it had been their habit to await the advent of especially beloved visitors at the corner between the cornfields. It was odd not to see Ben's and Tommy's dark heads and Caroline's sun-bonnet bobbing about in the sun.

"Odd and wrong," said Hilary decidedly. "Children ought to live in the country."

"Ben and Tommy and Caroline are at school in the country for most of the year," said Nadine tartly, "and they thoroughly enjoy the contrast of the London holidays."

"And the twins?" asked Hilary.

"The twins go to a little nursery school in Chelsea," said Nadine. "If they didn't they'd kill me. In the country there are no nursery schools."

"There are other things," said Hilary. "I am told that in the country the mortality among mothers is less high than in the towns. You can turn children loose in the country."

"You have no experience," Nadine informed him, "of what happens when the twins are turned loose."

She looked at her brother-in-law suspiciously. Who had put it into his head that country life was better for mothers as well as for children? Grandmother? If Grandmother had got it into her head that she and George and the children must all come and live in the country, then she was not going to enjoy her forthcoming visit.

"You'll be glad of a cup of tea," said Hilary, sensing agitation in her.

It was the chief thing that he knew about women: that they could always be calmed down by the fact, or even by the prospect, of a cup of tea.

But the beauty of the marshes, even more than the prospect of tea, was already calming Nadine. They had laid aside all terror today, and their mystery was that of beauty only. It was that moment of approaching sunset when the flaming patches of gorse, the wild marsh flowers, the sea-grasses, the crimson, peaty earth, the creeks and gullies of blue water were yielding to the last demands of the sun all that they possessed of glory. The line of the distant sea was jade-green, the sky turquoise. The old Castle, built upon a tongue of land jutting out into the Estuary to the east, had parted with its usual sombreness and gathered an amber warmth into its old stones. Beyond the Estuary the white cliffs of the Island had lost the hard, chalky look that had been theirs when the sun was high, and seemed fashioned all of pearl.

And now they were in Little Village, with the glinting Harbour to the right of them, the cottages among their fuchsias and tamarisks to the left, and before them the old oakwood that protected Damerosehay, with the broken gate leading into it.

"Is anybody ever going to mend that gate?" asked Nadine.

"I shouldn't think so," said Hilary. "It always has been like that."

"If that isn't Damerosehay all over!" said Nadine.

But she spoke more in pleasure than exasperation. It was because Damerosehay did not change that in this chaotic, tumbling, terrifying world it was a place of such comfort.

The moss grew thickly on the drive, and on the lichened boughs of the old gnarled oak-trees the new, coral-tipped young leaves were burning like candles. It was strange, thought Nadine, that creatures so gloriously fresh and young as those bright leaves could draw their life from anything so old and twisted as those oak-trees.... It gave one hope.... About the twisted roots of the trees a few late narcissus held up their white stars most proudly in the grass, and to the left of the drive the beautiful wrought-iron gateway that pierced the high red-brick garden wall gave her a glimpse of heavenly colour: flame-coloured tulips, forget-me-nots, deep red wall-flowers and golden broom. The scent of the flowers came over the wall in great gusts of perfume, and somewhere in the unseen garden a blackbird was singing in the ilex-tree.

Hilary's Ford gave a final bounce, collided with the mounting-block beside the front door and rocked to a standstill. Hilary drove abominably, and yet he never had a real accident, like so many expert drivers. The house of Damerosehay boasted a porch, added in the eighteenth century to the much older building, with a room built on top of it looking out towards the marshes. The porch was in itself like a little room, with benches upon each side and small windows framed in honeysuckle. It was the delight of every child who came to the house. The front door was of beautiful old mahogany, with a brass knocker and slit to the letter-box and a big brass door-handle. Hilary turned the handle, and they went in to the dim, stone-flagged, panelled hall, with the beautiful old staircase curving away into the dimness. Everything was just as it always was, with the old carved oak chest in its accustomed place with a bowl of glowing tulips set upon it, the dogs' leads hanging from their accustomed hook, set incongruously beneath the beautiful French mirror on the wall. And the smell of Damerosehay was just the same: the mingled scent of wood smoke, flowers, furniture polish, dogs and oil lamps. The Eliots were always going to install electric light, but somehow they never did. Something always seemed to happen to prevent them, such as a world war, or the absorption of available funds by the country drainage system, which always required to have a lot of money spent upon it, but yet somehow was never really satisfactory. Besides, the Eliots rather liked the soft light and the soft smell of oil, and were loathe to part with them; with the exception of Margaret, Grandmother's daughter, who did the lamps.

"Here's the Bastard," said Hilary, as a curious mass of grey fur, like an animated hearthrug, came scurrying from the shadows with frantic yappings and barkings of delight, cast itself at Nadine's feet and slobbered ecstatically over her shoes.

Nadine sighed patiently, for her shoes were new. Also she disliked displays of emotion, and could never feel for the Bastard that intense affection that was felt by other members of the family. The Bastard was of great age—seventeen years old—and had lived at Damerosehay all his life. He was an institution. No one knew what he was, but he was more like a sheepdog than anything else. He had become in old age immensely fat, and found it difficult sometimes to get his breath. He was also rather blind. But he still liked being alive, and Margaret spent hours brushing him, washing him, scenting him with delicate violet powder, dosing him and cooking his special food, staving off by every means in her power that desperate day when he wouldn't like mortal life any more and they would have in mercy to take it from him. But that day was some way off yet, for the mainspring of the Bastard's existence was a passionate devotion to the Eliot family, and he found his joy in life in the expression of it, so that he did not much mind his aches and pains or the indignity of his obesity.

It was otherwise with the chow Pooh-Bah, to whom the maintenance of personal dignity and the preservation of personal beauty were of prime importance. In this he was like Nadine, and they had always got on very well together. It was with real respect and liking that Nadine, having perfunctorily patted the Bastard, withdrew her feet from beneath his crushing weight and held out her hand to the dignified figure of the Chinese aristocrat, who was pacing to meet her with cordial but critical appreciation of her merits writ large upon his noble countenance. He, too, was old, though not so old as the Bastard, and the fur on his nose and the tip of his beautiful tail was white, but he still kept his graceful, regal figure, and the rest of his coat was still the colour of a ripe cornfield with the sun on it. He inclined his splendid head slightly to receive her respectful caress, as a king would graciously extend a hand to be kissed, and then led the way with dignity towards the drawing-room door, ushering them as a seneschal would do into the presence of the Queen.

CHAPTER

– 1 –

GRANDMOTHER SAT IN HER ARM-CHAIR by the wood fire in the drawing-room. In old days she had always got up to receive her visitors, but nowadays, with her rheumatism so much worse than it used to be, she could no longer rise gracefully from her chair, so she remained contentedly seated. She had always been beautiful, was beautiful now, and had every intention of remaining beautiful until the end of her days, and she did not in the least begrudge either the spending of a great deal of time and trouble upon the outer façade of beauty, or the curtailing of her activities by the elimination of those which she could no longer accomplish with grace. It seemed to her children and grandchildren that she did not mind growing old. There was nothing of desperation in the firm hold she kept upon her beauty, it was rather that she appeared to be taking good care of something entrusted to her care, but did not seem to regard it as an integral part of her.

"Nadine, my dear, I am so glad to see you," said Grandmother. Her voice had deepened with old age but lost none of its eager warmth, and it had gained that lilt of music that comes into the voices of the old when they are without querulousness. "You're alone, dear?"

"Yes, Grandmother," replied Nadine. "Did you expect me not to be?"

"I just thought, dear, that perhaps George and the children might have come with you, after all," said Grandmother, trying to keep the disappointment out of her voice.

"The whole family would have been too much to inflict on you," said Nadine lightly. "And George can't leave the War Office. I told you that, you know, when you rang up.... Darling, how are you?"

And Nadine bent to kiss her mother-in-law with mingled love, resentment and exasperation. She did not deeply love Lucilla, but she did not forget that in the past, when it had come to a battle of wills between them, Grandmother had won and she could never quite accept with acquiescence as did the rest of the family, the fact that this frail old woman, sitting here in this absurd old-fashioned room, and never even raising her voice, moulded the entire Eliot clan as wax in her fingers. Nadine was a woman of strong character, and the knowledge that since she had taken the name of Eliot she had scarcely ever had her own way made her at times feel like a cat with its fur stroked backwards.

Grandmother, Lucilla Eliot, had spent practically the whole of the greatest war in history either sitting in her arm-chair by the fire, or on really hot days sitting in her wicker-chair out in the garden under the ilex-tree, the Bastard lying at her feet with his chin propped on one of her shoes, Pooh-Bah sitting beside her. She had left the fire or the ilex-tree only to go to church, bed, to meals in the dining-room, or to pay a rare call upon an old friend. It was the opinion of her children and grandchildren that dear Grandmother had felt the war very little. Nothing that happened, not even the eruption of evacuees into her home, had ruffled her outward serenity, and she had made very little comment upon it. The change in her appearance that had taken place during the six years they put down merely to the passing of the years. Old people did not feel things very much, they said, and what a comfort that was!

But as a matter of fact the six years of the war had been for Lucilla a time of mental and spiritual activity and suffering as great as any she had known.... And she had had to go through it all without her beloved old maid Ellen, who had always been through everything with her before, and whom she had loved more than anyone had any idea of; except perhaps Hilary.

Damerosehay, that nearly twenty years ago had been bought by Lucilla as a sanctuary where the whole family could come to be re-made when the turmoil of life in the world had chipped bits off them, had through long periods of the war been obliged to say good-bye to its peace. The English Channel was to the south of the marshes, the Estuary, leading to one of the greatest of the naval ports, bounded them upon the east. Enemy planes had passed over day and night, guns had roared out at sea, and the old house had rocked to the explosions of bombs falling in the marshes. Lucilla was a brave woman, and physical danger had no terrors for her, but quiet was essential to her well-being, and she had suffered excruciating torture from the racket. Through long, noisy nights she had laid rigid in her bed, her hands gripping the sheets upon either side of her, trying not to cry just because the noise made her feel so terribly exhausted. Her one desire upon these occasions had been to be let alone, but she had never been let alone. Her daughter Margaret, and any visitors, evacuees or servants who might be with them at the time, had always come along in dressing-gowns to sit with her lest she should be frightened.... At least, so they said.... It was, as it happened, they who had been frightened, and their subconscious reason for coming had been to stay themselves upon her courage. This they had done, exhausting her still further. But she had given no signs of her exhaustion. She had kept them laughing through the night, telling them tales of her youth, and when the raid was over she had made them tea and sent them back to bed to sleep soundly until morning, while she lay awake too tired to sleep.

But the noise, and the necessity for bolstering up the others, had been as nothing to the torturing anxiety of those years. In the First World War Lucilla had lost two of her five sons, one of them her son Maurice, the great love of her life, and had suffered deep anxiety for the other three. In this war of the three sons left her, Hilary, George and Stephen, only George had been fighting, but the two sons of her son Stephen, the lawyer, went into the Services, and also David, Maurice's only son, whom she had brought up from his babyhood and who had meant to her quite simply the whole of her world. Stephen's sons had been killed, one in Norway and one in Greece, and day by day she had waited for news of David's death in the air. The first war had taken his father, this one would take him. On the first day of the war she had made up her mind to that, arming herself beforehand to face what would be the worst thing that could possibly happen to her. The fact that it hadn't happened, that by some miracle David had come through safely, had not altered the fact that for six years she expected it to happen, and through every day of those six years had never heard a ring at the bell or a step in the hall without steeling herself to face the shattering of her world. The perpetual anti-climaxes, when the ring at the bell had been only the butcher and the step only Margaret back from her Red-Cross working party earlier than usual, had been in themselves exhausting.

And then, for a woman of Lucilla's vivid imagination and deep sympathies, her own personal sorrows and anxieties had not been the only ones that she had had to bear. She had borne also as much as she was able of the sorrow of the world. For she had learned really to pray. For the first time in her life she had discovered prayer to be not what it had hitherto been to her, "the conscious occupation of the praying mind, or the sound of the voice praying," but a ceaseless offering up of the whole personality, of every thought and word and action, as sacrifice. And it was exceedingly tiring.... So that what with one thing and another Lucilla had spent a very active six years.... But sitting in her chair before the fire, or under the ilex-tree, knitting hour after hour for the Forces or for the evacuee children who surged about her, she had been careful to give no sign, either by word or look, of the extent of her endurance. It had been her opinion that in wartime old people were a great nuisance and the best thing they could do was to keep, at whatever cost, a tranquil exterior, and get on with their knitting. She was too humble a woman to assess her wartime activity at its true value.

But it had left its mark, and Nadine, who had not seen Grandmother for more than a year, was saddened at the change in her. She had to hold her tall, slender figure so rigidly, to keep herself from sagging, that she had lost some of her grace, her blue eyes were sunken and her face deeply lined. But she was still most beautiful, the undefinable elements of her beauty—her elegance and dignity and luminous vitality—seeming to have deepened in quality now that the more obvious loveliness had faded. And her fastidious daintiness was as adorable as ever, and to Nadine deeply touching because she guessed at what cost it was achieved. There was no Ellen now, and Margaret was the clumsiest creature who ever lived, so it must have been she herself who had dressed her lovely white hair so perfectly, and sewn such spotless lace at the neck and wrists of her simple black frock, with the faint scent of verbena clinging to its folds, and the task could have been neither quick nor easy for her rheumaticky hands.

"You're just the same, Grandmother," lied Nadine, as she bent to kiss her, speaking with as much intent to comfort herself as to please Grandmother.

Lucilla smiled as she returned the kiss, and did not contradict the lie. Indeed, she answered it with another:

"So are you, my dear."

Then they looked at each other and laughed with complete sympathy and comprehension; two beautiful women who had a very low opinion of the stark realities of life and a very high opinion of covering them up with a little persiflage.

Nadine straightened herself and looked about her. Thrones had fallen, armies had vanished into oblivion, great cities had been wiped off the face of the earth, but in the Damerosehay drawing-room not a single ornament had suffered a change of position. The Dresden shepherds and shepherdesses, lambs and cupids, stood just as they had always stood upon the mantlepiece, gay patches of colour against the great carved over-mantel, the Sheraton chairs stood in the same positions upon the same Persian rugs, the stiff, eighteenth-century chintz that covered the sofa and arm-chairs was the same, and the bowls of flowers stood where they had always stood. The drawing-room was not what it had been seven years ago; there were many more darns in the rugs, more cracks in the chintz, and the dents and scratches presented to the chair legs by the kicking feet of the grandchildren had been added to by those of the evacuees. Like Lucilla, it had suffered a slight tarnishing of the outward façade of its beauty, but the essence of it was unchanged.

– 2 –

There was a peculiar rattling sound in the distance.

"It's Margaret with that detestable trolley," said Lucilla, and her delicate old face went suddenly pink with annoyance.

"A *trolley?*" ejaculated Nadine. "A *trolley,* at Damerosehay?"

"Yes, dear," said Grandmother. "While dear Ellen lived I always had afternoon tea brought in properly, on the tea-tray, which was then placed upon my tea-table. But now that dear Ellen is dead Margaret brings in tea, and she's gone and got this trolley thing. She picked it up cheap at a sale, without telling me, she—But there, dear, what's the use? One can't hear oneself think."

The rattle and bang of the trolley approaching over the uneven stone flags of the hall was indeed a shattering sound even through the closed door, and Lucilla shivered dramatically. Nadine tensed a little, and Hilary moved to open the door with a twinkle of amusement in his eye.

Margaret entered, deprecating, shy, aware that Lucilla hated the trolley (though she never said so), aware that Nadine thought she really ought to try to do something about her clothes and hair (though she'd never said so), unhappy because of their disapproval, yet obstinately determined to stick both to the trolley and to the style of dress and hairdressing to which she was accustomed. A gentle yielding to the wishes of others was of the essence of Margaret, yet very rarely she would launch out on her own in the most startling way; as witness that sudden departure one afternoon (without telling Lucilla) to a sale, the having her fancy caught by a particularly hideous trolley, the standing up all by her shy self and bidding for it, the wheeling of it home through the lanes (she who so dreaded to be thought absurd) and the subsequent using of it in the teeth of Lucilla's unspoken disapproval. Lucilla could not understand these outbreaks of Margaret's.... Neither could Margaret... Hilary could. She had been a slave all her life long to Damerosehay and the Eliots, but in these little startling outbreaks, and in the glory of the garden that she had made, she went free. He set the door wide and smiled reassuringly at his sister. Lucilla was the great love of his life, but after her came Margaret. For besides his reverence for her selflessness, with its complete freedom from the least taint of bitterness or self-pity, his delight in her sudden flashes of independence, he had for her a deep fellow feeling. She, as well as he, was one of the homely Eliots.

Margaret was now sixty-three, though she did not look more than fifty. Like all keen gardeners, she had become weatherbeaten at an early age, so that when she got to fifty she could not well become more so than she was, and it merely remained for the coming years to keep her young with the joy in flowers and sunshine and good earth that grew increasingly day by day. She was tall, but bony and awkward in her movements, not soft and graceful like Lucilla. Her thick, rough, grey hair was cut short in a desperate effort to keep it tidy; yet it never was tidy. She wore heather-covered tweeds, faded by the sun and pulled out of shape by wind and rain, and a jumper deplorably knitted by herself in a shade of bright yellow that was all wrong with her tweeds. She liked knitting, though she did not do it very well, and she loved bright colours, though she was without discrimination in their use. Her woollen stockings were much darned, and her thick shoes made almost as much noise as the trolley.

"Hilary," said Lucilla, "help Margaret lift that trolley over the rugs. It has such silly little wheels, and they catch, and then the milk spills on the tray-cloth, and if there's one thing I can't stand it's a stained tray-cloth."

She spoke with deep apprehension, as though yet another international disaster threatened, and Margaret's face, bent in agonized concentration over the trolley, might have been that of a surgeon absorbed in a task of life or death.

Hilary's eyes twinkled again; he lifted his end of the trolley too high and sent a cascade of little buns catapulting to the floor. Lucilla opened her mouth to tell Hilary that he hadn't been paying attention to what he was doing, and to remind Margaret of how many, many times in the past she had told her *not* to pile the plates too full, remembered just in time that her children were grown up now—both in their sixties—shut it and said nothing.... It was strange, very strange, to be the mother of old people.... Because she herself felt so much younger than they were.

"How are you, Margaret?" asked Nadine.

Margaret started and flushed scarlet, because she had been so absorbed in the trolley that she had entirely forgotten to greet Nadine.

"I'm quite well, dear," she said in her soft, gentle voice, a very young voice, oddly touching in contrast with her elderly appearance. "And you? You look tired out. And the children? Is London agreeing with them?"

"Perfectly," said Nadine.

"George, when he wrote, said something about Ben having a cough," put in Lucilla softly.

"Just the remains of a cold. The children are splendid," said Nadine decisively, giving Margaret a dutiful kiss. "And if I look tired it's not London, but the splendidness of the children."

Margaret shrank a little from the kiss, not from lack of affection, but because she hesitated to touch the exquisite, flower-like face of her sister-in-law with her own weather-beaten cheek. She adored Nadine's beauty, even as she adored the beauty of the flowers in the garden. Nadine, misunderstanding the shrinking, was saddened by it. Though she regarded Margaret as an ancient museum piece beyond her comprehension, yet she reverenced her. She would have been glad if they could have achieved real friendship. But she knew they never would.

Margaret poured the tea into Lucilla's delicate Worcester cups, slopping it into the saucers a little as she did so. Hilary retrieved the buns from the floor, and they settled down to their tea with the dogs at their feet. Lucilla nibbled at one of Margaret's rather thick pieces of bread and butter, surreptitiously gave her bun bit by bit to the Bastard because somehow she could never fancy food that had been on the floor, and tried not to remember how dainty the teas had been when dear Ellen was alive. Margaret worked so very hard, with only intermittent assistance from Big Village to help her, was so desperately anxious to please always that it did not seem loyal to her to hanker after the old days.... But it was hard not to when one's tea was slopped over into the saucer.... Wrenching her mind away from the longing for Ellen that was always with her, like a persistent toothache, she tried to pay attention to what the others were saying. But they were talking about the deplorable state of the world, about that terrible bomb, about famine and inflation and chaos and death, and her mind shied away from their talk like a terrified horse. She couldn't do anything about it now, at eighty-six, except pray, and in between her prayers, now that the war was over, she wished they would let her forget sometimes that things had not turned out as well as one had hoped and enjoy the things that were left: the spring sunshine slanting into the quiet room, lighting up the flowers and the lovely ripe corn colour of Pooh-Bah's coat, the hot tea, the log fire burning on the hearth, whispering and fragrant, the feel of the dear old Bastard's chin resting on her shoe, the sound of the sea coming in the pauses of their talk.

"Don't!" she cried to them suddenly. "It's this that matters—this!"

"What, Mother?" asked Margaret, who never could follow the workings of another's mind unless it was explained to her very carefully and at great length.

"Beauty is truth?" asked Hilary, coming a little nearer.

But Nadine, without words stretched out a hand and gently touched her mother-in-law's. They had both been married and borne children. Lucilla knew always, and Nadine knew in her more domesticated moments, that it was home-making that mattered. Every home was a brick in the great wall of decent living that men erected over and over again as a bulwark against the perpetual flooding in of evil. But women made the bricks, and the durableness of each civilization depended upon their quality; and it was no good weakening oneself for the brick-making by thinking too much about the flood.

"You'd scarcely recognize the twins now, they've grown so much," said Nadine, watching for the little light of happiness that always sprang into Lucilla's eyes at any mention of her beloved grandchildren.

The flame leaped, then died.

"It's such a long time since I've seen them! Or Ben or Tommy or Caroline either," mourned Lucilla.

"Why Grandmother, George brought the older children to stay with you three months ago!" said Nadine.

"Four months," corrected Lucilla. "And that's a very long time, and he did not bring the twins."

"Only because they had chicken-pox, Grandmother."

"George and the children ought to have come down with you," said Margaret.

"I thought it would be best to interview Jill by myself," said Nadine. "Also I wanted a rest from George and the children."

Margaret, who had lost the lover of her childhood in the First World War and had idealized marriage ever since, looked shocked, but Lucilla agreed placidly: "One does."

"Who's looking after George and the children?" asked Hilary.

"My cousin Pamela Lyson is coping. She loves it for a few days, but not longer. She's elderly. She goes to pieces on the evening of the fourth day, but I'll be back then."

"I'm so glad you're going to have Jill, dear," said Lucilla.

"But I don't know that I am, Grandmother. I'm only going to interview her."

"As soon as I saw your advertisement in the paper, dear—and it was lucky that I did see it, for you never told me that you were inserting it—I went over to see Jill. Hilary drove me over. I remembered her as a sweet girl, but I was afraid the war might have changed her. But it hasn't. She's just the same, and exactly the influence the children need. I showed her your advertisement, and told her to answer it, and you should have seen her joy at the idea of being with her dear Ben and Tommy and Caroline again. The only difficulty, dear, is that, being a country-bred girl, I do not know whether she will want to take a permanent post in Town. She was in London for a time during the war, and it doesn't agree with her, she says, and I'm sure I don't wonder. So noisy and dirty now. Not like it used to be in the old days. But I told her I did not think it would be long now before you were all settled in the country."

Nadine flushed a faint and lovely pink—she had the rare gift of looking really beautiful when angry—and gripped her hands tightly together on her lap. Her feeling for her mother-in-law swung always between reverence and exasperation, according as the selflessness of Grandmother's autocracy, or the autocracy of her selflessness, was uppermost.

"But, Grandmother," she said slowly and evenly, "our living in the country is quite out of the question. George has this job at the War Office."

"I know you dislike the country, dear," said Lucilla, "but I think you should consider George and the children. Town life is always bad for children, and after all he has been through in the war George would have better health in good air. He could resign his War Office appointment."

"But, Grandmother. He couldn't afford to. We have the children's education to think about."

"My son George, dear, though a stupid man in many ways, has always had a clear head in practical matters. He would find ways of augmenting your income in the country. And you know, dear, you would have quite a nice little income to augment. You would have George's pension, and your legacy from your Aunt Anne. You did not tell me that your Aunt had died, dear—and, after all, why should you, for she was unknown to me?—but I saw the announcement in *The Times* and I saw her will, too, in *The Times.*"

"There's not as much as you'd think, Grandmother. Not with Income Tax."

"Income tax," murmured Lucilla meditatively, "comes in very useful. When people could quite well afford to do something they ought to do, but don't want to, they always plead income tax. The war flour is useful, too. When cakes don't rise there's a scapegoat handy."

And she secretly gave the Bastard the last bit of her bun.

No one's feelings were hurt. There were times nowadays when Lucilla uttered aloud the sentiments that she thought she was only thinking. This was obviously one of those times.

"Yes, dear," she said more loudly, with intention to be heard, "I've arranged about your interview with Jill. She's coming to see you this evening."

"But, Grandmother," pleaded Nadine, "I had thought I would go and see her. When one is interviewing anyone as important as a Nannie it is rather nice to see the sort of home they have."

"It isn't her home, dear: it's her aunt's."

"I know, but she's been there for some time, and it's her present setting. I should know much more about her seeing her there."

"It's too far for you to walk, dear, and the village taxi has broken down."

"I know, Grandmother, but I thought Hilary would be so kind as to take me."

"Certainly," said Hilary cheerfully.

"No, dear," said Lucilla firmly. "We can't take Hilary away from his parish duties and use him as a taxi two days running; it wouldn't be right." Suddenly she looked no longer firm, but pathetic and pleading. "I've arranged it all so nicely, dear. Jill is to come over with the Bread and go back with the Meat. Our tradesmen are always so kind and obliging. That's one of the good things the war has done—made us all more friendly together. I'd arranged it all so nicely."

Nadine yielded.

"That's all right, Grandmother," she said gently. "I'll see Jill here. It was sweet of you to arrange that for me."

Lucilla's lovely blue eyes were alight with love as she smiled upon her obedient daughter-in-law. That horrid tight feeling that came about her heart when people opposed her eased a little. It was a nasty feeling, and people would never oppose her if they knew how nasty it was.

"If we've finished I'll clear," said Margaret.

"I'll help you wash up," said Nadine with that too-bright willingness of the domestically wearied guest who hopes to goodness her noble offer will be refused.

"Don't bother, dear," said Margaret, making the answer that had now become codified in the Eliot family. "Not your first evening. Tomorrow you shall help me."

"Hilary," said Lucilla, "help Margaret lift the trolley over the rucks in the rugs that you made when you brought it in."

"Yes, Mother," said Hilary.

A bell rang.

"That's Jill," said Lucilla. "I have arranged, Nadine, that you shall see her in the dining-room."

"Yes, Grandmother," said Nadine.

– 3 –

The Damerosehay dining-room, in spite of its beautiful pan-elling, lacked the charm of the drawing-room, and was detested by all the Eliots except Lucilla, Hilary and Margaret. It was a chill yet stuffy room, and after one had eaten fish or onions in it one knew that one had for a very long time after. It had been Ellen's special pride, and because she had loved it so much Lucilla would not let it be altered in any way. It remained what Ellen had made it, a shrine of Victorian respectability. It had heavy mahogany furniture, heavy crimson curtains and carpet, heavy silver upon the sideboard. A massive portrait of Grandfather in his legal wig and robes hung above the mantelpiece, and his heavy, kindly face looked out with approval over the room that Ellen had created to his memory. Ellen had deeply respected Sir James Eliot, and it was largely owing to her that Lucilla, who had not loved him in the early days of their mar-riage, nor the children that she had borne him either, had become in the end a pattern wife and mother and had created that tradition of faithfulness in an accepted task, faithfulness at whatever cost, which was now the special tradition of the Eliots and Damerosehay.

Nadine knew the story of Lucilla's youth; and indeed it had been her story more than anything else that had reunited her to George. The influence of Ellen, maid and Nannie to the Eliots for a lifetime, had been, and was, deep and strong even to the third generation, and it struck Nadine almost like a blow in the face, when she entered the detested dining-room, to see Jill standing there like another Ellen, straight and stiff beneath the portrait of her father-in-law, looking an integral part of the room. She felt suddenly caught. When, compelled by the Damerosehay tradition, she had broken with the man she loved and come back again to her unloved hus-band, it had been with a scarcely recognized inner reservation. While David, who loved her, and whom she so desperately loved, was alive and free in the world, still loving and desiring her, the door was not shut. If it did not work with George, if it once more became utterly impossible, David was still there. She had never said this to herself in so many words, but the thought of that secret stair of escape was always with her. It was the rock to which she clung when it seemed as though her unhappiness would overwhelm her. And now, looking at Jill, it was as though the door to the stair, always ajar, began to close. For this was a woman without reservations. Jill made her afraid even as Hilary made her afraid. From Hilary's challenge she could escape, because she saw so little of him, but from Jill's she would not be able to escape. They would be together always, Mother and Nannie, even as Lucilla and Ellen had been together always, with Jill's single-mindedness a perpetual danger to her own lack of it. She paused for a moment, not knowing what to say, at a loss for perhaps the first time in her self-possessed life. It was Jill who spoke first.

"Good afternoon, Madam," said Jill.

Her voice was timid and soft, and at the sound of it Nadine suddenly lost that ridiculous feeling of panic and was herself again, a beautiful, well-dressed, self-possessed woman of the world interviewing a rather scared, dowdy little country woman who had applied to her for the post of Nannie to her children.... Jill, after all, was not in the least like Ellen. It had just been a fancy of hers.

"Good afternoon, Jill," said Nadine, shaking hands graciously. "It's nice to see you again. Do sit down."

"Thank you, Madam," whispered Jill, and perched herself stiff as a ramrod upon the extreme edge of one of the hard dining-room chairs.

Nadine sat upon another, and found that she also had to hold herself stiff as a ramrod. She had forgotten how uncomfortable they were! She was sure they had been chosen originally by Grandfather Eliot to teach deportment to the Eliot young. Sighing, and fitting her back as comfortably as she could against the panel of wood behind her, she resigned herself to looking like a seated Pharaoh, back rigid, feet together, and studied Jill.

Jill was twenty-four years old now, but in spite of marriage and widowhood she still looked like the child-nursemaid Nadine had briefly known in the Damerosehay nursery before the war. She was thin and undersized, with a plain, pale face redeemed by very beautiful eyes of a clear shade of green—the green that is seen in the curve of a wave upon a shadowed day. Her mouth was tender and her chin was strong. In her neat grey flannel coat and skirt and white blouse she looked already the Nannie she aspired to be. She wore no hat, and her two-coloured, lustreless, straight hair was arranged in a neat roll round her beautifully shaped little head. She kept her ungloved hands very still in her lap. There was nothing about her to challenge attention, and for a brief moment Nadine marvelled that any man had noticed her enough to marry her. Then she noticed again the tenderness of the mouth and the tranquillity of the hands. She opened her mouth to ask the usual questions, and did not ask a single one of them. All she said was, "Jill, you will love my children."

"Yes, Madam," said Jill simply.

"And help me to do my best for them."

"Yes, Madam."

Desperately Nadine groped after the questions she had prepared, but succeeded in capturing only one of them:

"Lady Eliot is afraid you will not be willing to live in London?"

"I'll be perfectly willing, Madam. I did tell Lady Eliot, when she asked me, that I liked the country best; but of course wherever the children are I will make myself contented."

Nadine smiled suddenly, aware that Lucilla stood corrected not of lying—for Lucilla never lied—but of a slight exaggeration to gain her purpose.

"I'm glad you feel like that, Jill," she said. "You see, General Eliot has an appointment at the War Office, and we have a very nice little house at Chelsea, and so we are not likely to leave London."

"I shall like Chelsea, Madam," said Jill. "There is the river and the gulls—like there is at the Hard."

"You love the Hard?" asked Nadine.

"Yes, Madam. I'm sorry my Auntie Rose is selling the Herb of Grace."

"Is she? I did not know that."

"Yes, Madam. She lost my uncle a little while back. It was to help her over his illness and the funeral and all that I left the day nursery where I was working. She don't feel she can keep on the inn alone. She's going to live with Edith, her daughter-in-law. You know the Herb of Grace, Madam?"

"I don't think I do, Jill. I know the little hotel at the Hard, of course, but it's not the one, is it?"

"No, Madam, it's farther on down the river. It's a nice old place, but it's lonely, and it don't get much custom. It didn't pay, through the war."

"I should think it would now that the war is over. People will be sailing again. There will be lots of white wings again, on the estuary and the river."

"Yes, Madam; but Auntie don't seem to feel she can tackle it."

"Yes, I understand. It's the war. None of us feel we can tackle anything. I don't feel I can tackle my children. When can you come to me, Jill?"

"Well, Madam, I'd like to get Auntie Rose settled with Edith before I leave her. In another month?"

Another month! Nadine's heart sank. She had been hoping for next week. Another month! But doubtless Auntie Rose's need was just as great as hers.

"A month from today," she said, firmly clinching it. "I'll write to you from London, Jill, and tell you the train. Have you had a cup of tea?"

"I'll have one when I get home, Madam, if you'll excuse me. I don't want to keep the Meat waiting."

"No, of course not," said Nadine, levering herself forward from her Egyptian position.

Whatever one did or did not do nowadays one had to keep on the right side of the Meat, or there'd be no perquisites for the dogs.

"I'll try to give satisfaction, Madam," said Jill as they shook hands, and then she slipped unobtrusively away into the shadows, opening and closing the door so softly that Nadine was hardly aware that she had gone until she found herself alone.

"I'll try to give satisfaction." It was years since Nadine had heard that old-fashioned remark. Because she had not heard it for so long it struck her as being rather a wonderful phrase. Satisfied. No one ever was. The whole world was crying out with hunger of some sort, physical or spiritual. To try to satisfy. Jill was right. That was all one could do.

She stood still for a moment, one hand over her eyes, desperately conscious of her own particular hunger. For rest. For peace. For David. Most of all for David, because it seemed to be only with him that she could find the other two. During the war it had been comparatively easy to put aside her love for David. There had been so much to do and bear, and one had been so keyed up to the doing and the bearing. Now, though there was still much to do and bear, one wasn't keyed up any more, and the circle of acute consciousness had narrowed from one's country to oneself again, and the personal problems once more pressed intolerably. And David was no longer a flier, seldom accessible to his family, and on his brief leaves seeming withdrawn from them into another element; he was back on the stage again, back in London, back in his old place in the family, Lucilla's favourite grandson, George's nephew. She saw him often, in the same little house in Chelsea where she had lived before the war, during the time of her separation from George, and where they had first fallen in love with each other, and every time she saw him the longing for the love she had put from her grew more intolerable.... Suddenly she hated it all; Damerosehay, Lucilla, George, the children, her duty.... How idiotic it all was! Life was going by so quickly, and she had never yet done a thing she wanted to do.

"Nadine!"

It was Lucilla's voice calling her, and automatically she obeyed and went out to the hall.

Lucilla was sitting on the chair beside the telephone, holding the receiver in her hand.

"It's someone ringing up, dear. But I really can't hear. I'm so deaf, you know. I'm no good at the telephone."

Her voice was full of distress. She hated these modern inventions, telephone and wireless; they did nothing but make a noise and pour out information one was generally better without. She pleaded her deafness as exemption from participation in these benefits of science, but her family noticed that her deafness only seemed to trouble her when it was a question of answering the telephone or turning on the news.

"No one's ill, are they, dear?" she asked anxiously, as Nadine took the receiver.

"No, I don't think so.... Why, it's George.... Hullo, old boy.... You all right? Children all right? You've only just got Grandmother's letter? What letter? What did you say? You can get off for a few days and come down with the children?"

"I think, dear, that this call is really for me," said Lucilla gently; and courteously, but firmly, she removed the receiver from Nadine. "It's Mother, George," she said, and thereafter there was silence while she listened to George. Her deafness did not seem to be troubling her just at the moment. "Yes, dear," she said at last. "Come down tomorrow and bring the children. A little holiday will do you good, and it will be nice for Nadine to have you here, too. You can manage a week? That's good. Dear boy, I'm so glad." Then, still holding the receiver, she turned to Nadine, a smile of sheer happiness irradiating her face like sunshine. "I wrote a little note to George, dear, after you had said over the phone that he would not be able to come down with you. I said to try his hardest and to bring the children. I thought a little holiday would do you all such good. It seems he's only just got my letter. It was delayed in the post. But it's all right, dear, they're coming—twins and all. George will drive them down tomorrow morning."

Lucilla's joy was so lovely a thing to see that Nadine could say nothing to quench it, but she found it difficult to force an answering smile, for if George was driving them all down in the car they'd be here by lunch-time tomorrow, and her period of peace was not going to last very long. Also, George had said something that she did not quite understand: "Only just got Mother's letter. Tell her I'd like to have a look at the old place."

He might, of course have been referring to Damerosehay, but she had a feeling that he was not. What old place had Lucilla suggested he should have a look at? She bent over and very gently took the receiver from Lucilla's hand, even as Lucilla had taken it from hers.

"You still there, George? Yes? Darling, bring my slacks down with you, will you? If we're staying a week I'd like my slacks. And a couple of shirts, too. The blue one and the yellow one. Pamela will see about the children's clothes. Goodbye, darling. Don't forget the slacks."

And she hung up the receiver. Lucilla hated slacks, and out of deference to her sensibilities Nadine had never worn them at Damerosehay. But now she was just going to.

– 4 –

All her life Lucilla had changed her dress twice in the day, once for tea and once again in the evening, and she still did so, even though what she still insisted upon calling dinner was now no more than Bengers for herself, bread and cheese for Margaret, and whatever else they could scrape up when visitors came. Until the war she had requested that the rest of the family dress, too, but now she could no longer insist upon that; they said they had nothing to change into, and in any case what was the point of changing when as soon as a meal was over you had to put on an overall and wash up? Lucilla alone, in the black lace dress she had had for fifteen years, bridged the gap between the gracious manners of the past and what she hoped would be the gracious manners of the future.

For Lucilla was not without hope for the future. She had lived long enough to know that the spring always comes back. Also she knew that if it was to be a flowering spring one must make one's preparations. She was making hers. She herself, she knew, would not see this spring, but her grandchildren and perhaps her children would, and it was for them that she prepared. She sensed in her children, and in David her grown-up grandson and his contemporaries, a deep and desperate fatigue. They seemed to her to be just standing about in the rubble and looking at it despairingly, not knowing what to do about it. They knew they ought to set about rebuilding, but they seemed too tired to make a start. They lacked initiative. When they could they had gone straight back to their pre-war jobs, as David had done, or to their old neighbourhood, as Nadine had gone back to that little house in Chelsea, automatically seeking the old grooves as a strayed cat automatically turns homeward. But though they were back in the old grooves they were back there without the old ardour. From the old homes and the old jobs the virtue had gone out. What they needed, Lucilla considered, was either new homes and new jobs, or else the infusion of some fresh spirit into the old things that should transform them like wine poured into water. Everywhere, in everything, there must be a rebirth, and it was her business as head of the Eliot family to do what she could to make it anew before she died. It might have been argued that her own fatigue was as deep as that of any of her family, and that at her age she had earned the right to sit back and let them plan for her rather than she for them, but Lucilla did not see it that way. For one thing, she realized that the old are to a large extent spectators in the game, and, standing a little aloof from the lives of their children, get them into a clearer perspective than they themselves can hope to do. And then, humble as she was, she could not help but be aware that the experience of a long life had put more sense into one of her little fingers than into the whole of the rest of the family put together. And lastly, Lucilla liked managing. She was a born organizer and, tired though she was, could no more refrain from organizing than a bird from singing. If in her rebuilding she should have to override the wills of others with her own she would do it without compunction, for in what she had planned there was no self-seeking.

Lucilla made her plans during those two periods of the day, at two o'clock and again at six-thirty, when she went to her room, rested, and changed her dress. They were blessed periods, and without them she felt that she could scarcely have gone on living. Increasingly as the years went by, her beautiful bedroom had become for her a sort of sanctuary. There was a deep peace in it—she did not quite know why, unless it was that for so many years it was here that she had prayed most deeply and most often; so often that now when she opened her bedroom door prayer brimmed up in her as automatically as it did when she crossed the threshold of Hilary's church at Big Village.

Having toiled up the stairs on this particular spring evening, Lucilla entered her room, shut the door and looked about her. In the old days Ellen would have been here, standing waiting for her by the window, one hand crossed over the other. Ellen would have helped her into her dressing-gown, and then she would have lain down on the sofa and watched Ellen get out her black lace dress from the wardrobe, shake out its folds, and then take the appropriate petticoat, shoes and handkerchief from their appointed places. All this Ellen would have done with the solemnity of a religious rite, and then she would have brushed Lucilla's hair with the silver-backed hairbrushes, and while she brushed they would have talked: about the children and the grandchildren and the dogs, about the delinquencies of the maids (if they happened to have any) or the daily help (if there was one), about the dreadful way the younger generation behaved and whatever the world could possibly be coming to. Easy talk, not appearing to go much below the surface of things, yet in reality going deep because the two women knew each other so well that with a lightly spoken sentence they could reveal to one another almost the whole of their unspoken thoughts. Well, Ellen's bodily presence was no longer here, and Lucilla missed it intolerably, yet as she moved about her room, doing for herself what Ellen used to do for her, she always found herself talking to Ellen, and her perplexities presently melted away as they had been wont to do when in the old days Ellen had applied to them the acid of her strong horse sense.

Today, following her usual programme, Lucilla took off her dress, put on her soft grey dressing-gown and lay down on the sofa. She prayed a little, and then she placed upon her lap the big black velvet bag from which she was never separated, and which contained her handkerchief, spectacles, bottle of eau-de-Cologne, the silver box which in the old days had always contained sugared almonds for the delectation of the grandchildren but which nowadays, when there weren't any sugared almonds or any grandchildren in permanent residence, contained merely Bisodol tablets for her indigestion and the current letters from her family. She searched through the bag and took out her spectacles and the last letter from her son George.

"I am afraid," she said, speaking to Ellen, "that I am perhaps not being quite straight with Mrs. George. I am working behind her back. Yes, I am. And I hate it when people do that with me. Yet what can I do? I have to think first of my son."

Lucilla's chronic difficulty in realizing that her children were not only grown-up, but elderly, was further increased in the case of her son George by the fact that he never had fully grown up. He was a brilliant soldier, a fine mathematician, he had won nearly every honour which it was possible for him to win in his profession, including the Victoria Cross, but yet there was a part of him that had never grown up. The part of his mind that he applied to the technicalities of his profession was keen and fine as tempered steel, but the part of it that he applied to religion, politics and domesticity had not developed very much since his school days. He was C. of E., a Conservative, a faithful and loving husband, a kind and loving father. But his religion had never consisted in more than believing in God, without having even asked himself what he meant by God, and in going to church to set a good example to the regiment or the children; and his politics were just a matter of believing that whatever "those damned Labour fellows" did was sure to be disastrous. His love for his wife was the unwavering worship of a good dog for his master, and his love for his children the protective, infinitely careful affection of a good master for his dog; in neither case was it very discerning.

He had been a very brave little boy, very loyal and very loving, and he was a brave, loyal and loving man. His courage and loyalty had always been obvious, but not his love, because he had been an inarticulate little boy and he was an inarticulate man. Only Lucilla understood the power of his loving and the suffering it caused him in his life, and only she had ever been able to solve his personal problems for him, because only she had succeeded in knowing about them without being told. As a little boy he had come to her room, fair-haired, blue-eyed and ruddy (he was one of the beautiful Eliots), and standing on one leg like a stork had thoughtfully wiped his nose on the back of his left hand. Then she had known there was something wrong. A little gentle probing on her part had revealed perhaps that he had a bad toothache or earache, had had it for days but hadn't said anything, and was only now standing on one leg and wiping his nose on the back of his hand because the thing had got to such a pitch that he really could not endure it any more. Nowadays when he came to see her it was much the same. He would stand beside her on the hearthrug in the drawing-room with his back to the fire, so that the warmth of it could not reach her (a habit of all the Eliot men), shift his weight to his right leg and thoughtfully rub his left ear. Then she would know that either the war was going worse than usual, that things were not as they should be between him and Nadine, that he was anxious about one of their children or that his war-battered body was really making it very difficult for him to keep his end up. Passing in a gentle flow of talk from one subject to another, she would know which it was, because when she reached the troubling one he would shift his weight from his right foot to his left and stop rubbing his ear. Then she would speak hopefully on the subject, not able to advise him, since he could not reveal his mind to her, and anyhow if it had to do with tanks she lacked technical knowledge but comforting him and clearing his mind by the mere fact that her love was taking the trouble to try to understand.... He loved her very much, as did all her children and her grandchildren.

It was easier to help him when he wrote a letter; not that he was a good letter-writer, for he was not, but because he had at least got to say something when he took a pen in his hand, while when he stood by her on the hearthrug there was no necessity. She unfolded the letter she had taken from her bag and read it again attentively:

"Dear Mother,

"Hope you and Margaret are well. How's the rheumatism? Better, I hope. Though I don't see how it can be in this weather. A lot of fog in Town. Seems to get into one's lungs. Filthy stuff, Town fog. Seems some while since I wrote. Sad falling off since I was a kid and wrote to you once a week. Do you remember? And you still write to me once a week, and don't you dare leave off, for I look for those letters. Have done, all my life. I'm a rotten correspondent. Dead beat by the end of the day. Haven't been feeling too fit lately. Nothing to worry about, but I'm not as young as I was. Looking forward to the day when they put me out to grass. Never had much liking for office life, nor Town life either. No good at it. But Nadine likes it, so must keep on for the present. She's well, though very tired. She's very keen on this house. Of course it's more home to her than it is to me, because she lived here when I was in India, and through part of the war, too, when I was hardly ever home. She's been repainting it all, working out fresh colour schemes, rearranging the furniture. Seems a bit comfortless to me, but I can see it's artistic. David got the paint for her and brought along some of his fellows from the theatre to help. They did most of the work, in fact. We see a certain amount of David. Nadine likes him and they have a lot of friends in common— writers and so on, all far too highbrow for me. The children are all right, but the house seems a bit full of them in the holidays, especially the twins. They need a garden. How's the Damerosehay garden? I'd like to run down and take a look at it sometime, and perhaps sail a bit and have a spot of fishing. I've a bit of leave owing. What the boys and I like about this house is that the river's handy. Can't sail on it, of course, or fish in it, but you can smell it. Simply must get out of Town in the summer holidays. I'd like to take the boys sailing. Criminal to keep boys cooped up in Town too much; or anyone, for that matter. And Ben has a bit of a cough. Nadine says it's nothing, but I don't like it. Put up at some river-side inn somewhere. Always had a liking for river-side inns. So have the boys. They're mad on boats. They get that from me. Well, good-bye, Mother. Take care of yourself. Love to Margaret.

> "Your loving son
> "George."

It was the longest and most revealing letter George had ever written to her, and the only one, so far as she could remember, that had ever contained even a hint of personal complaint. She read it again. He was feeling very tired, very ill. He was longing to leave the army. He hated London, and Nadine's artistic house where she had lived so long without him that it seemed to him her home but not his, with no place in it for him. And he did not approve of London for the children. And he did not get on with Nadine's friends.... Nor

David.... He had never got on with David. He did not know, of course, that when Nadine had left him and come home to England, leaving him alone in India, she had fallen in love with David, and he with her, and had only been waiting for the divorce which George had promised her to get married. Lucilla had succeeded in stopping the marriage, in reuniting Nadine and George, and had agreed with Nadine that George should never be told. That desperate, abortive love had remained, and always would remain, a secret between Nadine, Lucilla, Hilary and David. But George must sense something. He obviously did not like David and Nadine being so much together. ... And nor did Lucilla.... She did not know whether or not they were still in love, but even if they were not it was playing with fire to be together so much. Upon her very first reading of the letter Lucilla had known what she had to do.... Make George give up his work at the War Office and get the whole family to the country.... The only difficulty was, where in the world to find a house for them?

And then she had seen Nadine's advertisement for a Nannie, and had gone over to see Jill at the Herb of Grace, and discovered that the old river-side inn would soon be for sale.... George and the boys loved boats and the water.... It was a beautiful old house, and could easily be made into a very lovely home. It was old-fashioned, of course; but then, refrigerators and bathrooms and things were all quite modern fads, and in Lucilla's young days they had all got along quite nicely without them.

"Give me your word," she had said to Auntie Rose, "that you will not sell the house to anyone else until my son General Eliot has seen it."

And Auntie Rose had given her word.

And then Nadine had rung up asking to come and stay, and she had begged that George should come, too, but Nadine had refused for him without even asking him. That, for a moment had made Lucilla see red. She was a good and affectionate mother-in-law provided the women her sons had taken to wife did not attempt to manage them.... That was *her* prerogative.... Still seeing red, she had written that letter to George imploring him to take a little holiday and come down with the children. She had not seen the children for so long, she had said. She might not live much longer (this, though perhaps an unfair argument, was an irresistible one, she had discovered). As an apparent after-thought at the end of the letter she had mentioned casually that the Herb of Grace, an old inn on the river near the Hard, was for sale. She was not sure that George had ever seen it, and it was of great historic interest.

Yet perhaps she ought not to have gone behind Nadine's back like that. It was not really right to do evil that good might come, though so often, in dealing with daughters-in-law, it seemed that one had to. Ellen would have had no compunction about it. Ellen would have said that at all costs Mr. George and the children must have their country home, and Mrs. George be separated from Master David and that house in Chelsea that reminded her at every turn of the days when she had been going to marry him. She could hear Ellen's voice saying it.

She lay back and rested for a little while, continuing her plans for ensuring that George and the children saw the Herb of Grace before Nadine did and lost their hearts to it so completely that Nadine, in complete ignorance of its lack of modern conveniences, would not be able to refuse them their heart's desire. That should be easy. She had begun all right by seeing to it that Nadine interviewed Jill here and not there. She dozed off for a moment or two, and then she got up and began the slow, laborious, painful business of washing her hands, changing into her black lace dress and arranging her beautiful white hair afresh. Her few jewels—the hoop of diamonds that protected her wedding ring, her emerald ring upon the other hand, her lorgnette upon a thin gold chain and the little gold wrist-watch that David had given her—she always wore, but she added a few extra touches tonight because Nadine was here. She put on her best, very ancient, satin petticoat, the one that rustled with that lovely rustle that no modern garment seemed able to achieve. She took out her loveliest lace handkerchief and scented it with eau-de-Cologne, powdered her nose very carefully and put a little posy of flowers into her waistband. The gong went just as she had finished her preparations, and she crossed slowly to the door, enjoying the rustle. The Bastard was waiting for her on the mat outside, and followed her stately progress down the stairs, wheezing heavily and with great importance. Pooh-Bah was waiting for her on the mat at the foot of the stairs, and both dogs fell into line and paced behind her to the drawing-room door. Nadine and Margaret (Hilary had gone home) were waiting for her in the drawing-room, and to please her they had made a little effort. Nadine had knotted a light gauzy scarf about the shoulders of her black dress, and looked superb and Margaret had changed her yellow jumper for a pink one and put on her pearls. The fact that she had not changed from her gardening shoes to her slippers was, Lucilla knew, a mere oversight and she did not mention it.

"Is dinner ready?" she asked, smiling at them with loving approval.

"Yes, Mother," said Margaret, and they passed in procession to the dining-room.

Nadine was very tired, and hysterical laughter rose suddenly within her as the three of them sat down to their Bengers and sardines. The massive silver on the table, the lighted candle and the flowers, the beautiful china, Grandmother's toilet.... And Bengers and sardines.... Then she choked down her laughter. For Margaret had made a special effort tonight. She had grilled the sardines and mashed some potatoes, and stewed a few prunes that were so very withered that she had surely been hoarding them for a very long time as a special treat for an honoured guest. And Grandmother, eating her Bengers very slowly so as to make it last out through the two courses her daughters were consuming, ate it with such an air that Nadine could almost see the ghost of the butler whom once she had looming behind her chair, and, looking down at her plate, was suddenly astonished to see a sardine there instead of a wing of chicken.

"They do say," said Lucilla in her lovely musical old voice, "that now the mines have been swept away the fishing-fleets will be able to get out again and we'll have plenty of real fish. It would be nice, wouldn't it, to taste a Dover sole again?"

"You're right, Grandmother," said Nadine warmly, and with what Margaret thought unnecessary depth of conviction.

But Lucilla knew, from the warm current of sympathy suddenly set flowing between her and her daughter-in-law, that Nadine was referring not only to Dover soles. She was apologizing for that stifled mirth that had not gone unobserved by Lucilla, and she was saying that she recognized Lucilla's efforts at preservation as what they were, not so much the salvage of useless trash from a lost past, but paving stones set upon the quagmire of these times, leading to a new dignity whose shape she could not guess at yet.

CHAPTER

– 1 –

ADINE SLEPT THAT NIGHT as she had not slept for weeks. That was a gift that Damerosehay usually seemed able to give—sleep. The timelessness of the place loosened one's hold upon the cares of today and the silence took them and hid them away. Nadine's small single room faced over the marshes to the Estuary, and after she had undressed she stood at the window watching the lights of cottages twinkling out on the marsh and the light of a great ship passing beyond in the darkness. Then she got into bed and lay for a little listening to the soft rustling of the reeds. Then she slept, and knew nothing more until she woke in the half-dark and heard that muted orchestra of strange cries with which the seabirds welcomed the dawn. Then there was silence again, and she slept once more until she woke in a blaze of sunshine and found Margaret in a blue overall setting a breakfast tray beside her bed.

"Mother has hers in bed nowadays," said Margaret, "and I thought you'd better, too. It'll rest you. George and the children will be here by lunch."

Their eyes met and they laughed.

"And don't you need rest before the invasion, Margaret?" asked Nadine.

"I'm strong, you know," said Margaret. "It's a good thing," she added as a plain statement of fact, with no sarcasm. "I'm afraid it's only just toast and marmalade and coffee. I'm keeping the bacon and eggs for George and the children for lunch. Is gooseberry tart still the twins' favourite pudding? I've one bottle of gooseberries left."

"Unfortunately, yes," said Nadine. "It's extraordinary what children can digest."

"I'll do a milk pudding, too," consoled Margaret. "Now don't get up till you feel inclined. Have a good rest. My daily is coming up from the village this morning, and she'll get the bedrooms ready. Have I forgotten anything on the tray?"

Nadine could see several things, including the marmalade spoon and the teaspoon, but she forbore to mention it; for where would they all be without Margaret?

"Has it made you happy, Margaret?" she asked.

"What?" asked Margaret.

"Slaving for the Eliot family."

"I'm happy," said Margaret. "Aren't you?"

"No," said Nadine, pouring out her coffee.

They looked at each other, separated by that intangible barrier of a whole world of experience that lies between a beautiful woman who has married and borne children and possessed every blessing that the world prizes, and a plain woman who has had none of it.

"What is it that you haven't got, Nadine?" asked Margaret bluntly.

"Some saving grace," said Nadine. "Something that you have and I have not. Some sort of astringency. I don't know what it is.... You do make good coffee, Margaret."

Margaret flushed with pleasure and went away, and Nadine helped herself to marmalade with the blade of her knife and stirred her coffee with the handle and ruminated dreamily in the warm spring sunshine. An astringent grace. Not one of the softening graces. Astringent, like an herb. "Herb of Grace." Why, that was the name of the inn. Jill's inn. Jill's herb. Oh, thank God for Jill! How wonderful it would be to have a Nannie!

She drank her coffee and ate her toast with glorious slowness, and had her bath and dressed in heavenly leisure. Her violets, that the children's friend had sent her, were too faded to wear now, but they were still fragrant. Nothing astringent about violets, she thought; and they were her favourite flower. That unknown girl had sent her a very suitable gift. She opened her door and went out into the passage. The room next to hers was the little room over the porch that David always used when he came here. She walked past the door, then turned back, opened it and went in. Lucilla always kept this room exactly as David liked it, and never put anyone else to sleep here if she could help it, so that it was always waiting for him. It was an austere little room, holding just a few treasures: some rare books, an exquisite Chinese model of a galloping horse in blue-green china and a reproduction of Van Gogh's painting of a lark tossing over a wind-blown cornfield. The galloping horse, the tossing lark, bathed now in early morning sunshine, were the very epitome of happy freedom. Nadine felt suddenly desperate. Freedom and happiness. And they had turned their back upon them both.

She had left the door ajar, and now, hearing a soft rustle behind her, she turned. Lucilla was standing in the doorway, her blue eyes full of pity and anxiety, but her sweet mouth very determined. But she uttered no reproach at finding Nadine on forbidden ground.

"I'm going out into the garden, dear, to stone the raisins for Tommy's favourite cake."

"I'll help you," said Nadine.

"I'm putting Ben and Tommy in their usual room," said Lucilla, as she slowly descended the stairs, Nadine following meekly after. "And would you mind, dear, if I had Caroline in my dressing-room, as I used to do when she was a little girl and lived with me?"

"Of course, Grandmother," said Nadine.

"The twins shall sleep in the old nursery, George can have the blue room and you shall stay where you are. A room to oneself is the best rest of all when one is tired, I used to think when I was married.... Does George snore, dear?"

"Yes, Grandmother."

"I guessed as much. He's very like his father. Bring the garden chairs, dear. It's so warm that I think we could sit under the ilex-tree to do the raisins."

They sat together in the sweet spring sunshine, with the dogs at their feet, the blackbird singing over their heads and the garden a blaze of glory before their eyes, and Lucilla, chatting casually about this and that, was very sweet and loving to her daughter-in-law. But Nadine did not suppose that her trespass of the morning would be overlooked. Nor was it.

"It was a great triumph to get these raisins," said Lucilla. "I do so wish David would marry some nice girl. It would do him so much good. He has been through so much, poor boy, and a nice girl-wife to make him young again is what he needs. Do you like doing the raisins with your finger and thumb, dear? Wouldn't you rather have this silver knife?"

Nadine's heart missed a beat, but she kept her face expressionless and her voice casual.

"No, thank you, Grandmother. I belong to the finger-and-thumb school of thought. Have you anyone in mind?"

"No, dear. I see so few young people nowadays, I don't even seem to see much of my dear David now, he is so busy. You see him much more often than I do. Have you noticed him with any nice girls?"

"With hundreds, Grandmother, but I haven't noticed him falling for one more than another."

"It's such a pity," sighed Lucilla. "It's as though something were holding him back. As though he needed to be set free in some way."

There was a little silence.

"Set free?" murmured Nadine.

"Freedom and happiness are always on ahead," said Lucilla. "Never behind. There, dear, now you've upset the raisins. Never mind, we'll soon pick them up again. What was I saying? Oh, yes, David's marriage. As you know, dear, the whole family decided that this house should be David's at my death; partly because he loves it so, and partly because he is best able to keep it up as the family home for all of you. But I've set my heart on his having it before my death. I want him to come here with his bride; and then Margaret and I can go and live at Big Village."

Nadine was speechless. Lucilla and Damerosehay were in her mind so inseparably one that she could not visualize Lucilla living anywhere else.

"I've planned it all," said Lucilla. "You know that pretty little cottage near Hilary's vicarage—Lavender Cottage, where Miss Marble lives? Miss Marble is getting too old, now, to do for herself, and she wants to go and live with her niece at Bournemouth. She's given me the first refusal of her cottage. I thought it would be nice for Margaret to have just a small place to look after, for she has worked much too hard for us all in this great house. And Lavender Cottage has a lovely little garden for her. And then in my last illness she'll have Hilary handy, only just across the road. And when I die she can either stay in the cottage or move across to Hilary, just as she fancies."

"But, Grandmother," gasped Nadine, "won't it break your heart to leave Damerosehay and all your treasures?"

"No," said Lucilla. "It was for my children's and my grandchildren's sake—and especially for David's sake—that I came to Damerosehay. For their sake I've lived here happily, and for their sake I'll leave happily. I'll take a few of my things with me to Lavender Cottage, and the rest I'll leave here for David and his wife."

"I only hope, Grandmother," said Nadine, her pent-up pain surging out in sudden bitterness, "that this wife of David's will appreciate Damerosehay and its treasures. You know, it's all a bit out of date."

It was a cruel thing to say, and the moment she had said it Nadine could have bitten her tongue out. She dared not look at Lucilla's face, but she saw her brace her shoulders, and saw her fingers fumbling over the raisins. It was a comfort to have Margaret appear at this moment with the eleven o'clock cups of tea. When she went away again they talked of other things until the raisins were done, and then they went indoors to wash their hands, and Nadine went up to her room.

– 2 –

She stayed there writing letters until the sound of a car's wheels crunching on the drive, and then a wild commotion of barking dogs and shouting children, told her that her family had arrived; and even then she lingered a little, that Lucilla might have the joy of welcoming them without her; that much reparation for her cruelty she could make. She gave them ten minutes, and then she went downstairs.

They were all with Lucilla and the dogs under the ilex-tree; George, Ben, Tommy, Caroline, the twins Jeremy and Josephine and Mary the pekinese, and they were all, George included, behaving as though this were the first day of the holidays and they were just home from school, with Lucilla the centre of their joy.... And Lucilla looked utterly, radiantly happy.... But not too happy to see Nadine approaching and to yield to her instantly the place that was hers by right.

"Look! There's Mother!" said Lucilla, and put a twin off her knee and turned aside to pick up a fallen ball of wool.

And Nadine, after twenty-four hours rest from her family, looked upon them with a sudden warming of the cockles of her heart as they surged about her. She put her hands on George's shoulders and raised her face for his kiss with sudden pride in him. He was a good-looking man. He had kept his upright, trim, soldierly figure, and his iron-grey hair was still thick, with a crisp wave in it. Though his face was tired and lined there was no slackness about it, and his eyes as they smiled down at her were infinitely patient and kind. He was a good man, and she remembered that it was for his solid worth that she had originally married him, and not for the sensitiveness and intuition that she now so unreasonably demanded of him because she loved them in David. And Ben had them. Turning to her eldest son, seeing his sudden smile flash out like light over his thin, dark face, she noticed for the first time the likeness to David that Sally had realized almost at the first glance, and for the first time it occurred to her that she might in the future find great comfort in her eldest son.

And then the violence of one of Tommy's bear-hugs enveloped her and she forgot Ben. For Tommy was her favourite child. She adored his beauty, his vitality, and the love of adventure that he had inherited from her. His toughness, too, was to her a restful quality, making it impossible for her to hurt him, as she so often hurt Ben and Caroline. And the simplicity of his self-seeking, not tangled up, as was hers, with a hampering sense of duty, also rested her. You knew where you were with Tommy. He meant what he said and did what he wanted to do, and hid from you nothing whatever of his likes, dislikes and distresses. Not that he had many of the latter. His health was of the rudest, and nothing except the thwarting of his will had any power to put him out.

"Mother?" whispered Caroline.

And Nadine put Tommy forcibly from her and turned to kiss her plain, precise, anxious little daughter. How she had come to have such a child she never could imagine. Caroline wasn't like her and she wasn't, in looks, like George. She wasn't like anybody in the family. She was a mixture of Queen Victoria when young and a tabby kitten, and Nadine could never manage to feel for her anything more than the natural affection of a mother. Though she found her very useful. Her conscientiousness and motherliness made her invaluable in caring for the twins.

The twins! She felt tired again at the very sight of them, though a glow of maternal pride went through her as she looked. They were taking no notice of her. Jerry had climbed up into the ilex-tree, where he was greening the seat of his new turquoise-blue knickers and making the most earsplitting noises. José, set down from her grandmother's knee, had betaken herself to the iris bed with Mary in her arms.

"Jerry," said George, "come down out of that tree and kiss your mother."

"I can't," said Jerry. "I'm an air-raid siren."

"Do as I tell you, Jerry," thundered George, who expected military obedience from his children but seldom got it from his youngest.

Jerry's only reply was an excruciating up-and-down wail.

"I think, dear," said Lucilla gently, "that you had better sound the All Clear and come down. There's gooseberry tart for lunch."

Jerry shrieked wildly upon one note and fell from the tree, hooking his white shirt on a branch and ripping it from top to bottom. Arrived upon the ground, he did not kiss his mother, but made a bee-line for the dining-room.

"José!" commanded the thwarted George. "Kiss your mother."

José raised her lovely little flower-like face above the spikes of the iris leaves and smiled at him tolerantly.

"Just a minute," she said. "Mary, stay there. You're Moses. Lie *down*, Mary. Lie *down*. Mother, you're Pharaoh's daughter. Come and find Moses."

Nadine found Moses and was kissed. José was on the whole an easier child to deal with than Jerry. If you did what she wanted, then she would do what you wanted, whereas Jerry, like Tommy, regarded the attainment of his own will as a dead end.

As everybody was hungry and the food was good, the luncheon hour was irradiated by the harmony that comes when everybody is doing what they want to do. Lucilla waited until the children and George were well into their second helpings of pudding before making her next move for their good.

"I think Nadine looks rested already, don't you, George?" she enquired.

George wiped his moustache with his napkin and considered his wife, the kind lines crinkling round his eyes.

"Breakfast in bed?" he enquired.

"Margaret always spoils me," said Nadine.

"I think, dear, that a rest on your bed would be nice for you this afternoon," said Lucilla. "I'll rest, too, and Margaret has a meeting, I believe. George will look after the children, won't you, George? You might run them over in the car to the Hard, dear, and look at the old inn I told you about—the Herb of Grace. It would be nice for the children to see it, for it has great historic interest."

"Will tomorrow do as well?" enquired George, who had been driving all the morning and was tired. "Looks as though it might turn to rain this afternoon."

"Oh, no, dear; the glass is quite high still, though rain is foretold for tomorrow. The children would enjoy it, I think. There's not only the inn for them to see, but dear Jill, who was so good to Ben and Tommy and Caroline when they were little. And then there's the river...."

At this there was a whoop from Tommy, and Ben's face kindled with delight.

"Very well, Mother," said George.

"I rather think I'll come, too," said Nadine. "I should like to see Jill again. There are a few things I forgot to say."

"You could write her a little note, dear," said Lucilla. "And George will take it, won't you, George? Nadine really does need the rest very badly."

"By all means," said George. "I'll take the elder children and any number of notes, but I do jib at taking the twins. They get underfoot in the car to an astonishing degree. Couldn't they play in the garden?"

"They could dear," said Lucilla. "But I think it would be paying a pretty attention to Jill to take them to see her, since she is to be their Nannie."

"Put her off entirely, I should think. Better keep 'em out of sight till she's committed to it."

"Oh, no, dear. Jill will love to see dear José and dear Jerry."

Lucilla's hand trembled a little as she helped herself to toast. The way in which modern parents discussed their offspring in front of them chilled her to the bone; especially if the remarks were of a type to make the darlings think they weren't wanted. Not that the twins appeared to have taken their father's remarks to heart. They were completely absorbed, Jerry in gooseberry tart and José in spilling lemonade down her blue smock with what appeared to be deliberate intention.

"I'll take them," said George resignedly. "You have a good rest, Nadine. I'll manage."

Nadine did not fight it. The memory of the cruel thing she had said was with her still. She did not know why Lucilla was so bent upon keeping her from seeing the Herb of Grace, but it was not in her to hurt Lucilla any more that day.

– 3 –

The twins had not taken their father's remarks to heart for the very good reason that they never paid the slightest intention to anything that he said. They never paid any attention to anything anybody said. Separated by a considerable gap of years from Ben, Tommy and Caroline, they lived together in the bright world of their own imaginings, as though inside a rainbow soap-bubble, and had only a casual glance to spare for the people and things outside. They were kindly disposed towards the people and things outside, but nothing and nobody was very real to them until he, she or it had been drawn inside their bubble and metamorphosed by their imaginations into something that, though the same, was different, like the beast in "Beauty and the Beast" when he became a handsome prince. When they were drawing someone into their bubble in this way, as a spider draws a fly into his web, they would become suddenly most endearing, as though a little sugar were necessary for the enticing of the victim. And then the latter would think himself popular with the twins.... But he would be entirely mistaken.... All the affection of which the twins were as yet capable was given only to each other.

But though they never listened to anything he said, they liked their father. Of all the people outside the bubble he was the one to whom they were most kindly disposed. Not only was his bulk useful to them, as being easily transformable into that of an elephant, a policeman or a petrol-pump, but it gave them a feeling of safety. He was the rock from whence they were hewn, and when some wind of the outside world caused the walls of their bubble to shiver and quake, presaging that dread day when the bubble would cave in altogether and stark reality be for ever with them, they would seek shelter beside George like chickens beneath their mother's wing. They did not feel this way about Nadine. To them she was still no more than that which she had been from the beginning: the source of nourishment. It was only at meal-times that she was important. George unconsciously resented this on Nadine's behalf, and was always trying to make them pay a more courteous attention to their mother. But it was no good. The twins were at all times entirely allergic to good influences. A good influence is no use at all as a protagonist in an imaginative drama.

"I'm going to sit by Daddie!" yelled Jerry as he came tearing down the stairs after lunch, arrayed in the sunshine-yellow outfit which had replaced the ruin of the blue knickers and white shirt of the morning. The car, seen beyond the open front door, had become for him in the moment of descent down the stairs a goods train. Father was the driver, himself the stoker, José the coal, and Ben and Tommy and Caroline the goods.

"Me, too!" yelled José, knowing without being told that she was now coal, and making the kind of noise that coal does make falling down a chute. She also, now, was arrayed in sunshine yellow. She *had* spilled lemonade on the blue smock with deliberate intention. If Jerry made a mess of himself, she always made a mess of herself, too, because she could not endure to be dressed in a different colour from her other half.

"Young toads! You sat by Daddie coming down," said Tommy bitterly, he having earmarked this post of honour for himself, because by watching George he was teaching himself to drive the car.

A smile flickered across Ben's face, not his lovely, living smile, but the deprecating, shadowy smile with which he confronted life's major disappointments.... One can see the country so much better from the front.

Caroline said nothing, but slipped her hand into her father's. She wanted to sit by him because she loved him more than anyone in the world. George pressed her hand and dropped a kiss on the top of her head. Her devotion touched him very deeply, and because of it she was his favourite child.... Though he would have been considerably astonished had he known that her love for him was less that of a daughter for her father than of a mother for her child.... Lucilla, sitting on the hall seat with Nadine to see them off, and watching the little drama, was well content. Caroline was unlikely to marry—too plain, poor child—she would stay with George always and be the prop of his declining years. Lucilla felt that she could die happy, leaving George in Caroline's capable hands.

"I'll have my Elf," said George, this being his particular name for his eldest daughter.

But at this the twins exploded into such a passion of grief and rage that the old house all but rocked with it.

"Stop that noise at once!" shouted George, unheard above the din.

Nadine put her hands over her ears and hoped to goodness Jill would know what to do about these awful passions of the twins; they were simply getting on her nerves.

"In a royal procession," said Lucilla, who understood her grandchildren better than anyone, "the King and Queen always sit in the back of the car, with outriders to either side. Tommy and Ben would make splendid outriders. Sit to the left of them, Ben, and you'll be the first to see the pond where the red and white water-lilies grow, and then the turning to the Hard, and the river. Tommy, those woods to the right, opposite the ponds, are still full of the shell-cases they hid there in the war. Miles of them, they tell me, looking just like bones, rows and rows of vertebrae. You're so fond of bones, dear. Caroline, my darling, give me a kiss before you go."

Somehow, in spite of the noise, her gentle voice reached the ears of all five of her grandchildren. The twins' yells ceased as though a tap had been turned off, and in no time at all the family had settled themselves in the car in the positions she had indicated.... Nadine dropped her hands thankfully to her lap, then picked up Mary, her pekinese, and went upstairs to rest. Lying on her bed, with Mary stretched sweetly upon her chest, she fondled the little dog's silky ears and thought how much easier dogs were than children, and wondered how on earth Lucilla did it, and if she'd be any more efficient as a grandmother than she was as a mother, until she fell asleep.

CHAPTER

– 1 –

GEORGE, AS THE CAR SLID DOWN THE DRIVE through the oak-wood, felt suddenly happy and at peace. Those three worries, that nagged at him night and day like toothache—the state of the world, his inability to be to his adored wife the husband that she wanted, and the unsatisfactory state of his own health, that made him fear he might die and leave her to grapple single-handed with all these children—found ease. The beauty of the spring flowers growing in the grass beneath the old oak-trees, the scent of the gorse blowing in from the marshes, the warm sun, the sea wind—these things were not affected by the state of the world. Though apparently so fragile, their quality was more durable than the quality of anything that man could make, and encompassed by them George felt that he, too, would last out, at least until the children were well launched in life, if he could live always in this country air. The children! The success of his paternity was very obvious to him at this moment, and comforted him for his failure as a husband. Here was his funny little Elf beside him, giving him that loving, trustful smile of hers whenever he looked her way, that smile that always made his protectiveness swell like a balloon inside his chest, and his two fine sons behind, still disgruntled because they had not been able to sit next to him. And the twins! Though their roars had ceased, there was still a backwash of sobs from them (not grief-stricken now, merely automatic), and all because they had not been allowed to sit next to their father.

George squared his shoulders as they swung out into the road and hummed "Onward, Christian Soldiers" through his teeth, as was his habit when happy. The twins bowed to right and left with shattering dignity. Caroline kept an eye on her father's driving, for she did not really consider him safe with a car if she were not there to look after him, and was always careful to warn him of anything approaching round the corner. Tommy, who had decided to be a surgeon when he reached man's estate, was occupying himself making a sketch of his stomach on the back of an envelope, until such time as they reached the shell-cases in the wood.

Only Ben was aware that this drive was not just another of the many drives they had with Father, but something that had a special significance. This wasn't just a drive to see Jill and an old inn, it was a drive to some important change in their lives. He did not know how this idea had come to him. Perhaps from Grandmother. Ever since the days when as small children he and Tommy and Caroline had lived at Damerosehay he and Grandmother had been very close to each other.... He often knew what she was thinking about.... This sense of expectation thrilled him, keyed him up, gave him that glorious feeling of being in the right relation to everything and everybody near him, so that the touch of the sun on his face, the pressure of José's warm little body against his thigh, were not just sensation, but a claiming of him that locked him into his place in the pattern of things and banished that feeling of futility that so often made his life a misery to him. Happy and excited, he flung an arm round little José and smiled down at her.... Outraged, José removed his arm, as though its presence about her were a sort of sacrilege, drew herself up stiff as a ramrod and bowed to a rabbit scampering beneath the hedge. Beyond her, Jerry raised his hand to the salute as they passed a cow looking over a gate, and beyond Jerry, Tommy was gazing with knitted, puzzled brows at the envelope held in his left hand, while with his right hand he violently prodded his chest as he tried to remember exactly what happened at the junction of the stomach and the small intestine.... Ben decided, not for the first time, that all his family were quite mad, and turned his attention, as Grandmother had advised, to the view.

It rewarded his observation, and in five minutes he had forgotten his family, the car, their destination—everything whatever except the ebb and flow of colour, the strong swing of the sky overhead, the circling of clouds and birds' wings, the flowing green curve of the meadows and the deep-welling life within him beating almost painfully against some closed door inside; until the door yielded and he poured himself out, drawing in again in exchange the colour into his blood, the movement into his muscles, the strength into his bones and the quality of this spring world into his quality, to be a part of him for ever. When he got home again he would try to paint what he had seen, or write a poem about it, letting the colour and movement and strength flow out of his blood and muscle and bone upon the paper. But he would not show his work to either his father or his mother.... He had learnt not to.... For George, who wanted his eldest son to follow him into the Army, would, in spite of his astounded admiration for his son's cleverness, rub his ear and look worried, the fear that Ben was not developing according to plan showing only too clearly in his eyes, and Nadine, who had decided on the diplomatic service for Ben, would glance at the painting or poem with the same tolerant, amused inattentiveness that she bestowed upon the twins' games, and he would feel, as usual, utterly and completely futile.

He had sometimes shown his drawings to Grandmother, who, though she did not understand art, understood Ben, and was incapable of word or look that could wound him. And he very often showed them to David, whose intense interest was, he knew, unfeigned. David could not draw a line to save his life, but he knew all about drawing loveliness into your blood and bones and then pouring it out again, and between him and Ben would come that quick leaping up of sympathy that seemed to Ben a much closer brotherhood than the brotherhood of the flesh that linked him to Tommy. He would no more have dreamed of showing anything he had done to Tommy than to a boa-constrictor. Though he got on well enough with Tommy. They were at one in their tolerant, amused affection for their father and their adoration of their mother, and for the rest they let each other alone and went their separate ways.

There was no lovelier country in all the world than this, thought Ben, looking across the fields where the gulls were following the plough to where beyond the blue of the Estuary the Island lay half-hidden in rosy mist, with its uplands just emerging from the mystery, like the mountains in some Japanese colour print. Ben thought of the Island as a great brooding Daemon over the landscape. He always felt aware of the Daemon even when he could not see him, just as he was always aware, whether he saw it or not, of the old Cistercian Abbey whose ruins were beyond the River and the Hard.... They had this countryside in their charge, these two Presences.... Speeding past the ploughed fields and the green meadows and the little streams with their floating gardens of flowers, they passed the towering grey walls of a roofless ruined chapel, and then the old and mighty barns, with red-brick walls and golden roofs, that had been built where once had been the monks' ox-farm and sheep-farm, and that bore still the old names of the Bouvery and the Bargery.

Then they were in the deep woods, and the scent of the primroses and wood-sorrel drifted to them, and George slowed down the car that they might feast their eyes upon the fresh spring green over their heads, and hear the cuckoo calling, and watch for the flash of a jay's wing or a sight of a squirrel's cage high in a tall tree. Even Tommy (until his attention was caught by the shell-cases) looked and listened, and the twins suddenly forgot the royal blood in their veins and were Rat and Mole in the woods. In London lately they had forgotten about Rat and Mole, but now they remembered the book that Grandmother had read to all her grandchildren in turn, and that was now a classic in the Eliot family, and sudden ecstasy seized them. They did not need to tell each other of what they were thinking, they were too much one for that, but as one child they brought their paws up over their snouts and began to make the most extraordinary noises.

"Are those children going to be car-sick?" George asked Caroline.

Caroline glanced anxiously back over her shoulder.

"Scrape, scratch, scrabble and scrooge," said José.

Caroline's face cleared.

"It's all right, Daddie. They're only playing at 'The Wind in the Willows.'"

"Onion sauce! Onion sauce!" said Jerry.

In their games he was Mole and José was Rat because she had "a brown little face, a grave, round little face, small neat ears and thick, silky hair." Tommy was Toad because of his boastful ways, and Ben was Badger because of his kindness to the younger brethren. "Mr. Badger, he's a kind-hearted gentleman, as everyone knows." Caroline was the jailer's daughter, "a pleasant wench and good-hearted."

Ben was watching eagerly now, as Grandmother had bidden him, for the gleam of water. There it was, between the trunks of the trees—the lovely lake of Frieswater. In the summer it would hold a shield of red and white water-lilies upon its breast, but they would not confront the sun with a greater splendour, Ben thought, than did the glinting surface of wind-rippled light. David had said the light of the sun upon the wind-blown ripples seemed to him sometimes like the light of creative genius. "The wind bloweth where it listeth," and sometimes at the touch of the mystery there is a flash of reflected light from the soul of a man, and a new life born from the flash; but sometimes the ripple passes lightless as the wind goes on no man knows where, even as no man knows from whence it came.... Something like that David had said.

They drove slowly on until Ben cried, "Stop, Father! The turning to the Hard."

George obediently stopped, and they sat in silence looking at a scene that even Tommy loved intensely. The Hard had once been a flourishing shipbuilding town that had made some of the greatest of England's ships. Nelson's *Agamemnon* had been built there, and many a glorious East Indiaman. Now there was nothing left of it but one enchanted, fairy-tale street, a double row of old brick cottages with tumbled, weather-worn red roofs facing a steep path bordered with green turf that sloped to the river. Once this place had hummed with noise: the ring of hammer upon anvil, the rasping of the saws that hewed the oak logs into the great ships' timbers, the clatter of the hammers and the whistling of the men at work upon a ship in the slips. Now there was silence: no sound but the whisper of the wind and the crying of the gulls who swooped and circled over the water. They could see the river down at the bottom of the little street—a wide, tidal river sparkling and glinting in the sun. White swans rested upon it and small ships rocked at anchor. Beyond was a glorious stretch of green and tawny marshes, threaded with channels of blue water, and beyond were woods sweeping to the skyline. Not far away, unseen yet present to their thoughts, was the ruined Abbey, whose bell in the old days had been heard by sailors far out at sea. The shadows of the clouds passed over this scene like the shadows of great wings, and the peace of the place was indescribable.

Tommy came to first, his eyes yearningly upon those small boats rocking at anchor.

"Only damn fools live in London," he said violently.

Ben, who could quote whole chunks of "The Wind in the Willows" from memory, echoed the thought that he knew was in Tommy's mind:

"'Believe me, my young friend, there is *nothing*—absolutely nothing—half so much worth doing as simply messing about in boats. Simply messing—messing—about in—boats—messing—'"

"That'll do," said George sharply, for he felt this sort of conversation to be somehow disloyal to Nadine. "Eyes right, Elf. Where's this inn of Grandmother's we've got to take a look at?"

Caroline, he knew, would have had the forethought to ask how to get there. Caroline was the only member of the Eliot family who ever had this kind of forethought.

"You go through a gate between a barn and an oak-tree," said Caroline, "and then straight on along a lane."

The barn was facing them, and the old, storm-twisted oak tree bent over the gate to lay its branches on the roof of the old barn. It was studded with new green leaves, coral-tipped, and they made a sort of canopy over the gate. Ben was out of the car in a flash and had opened it.

"Always thought this gate led into a farmyard," said George as he drove forward.

"I didn't," said Caroline softly. "I always had a feeling it led somewhere wonderful, but was afraid to go and see, in case it didn't."

– 2 –

Ben had closed the gate again, but he did not get back into the car, he jumped up on to the running-board and swung there, lithe and graceful, beside his father. His eyes met his father's, and they were brimming with light. George glanced at Caroline, and saw that her cheeks were bright pink with excitement. Behind him Tommy was giving his famous imitation of quacking ducks faced with a lovely mess of really dirty weed, as was his habit in moments of happy anticipation, and the twins had ceased to be Rat and Mole and were giving their equally renowned interpretation of an express train screaming with joy as it rushes headlong into a tunnel. But George, though the noise from behind smote with violence upon the back of his head, forbore to silence them. For really he didn't blame the kids. His own heart was beating rather faster than usual.

The lane was narrow and winding, only just wide enough to take the car. It must have been of a great age, for it was very deeply sunken in the earth. Upon each side were grassy banks covered with primroses and dog-violets, with above ramparts of golden gorse. Oak-trees grew in the unseen field upon their right, and their wind-blown branches stretched over their heads, turning the lane into that tunnel which had immediately changed the twins into the train. Looking up through the flame-tipped, burning young green and the grey, lichened twigs, one could see the blue sky. Somewhere overhead a lark was singing madly.

They went on a little farther, and the lane turned off downhill to the left. It changed its character now. To their right, above the steep bank of primroses, was a most enchanting wood.

"The Wild Wood! The Wild Wood!" cried José when she saw it. "The Wild Wood where Mr. Badger lived!"

To the left was an orchard of old gnarled apple-trees with a gate leading into it. These trees, too, leaned over the lane and made a tunnel of it. Beyond the gate, in the lovely orchard, a rough track bordered with clumps of daffodils led away downhill. Down at the bottom of the lane, framed by the trees as in a picture-frame, was a blaze of sunlight and the river.

Complete silence fell suddenly upon everyone, even the twins. The car slid down the lane, passed out into the sunlight and stopped. And still no one spoke.

In front of them the lane merged gradually into a beautiful fan-shaped little beach of smooth pebbles upon which the river lapped in gleaming ripples. To right and left of this beach a stout stone wall had been built, and it swept away to each side, taking the curve of the river-bank. A little rowing boat, tied to a ring in the left-hand wall, rocked upon the ripples. Small stout ferns grew in the crevices of these walls and festoons of brambles hung over from above. To right and left flights of worn stone steps were built against the wall. The steps to the right led up to a small gate, painted green, that led into the wood, those to the left to another small gate, painted blue, leading into the garden of the inn. This garden, merging gradually into the orchard upon the landward side, had old-fashioned box-bordered flower-beds that were a tangled mass of scented red wallflowers growing round rose bushes, gooseberry bushes, rosemary bushes and currant bushes, all incongruously but gloriously mixed together upon either side of the stone-paved path that led to the inn door. The inn itself was a fair-sized old house, with bulging, whitewashed, buttressed walls and a steep, uneven roof of amber tiles patched with golden lichen. Windows looked out of the white walls and the wavy roof at the most odd, unexpected levels. There did not seem a straight line anywhere, and yet the old place gave no impression of decay. On the contrary, it looked immensely strong—as strong as a fortress—glowing and safe, friendly and warm, and most deeply alive. The front door was of very old oak, and looked as though it had once been a ship's door. Over it a painted sign was fastened to the wall of the house. It was dim and weather-worn and from where they sat in the car they could not see anything of it except a soft blur of blue and green. Yet they none of them seemed able to move. The beauty of this place had laid a spell upon them. It seemed too good to be true. They were afraid that if they moved it would all vanish.

Tommy, as ever, recovered first.

"I believe there's a boat-house round there to the right," he said. "I can see a bit of it. One would get to it through the wood."

"There doesn't seem to be anybody about," said Ben.

"Let's go and knock on the door," said Caroline.

Then they all tumbled out of the car and ran up the steps to the blue gate, and through into the garden. They walked up the paved path to the old ship's door, George coming last, holding Jerry and José firmly by the hand. Yet the twins were still astonishingly quiet. Accustomed as they were to being in fairy-tales of their own concoction, this fairy-tale that had suddenly encompassed them without any volition of their own was slightly bewildering. They couldn't imagine what was going to happen next, and awaited it in breathless silence.

The whole family stood in a group looking up at the signboard. It had upon it a delicate design of blue flowers and narrow green leaves. Above the flowers were the words, Herb o' Grace o' Sundays, and down below, where the roots of the flowers were shown stretching down into the earth, in much smaller letters, Maison Dieu.

"Gosh, but it's old!" ejaculated Ben. "Why it's a Pilgrim Inn!"

His relatives looked at him expectantly. It was always to Ben that the Eliots turned for enlightenment about odd, unexpected things. Tommy could always tell all you wanted to know about internal combustion engines and the working of your own digestive organs, or how to put in a new fuse or mend a puncture; but Ben had the kind of mind that stored up odds and ends of information about the habits of birds and the derivation of names and the sources of legend. In London he spent a lot of time browsing in second-hand bookshops, or among the books in David's flat; for David had that kind of mind, too.

"H'm?" enquired George.

"There were always hostels for pilgrims near the great Abbeys and Cathedrals," said Ben. "They were called Maisons Dieu. They're the very oldest inns of all. Very few of them left now."

"And Herb o' Grace o' Sundays?" asked Caroline.

"It's the narrow-leaved rue," said Ben. "The country people used to grow it over the graves in the churchyards."

"Why?" asked Tommy.

But for once Ben was stumped, and chuckling at having caught him out, Tommy knocked loudly upon the door. A light step sounded inside and it swung open, revealing Jill standing on the threshold, dressed in a green overall with blue flowers on it, her eyes soft and bright with welcome. Without a moment's hesitation Caroline flew into her arms. She had never forgotten Jill. It was Jill's and Grandmother's unfailing tenderness that had given to her rather insecure childhood a stability it would not have had without them.

"Miss Caroline! How you've grown, dear! And Master Ben and Master Tommy, too," said Jill, holding Caroline to her with her left arm and holding out her right hand to Ben.

He gripped it warmly. He hadn't forgotten her, either, or how the obviousness of her remarks had always comforted him, drawing attention as they always did to the eternal verities, like growth and the weather. Tommy grinned at her, remembering how she had never given him away when he ladled his porridge into the marmalade pot.

"Good afternoon, Sir," said Jill to George. "It's a lovely fine day, isn't it? Warm for the time of year."

"Good afternoon, Jill," said George, and the immense relief he felt at the sight of her made him suddenly look ten years younger. "Here you are," he added, and swung the twins forward, and Jill received them, a hand held out to each, as a fresh runner receives from a spent one a couple of valuable but fatiguingly heavy packages, that must be carried along to the end of the way though the heavens fall. She braced her shoulders, looking at the twins, and then she smiled as though she felt herself equal to it.

"Jerry and José," she said softly, smiling at them. "And I'm Jill. Three J's. We'll be happy."

And the twins, still most extraordinarily well-behaved, smiled back at her. They liked the firm clasp of her hands, her even voice, her steady eyes. They knew instinctively that she would always be the same—not hugging them one moment, and scolding them the next, and neither for any apparent reason, but reasonable and even-tempered and to be relied upon, like the ground beneath their feet.

"Will you come in, please, Sir?" invited Jill. "The kettle's on the boil and I've just baked some scones."

"We didn't mean to put you to any trouble, Jill," said George. "We've really come to bring a note from my wife and to ask your aunt if we may look at the inn. It's of historical interest, I understand, and Lady Eliot thought we ought to take a look at it before it changes hands."

"Auntie Rose and I will be pleased to show you over, Sir," said Jill. "But you'll have tea first, won't you? It's no trouble, and the children will be hungry."

George, handing her Nadine's note, liked the way she spoke to him, with no shyness or coquetry, respectfully, yet showing him firmly that she put the children's hunger before his own desire for archaeological research.

They all trooped in, the old ship's door shut behind them, and immediately they had a wonderful feeling of being most royally and loudly welcomed, almost as though some generous, glowing personality had shouted aloud at the sight of them. They looked round, but there was no one with them in the stone-flagged passage except Jill. To their right beautiful oak panelling reached from floor to ceiling, to their left an oak partition reached not quite elbow-high, and they looked over it between old oak posts, strangely carved with birds and beasts, into the bar. A few steps farther and the partition ended, giving entrance to the bar. It was the most attractive bar parlour George had ever set eyes upon. The bar itself, with a door behind it that evidently led through into the kitchen, was against the inner wall, facing the wide window set in the huge thickness of the outer wall, and looking out upon the garden. The ceiling was not so low as the ceilings of old houses so often are, and was whitewashed and crossed by strong oak beams. There was an open fireplace in the wall opposite the partition, with spotted china dogs upon the mantel, and two old settles with crimson cushions to either side of it. There were crimson curtains at the window and red rag rugs on the snowy stone floor. There were other treasures, too—a grandfather clock, very old brass spittoons, old sporting prints upon the walls—but George's eye was caught away from them by the glory of the staircase that exactly faced the front door. It was of black oak and highly polished with age, each stair sagging in the middle like a bent bow. It sloped up between high panelled walls, then divided and curved away to right and left beneath an alcove in the panelling, where there must once have been a cupboard, and that held now some strange little carved figure that he could not make out in the dim light. The sweep of this dividing staircase was most wonderfully beautiful and gracious, and gave one a feeling of welcome, like strong arms held out—the arms of that glowing personality who had welcomed them in. And Ben noticed, though George did not that the whole structure of the staircase, with the arms held out beneath the upright panel, was like a cross.

"We go this way," said Jill, and lifted the latch of a door that was so a part of the panelling to the right of the passage that they had not seen it until she opened it. "It's Auntie Rose's parlour," she said with pride, and stood back for them to enter.

George exclaimed in delight. It was a lovely little room, panelled in green-painted wood, with two windows—a small one looking over the garden through which they had come, and a large one looking out over another patch of garden, that was now a swaying mass of daffodils, over the low wall to the river, with the marshes and the woods beyond. The room was full of silvery light reflected upwards from the river. There was a floor of dark oak, and fine old candle-sconces upon the walls. It was furnished according to the taste of Auntie Rose, with a modern "suite" upholstered in puce velvet, lace curtains at the windows a very distressing carpet, innumerable embroidered cushion-covers and antimacassars, and pictures in gilt frames of gentlemen in cocked hats bowing to ladies in crinolines, all of them with exactly the same face. The fireplace was truly terrible—a heavy overmantel trimmed with red velvet and a surround of imitation black marble—but George noticed that the basket grate was old, and that the black marble was obviously a superimposed structure.... Yet through these things the beauty of the room shone like sun through the mist.

"What Mother could make of this!" exclaimed George suddenly to Ben, and Ben nodded.... He had already seen in his mind's eye just what Mother would make of it.

"This house is just like Damerosehay," cried Caroline in delight.

"It's not in the least like it," retorted Tommy, a little contemptuously, and Caroline flushed painfully.

Ben took her arm and pinched it comfortingly.

"Exactly," he whispered.

He knew what she meant. Both old houses gave one the feeling of having been built from inside as well as from outside, as though the men and women who had made them were not only the actual masons and carpenters, but those who had lived in them, too, and both alike had not manufactured them: they had put them forth bit by bit from their own souls and bodies, like a squirrel building his cage in a tree or a badger his holt in the ground. And the strength of their blood and bones still lived on in the wood and stone of each house, plain for all to see, and something of their spirits lived on in the spirit of the house; and the spirit of the house, though so ancient, was not yet full-grown; it waited on those who would come for the perfect flowering. It was like that at Damerosehay, and it was like that here.

"What aspect?" asked George.

"South," said Jill. "The river takes a bend here, you see, Sir, so that this room looks due south and gets all the sun. The front of the inn looks west, and the sunsets are lovely behind the wood. This way, Sir. Tea's ready in the kitchen."

She opened a door in the east wall, beside the fireplace, and they went through into a small, square room panelled in dark oak, that also looked towards the river. It was uncarpeted and there was nothing in it except a few boxes and a sewing machine.

"It's just a passage room, and we don't seem to have much use for it," said Jill apologetically.

"A library and studio combined," said Ben. "Lined with books. A table in the window. There'd be a good light if one wanted to paint or write, or anything like that."

"Good place to store fishing-tackle," said George.

"Put up a partition," said Tommy. "Make a passage out of this end. You could have a door with green bottle glass in it, to give light in the passage. The bottom part of the bookshelves could be cupboards. I could keep my bones there, and work at my anatomy at the table in the window."

George and Ben said no more about painting or fishing-tackle.

Tommy always had what he wanted. This room was now dedicated to books and bones.

"There are two kitchens," said Jill. "One behind the bar parlour, where we do all the work, and one through here where we live."

She opened a door opposite to the one by which they had entered, and they went down two steps into the most glorious room of all, the living-kitchen. It was a large room, stonefloored, with whitewashed walls and great beams crossing a whitewashed ceiling, with a fine old oil lamp hanging from the central beam. There was a wide fireplace with a fire burning in it and a kettle singing on the hearth, and two wide windows, one looking south towards the river, the other east on to the stable yard. The room was furnished with old furniture: a splendid oak table, a huge dresser with blue willow pattern china upon it, a tallboy, high-backed, rush seated chairs and a rocking-chair. There were some fine bits of Bristol ware upon the mantelpiece, flowered chintz curtains at the windows, strips of plain matting upon the floor and pots of geraniums upon the window-sills. The table was laid for tea with a blue-and-white check tablecloth, willow-pattern china, a home-made cake, scones and honey. The room was gracious, lived-in, warm, glowing and altogether glorious.... And extraordinarily familiar.... Standing there in the sunlight and firelight, George and the children felt as though they had come home. They looked at each other, but they could not speak.

"Auntie Rose did think of running the inn as a guest-house at one time," said Jill. "That was after they put on the buses to Radford and people starting going there of an evening, instead of coming here, so that as an inn it wasn't a paying concern any more. But she didn't feel equal to it. It would have made a good guest-house. The bar parlour the dining room, the green parlour the lounge and this kept private, for the family."

"A lovely guest-house for tired people," said Caroline, with shining eyes. "I could leave school and help Mother run it."

"One would be a fool not to keep this room exactly as it stands," murmured George. "Jill, is the furniture as well as the house for sale?"

Jill looked doubtful.

"Auntie Rose is very attached to all the things in the parlour," she said. "The pictures were her wedding presents, and all the cushions and antimacassars she embroidered herself, and that lovely suite she and uncle bought for their silver wedding. But I don't think she sets much store by the things here. They're old, and shabby, too, and belonged to her mother-in-law. Nor yet I don't think she cares much for anything in the bar parlour. That's all shabby old stuff, too."

"I wouldn't dream of asking your Aunt to part with anything in her parlour," George assured Jill. "It's these things here—"

"Auntie's in the other kitchen," said Jill. "We'll ask her."

They went through into the farther kitchen, but Auntie Rose had disappeared, This kitchen, too, was delightful, with a north window looking out into the orchard and an east window looking on the stable yard. It had the same whitewashed walls and the same oak beams crossing a whitewashed ceiling, but here the wide hearth had a cooking range in it, the long table was of scrubbed deal and the dresser of pitchpine. But there were brass pots and pans on the mantelpiece, bunches of herbs and another fine old oil lamp hanging from the ceiling, a cuckoo clock upon the wall, queer old bulging cupboards everywhere; and, best of all in the children's eyes, an open door in one corner showed the beginning of a stone turret staircase winding away into the darkness to one knew not what.

"Auntie must have stepped outside," said Jill, and opened a door in the east wall that led into a porch like the one at Damerosehay—a porch as big as a little room, with seats upon either side.

They went through into the stable yard, and George saw with satisfaction that the rough road leading from the lane through the orchard to the stable yard was wide enough for a good-sized car, and that some of the stable buildings would be easily convertible into garages. This yard was beautiful, with its old rounded cobbles and green-painted pump. The stable buildings were of mellowed, garnet-coloured brick, roofed with those same amber tiles that roofed the inn. The place reminded George of an old London mews, for opposite the house a flight of steps built against the wall led up to what had obviously once been a coachman's living-quarters. There was a beautiful wrought-iron hand-rail, protecting the stairs, with a small balcony above, upon which opened two windows, one on either side of a green door.

"There's a bit of vegetable garden behind the stables," said Jill. "Lovely onions."

And then Auntie Rose came towards them from the orchard, with a little basket of bantam's eggs.

"For the children's tea," she murmured in her soft, yet brisk old voice. "They'll be hungry, the dears. And in London, so they tell me, you've but the one egg a month, and that addled, as likely as not."

"This is Mrs. Spelman, my Auntie Rose," said Jill to George.

"The General's taken a real fancy to the place, Auntie."

"I'm pleased to hear that, Sir," said Auntie Rose. "I've not put it in the agent's hands yet, or advertised it in any way. Lady Eliot, she wanted me to give you the first refusal."

"Lady Eliot—what did you say?" asked George.

"It was an honour to see her ladyship," said Auntie Rose. Came herself, she did, to see Jill and tell her to answer Mrs. Eliot's advertisement. So anxious, she is, to have you living in the country near her. Yes, Sir, I said you should have the first refusal. I was glad to oblige her ladyship. Is the kettle on, Jill?"

They were all going back into the house. George came last, moving like a sleep-walker. He took out his handkerchief and mopped his forehead.

Auntie Rose presided very charmingly over the tea-party. She was of the old school, and respected what she still called "the gentry," and because of her respect felt perfectly at home with them. Feeling no necessity for proving herself as good as anyone else, she was just herself, and, contentedly established in the familiarity of herself, was happy.

And Auntie Rose's self was delightful. She was a little, round woman with rosy cheeks and blue eyes and white hair done up in a bun on the top of her head, marvellously attired in a grey-brown tweed skirt, a purple satin blouse and high button boots. She had not moved with the times, and was as restful as are all things and persons who seem impervious to change. She was about as restful as the Herb of Grace itself.

"Mrs. Spelman, how can you endure to leave this beautiful place?" asked George, drinking hot, strong, sweet tea poured out of a large brown earthenware tea-pot, and wondering why tea always tastes so much better when it is poured out of a brown tea-pot than out of any other kind.

"I'm gettin' old, Sir, and it's a burden on me now. I'm lookin' forward to takin' me ease with me daughter-in-law. And as for beauty Sir, I've never let that trouble me. Jill, now, she's the one for beauty—lettin' a saucepan boil over while she looks at a rainbow—

but, then, she's had the time for it, while I've had too much to do between dawn and sunset to waste me time lookin' at 'em.... Another egg, dearie?"

Jerry graciously accepted another bantam's egg, and Tommy helped himself to his sixth scone. George, remembering the lunch they'd had, was ashamed of them.

"It's all right, Sir," Jill, who was sitting beside him, said softly. "There's plenty, and country food is good for children. Master Ben and Miss Caroline will soon put on weight when you've settled here, and Master Ben will lose that nasty cough."

"It's nothing," Ben said, smiling at her.

George looked at his two eldest. Yes, they were too thin and fine-drawn. And though Nadine said it was nothing, he had been worried about Ben's cough for a long time now. They had taken their full share of family anxiety through the war. Care-free country holidays were exactly what they needed. "Messing about in boats... simply messing about in boats."

They ate all there was to eat, and then Auntie Rose took them up the turret staircase. Half-way up there was a small arched door in the stone wall. It was of very old oak studded with nails, and looked as though it might lead into a dungeon.

"What's in there?" demanded the twins as one child.

"Only my storeroom, ducks," said Auntie Rose.

"Let's see," commanded the twins.

Obediently Auntie Rose fished a large key out of her capacious pocket and unlocked the door. She had scarcely got it ajar when the twins were inside, squeaking with delight, enchanted by this room as nothing else at the Herb of Grace had enchanted them yet. George was at a loss to understand their pleasure. The little room was attractive in its strange, octagonal shape, and its narrow lancet windows were attractive, too; but the stone floor was very worn, and the room was papered with a rather dirty mustard-coloured paper with chocolate-coloured lozenges upon it. Slatted shelves, bulging and stained with age, were nailed round the walls and supported a large assortment of black bottles and brown crocks, of all shapes and sizes, filled with Auntie Rose's home-made wines, pickles and preserves.

"I keep it locked, so that no one shan't get at me wines," explained Auntie Rose. "All me own make—cowslip and elderberry wine and sloe gin. There's a big cellar down below, Sir, for the stout and cider and beer—what there is of it these days. The cellar door is behind the bar."

"What beautiful Easter eggs on the paper!" cried José in ecstasy.

"Wizard!" exclaimed Jerry.

But no one else seemed to like the little room much, except Ben, who lingered at the door a moment, feeling in the room some indefinable attraction; almost as though there were buried treasure here.

They went on up the staircase to see the rooms upstairs. There were eight of them altogether, with several large attics up above in the roof. Upstairs was an enchanting place, with odd corners, surprising little flights of steps, unexpected windows and deep cupboards. The refracted light of the sun upon the river danced on the ceilings, there was the murmuring of birds beneath the eaves, the smell of lavender and furniture polish. The walls were papered with old-fashioned flowered wall-paper, bright and gay, and there was some priceless old furniture to which Auntie Rose seemed entirely indifferent, if not actively hostile.

"It all belonged to me mother-in-law," she said. "Barrin' me lovely brass bedstead."

Casually she mentioned the price she had been advised to ask for the house, and it was surprisingly reasonable. Provided she might have her precious "suite" and the hideous brass bedstead, she was prepared to sell all the rest of the furniture. George began making frantic calculations upon the back of an envelope. They'd get a good price for the Chelsea house. They could borrow from the Bank. It could be done. Run as a guest-house (but he liked the old-world "inn" better) the place was bound to pay. Nadine was a wonderful organizer, and, abandoning himself to wishful thinking, he assured himself that she'd not get overdone, for help was more easily come by in the country than in the town, and he'd be there to help her. The words "there to help her" sang in his mind like a song. Together, working together, planning together, coming closer to each other than they had ever done in their difficult married life of constant separation, estrangement, difficult adjustment; and then separation again, and estrangement again, and bitterness and sorrow, and always in his soul that desperate longing to be loved by Nadine as he loved her—whole-heartedly…. He stumbled upon one of the unexpected steps, dropped the envelope, and entirely forgot to ask Auntie Rose if there was a bathroom.

"May we go down the front stairs, please?" Ben was saying when he came back to awareness of his surroundings. "I want to look at the deer."

"What deer, me love?" asked Auntie Rose.

"The one in the alcove where the stairs branch," said Ben. "I saw it from below."

"You mean the little old stone goat?" asked Auntie Rose. "It's nothin' to look at, dearie. Just some rubbishy old thing me husband dug up in the onion bed. 'Throw it in the river, Fred,' I said, but he would put it there in that cupboard place. After he died I'd meant to throw it out, and then I hadn't the heart. Set store by it, Fred did. He'd take queer fancies for all sorts of rubbish, Fred would. Odd chap, he was, though a good husband, and, in the trade though he was, only took a glass too much once in a way as a matter of business. There it is, dearie."

They had come half-way down the lovely branching staircase, and stood before the alcove in the panelling, looking at the little stone figure that Auntie Rose had thought was a goat. But Ben, even from below, had known better. He stood now looking at it with reverence, while the others, after a cursory glance at what seemed to be a bit of carved stone of no particular attraction nearly worn away by weather, looked at Ben, puzzled by his rapt attention. He stretched out a hand as though to touch the creature, then drew it back as though he felt his touch might be a profanation.

"Pick it up, ducks," said Auntie Rose with slight impatience. "It won't bite. Stone, it is."

Ben took the little image very gently into his hands.

"It's a deer all right," he said. "Look at the curve of the neck, the antlers." Suddenly he caught his breath. "Look at the way the antlers are carved, holding up a cross."

"H'm?" said George.

"Yes," insisted Ben. "Look."

His thin, sensitive fingers passed over the little figure like the fingers of a sculptor over the clay, and for a brief moment the brightness of his vision compelled the others to see what he saw: a beautiful white deer with a proud neck and a delicate pointed face beneath the spreading antlers that unmistakably branched inwards to form a cross. Then the sudden flash died to a spark that enabled his own sight only, and the others saw what they had seen before—just a worn stone image of some little animal with horns; only they saw now that it was possibly a deer, and that the horns were undoubtedly twisted in a rather unusual way.

"Must be very old, though," said George, with respect.

"This was a Pilgrim Inn," said Ben, putting the little deer gently back into his niche. "I expect, if we knew where to look, we'd find frescoes of lives of the saints hidden under the wallpapers, and perhaps more holy images that tumbled off the roof into the garden." He looked at Auntie Rose. "Was this the only one you ever found?"

"Fred found a few odd broken bits, diggin' the garden, an' brought 'em in. But them I *did* throw out when he was gone. Not one of them had a head to it, even. He'd only kept 'em because of some old wives' tale his great-grannie had told him when he had the scarlet fever as a lad."

"What tale?" demanded Ben sharply.

Auntie Rose rubbed her nose, trying to recollect it.

"Somethin' about some old monk from the Abbey who had a fancy for birds an' beasts. He built a Chapel in the woods, Fred's great-grannie told him, an' he'd feed the creatures there, an' tend to 'em when they were sick. Just some tale the old great-grannie made up to keep Fred quiet when he had the fever on him. But Fred, he believed it. He'd swallow anythin', Fred would. An' he got the notion that old monk had carved the animals that fell off the roof, an' those birds an' beasts there on the wooden pillars. Only a man who loved the creatures, Fred said, could get 'em so life-like. Loved animals, Fred did. Wouldn't never shoot anythin'.... Soft he was."

Ben let out a sigh of exasperation.

"Auntie Rose, you oughtn't to have thrown away the other holy images, even though they had no heads."

"Is that a holy image?" asked Jerry, gazing round-eyed at the deer.

"Yes," said Ben.

"What's a holy image?" asked José, also round-eyed.

"Something someone makes for the love of God," said Ben steadily.

George and Tommy both shot up their left sleeves and looked at their wrist-watches—the invariable custom of both of them when embarrassed. The twins and Ben were continually embarrassing them; the twins by the questions they asked, and Ben because he never evaded their questions, but answered them with the truth as he saw it.

"Then a house could be a holy image," said Jerry.

"Yes," said Ben.

"Then this house is," said José.

"Yes," said Ben.

"Gosh, it's late!" interrupted Tommy firmly.

"Better be getting along," agreed George. "Mother will be anxious. Thank you more than I can say, Mrs. Spelman, for your kindness and patience, and the splendid tea you gave these children."

"A pleasure, Sir," said Auntie Rose as they went down the stairs. "And I'll be hearin' from you?"

"As soon as possible. But I must consult my wife, of course."

"Of course, Sir."

They trooped out into the garden and saw the wood all lit up by the westering light, as though a thousand candles had been lit upon the trees that stretched their shade deep beyond deep in the dark wood. The water was all a-glint, too, and the colours of the flowers burned pure and still. The sky was a deep blue-green overhead, and three wild swans were flying up-river to their home. There was no sound in all the world but the beat of their wings and the soft lapping of the water against the old stone walls. They stood for a moment at the gate at the top of the steps, and the peace held them silent. Then Tommy clicked the gate open, Jill kissed the twins, and they went down the steps to the car.

– 3 –

Driving home, the children kept up a perfect racket of excited chatter, but George felt worse and worse. What on earth was Nadine going to say? How on earth had it all come about? What had he said, what had anybody said, to start them off on this wild idea of buying the Herb of Grace and turning it into an inn? He couldn't for the life of him remember. He was, of course, not committed to anything; it was perfectly possible to back out.... But, appalled though he felt, the prospect of backing out made him feel worse still.... How could he disappoint the children? They were nearly off their heads with delight. How could he disappoint himself? Entering the Herb of Grace had been to him homecoming; just that. But it must be as Nadine wished. Everything, always, must be as Nadine wished; that was the guiding principle of his life. But she wouldn't wish to live at the Herb of Grace; he felt dead certain of that; and he wished to goodness the expression of her wishes were over. It wasn't going to be pleasant, the first half-hour after they reached home. He wished she'd been with them this afternoon, or that she'd seen the place before they did; for if she had they'd never have got themselves into this mess.... Then a curious suspicion flashed into his mind. Had Lucilla, or had she not, seen to it that Nadine should not see the place before they did, should not accompany them this afternoon? And what was this Lucilla had said to Auntie Rose about giving him the first refusal of the place?... Undoubtedly his saintly old mother was up to one of her deep games here. Abruptly his wearied mind ceased from thought. He'd say nothing when they got home. He'd just let things take their course.

They started to take them as soon as the car drew up at the front door of Damerosehay, and Lucilla and Nadine and Margaret, coming out to welcome the travellers, were told by Jerry at the top of his voice, "There's a lovely house with a wild wood, and Daddie's going to buy it, and we're all going to live there!"

"What nonsense you talk, darling!" said Nadine.

"But it's true, Mummy!" yelled José, and then all four children began to talk at once, so that no one could hear a word.

"That'll do, darlings," said Lucilla, somehow or other managing to quell the riot without even raising her voice, as was her miraculous habit. "Supper is ready. Wash your hands quickly and come along."

Hands were washed, and they all trooped into the dining-room. It was, of course, long past the twins' bed-time, but as they were much too excited for sleep Lucilla decreed that they should absorb their biscuits and milk with their elders, what time those elders were attacking stewed rabbit, rhubarb and cheese-straws—an unusually magnificent repast to which Margaret had mounted, as though upon eagle's wings, because George was present. The moment the pangs of hunger had been slightly allayed the children started talking again, and once more it was difficult to disentangle one thing from another.

"Let Tommy tell us," suggested Lucilla.

Tommy's jaws, champing upon rabbit, stilled for a moment in surprise. He was no raconteur, and it was generally Ben who was called upon for a coherent story. But he was subtly flattered by his grandmother's choice of himself, and pausing only to remove an obstruction from his mouth and identify it as a piece of the tibia, he plunged into enthusiastic narrative, his rosy face ablaze with excitement, his bright, dark eyes fixed upon his mother, whose darling and pet he was.... Lucilla had known what she was doing when she directed the full battery of Tommy's guns upon his mother's heart, for the disappointing of Tommy was a thing of which Nadine had never yet found herself capable.

"You're taking things too much for granted, old boy," George's voice cut in upon Tommy's enthusiastic description of the little room where he was going to keep his bones. "Mother has not seen the house yet. She may decide it's not quite her cup of tea."

Tommy waved this interruption aside as unworthy of attention and plunged into a description of the boats they would have in the boat-house.

"It all sounds lovely, but wildly beyond our means," said Nadine, when it was next possible to get a word in edgeways.

She had gone rather white, and was crumbling her bread and not getting on with her rabbit.

"That's all right, Mother," said Tommy. "Father's going to leave the Army and we're going to run it as an inn. We'll simply coin money."

"Will we?" asked Nadine. "I suppose there was electric light laid on, George?"

George wrinkled his brows, tried to rid himself of some sort of vague vision of beautiful oil-lamps hanging from equally beautiful old beams, but was saved from the necessity of answering by Ben, who had been devouring rabbit at great speed while Tommy talked, but now laid his knife and fork down on his empty plate and with shining eyes began to tell them a few facts about inns, which he had picked up from a book David had.

"Ours is a Pilgrim Inn, Mother—a Maison Dieu. All the rooms would have been called after different saints. The old inns all gave their rooms names, you know. The secular ones were named after flowers, mostly. I wonder who painted our sign? Great artists painted the inn-signs sometimes, Mother—Hogarth, Morland, David Cox. You know, Mother, the early plays were given in inn yards, and the modern theatre takes its form from the galleries that ran round the yard.... I tell you what. Next Christmas we'll act a play at the Herb of Grace! Wouldn't it be a lark!... When the guests come we won't allow tips, of course. They never had tips in the old days. The tip didn't come in till the thirteenth century. Mother, do you know the difference between an inn and a public-house? The inn is bound to give shelter, rest and food to the wayfarer, at any hour, but the public-house is not. Mine Host always greeted the guest and gave him a complimentary glass of wine. Father'll be good at that, and you'll be a wonderful hostess, Mother. We'll have to have a hall porter, a waiter and garage mechanic, but we'll give them the old names—chamberlain, drawer and ostler."

"You'll be chamberlain," interrupted Caroline suddenly, her cheeks as pink as Tommy's. "I'll be drawer, and Tommy ostler."

"You're at home very little," Nadine reminded them dryly.

"We're at home in the holidays," Tommy told her; "and the holidays—Christmas, Easter, the summer—are just when visitors will come. *We'll* do all the work, Mother—Father and us. You won't have anything to do except look lovely. We'll get a cook."

"Where from?" asked Nadine. "And was there a bathroom?"

No one seemed to know, and there was a short silence, broken by José.

"There's a river," said José. "A river for Rat."

"And a Wild Wood," said Jerry.

"And a Person with Horns in the Wild Wood," said José. "It lives in the Chapel in the woods that the man made who liked animals."

"What does she mean?" demanded Caroline.

"She's mixing up the deer in the alcove with the story Fred's great-grannie told him," said Ben, and his eyes met his grandmother's, and she knew that sometime, when they were alone together, he would have something to tell her—some old legend, such as they both delighted in. Meantime supper was finished, and smiling at him, she got up.

"Well, children," she said, "Mother will see about it in the morning."

Nadine, not committing herself, white-faced and tight-lipped, went upstairs to put the twins to bed, Margaret and Caroline to the kitchen to do the washing up, Lucilla to the drawing-room with her son and grandsons. There she immediately suggested bridge, and George got no chance at all to ask her what on earth she had been up to.... Nadine did not return.... They played for an hour, George continually forgetting what was out, and then he could stand it no longer, pleaded a headache, went upstairs and knocked at Nadine's door.

"Come in," said Nadine.

He went in. She was sitting up in bed with a book in her hands, a frilly dressing-jacket round her shoulders. In the light of her bedside candles she looked absurdly young and altogether lovely. The blood drummed in George's already aching temples and he caught his breath. He went to the foot of the bed and gripped the old-fashioned brass rail tightly in both hands.

"Nadine!" he whispered.

"I don't believe you've even unpacked yet, darling, have you?" she asked in a light, hard voice. "And I don't believe Grandmother told you she'd put us in separate rooms."

Her cruelty was like the lash of a whip in his face, and he went white. An agony of pity and remorse seized her. That was the second detestably cruel thing she had said today. What was coming over her? What was happening to her?

"George! George! I'm sorry!" she cried. "I didn't mean to speak in that hateful tone. Come here, darling. Come and sit on my bed and let's talk."

He came slowly and sat beside her, and she chafed one of his cold hands between her warm ones and murmured endearments as she would have to the twins. But she couldn't undo it. Once again, as so often before, she had made it clear to him that his lifelong passion was to her nothing but a burden that she must bear.... And never by look or word had he ever let her guess what a lifelong burden to him must be her lack of response to his love.... In giving up David she had made for him an immense and splendid sacrifice, yet it seemed to her at this moment that she perpetually rendered it useless by her cruelty. What was the matter with her, that the quality of that action seemed powerless to affect the stuff of her daily living? Lucilla, whose early history had been so like her own, had made her unloved husband utterly happy, and had come in the end to love him. Lucilla had succeeded where she was failing. Something or other Lucilla had done, consciously or unconsciously, which she was not doing. As she had thought this morning, something was lacking in her—some herb of grace.

"Nadine," said George miserably, "about this damn inn. Mother has been up to something about it, but I give you my word I don't know what. When I started off this afternoon I'd no more idea of buying the place than of buying the Albert Memorial. But when I was there.... I don't know what happened.... The place gave us such a welcome... like a personal welcome...."

"I believe you," said Nadine. "I've never known you get entangled in Grandmother's schemes for our good other than unconsciously. You liked this house?"

"It felt like home," said George wretchedly.

"Then we'll buy it, and, if you'd like to do that, run it as an inn."

He gazed at her in stupefaction.

"You've never had a home," said Nadine. "All those furnished houses we've lived in since we married, that detestable Indian bungalow where we quarrelled so badly—they were none of them home. The Chelsea house was my home, but not yours. The Herb of Grace will be our home, yours and mine. Our first."

A ridiculous desire to weep kept George silent, but he crushed her hands in his till she nearly yelled with the pain.

"You haven't even seen the place," he muttered at last.

"We'll go tomorrow. Just you and I."

"You may hate it."

"No, I don't think I shall. I need it—the Herb of Grace...."

Then he began talking, as Tommy had done, as Ben had done, with shining eyes like Caroline's, pouring out his plans for the boathouse, the house, the garden and the orchard. She listened, smiling agreement, while her exhausted spirit cried out in terror within her. How *could* she do it? She was so desperately tired.... And she'd only just repainted her beloved Chelsea house.... A little of her deadly fatigue must have showed in her face at last, for he jumped up, full of contrition.

"You're dead beat," he said, bending to kiss her. "Selfish beast that I am. Get a good sleep, darling, and we'll go and see the old place in the morning."

And he went off jaunty as a schoolboy, and she blew out the candles and lay staring with desperation into the dark. Before he came to her she had been steeling herself for refusal, resolutely steeling herself against the passionate enthusiasm that she would never have allowed to develop had she been with them—and how well Grandmother had known that!—steeling herself even to the point of disappointing her adored Tommy. And then she had said that cruel thing to George, and her horror at herself had betrayed her.

"Hoisted with my own petard," she said.

The night-wind stirred in the rushes outside her window, ruffling with its light whisper the deep, calm peace of the night. Was she sorry? Her body began weeping from sheer weariness, yet she felt her spirit move within her, and with eagerness, like someone going home. She sobbed herself to sleep, yet when she slept she smiled.

CHAPTER

– 1 –

ℕO, SHE WAS NOT SORRY, she decided five months later, as she sat working at her housekeeping books at her escritoire, set in the window of her upstairs sitting-room. It was a lovely little room, and perhaps had once been a powdering closet. It had been a box-room in Auntie Rose's day, and had been papered with church almanacks, but through the almanacks Nadine's quick eye had seen the ridge of panelling, and the first thing they had done in this house had been to strip off the almanacks and disclose it. Now the panelling had been painted cream colour and the little room furnished with Nadine's eighteenth-century escritoire, a Sheraton chair with a tapestry seat, a comfortable little arm-chair, and a corner cupboard with glass doors holding some precious bits of china. That was all the furniture there was room for, but there was a white sheepskin rug on the polished oak floor, a little old mirror hung on the wall and there was a vase of late autumn roses on the escritoire. Beside Nadine, in her basket with its powder-blue cushion, Mary the white pekinese lay fast asleep.

The powder-blue curtains framed a view that in the past five months had mysteriously become part of Nadine's very soul; which was odd, for views had not hitherto meant much to her. But, then, she said to herself, they had none of them been *this* view. She laid down her pen, propped her chin in her hands, and feasted upon it. Just below her the strip of garden that stretched from the house to the river wall was a blaze of colour: purple and white Michaelmas daisies, scarlet dahlias and early yellow chrysanthemums. They were enjoying an Indian summer, and in the bright, warm sun the butterflies were sunning themselves on the Michaelmas daisies, and two slim willow-wrens darted from flower-clump to river wall and back again, appearing too happy to stay still. The river was blue, and almost as still today as the tawny marshes, and, beyond, the golden October woods swept to the blue of the sky. Through the open window there came no sound, except the soft lap of the water against the wall, and the tap of a hammer, where in the boat-house Ben was messing about with boats.

At the sound of that busy hammer Nadine's face softened with sudden tenderness and compunction. Ben had not been able to go back to school this term. Lucilla had insisted that his mother take him to see a doctor about his cough, and the doctor had said that his lungs were not satisfactory. Nothing to worry about, said the doctor, a few months of laziness and fresh air would probably put things right; but there might have been something to worry about if Lucilla had not taken action, and Nadine was ashamed.

"I'm a poor sort of mother," she said to herself now. "I've got too tired to want to bother about anything. It was a good thing for Ben's sake that we came here. And George's, too; he's a new man."

Yes, this move had justified itself, even though after the wild activity of the past few months she was, if possible, even more tired than she had been before. Yet it was chiefly her body that was tired now, her mind, that had been so weary and fretted in London, had been wonderfully rested by this house that was now her home. Hardly knowing what she did, she stretched out a hand and laid it upon the panelled wall beside her; it was warm in the sun, as though it were alive. Increasingly, as she lived here, Nadine had a feeling that this house had a personality of its own—some sort of great angel who grew with the growth of the house and was enriched, or otherwise, by those who lived here; and she felt, too, that this angel was well-disposed towards her. It was a genial sort of angel, and remarkably patient. When she first arrived, with everything to do and feeling herself without the strength to do it, she had bitterly hated its body, the house, and it had suffered her hatred with the gentleness of an old dog who knows he gives offence with his matted coat, yet cannot unaided mend matters, though he would die to please you. But her hatred had not lasted long, for the response of the house to her onslaughts upon it had been so swift that the bitterness had ebbed away, and in its place had come the deep, companionable love of those who strive together for the glory of God.

That had been Ben's phrase. "For the glory of God!" he had cried, as he stripped the almanacks from the panelling, and he had shouted it again at the top of his voice when he and Tommy had torn away the terrible overmantel and surround in the drawing-room, and revealed behind it a perfect Adam mantelpiece. George had protested at this battle-cry, but Ben had stuck to it. This house was Maison Dieu, and the stripping away of all that was unworthy, and the building up of new beauty, was in the nature of a crusade.

And the house had agreed, and collaborated. Nadine had a supreme gift for furnishing and decorating, but never had she so enjoyed putting her gift to use as she had during the last few months. The Angel had seemed to work with her, telling her what to do and how to do it, as though he, too, were an artist.... And it had been the house itself that had attracted to her assistance Malony, Annie-Laurie and Smith. Nadine suddenly began to laugh as she thought of these three, after Jill her chief prop and stay, and, dreaming in the sun, she went back in memory to the first weeks at the Herb of Grace, and the blessed day of their arrival.

– 2 –

After the first few days she had declared with bitter passion that she would not stay in this house, *she would not*, unless a bathroom and a resident lamp-cleaner were put in and the mice put out. She realized it would be impossible to install electric light for a long time to come, and she agreed with George that lamplight and candle-light were very beautiful, but she was not going to do the lamps herself. Nor was she going to live here without a bathroom. Nor with the mice. And if George did not wish her to leave him again he must see to it. Having delivered herself of this ultimatum, she took a headache to her room, lay on her bed with it and cried. George meanwhile spent the morning touring the neighbourhood in the car and interviewing every plumber he could find, only to be told by each firm that though it would be delighted to undertake the General's order at some future period, baths at present were unobtainable. George bought ten mouse-traps and came home very crestfallen, to find Caroline helping Jill prepare lunch, while Ben and Tommy, as hungry as hunters after a morning's hard work in the garden, were laying the table in the hope that that would hurry things on; but Nadine still in her room. It was the beginning of the summer holidays, so the children were at home, with the exception of the twins, who were staying at Damerosehay in the care of Lucilla and Margaret, so as to set Jill free to help get the house in order and smooth out all disharmony with the oil of her gentle common-sense.

"We'll send Mrs. Eliot her lunch up on a tray," she said now to the miserable George. "You shall take it yourself, Sir. Tired out, she is. What beautiful mouse-traps, Sir! I don't know when I've seen finer mouse-traps than those."

She laid the tray swiftly and deftly with a special invalid lunch, setting a little vase of flowers upon it, and George tramped up the stairs with it, and carried it with heavy tread to Nadine, and set it upon the table beside her bed, upsetting the vase of flowers as he did so.

"How sweet of you, darling!" she said, mopping up the water, and hating herself now for her tears and her temper; in the old pre-war days she had never cried. "Did you have any luck about the bath?"

"No," said George, "but I bought ten mouse-traps."

"How splendid!" said Nadine. "What are you going to bait them with? We eat all our cheese ration."

Again she hated herself, but George was not hurt this time by her sarcasm, for his attention was distracted by the most extraordinary chugging noise that came drifting in through the open window. He turned and looked out.

"What the dickens!" he ejaculated.

Nadine, eyeing the perfectly fried fillets with approval, and thanking heaven that Jill knew how to cook as well as how to look after small children, glanced indifferently at the strip of river framed by the window. Then her indifference changed to interest, and she slipped off her bed and went to stand by George. The most astonishing Heath Robinson contraption was chugging up the river. It looked as though it had originally been a coal barge, though it was now fitted with a motor engine, and carried instead of coal the most extraordinary assortment of oddments that Nadine had ever seen. In the centre of the barge was a bathing-machine, its little windows hung with gay flowered curtains. Behind the bathing-machine was strung a washing-line from which brightly coloured female undergarments fluttered out over what was apparently a vegetable garden planted in the stern of the boat. The front of the boat was filled with the most amazing assortment of machinery, above which towered a flagpost from which fluttered the Union Jack. At the top of the flagpost was a curious bunch of scintillating brightness that at this distance could not be identified as anything in particular. There appeared to be a crew of three, a male figure dimly discernible among the machinery, a female figure tangled up in the washing, and a cat cleaning its whiskers on top of the bathing-machine. The boat had been travelling slowly downriver, but at sight of the Herb of Grace it slackened speed, and it appeared that the crew were shouting remarks to each other. Then, with much noise, they steered for the shore and came to anchor beneath the garden wall. The lower part of the craft was now hidden from the astonished gaze of Nadine and George, but they could still see the flagpost with its flag, and the brightness above that now revealed itself as a bunch of bells, that chimed softly and sweetly as the boat rocked to stillness; also the tops of some flourishing tomato plants growing in the vegetable garden, and the cat on top of the bathing-machine. The latter was an immense tabby with a white shirt-front, and it now ceased washing itself and gazed at Nadine and George with speculative interest. The top of a ladder now appeared above the garden wall.

"Must be a sort of circus," said Nadine.

"Great Scott!" exclaimed George. "They're coming ashore!"

The man came first, climbing off the ladder on to the top of the wall with the nimbleness of a monkey. And he was like a monkey to look at. He had a brown, sad, puckered face, and dark hair cropped short. He was small in stature, thin and wiry, clothed in dark-blue dungarees and sweater, with a bright red scarf knotted about his throat. No less nimble was the girl who followed him, though much better looking. She looked at this distance about eighteen years old, very thin, light and graceful in her movements, with a little, sunburnt face, delicately pointed at the chin, and wonderful, shining gold hair twisted in plaits about her small head. She wore a diminutive jade-green skirt and a yellow jumper, and her thin, brown legs were bare. When the two of them were upon the wall the cat passed a paw thoughtfully behind its left ear, then took a flying leap and landed behind them. With the agility of tight-rope walkers the three of them then marched in single file along the top of the wall and vanished in the direction of the front door. A moment after there was a knock, the heavy tread of Tommy marching to open the door, and then voices.

"Hadn't you better go down, darling?" queried Nadine.

But George was gazing like a man mesmerized at the bunch of bells and the Union Jack and the tops of the tomato plants. There was a racket on the stairs, and Tommy burst in.

George swung round.

"Don't make such a damnable noise!" he shouted loudly. "Do remember that your poor mother has the most frightful headache."

"Sorry," shouted Tommy, equally loudly. "Come along down, Father. There's a splendid chap here—a sort of tinker. Mends anything. We've asked him to lunch."

"Asked him to *lunch?*" exclaimed Nadine.

"Of course, Mother. This is an inn, you know, not a pub. We're bound to give shelter and refreshment at any hour."

"Did he ask for lunch?" demanded George.

"No. He asked for beer, and to sharpen our scissors and knives and sell us tomatoes. I had to tell him we hadn't got the beer in yet, but we were having cider and Spam for lunch, and he said he could make do with that. The girl's jolly nice, too. Awfully pretty."

"Go down at once, George," said Nadine, her hand to her head. "And get rid of them."

"You *can't* get rid of them," said Tommy indignantly. "This is an inn, I keep telling you."

George went, followed by Tommy. Nadine carried her tray to the window, put it on the broad sill, sat down and began to eat her fish. She felt much better after she had eaten a little—in fact, almost well. It was delicious fish, but it would have been improved by a baked tomato. Nadine was of the school of thought that considers fish and tomatoes as inseparable as bacon and eggs. She finished her fish, ate the little junket that Jill had sent up with it, and then looked thoughtfully at the tops of the tomato plants showing above the garden wall. She'd just slip down, she thought, and see if the tomatoes were worth buying. As she went down the stairs she heard a great clatter of knives and forks and conversation coming from the kitchen. George, evidently, had not found it possible to overrule Tommy's invitation to lunch. She went out through the old ship's door and round into the garden. Standing by the wall, she found herself looking straight at the bunch of little bells at the top of the flagpost. They were pretty bells, and she could fancy she still heard that fairy chiming coming from them. Then she took a look at the rest of the boat. It was most attractive. The bathing-machine, a large one, had been divided to make two tiny cabins and a kitchen-living-room. The kitchen had a little oil cooking-stove in it, a tiny dresser with pretty china and some bright pots and pans, a table, a seat that let down from the wall and a shelf for books. In each cabin was a bunk that could be used as a seat in the day-time, and from the roof of each hung an oil-lamp. Nadine noted that these lamps had been well polished and well cared for by someone who evidently understood their tricks and their manners very well indeed.

Then she turned her attention to the vegetable garden in the stern. It had two beds, one planted with tomato plants bearing beautiful, ripe, red tomatoes, and the other with lettuces and radishes with a border of pansies round the edge. These beds had been made—Nadine gazed and gazed again—by filling two large baths with earth. *Two large baths.*

Her headache vanished as though it had never been. She did not hesitate. She hastened to the kitchen and entered upon a scene of conviviality that would scarcely have met with her approval had there been room in her mind for anything except baths. George, her children, Jill and the two strangers were seated at the kitchen table drinking cider and devouring Spam and salad off the beautiful willow-pattern china as though they had known each other for years. The cat was under the table, also partaking of nourishment off a willow-pattern plate. George, it was true, looked a little self-conscious, but he seemed to be enjoying himself all the same, and everyone else was completely at their ease; with the exception of Mary the pekinese, who was sitting on the window-sill gazing at the cat and frozen stiff with horror at finding herself in such plebeian company. There was a vacant place at one end of the table, opposite George, and as soon as she saw Nadine, Jill got up and pulled the chair back.

"We hoped you would feel well enough to join us, Madam," she said. "You had such a light lunch. Could you fancy toast and a cup of coffee? It won't take a minute."

"Yes, I could, Jill. Thank you," said Nadine, and took the empty place.

She was not quite sure that they had been hoping she would join them, but Jill could always be relied on to say what would best help everyone over an awkward moment.

"My wife," said George, red-faced but courtly. No matter how flustered, he was always a good host. "Mr. - er—"

"Jim Malony," said the monkey-faced man, and, standing courteously, he bowed to Nadine with the most surprising grace, his bright yet sad, dark eyes twinkling with friendliness. "And this is my daughter, Annie-Laurie."

Annie-Laurie turned her little brown face towards her hostess and smiled shyly. She had a queer, crooked smile like that of a beseeching child; though at a second glance one saw that she was very far from being a child. Her beautiful bright blue eyes were deeply and maturely anxious, and though her crooked smile had a child's appeal, it died very abruptly, and her lips in repose had a woman's hard control. It was a resolutely sealed-in face, yet the hidden wretchedness was not quite masked by the bravery. Nadine was not a naturally maternal woman, yet she had borne five children, and at sight of that face she felt a stab of pain at her heart. She glanced at Jill, heating coffee at the kitchen stove, and their eyes met pitifully.... There was undoubtedly something very wrong with this girl.... And yet at the same time there was something very right with her—a direct simplicity in her beseeching, a vitality that leaped like a pure flame. Nadine answered the smile, but for once found herself without words.

The rather painful little pause was broken by Tommy, who indicated the region below the kitchen table with a gesture.

"The cat Smith," he told his mother. "Enjoying the trimmings of your fillets."

Then the conversation flowed on again where Nadine's entrance had interrupted it, rich and racy, upon the subject of fish, boats, rivers and river-side inns. It was sustained chiefly by Tommy and Jim Malony, but George, Ben and Caroline flung in eager questions now and then. Annie-Laurie said little. She ate daintily, and every now and then she smiled at her father, with the tenderness of a woman who has heard her man's tales many times before but is glad to see him happy in their repetition. Her attitude to him was scarcely old enough to be her father, for in spite of his puckered face he was obviously a youngish man. Nor was she in the least like him: she was very fair beneath her sunburn. His attitude to her was obvious in every glance he sent her; it was lovingly anxious, protective, like that of an adoring old watch-dog. He was a born raconteur. Jokes, vivid little anecdotes, shreds and scraps of information about all sorts of out-of-the-way subjects kept them enthralled. He talked in a husky, croaking voice that was yet unusually articulate, and his Irish brogue seemed too rich and glorious to be true.

And Nadine did not think for a single moment that it was true. She no more believed that Jim Malony was an Irishman than she believed he was what Tommy had said he was, a tinker. She did not know what he was. She was utterly nonplussed by the pair of them. They were not of the class that she was accustomed to describe as working-people, nor were they exactly gentle-folk. What on earth were they?

"Troubadour..."

It was Ben who had spoken. He was sitting next to his mother, Annie-Laurie upon his other side, and now that she had finished her Spam and salad he had turned to her and was shyly and kindly trying to talk to her.

"Your father is like a sort of troubadour," he said. "You know, one of those men who travelled from house to house in the old days, telling wonderful tales and cheering everyone up."

"He's always cheerful," said Annie-Laurie. Her voice was clear and charming, educated, without the trace of an Irish accent, and when she turned to smile her crooked smile at Ben an unsuspected dimple appeared in her left cheek. "It seems the right place for a troubadour, this old house. They were the ancestors of the strolling players, weren't they? And the old players liked best to play at inns."

"They played in the inn galleries," Ben agreed enthusiastically.

"And stepped on to their stages out of the lovely old rooms with their flower names: Fleur-de-Lys and Herb of Grace."

As she spoke she turned to smile at her hostess, and Nadine marvelled at her knowledge and her grace.

"Do you like flowers, Annie-Laurie?" she asked. "You have some lovely pansies growing in the garden on your house-boat."

"I like flowers, children, birds and animals," said Annie-Laurie— "anything that needs looking after. My pansies are pretty, but you can't grow many flowers just in a bath. It was because your garden was so lovely that my father and I stopped and had a look, and then the old house looked friendly; like a person. And it looked so safe, too; like a fortress. We hoped it was an inn, and we came round to the front to see. But I think perhaps you are only using it as a private house, and that we ought not to have asked to come in?"

"That's all right, Annie-Laurie," Nadine assured her. "It is going to be an inn one day, when we have got things straight. We have only just moved in, and nowhere—simply nowhere—can I find a bath to put in the bathroom we want to make."

"Bath, is it?" enquired Mr. Malony. "Glory be to God, Ma'am, I've two baths!"

"Mr. Malony," said Nadine, "I will pay you any price within reason you like to mention for those baths, and if you are a sufficiently skilled workman to help our local plumber put them in for me, I will double it."

"Ten quid the pair?" suggested Malony instantly. "Let you give us twenty quid and our food, now, and I don't know but what Annie-Laurie and I won't stay here until you've got the place to your liking. There's nothing Annie-Laurie can't do—cook, clean lamps, wash, iron, sew—and, glory be to God, there's no mouser to touch Smith in the whole of the United Kingdom. Done, Ma'am?"

"Done," said Nadine.

– 3 –

And they were still here, sleeping in their house-boat that was anchored now beyond the boat-house at the edge of the Wood, spending their evenings there, but having their meals at the Herb of Grace, and toiling there from morning till night. They were invaluable. Malony, with such tact and humour that he gave no offence in the process, had helped a local plumber to install two bath-rooms, one for the guests and one for the family. Procuring the paint from no-one-knew-where, he had repainted the house from top to bottom quite superbly. He had worked in the garden with Ben and Tommy, assisted George to get the garage into order, scrubbed floors, washed up, cleaned shoes, polished silver, carried luggage—done anything and everything that his quick eye saw needed doing. In spite of the sadness of his face he was always cheerful and good-humoured. They had already had a few guests—friends who came to give them a good send-off—as well as casual droppers-in—men from the Hard coming for a pint when the day's work was over, picnic parties and river-folk —and Malony had known exactly how to deal with all of them. With a green baize apron tied round his middle he shared the duties of hall porter (only the children insisted upon the old name of chamberlain) with Ben, and attired in a white apron or a leather one he was Tommy's better half as waiter or garage mechanic; though woe betide him if he forgot to refer to himself as drawer or ostler. And upon the very rare occasions when there was some liveliness at the inn at night George had found him the most excellent chucker-out. And when Jill was helping Nadine with the cooking (for they had no cook as yet) he minded the twins with a skill that came little short of genius.

Annie-Laurie was as valuable as Malony. She took over entire charge of the lamps, and all the duties of a chambermaid. She was very nearly as good with the twins as Jill and Malony, and she was deeply attached to Mary the pekinese. But though she was friendly, she was not very forthcoming. She replied courteously and sweetly when spoken to, but she never told anybody anything, and all of them except Nadine found her reserve difficult to live with. But Nadine liked it. She liked Annie-Laurie, and she believed that Annie-Laurie liked her. There was a deep, unexpressed sympathy between them.

As for Smith, he was an animal of parts. He was an excellent mouser, prompt and efficient in the execution of his duties, but not lingering over them in the painful manner of so many mousers. He was clean, dignified and benevolent, and even Mary eventually found his presence at the Herb of Grace an added amenity.

Malony had himself given Nadine and George a short sketch of his history. He had begun life as plumber and house decorator, which was how he had come by the baths, but a bad bout of pneumonia had left his lungs weak, and strengthening sea air having been ordered by his doctor, he had started a bathing-machine business. He had owned twelve bathing-machines and done very well out of them; which was how he had come by the bathing-machine. But the bathing business palled on him. He had a longing to see the world. He also had a pal who was a bargee, but who was sick of it and wanted to settle down. They did an exchange, the pal taking over six of the bathing-machines and Malony the barge, which he made into an excellent house-boat with the help of one of the bathing-machines and an engine which another pal gave him in exchange for the remaining five. Smith had been the bargee's cat, and had come into their possession with the barge. Since then he and Annie-Laurie had just been seeing the world, picking up a living by doing odd jobs of work at river-side houses. Annie-Laurie was his only child. Her mother had died at her birth. She was the living image of her sainted mother. She had had a very good position at a dressmaking establishment, but had thrown it up to look after her father in his illness. This tale, admirably and amusingly related, George swallowed in simple faith after adding a few grains of salt; but Nadine did not believe a word of it.

But her unbelief had not prevented her from agreeing wholeheartedly with George's proposal that they should turn their unused coachman's quarters into a comfortable little flat, suitable as a winter home, and invite Malony and Annie-Laurie to stay with them for always. Whoever they were, she liked and trusted them, and last night she and George had made the proposal, and after one hurried strange glance at each other they had asked if they might think it over. They had given no answer as yet. Annie-Laurie had been very quiet all day, and Malony had made his jokes with difficulty. Nadine looked at her watch. It was 3:30. In another hour or so their first real guests would be arriving; for the personal friends who had hitherto stayed with them had hardly counted. But these two—John Adair and his daughter—were strangers. And important strangers, too. The familiarity of the name John Adair, when she received his brief business-like note asking for accommodation for an unlimited period, had sent Nadine to her *Who's Who*, to find to her dismay that he was what she suspected—John Adair the painter, a wealthy and famous man who would require to be fed as such; and she still had no cook. And the bath-water still showed a tendency to come out of the tap a curious shade of yellow-brown, and not always as hot as might be wished. A crease of anxiety showed between Nadine's eyebrows as she looked at her watch. She had an uneasy feeling that the offer she and George had made to Malony and Annie-Laurie had upset them in some way, and that they might perhaps take themselves off just at the moment when they were most urgently wanted.

There was a tap at the door.

"Come in," said Nadine.

Annie-Laurie entered softly and came and stood by Nadine's chair. She looked neat and fresh in her flowered overall, but her old-young face looked strained and weary.

"Yes, Annie-Laurie?" asked Nadine.

"If you please, Mrs. Eliot, my father and I think it would be best if we were moving on now."

"But, Annie-Laurie, you surely won't leave me just when I have guests coming?"

"We'll stay another week."

"A week's not long. Mr. and Miss Adair are coming here indefinitely."

"My father says—just another week."

"Then you have decided not to accept the General's offer of staying with us permanently?"

"No."

The monosyllable dropped bleakly, and looking up at Annie-Laurie's face, Nadine saw it desolate. She pulled forward the little arm-chair.

"Sit down, Annie-Laurie, and let's talk this over."

"It would be best for us not to stay," said Annie-Laurie wretchedly; but she sat down.

"Listen, Annie-Laurie," said Nadine. "I am very fond of you. I—love you, I think."

She had not known she was going to say that. She wasn't the sort of woman who said that sort of thing. She had not even known until she spoke, that she did love Annie-Laurie. But it was true. Astonished, bewildered, she put out her hand as though for support against the sun-warmed panelling. And again she had that sensation of a warm and living personality—the personality that had prompted her to speak as she had. She glanced at Annie-Laurie. The girl's face was white, and wore again that sealed-in look that had struck Nadine so painfully on the day of her arrival.

"Your father would like to stay. It is you who had decided against it," said Nadine.

"How did you know that?" whispered Annie-Laurie.

"I felt it, somehow. Why, Annie-Laurie? I know you are fond of me."

A curious pulsation passed over Annie-Laurie's sealed face, as when the first breath from the south passes over a frozen world. It passed, but she could not regain the old stillness. She struggled, but Nadine's warmth had pierced right through her defences, and beneath them the life was painfully quickened. But she did not cry. She pushed her thin hands up into her lovely gold hair and held them there as though she carried in her head a burden too hard to bear, and her eyes seemed dumbly beseeching Nadine to deliver her from its weight.

"You'll have to try to tell me a little about yourself, Annie-Laurie," said Nadine gently. "That tale your father told us, the plumbing business and the bathing-machines and all that nonsense, I didn't believe it. Nor do I believe that he is Irish. Tell me the truth about him."

Annie-Laurie's hands slipped to her lap. They were trembling, and she clasped them tightly. But Nadine had helped her over the first hurdle, and she could speak now.

"He was a comedian. He was on the halls, and in pantomime. We did acts together. He sang Irish songs and I sang Scotch ones, and we both danced, and he told funny stories. It got sort of second nature with him to talk Irish. He was an engineer before he went on the halls. He's clever. There's nothing he can't do, nothing he doesn't seem to know. We made a lot of money at one time. We had—everything."

Music-hall artists. Nadine was surprised at herself that she had not guessed that before. Ben, with his usual intuition, had described Malony as a troubadour, and had been wiser than she. Their bizarre appearance, vitality, adaptability and imagination were explained now. But the change-over from engineer to comedian was odd.

"What made your father go on the halls?" she asked.

"He couldn't keep his engineering jobs."

"Why not?"

"They didn't satisfy him—and then he drinks sometimes," said Annie-Laurie.

Her hands had stopped trembling and her face was quite expressionless.

"But not now," said Nadine.

"Not since we've been here," said Annie-Laurie. "Something new, something that interests him, and he's all right for a bit. But when he gets accustomed to anything—"

"And that's why you think you ought not to stay with me?" asked Nadine gently. "You think he'd disgrace the Herb of Grace?"

"Not only Jim—Father. I would. I've been in prison. Wherever we go, whatever we do, it comes out."

The desolation in her voice seemed to open a sort of pit at Nadine's feet. She was shamed. Women like herself, sheltered, indulged, secure, beloved; and yet they dared to find life hard, they dared to pity themselves because the path they trod was strewn with pink rose-petals when their own choice would have been crimson. She hated herself. Her hatred choked her, and she could not speak.

"So you see why we must go," said Annie-Laurie.

Nadine took a quick decision.

"There's no need to go, Annie-Laurie, if you would like to stay."
Annie-Laurie stared at her incredulously. "Whatever it was that you did, that is in the past. It is what you are now that matters, and what you are now I trust. I trust you, Annie-Laurie; both you and your father."

Annie-Laurie took a deep breath.

"He's not my father."

Again Nadine put out her hand as though for support, and again the old woodwork warm in the sun was like the clasp of a reassuring hand. Yet really, she told herself, she ought to have guessed that, with Malony so obviously younger than he looked. And Annie-Laurie, perhaps, much older.

"How old are you, Annie-Laurie?" she asked.

"I don't look it, but I'm over thirty," whispered Annie-Laurie.

She was looking at her hands clasped in her lap, her head bent, and Nadine could not see her face. She, too, looked at Annie-Laurie's hands. The knuckles were showing white through the sunburnt skin. She stretched out her hand and put it over them.

"I had to tell you," said Annie-Laurie. "I had to—after you'd said you trusted me—even though—"

"It's all right," said Nadine. "You can still stay, if you want to. You do want to, don't you?"

"Yes," said Annie-Laurie.

"Why?" asked Nadine.

"Because of you... and the house." She looked up at last, her adoration warm in her eyes, but her relief a thing of such intensity that she could not speak of it. "He stuck to me through it all," she said.

"You can't marry him?" asked Nadine.

"It's not possible," said Annie-Laurie. "But we're not really doing anything wrong—I can't explain—"

"Listen, Annie-Laurie," said Nadine. "What you have told me is between us. I will not speak of it to anyone—not even to my husband. And I will not speak of it to you again, either; but if at any time you would like to tell me more about yourself, then I shall be glad to hear it." She paused, but there was no answer, and Annie-Laurie was once more looking at her hands. "For your own sake, not mine."

Annie-Laurie looked up speechlessly, and the light and warmth that had been in her face were gone. She was sealed in again.

"Very well," acquiesced Nadine. "That's settled, then. And keep a firm hold on your Jim. We don't want him to start drinking."

Annie-Laurie stood up, her usual poised and steady self, and smoothed her overall.

"I don't think he will... not here."

"Is 'here' so different from other places?"

"Yes. You're different. The General and the children, and Jill. He likes you all... and the house."

"What is it about the house that attracts you so much?" asked Nadine.

"It's so safe," said Annie-Laurie, "Seeing it that day from the river—well, you know what it looks like from the river, towering up above that grey wall. I thought that morning—one could be safe there."

"You're safe here," said Nadine gently. Annie-Laurie folded her lips tightly, and Nadine saw that she was about at the end of her tether. "Run along now," she said lightly. "Those guests will be here soon, and you've the tea to get."

Annie-Laurie vanished, and Nadine turned at once to her housekeeping books, to stave off what she knew was coming. But it was no good. By the time she had added up the butcher the reaction had set in. What on earth had she done? Well, why ask that? She knew perfectly well what she had done. She, the respectable wife of a distinguished husband, the mother of five young children, two of them boys at the most impressionable age, had of her own deliberate choice taken into her household a man who at any moment might start drinking and a girl who had been in prison, and the relationship between the two of them, though Annie-Laurie had assured her they were doing "nothing wrong," was, to say the least of it, odd. She put the meat aside and tackled the fish, but the fish didn't make her feel any better. She felt cold all over, and was astonished, when she looked up, to see that the sun was still shining. She had been mad, she told herself—stark staring mad. Well, it was too late now. The thing was done, and she must abide by it. What on earth would Lucilla say if she knew? She could not imagine what Lucilla would say; she only knew that Lucilla must never know. No one must know. She was used to keeping secrets—there was David. But how she hated concealments! They made one feel imprisoned, walled in.

Poor Annie-Laurie! What was walled in there? The girl was obviously, mentally and nervously, in a bad state, and also afraid, or she would not have spoken as she had about the sense of safety that the house gave her.

"Well, you've done it," said Nadine to the house. "You pulled them in here to yourself just as you pulled in George and the children. You've got to defend us all now... 'from all adversities which may happen to the body, and from all evil thoughts which may assault and hurt the soul.'"

She realized that she was praying, and was astonished at herself, for it was not her habit to pray, and far away, like an answer to her prayer, came the distant chiming of bells. This faint chiming was now one of the special sounds of this place, a part of it, like the slap of the ripples against the river wall, the crying of the gulls and the beat of the swan's wings overhead. It came from the bunch of bright bells that hung on the top of the mast on Malony's boat. Sometimes the wind made them chime, and sometimes Malony tramping about and rocking the boat. The sound was extraordinarily beautiful, and to Nadine at this moment reassuring.

– 4 –

That was not the last of Nadine's shocks that afternoon. A mere half-hour later there came the sound of a car, and then George's genial voice raised in welcome. Mary, barking wildly, exploded into a white fountain of fur in her basket. However deep her slumber, the advent of strangers never failed to explode her like a match set to a fuse.

"Be quiet, Mary!" said Nadine, as Mary leaped from her basket, ricocheted across the room and started bouncing herself back and forth against the door; but she spoke only automatically, for Mary, set off, was like one of those old-fashioned alarm clocks that cannot be stopped until they have finished.

Nadine took her powder compact and her lipstick from her bag and attended carefully to her face before the mirror. She always refused to be hurried. Hurry was so ageing. Then she opened her door, and with Mary bouncing about her passed with her loveliest grace and dignity down the gracious curve of the stairs to greet her guests. They were laughing and talking with George in the bar-parlour, now called the hall, where he was shaking cocktails, for a free drink on the house upon arrival was a tradition that George delighted to keep up, but they looked up and saw her, and paid her beauty that homage of a quick, surprised silence that she was now so used to that she hardly noticed it.

"My wife," said George, with his customary pride.

Oddly enough, it was the girl whom Nadine saw first, and saw with a pang of utterly unreasonable fear, followed immediately by a pang of equally unreasonable dislike. For what could there be to fear in this child, or to dislike either? She looked a thoroughly nice girl, Nadine decided on second thoughts, and though, with her height, her big bones and her haphazard features, she couldn't, in her hostess's opinion, be called beautiful, her hair and her tawny eyes were lovely. And though she had no style, she had her own charm, Nadine thought, as she shook hands with her. In her golden-brown tweeds and honey-coloured jumper she looked like some loving, faithful sort of animal—a retriever or a pony or a young lion who had been born without carnivorous propensities.

"I hope you'll be happy here," she said to the shy, friendly Sally.

"It's a beautiful place," said Sally. "Sort of—set apart. It's like seeing a picture in an exhibition of some strange, shining, dream place and stepping over the sill of the frame and finding yourself safe inside it."

Safe. She, too, used the word safe. What a lovely deep voice she had!—a singer's voice, it's charm increased by the Scotch lilt. Yes, she was attractive.

"We've met before, Mrs. Eliot," said John Adair.

Even while she was speaking to Sally she had known that, had been aware in all her quickened senses of his compelling vitality. Now she turned to him.

"In the train once," she said. "What a coincidence!"

"I'm no believer in coincidence," he told her, holding her hand in a warm, friendly grasp, his strong, ugly face creased with amusement. "And I don't leave things to chance."

So he had come here because of her. How in the world had he found out who she was, where she lived? In her youth she had been used to being the happy quarry of many cheerful huntsmen, and she had played the game of enticement, evasion and withdrawal with a wicked glee, but the bitter pain of her break with David had left her no heart for love as a game, and with her power of attraction weakened by her indifference. But now something of the old delight stirred in her again. Her answering laugh had in it the ring of genuine amusement, a ring that had been absent for so long that it positively startled George, and for a moment she looked a girl again. Recovering from the shock, George smiled broadly. A little amiable flirtation would do Nadine as much good as a bottle of tonic. He had no fear of this man. Though George was unaware of the subtleties of character or of situation, he could sum up the general lay-out pretty shrewdly. He recognized in John Adair a man very happily possessed of an exceedingly successful career, and a successful careerist in the early sixties hoarding his strength and his powers for the one purpose, had no use for the damaging emotions, only those that refresh and invigorate. Nadine might think the fellow had fallen for her.... Well, he obviously had, but probably only because he wanted to paint her.

Nadine gently withdrew her hand and became the perfect hostess of a guest-house.

"Let's sit down while we have our cocktails. Then I'll show you your rooms. In there is the drawing-room. Tea will be served presently. It's so warm I believe you could have it in the garden. We put up tables among the Michaelmas daisies, by the river wall. You are our only guests for a couple of days, and then there are two men coming for a week's fishing, and some week-end people. We never take more than six guests though people come and go for meals and drinks. You have come for as long as the Herb of Grace gives satisfaction, haven't you?"

"You see before you two homeless vagabonds," said John Adair cheerfully. "Lease of flat fallen in. Couldn't find another. Furniture stored."

"What about your painting, Sir?" asked George.

"I've kept the studio. The owner of the flat didn't want it. I can go backwards and forwards to Town when I need to. But, as it happens, I've finished my commissioned portraits, and I'm going to take a bit of a holiday."

"That doesn't mean that he's going to stop painting," said Sally. "He can't. The back of the car is so full up with all his painting things that we could bring hardly any clothes or books. He means that he's just going to paint what he wants to paint."

John Adair's eyes went to Nadine's face, and he appeared to be pondering upon it.

"And where is he going to paint?" asked Nadine, with a suspicion of dryness, for his look now as he regarded her had become slightly impersonal; he might have been a window-dresser wondering how to arrange the goods to the best advantage.

"Have you an attic with a north light?" he asked.

"Well, as a matter of fact, we have," said Nadine, slightly outraged, "but—"

"Never say 'but,'" said John Adair, with twinkling eyes. "It is not only one of the ugliest words in the language, it is also a singularly depressing word, connoting irresolution and heard upon the lips of those who are half-hearted in their undertakings, unhappy people who never go the whole hog, and with whom I should be most grieved to see you ally yourself.... This is an extremely good drink, General; you've gone all out with this cocktail.... Mrs. Eliot, *have* you an attic with a north light?"

"It's yours," laughed Nadine. "I'd wanted it to store the apples in, but I can't have it."

"No, I'm afraid not."

"It's a bit dusty, but Malony, our house man, shall sweep it out."

"Thank you very much. This evening? I'd like to settle in as soon as possible."

Yet, though his words were brusque, his tone was courteous, and his twinkling eyes upon her were now once more so full of animation and delight that she did not resent being stampeded. When one is very tired, she thought, the masterful people who tell you what to do can be very restful.

On their way upstairs she showed them the drawing-room, which she had now made a place of tranquil beauty. It was very simple. She had been lucky enough to get hold of some old green brocade for the curtains, which she had lined with peach colour. The arm-chairs were upholstered in pale green, and Lucilla had given her a couple of Persian rugs from Damerosehay for the floor. There was some old glass on the Adam mantelpiece, plenty of books in a tall, glass-fronted book case, an old rosewood piano and bowls of flowers. The only picture was a painting of Ben's. He had not showed it to her, but she had found it in the little room next door, where Ben painted when Tommy was not at home to litter it up with his bones, and to please him—for she was full of sorrow just then for her neglect of his cough—she had framed it and hung it in the drawing-room. It showed a herd of red deer racing through a village street at night, under the light of the moon... and leading the red deer was one white one.... Ben had drawn the street from the one at the Hard, and he had got very well the contrast between the peaceful old houses dreaming under the moon and the swift movement of the deer. The flying clouds overhead seemed no swifter in flight than the red deer and the white one was like a fallen moonbeam; indeed, the light in the picture came from him rather than from the moon. But Nadine did not think it was very good; the anatomy of the deer seemed a bit odd in places.

But after just one delighted glance round the room John Adair was in front of it.

"Who did that?" he demanded.

"Ben, my eldest boy," said Nadine, "You know, in old days it was a common occurrence for people in these parts to wake up in the night and hear the deer from the Forest galloping down the village street. When he heard it, that captured Ben's imagination. Also we've got in the house a funny little stone image of a deer that was dug up in the garden, and that has captured his imagination, too. But I'm afraid the picture is not very good."

"It's damn good," said John Adair, almost with violence.

"But the drawing—"

"Faulty, of course; he's had no teaching. But he's got it—the light."

"Yes, the moonlight is lovely," said Nadine.

John Adair snapped his fingers impatiently, for that was not the light that he had meant.

"How old is this boy?" he asked.

"Sixteen," said Nadine.

"At school, of course?"

"Actually he's at home just now. He's not too strong, I'm afraid. The doctor said he must have a term or two off and keep out in the air as much as possible. It's so bad for him, missing school like this."

"For this boy, probably the best thing that could have happened," said John Adair, tapping the picture with his finger. "I'll soon correct the faulty drawing."

"You mean—?" asked Nadine.

"We'll share my studio, your son and I. You, too, of course. I'm going to paint you for next year's Academy."

Nadine looked the picture of incredulity.

"I've no time for such nonsense," she laughed.

"You'll find the time," he assured her, "and you knew, the moment you saw me here, that I had come to paint you."

She did not deny it. What was the use? No conventional insincerities would deceive this man.

"How did you know where to find me?" she asked.

"That day in the train you dropped a letter headed 'The Herb of Grace.' Then when Sally and I were searching for a roof over our heads she showed me the advertisement of your inn in some paper or other. I made a few enquiries, and heard that General Eliot had an exceedingly beautiful wife. Then I put two and two together. And here I am."

Sally, at the window, had been gloating over the view. Now she gave an incredulous cry of delight.

"It's the twins!" she cried.

John Adair and Nadine joined her at the window, and beheld the twins and Jill coming through the garden.

"You're the mother of my children," she said, turning eagerly to Nadine. "Of the Chevalier, the Pirate, Kate Greenaway and the twins! I used to see them in the greengrocer's shop at Chelsea."

"Was it you who sent me the bunch of violets?" asked Nadine.

"Yes, I did."

"Thank you," said Nadine. "It's odd, isn't it, that we should be together here? That *is* a coincidence, if you like.

They looked at each other, and Nadine saw a tiny shadow of fear in Sally's eyes. It was gone in a moment, but unmistakable. So Sally was a little bit afraid, too, and was probably as unaware of the reason as she was herself.

"I say again, there's no coincidence," said John Adair behind them. "You stepped into a picture, Sally, so you said, when you came into this house. The great masters, no matter how densely populated their canvases, never get a single figure there without deliberate intention."

CHAPTER

– 1 –

$\mathcal{J}$OHN ADAIR AND SALLY had been at the Herb of Grace for a fortnight, though it seemed longer, so much a part of its life had they become, and so quick was Sally at making herself useful wherever she might happen to be. She liked being useful, especially when it meant minding the twins. This morning she had been aware of a slight atmosphere of strain in the house. The two fishermen were now in residence, and though they were quiet, elderly men, absorbed in fish, they nevertheless ate a lot and seemed dissatisfied if fed only upon the fish they caught. And today a relative of General Eliot's, who had been ill and was visiting Lady Eliot at Damerosehay, was expected to lunch.... And Nadine still had no cook.... Sally had already offered to cook for the period of her stay, but Nadine had received this offer a little brusquely; her pride would not let her accept quite all that much help from a guest. Sally could understand that, and so this morning she had just offered to look after the twins while Nadine cooked and Jill did the children's washing. Nadine's pride permitted her to do the flowers, mind the twins and exercise Mary, for these were holiday employments that took her out of doors. And she loved the twins. It was convenient for a woman to be born as naturally selfless and maternal as was Sally, thought Nadine. She would make a good wife and mother with very little effort on her part.

Sally gave the twins their morning lessons in the drawing-room first. They did not like acquiring information, and generally behaved like demons in the process, but she promised them that if they were good they should take her afterwards a long way inside the Wood, whose real name, Jill said, was Knyghtwood, and they gave quite a good imitation of a couple of cherubs. They'd have given an imitation of anything to go to Knyghtwood… right deep in. When they went with Jill, though they went a good way, they never seemed to have time to go just quite far enough; she always had to get home to do something or other. And Father and Mother never had time to explore more than just the fringe. And with Ben they never got far enough because he was making a picture of a part of the wood that he liked especially, and as soon as he got there he stuck. But Sally, they felt, being both leisured and inartistic, could be relied on to go right deep in… right past Ben's place to the place where the Fairy Person lived.

Lessons finished, she took them upstairs to their lovely nursery and put on their stout little walking-shoes and their Fair Isle cardigans. They could have done this for themselves, but she loved to do it. She liked the feel of their wriggling little feet in her hands, and the warmth of their bodies in her arms made her feel even gladder than usual that she was alive. Holding a child in your arms gave you much the same feeling as pushing your finger down into the earth when you were gardening, or having your horse nuzzle the palm of your hand for sugar. Quite suddenly you felt that your life not an isolated thing, but existed in all other lives, as all other lives existed within yours. There wasn't anything anywhere to which you could say, "We don't need each other."

Taking her arms from around José, she looked up, and her eyes met those of Annie-Laurie, who was making the twins' beds. In the older girl's face there was a look of anguish, immediately and quickly sealed in again when she saw herself observed. And not only anguish but something rather like hatred. Sally suddenly felt shaky at the knees. Nadine, she knew instinctively, did not really like her, and now it appeared that Annie-Laurie actually hated her. She was not surprised at Nadine's dislike, for she didn't like herself, but the hatred did surprise her, and horrified her, too, for that glimpse of it had been like a brief glimpse of darkness. Then her shock, her horror, were forgotten in a surge of compassion. Did Annie-Laurie live in that darkness? Annie-Laurie was answering her compassion now with a look that said, "I don't need you." But that wasn't true. They were together in the picture.

"Annie-Laurie, will you show me your house-boat one day?" she asked.

"There's nothing to see," said Annie-Laurie curtly.

"Please," said Sally.

"It's our private little house, my father's and mine. Not even Mrs. Eliot has seen it."

The rudeness of this hurt too much for Sally to be able to find any answer. She smiled, her face surprised yet humbly patient, like that of a child when it is hurt, collected the twins and went downstairs to find Mary and her mackintosh and boots. The care of a snow-white pekinese in the country was, Nadine had discovered, no sinecure. She had become so tired of having to wash Mary every time she had been in Knyghtwood that she had now made her four little mackintosh top boots, and a curious mackintosh garment that protected her furry under-carriage and tied with bows on top of her back. Mary detested these garments, and rumbled aggressively all the time she was being put into them, her rumbles accompanied by a flash in the eye which led everyone to feel it was just as well that they could not understand what she said.

– 2 –

The party of four set out. The cat Smith came a little way with them, treading with delicate precision and swinging a slow, rhythmical tail; but not too far, for he was urban-minded, and not really at home in Knyghtwood. Sally had so far explored only the fringes of it, and she was almost as excited as the children.

"With Jill we've been as far as the big oak," said Jerry. "And with Ben we've been as far as his special place, where the Person is who plays the pipes; but with you we're going right deep in to the Place Beyond, where the Fairy Person with the horns is."

Sally was interested. They had probably got Pan playing his pipes out of "The Wind in the Willows"; Ben had made himself a little pipe, and played it in the wood sometimes, when he thought there was no one about to see and laugh at him, and they had perhaps heard his music; but where did the Place Beyond come from, and who was the Person with the horns?

"Who is this Fairy Person?" she asked.

"We saw his pointy face looking at us out of the wood that first day we came," said José. "We couldn't see more of him because he was hiding in a holly-tree. Then he went away, and we haven't seen him again. We want to."

"What's the Place Beyond?" asked Sally.

"What the other places aren't," said Jerry, a little impatient with her stupidity.

"But how will you know it when you get there?" persisted the obtuse Sally. "I mean, there are so many places that aren't what other places are."

The twins looked at her pityingly.

"Because it isn't many places, it's one place. It's in the middle."

Sally gave it up and looked about her at the wood. It was, she thought, the loveliest wood she had ever seen, and full of deep peace. The woods across the river were beech woods, but this was chiefly birch and alder, with willows growing next the water, and brambles and crab apples, wild cherry and stunted oaks growing up the inland slope. The willow shoots were wands of gold, the birches and oaks silver, the brambles gemmed with bright leaves, the mosses and lichens saffron and coral and jade. The river to their left showed only as a suffusion of silver light, while overhead the patterning of branches against the sky cut from the immensity fragments and patches of blue that yet seemed each of them to hold something of the glory of the whole. There were small stirrings of unseen wild things going about their business in the undergrowth, and the rustle of wings, but the sound seemed only to intensify the deep stillness. Such autumn days have a holiness that spring lacks, thought Sally. They are like old serene saints for whom death has lost its terror.

Jerry and José were now Rat and Mole. They ran along making little squeaking noises, and dropping now and then to all fours. Mary was the spirit of all her hunting ancestors fused into a white flash of speeding light; she was here, there and everywhere, hot upon exciting rabbit smells. Sally strode along with her hands deep in the pockets of her golden-brown tweed coat, her chestnut head gleaming, her face a little flushed with her joy. The hurt that Annie-Laurie had dealt her, together with all things of darkness, she had left behind at the green gate. The air of this wood, clean and sweet though it was to breathe, was yet somehow resistant, woven of some sort of heavenly loveliness that could not be interpenetrated by anything that was contrary to its nature. The Herb of Grace gave one a sense of defence against all that might happen to the body, but here one felt defended from all evil thoughts which might assault and hurt the soul. It had an inner safety. An old phrase came to her, "The armour of the house of the forest." That was what the early Christians had called it, when they fled there to find safety from persecution. And yet, according to the twins, it was only the courtyard; there was a Place Beyond.

Mary suddenly swerved away uphill to the right, Rat and Mole following. Sally took her hands out of her pockets and ran after them. At the top of a grassy bank there grew an oak-tree, a splendid old giant to whom one must obviously pay one's respects before one passed any farther, for he dominated this bit of the wood in a very kingly way. Standing in a group together, Sally and the twins and Mary did homage. Just as they were turning away again Sally's eye was caught by some narrow green leaves growing at the foot of the oak.

"Look!" she said. "They're like the leaves on the inn sign-board. Is it the herb of grace, José?"

"Yes," said José. "Ben said so. Rue. Herb o' Grace o' Sundays. But it hasn't any flowers."

"It'll have them when the spring comes," said Sally, and she touched the leaves gently with her finger-tips. Then she picked a spray of leaves and put it in her buttonhole.

They ran down the bank and went on, and the enchantment and silence of the wood were threaded through by the sound of running water. Presently they came to it—a stream that ran down through the wood towards the river. The water was amber in the sunlight, red-brown in the shade, tinged with iron, but crystal clear, so that one could see all the pebbles on the bottom. The stream was a wide one. and in the centre of it was an island fringed with loose-strife and bog myrtle, with a clump of thorn-trees and sloes in the centre of it. It was reached by a bridge made from the fallen branch of a tree over-grown with clumps of fern. The sunlight fell softly on this island, lighting up the grape-dark sloes, the tiny ruby berries on the thorns, drawing up the scent of the bog myrtle and wet ferns.

"It's Brockis Island," said José. "Brockis means badger, Jill says. This is Ben's special place. He's painting it. He says Pan comes here. And one day we heard pipes; we did really."

"Pan has horns, too," said Jerry. "But not such nice horns as the Fairy Person's."

"Ben put the bridge there," said José, "so that we should not get wet going to the Island. We think no one knows about the Island except us."

They crossed the branch, pushed their way through the bushes upon the farther side, and found themselves facing a small natural archway made by two old thorn-trees leaning towards each other. The archway was just the right size for children, and Sally had hard work to get through it, yet once through she caught her breath in wonder, for inside was a small perfect green lawn so thickly surrounded by trees that one could see nothing through them, and with the berry-jewelled branches arching overhead to make a roof. It was a sweet and secret place, a perfect little house for children. The sunlight striking through the roof overhead gave to every leaf and every blade of grass something of itself to treasure in a green loving-cup, or hold triumphantly erect upon a spear-point. Perfect as it was now, shining and jewelled, Sally thought it would be even more wonderful in the spring, when the primroses were out and the fruit blossom made a pink-and-white roof against the sky.

"Look!" said Jerry, pointing.

Between the roots of an old thorn-tree, veiled by bracken fronds of palest gold, was the entrance to someone's home. Mary, barking wildly, charged up to it as though she meant to leap down inside, but at the doorstep halted, spun around in a furry flurry and subsided with chin on paws, black eyes sparkling, hind parts elevated, well-braced legs and trembling tail. Rat and Mole dropped to all fours, and Sally sat back on her heels, looking with shining eyes at the badger's holt.

"He's stripey," said Jerry, "with whiskers."

"Ben's seen him," said José. "Once when he was here by himself."

"Dear Ben," said Sally. "Look! The herb of grace is growing here, too; just one root of it beside Badger's front door."

José put her paws over her snout and squeaked.

"Come out, Badger!" she called. "Come out and play with us."

But Jerry dealt firmly with her.

"Stop that, José! If we play at Rat and Mole and Badger we'll be here all the morning, and never get Beyond."

He seized a bit of fallen wood, flung a leg over it, galloped once around the green lawn, neighing loudly, and proceeded to crash through the bushes upon the farther side. José, quick as lightning, copied him, and Sally, dashing after them and seizing them by their disappearing tails, was only just in time to prevent them plunging into the stream on the other side of the island, where there was no bridge.

"I'm your horse," she said. "A mighty war-horse. You'll cross this rushing river one by one upon my back."

This was a good idea. Sally, a hardy creature who never caught cold, took off her shoes and stockings and waded across with them, carrying Mary in her arms upon the second crossing. Then she sat down upon the farther bank, dried her feet with her handkerchief and put on her shoes and stockings again. When she looked up they had all three disappeared. Of course. They were knights on horseback now. They would go fast.

– 3 –

The narrow path through the wood that they had followed had ended at Brockis Island. There was no track through this part of the wood, and the trees grew more closely together. Sally walked on, keeping the gleam of water upon her left. She did not feel anxious—she'd be sure to come upon the twins sooner or later. And it was good to be alone for a little with this beauty. She saw some wonderful things as she walked: a stick jewelled with scarlet moss-cups, a jay's feather lying on a cushion of green moss, a charm of goldfinches tossing above a clump of thistles. And as the shade deepened so did the mystery of this place, and the sense of holiness that was the autumn's gift. Her heart beat a little quicker.... Surely she was coming to somewhere.

There was a brighter gleam of sunshine, and she came to a clearing in the wood. She shut her eyes for a moment, dazzled, and opened them upon the landscape of a vision or a dream; the same landscape that she had remembered from some picture when she had first seen Ben. Only now it was not a vague, illusive memory of something that she saw, but a clear and distinct picture. A second, smaller stream ran through this clearing, seeping silently through a wide bed of smooth, rolled pebbles. The bog myrtle grew here, too, robed in silver light, beautifully massed against the deep shade of the wood beyond. She saw the shapes of many birds all about her—swans upon the river to her left, a heron in flight, small birds singing in the branches—and she saw the animals clearly, too: a rabbit, a bear, deer, many dogs, one of them very old and bowing his head as though in reverence. And there upon his great white horse was the Chevalier, the sunlight gleaming upon his hunting-horn and the rich colours of the silk and fur that clothed him, and he was gazing with a rapt face at something which he saw and she could not see. But his face was not Ben's face this time; it was a fair face with clear-cut features—the face of a much older man.

The colour, the light, were so heavenly that she could not look any longer. Against her will her mortal eyes closed, and when she opened them again the scene was of this earth.

Yet there were birds still: she saw a swan upon the water and heard the cry of the seagulls. And two dogs were still there: a funny old mongrel like a grey woolly hearthrug and a majestic and incomparable chow. And the Chevalier was still there, gazing with that deep absorption at something that was clear to him but hidden from her. But the great white horse, the hunting-horn, the garments of silk and fur, had vanished. He was a man of this century, on foot in the woods. But his face was the same, and she had always known it.

Though she did not move, he was aware of her and turned round. His eyes looked dazed for a moment, and then puzzled recognition dawned in them.

"Haven't we seen each other before somewhere?" he asked.

She came forward, her hands in her pockets, her face lifted to look at him with the unself-conscious absorption of a trustful child.

"Yes, at a party in London. I'm Sally Adair. My father and I are staying at the Herb of Grace. I knew a relation was coming to lunch, but I didn't know he was you."

"And I knew John Adair and his daughter were guests at the Herb of Grace, but I didn't know the daughter was Sally the Shepherdess.... Why, the old Bastard likes you!"

The chow, gazing at her with imperial consideration, had not yet made up his mind about her, but the Bastard was leaning his old head against her knee. She caressed his rough fur.

"He's the one who's just the same," she murmured. "The one who had bowed his head and was worshipping."

David looked puzzled, as well he might.

"The sunlight got in my eyes, and I saw a strange picture," she explained—"a picture of all sorts of birds and animals in a wood."

"One sees the oddest things in woods," agreed David.

"What were you seeing?" asked Sally.

"Nothing out of the ordinary. Just a kingfisher. Though actually a kingfisher is a bit out of the ordinary, isn't he? A heavenly bird."

"What we ought to be seeing," said Sally, "are the twins and Mary. I brought them out for a walk, and now I've lost them."

"Those twins!" said David with sympathy. "Many's the time I've lost them. If they turn into anything that gets a pace on, like a speed-boat or a motor-bike, it's all up."

"They were knights on horseback," said Sally.

"Not so bad as a speed-boat," said David cheerfully. "I suggest that if we tramp on to the edge of the wood, where I've left my car, singing 'Gaily the Troubador,' they might think the time had come to ride home from the wars. Do you know the 'Troubadour,' by the way? Grandmother brought us up on all those old songs; 'Clementine', and 'Wrap me up in my Tarpaulin Jacket,' and the rest."

"Of course I know them," said Sally. "My Scotch Nannie sang them all to me when I was little."

And as they swung inland and began to climb up the slope of the wood, the two old dogs at their heels, her deep contralto voice rang out in the air of the 'Troubadour'. David was silent for a moment, astonished at the loveliness of her untrained voice, then he joined in. Another couple might have felt themselves ridiculous, singing the sentimental old ballad together at the tops of their voices, but neither Sally nor David suffered from self-consciousness. They tramped on singing, through waist-high bracken, until the trees thinned and they came out into a narrow, winding lane, high up on the brow of a hill, with a beautiful patchwork of pasture and shorn harvest-fields rolling away towards the distant silver line of the Estuary, with the Island opal-tinted and celestial beyond. David's silvery-grey car waited at the edge of the wood, but there was no sign of the twins.

"You'd have thought the row we made would have fetched them, wouldn't you?" said David.

"I suppose the Place Beyond was not that lovely hollow where we met each other, but beyond again," said Sally, and she explained about the twins and the Fairy Person whom they expected to find in the place that is not what other places are because it is the one place, in the middle.

"Like the hub of a wheel," said David, opening the door of his car. "Sounds very deep. And I shouldn't like to intrude on the twins in the place—if they've found it. We'll sit and talk in the car, and every now and then make a noise like an air-raid siren to let them know where we are. Jerry likes the noise of a siren. The only person of my acquaintance who does."

"What is the wood like beyond the hollow?" asked Sally, as they settled themselves in the front of the car with the two old dogs comfortably installed at the back.

David laughed.

"I can't tell you. I don't know this wood." Then he looked at her teasingly. "I believe you're taking this mysterious place of the twins quite seriously. You're disappointed because you didn't get there, aren't you?"

Sally flushed, but she did not deny the charge.

"Yes, I am," she said stoutly. "Though if I'd got there I don't suppose I'd have seen whatever it is the twins are seeing. Children have vision."

"Imagination," amended David.

"It's the same thing," said Sally.

"Not quite, I think. Imagination comes from yourself and can deceive you, but vision is a gift from outside yourself—like light striking on your closed eyelids and lifting them to see what's really there."

"Or only half see it," said Sally sadly. "So that you can't express it at all."

"Keats had a good idea of the difference between the imaginative man and the visionary," said David. "'Every man has his speculations, but every man does not brood and peacock over them till he makes a false coinage and deceives himself. Many a man can travel to the very bourne of heaven, and yet want confidence to put down his half-seeing.' You'd be like that, I think. As for me, I brood and peacock."

Sally laughed.

"I don't see that a visionary who can't say what he has seen is of much use."

"Pens and paint, a good voice production and grease-paint and things aren't the only means of expression. Some people express loveliness just by loving. It's the better way. You don't get that bitter contrast between the artist and his works that shocks people so."

"Don't disparage artists, please. The great ones—they're utterly selfless. 'I would write from the mere yearning and fondness I have for the Beautiful even if my night's labours should be burnt every morning, and no eye ever shine upon them.'"

"Writers and painters have a medium that can foster self-effacement. Actors haven't. An actor can't hide himself behind paper or canvas. If you're not there your art's not there. That's why we actors are often such self-centred objects. I wish I was a painter, like your father."

"Father's not selfless," laughed Sally. "Nothing would induce him to paint a portrait that would be burnt in the morning. He likes material rewards. He's clever. He has a most uncanny insight into people, their real selves and their motives, but he's not a genius."

"'A prophet is without honour in his own country.'" laughed David. "And what's a genius?"

"A man of imagination who has vision, too.... Or a child.... You said children had only imagination, but I think that sometimes they have both. And I think you have, too."

"No. I'm no use at all." He spoke with bitterness.

"People say that when they need a good holiday," said Sally sagely.

"Well, I'm taking it. Indefinitely."

"You've been ill, haven't you?"

"I'm ashamed to say I had what they call a nervous breakdown. A thing I've always despised in others."

"I'm so sorry, but I expect it was a blessing in disguise," said Sally, with practical sympathy. "It's made you take a good holiday; and it's humbling, isn't it, to find that one isn't as strong-minded as one thought one was? Are you staying in those seamarshes that you told me about?"

"Yes. With my long-suffering grandmother. People talk a lot of nonsense sometimes about the old being a burden to the young, but in my experience it's the other way round. It's the old who do all the propping and sustaining. You'd like my grandmother, and she'd like you. I think you'd better meet as soon as possible. What about this afternoon? I could drive you over to Damerosehay to tea and bring you back afterwards. I promised Grandmother to take Ben over. They're *en rapport*, she and he. Would you like that?"

"Yes, I'd like that," said Sally. "Only first we've got to have lunch at the Herb of Grace, and we can't go back to lunch without the children."

David made a noise like an air-raid siren, and then they talked a little about John Adair's pictures and Sally discovered that David had never met her father.... So that sketch made at the rehearsal had been made without his knowledge.... Then the siren sounded again, and presently there was the pattering of small feet in the wood. Then the twins emerged with lips stained with blackberry juice and leaves in their hair. They were earthy, and trailed behind them clouds of glory in the shape of unravelled wool ripped from their little cardigans. Their cheeks were very pink and their eyes very bright, but strangely unfocused, like the eyes of babies, who have not yet adjusted themselves to a new environment. Mary, incredibly dirty, and with one boot missing, bustled in the rear. They replied with sweet, vague smiles to David's greeting and climbed immediately into the back of the car with the two old dogs, about whose necks they flung their arms and against whose furry faces they leaned their cheeks with a warmth of affection never bestowed upon their immediate family. Mary, whose arrogant youth despised the decrepitude of Pooh-Bah and the Bastard, placed an imperious little paw upon the running-board and barked to Sally to pick her up. David, suffering from the extraordinarily sharp pangs of hunger that afflict those with overstrained nerves, started the car for food with a sigh of relief.

Sally, with Mary in her arms, turned round to the twins.

"Did you get there?" she asked them eagerly.

They smiled at her with the amused tenderness of a mother whose child asks a question to which the answer would be beyond its comprehension, nodded, but remained silent.

"Oh, please tell me what it was like!" pleaded Sally.

They smiled again, but vouchsafed no answer.

"Did you see the Fairy Person?" asked Sally,

They nodded, and pursed their blackberry-stained lips together like tight dark rosebuds.

Sally looked down at Mary in her arms. The little dog's body was hot with excitement, and its heart beat fast beneath her hand. It made a leap for her nose, and kissed it, but did not utter.

"Just wasting your time," said David. "Much better talk to me. I'll answer any question you like to ask to the best of my ability."

"What exactly is the Herb of Grace?" asked Sally. "Why did the builders of a Pilgrim Inn call their house after it? Why in old days did the country people plant it in churchyards? Why is it growing in the wood beside a badger's holt? What *is* it?"

"Obviously something without which you can be neither a pilgrim nor a badger," said David. "Nor get to heaven. The rue is a bitter-leaved herb. Herbs are astringent. Rue is repentance. Ruth is compassion. Old Don Quixote was the knight of the rueful countenance, and he was a pilgrim, poor old chap!"

"And Badger was compassionate," said Sally. "He was so good to Rat and Mole when they were lost in the Wild Wood. Do you remember? And he shared his porridge with the little hedgehogs.... But you haven't really answered my question."

"Don't hurry me," said David. "I'm getting there gradually. (Glad you were brought up on 'The Wind in the Willows,' by the way.) Astringent—that means contraction. Bitter to taste. Repentant. Compassionate.... I've got it.... Single-mindedness."

"But I've always thought of single-mindedness as a sort of concentration," said Sally.

"Yes. Contraction. Everything gathered in for the giving of yourself. The whole of you. Nothing kept back. No reservations. No loopholes of escape. Like a diver taking the plunge or a man banging a door shut behind him that locks itself so that he can't go back."

"And you couldn't do that without repentance," said Sally thoughtfully. "I see that. You'd have to humble yourself before you could let go like that. Pride can't let go. But compassion?"

"That's at the root of all giving, don't you think? At the root of all art. You can't hoard the beauty you've drawn into you; you've got to pour it out again for the hungry, however feebly, however stupidly. You've just got to."

"And you said a little while ago that artists are selfish."

"No, I didn't; I said they were self-centred. That's not the same thing. Rather than not tell what they've seen they're prepared to die of the telling; but they aren't in the least interested in anyone else's death-bed."

"I hadn't realized single-mindedness was so complicated."

"It isn't. It's very simple. It's what T. S. Eliot calls the 'condition of complete simplicity costing not less than everything.'"

"Then only very few wear the Herb of Grace," mourned Sally.

"More than you think, perhaps.... You've got it in your buttonhole yourself.... One knows them when one sees them. There's a look in the eyes. Have you met my Uncle Hilary?"

"No, not yet."

"He's an extreme case. But I should say that if once—only just once—one had succeeded in giving without reservation, then you'd have got one foot on the pilgrim's way, you'd get a glimpse of—something." He paused and looked at her with sudden amusement. "If this is only the second conversation we've had together—and I believe it is—we seem to have skipped a good many preliminaries."

"It was meeting in the wood," explained Sally. "I believe that wood is a very direct route to wherever it is one is going. Some places are like that; they seem to hurry you on."

"Where to?" asked David amusedly.

She had spoken impulsively, and she could not answer. He did not want to go where she wanted to go. Forgetting this, she had been for a little while in the seventh heaven of happiness. But now she was in pain, in actual physical pain, as though her heart was being squeezed. As they talked, her slow brain had been stretched to the uttermost; but he, she realized, had been talking to her as one talks to an intelligent child, asking her questions to which he already knew the answers, delighting in the testing of her intelligence, but not on equal terms with her. His question and answer had come with the swiftness of a fencer's passes.... Just a game.... She held Mary tightly in her arms and pressed her cheek against the little dog's soft head for comfort. Glancing at her, surprised at her silence, David saw her with blanched face beneath her sunburn, looking as she had looked when he had thought she was going to faint in the heat of Jan's drawing-room. The walk must have tired her out. Couldn't be as strong as she appeared, he decided.

They were slipping now down the delectable lane that led to the Herb of Grace, David looking about him with delight, and as they neared the river they were greeted with a drift of music, like the chiming of fairy bells, very distinctive, a sound that once heard could not be forgotten.

"Whatever is that?" demanded David, startled. "I've heard that before somewhere. Whatever—"

"It's the bunch of bells that hangs on Annie-Laurie's house-boat," said Sally. "It chimes like that whenever anything rocks the house-boat."

"Annie-Laurie. What Annie-Laurie?" asked David sharply.

"Annie-Laurie and her father are the prop and stay of the Herb of

Grace," said Sally. "I suppose you'd say they're chambermaid and boots, though they're not quite the type—they're puzzling people. They live in their own house-boat on the river."

"Glad Nadine's got help, puzzling or not," said David.

But he looked for a moment vaguely disturbed; until they drew up before the inn and the beauty of the place overwhelmed him with delight. He had his back to the inn, and was helping Sally out of the car, when Nadine appeared at the open front door.

"There's Mrs. Eliot," said Sally.

His face set suddenly into hard lines. For a fraction of a second he was completely still, as though steeling himself for something. Then he turned round.

"David?" said Nadine.

She came slowly down the paved path between the chrysanthemums and Michaelmas daisies, graceful and most lovely, her eyes blazing with hunger in her carefully composed face.

"Hullo, Nadine," called David cheerfully. "You've got a jolly place here." And he ran up the steps to join her. They had both of them forgotten Sally's existence. She saw that they had, and turned away and busied herself in getting the children and dogs out of the car.

"Run round to the back," she said to the twins, "and ask Jill to make you clean and tidy again. Take Mary with you."

She heard her voice coming from some great distance, and had a horrible feeling of isolation and unreality, as though she were separated even from herself and falling through some dark limbo where there was neither handhold nor foothold, but only emptiness. She was terrified. She did not quite understand that she had given herself to this man with that completeness of which they had just been talking. She had leaped, like the diver, but there was nothing there to receive her. Then abruptly the nightmare feeling passed and she found herself standing on the paved path, looking back towards the car, and she did not know how she had got there.

The children and Mary had disappeared, and the stately chow had presumably followed Nadine and David into the house; but the old furry mongrel, the Bastard, the one who had liked her and leaned his head against her knee, remained. He was trying to get himself up the steps but his age and his rheumatism, combined with the fact that he had already been for quite a considerable walk in the wood, were making it difficult. Sally ran to him, and reached him just as he sat down suddenly at the top of the steps to rest. She sat down beside him. He looked up at her, his eyes bright with affection behind the mat of hair that fell over them, yards of pink tongue hanging out of the corner of his mouth, and wheezed apologetically.

"Yes, the morning has been a bit too much for you." Sally agreed. "But you've always been everywhere with him. You couldn't possibly be left behind. I see that."

The Bastard gave her another of his bright glances, swung up his tongue and kissed her on the chin. They sat side by side, much attracted by each other, and also deeply united by the bond of this mutual love for a man who had forgotten all about both of them; until a whiff of rabbit stew from within put new life into the Bastard, and he arose and led the way indoors.

CHAPTER

– 1 –

NADINE HAD A WAY WITH A RABBIT that was little short of genius, and when she had finished stuffing it with prunes, and doctoring it with herbs, and one thing and another, the dish was scarcely recognizable as rabbit at all and was worthy of the grand French name with which she sought to disguise its humble origin. Her apple cream, waiting upon the side table, looked superb, too, and George had succeeded in capturing from somewhere some quite extraordinarily good sherry. The talk at lunch was good, too, for John Adair and David always had plenty to say, and the wit to say it well, and the two elderly fishermen, once they could be prised off fish, were men of experience and intelligence. Nadine and Sally talked with unusual animation, and even Ben, who had been deeply happy since the arrival of John Adair, wasn't afraid to shove in his oar now and again. George, always at home in the role of host, said little, but radiated glad hospitality, and Annie-Laurie and Malony waited with their usual almost slick deftness; and the room was full of flowers and the lovely mellow light of a perfect October day.

And yet there was something wrong with this luncheon-party, and John Adair was highly intrigued. His keen eyes went from one face to another, missing no shadow of expression, his ears stood alarmingly out from the side of his head, intent upon catching any slightest inflection of a voice that should give him some clue to the emotions of these people, should show him their place in the picture framed by the old walls of the Herb of Grace. Yet all the while, as he watched

and listened, the flow of his own talk sparkled in and out of the conversation of the others, throwing it into that clear-cut relief that he
required for his observations.

"Father's on the war path again," thought Sally. "He's in one of his
detective moods."

"That's a damn clever fellow," thought David uneasily.

He was so accustomed to getting on well with everyone that this
sensation of unease was unpleasantly unfamiliar. Instinctively he
knew that, for the moment at any rate, John Adair disliked him. He
did not return the dislike. On the contrary, he liked the artist immensely. He liked his fierce red beard, his haphazard features, his
clear, brown, tawny eyes. This would be the lion of a fellow to deal
with if one got seriously across him.

"Which you will do, young man," thought John Adair savagely, "if
you harm Sally. Touch my girl to her hurt and I'll tear you limb
from limb."

He was astonished at the violence of his reaction to the fact of
Sally's love. He had not been seriously disturbed by his discovery of
the love between Nadine and David, even though the woman was
one by whom he was himself much attracted, for he had never been
in the habit of letting his affections disturb him at all seriously. As
long as a love served his art (and his tendresse for Nadine was en-
abling him to paint a damn good portrait of her), well and good, but
as soon as it threatened to disturb his single-minded devotion to his
craft, then he stamped upon it (and incidentally upon the woman,
too) thoroughly and at once. No woman he had ever come across
was worth one faulty stroke of a brush upon canvas.... Except Sally;
though he had not known it until this moment.... Sally was bone of
his bone, flesh of his flesh, and he knew now that he would give his
right hand—his painter's right hand—and go maimed for the rest of
his days, in art as well as in body, to save her from this pain. What a
child she was! What a naïve child!... She couldn't hide it.... She
hadn't even the wit to realize that her very avoidance of David's
glances, her diffidence when he spoke to her, gave the show away by
their unnaturalness. Yet, child that she was, she was putting up a
good show, and he was proud of her. She was forcing herself to talk
with unusual animation, and she was most sweetly and touchingly
deferent to the woman whose tenacity was blocking her happiness.

Tenacity. He had stumbled upon the word unaware, yet he
thought it was the right one. It occurred to him suddenly that

Nadine was holding the man against his will. At first he had been aware only of the love between them and had speculated as to its depth. They were both obviously capable of passion—Nadine had it in her face, David could not have been the actor he was without it—yet he did not think that they were lovers. The hunger in Nadine's eyes was that of a woman unsatisfied, and there was an austerity about David Eliot that seemed somehow to forbid it. They had, he thought, turned from an impossible love, the man with clean, clear-cut decision, and with the strength that obviously was part of his character, the woman with some reservation. Did she know she was still holding on? He could not be sure of that yet. Did she know the man wanted to be set free? Obviously not, or she would have set him free, for her pride was considerable; she was a woman accustomed to be wooed, not to woo. Her blindness surprised him, for now that he had got David thoroughly under the microscope there seemed to him little doubt as to his state of mind. He loved her, obviously, and would do probably in some sort until he died; but in his eyes as he looked at her there was a steady patience—the same sort of patience that he had seen in the eyes of men lying with smashed limbs imprisoned in plaster, waiting for freedom. He judged him to be a man of such tempered loyalty that it was not in his power to free himself. He was a fine man, John Adair decided suddenly, and he would not have disliked him had he not been indifferent to the charms of his child, who was bone of his bone and flesh of his flesh; in fact, a bit of himself.

"Egotism," he said, apropos of something entirely different, and getting into his lecturer's stride, "is the foundation stone of our present so-called civilization. We've built up the whole thing on a morality based upon self-interest, and then we're surprised to find the foundation stone disintegrating into as many particles as we are egos, and the building with it."

"No hope?" enquired one of the fisherman, cheerfully helping himself to more apple cream.

"One might try the application of the Herb of Grace," suggested David.

"H'm?" asked George.

David smiled at Sally.

"Miss Adair and I decided this morning that the astringent rue is the grace of single-mindedness."

"You can define single-mindedness till the cows come home," said the second fisherman, "and still be no farther on."

And he regarded what was left of the dish of apple cream with a speculative eye, for he was a slow eater and hadn't yet got through his first helping.

"Miss Adair and I got quite a way, thank you," said David cheerfully. "And we boiled it down to a complete letting go. Abandonment of the ego for something greater."

"Let go," said John Adair, thoughtfully stroking his beard, his eye on Nadine.

"Annie-Laurie," said Nadine, detaching herself composedly from his gaze, "you'll find another dish of apple cream in the larder. Will you bring it, please?"

"Yes, Madam," said Annie-Laurie.

Her very distinctive voice fell into one of those queer silences that come suddenly at twenty minutes past the hour, and once again David looked at her with quickly concealed yet painful speculation as she left the room. He had had a severe shock, John Adair had noticed, when he had first set eyes on her, and he had been careful not to look at her again; until now, when the further shock of her voice had startled out of him that quick, anxious glance. What did he know about the girl? She, at sight of him, had obviously had a shock, too; for that sealed-in look of hers had now bitten so deep that all the contours of her face were painfully sharpened. Forgetting about Sally for the moment, John Adair pulled at his beard in high delight. Who'd have expected to find such an interesting bunch of personalities in this back of beyond? From the moment that he had set eyes on Malony and Annie-Laurie they had interested him intensely. The girl's mask of a face, the man's tragi-comic monkey's countenance; they were both of them worth a portrait when he'd finished with Nadine.

"Could you spare me a short sitting this afternoon?" he asked her, as they all sat in the garden by the river wall, drinking their coffee.

"I am afraid I am not free this afternoon," she said.

She was lying back in her deck chair, her hands clasped gratefully about the warmth of her coffee cup, a little smile lifting the corners of her lips. David was beside her, and she was drenched in sun. The hunger had gone from her face, and for the first time in John Adair's acquaintance with her she looked happy. Just for the moment she had put her trouble from her, and was warm, and with David. John Adair knew what her refusal meant; today was David's.

And David knew, too, and did what he could.

"Nadine, will you show me the house before I go?" he asked gently.

"Go?" she asked in a low voice, yet sharply. "You'll stay till after supper, surely?"

"I promised to take Ben over to have tea with Grandmother, and I've asked Sally if she'll come, too. Grandmother would like her, I think. I'll restore them both in time for supper."

"And stay for it yourself?"

"I can't do that, Nadine. Old Hilary is coming to supper at Damerosehay."

"For a man who's supposed to be suffering from a nervous breakdown you seem to be living in rather a whirl of social gaiety."

He laughed.

"I'm here for some while, Nadine."

It was a private conversation, indulged in under cover of a loud-voiced, indignant discussion upon the iniquities of income tax that was being carried on by George, John Adair and the fishermen. But John Adair, while trumpeting upon income tax as loudly as any absorbed the whole of it into his protuberant right ear. He lifted an eyelid in Nadine's direction. Her momentary look of happiness had vanished, and there was a trace of bitterness in her face as she looked at Sally, sitting on the river wall talking to Ben. For so experienced a man, David had really been extraordinarily tactless, and the measure of his tactlessness was the measure of his present indifference to Sally. Again he hated the fellow.

– 2 –

Yet in spite of her tenacity he did not on Sally's account feel any bitterness towards Nadine. Indeed, he was astonished to find himself possessed of a perfectly genuine heartache for her. He would, he found, have given a good deal to have that fleeting look of happiness habitual with her, even though as a happy woman she would have been far less interesting to paint. Yes, within the bounds set by reason and age, he loved her.

"Still not free this afternoon?" he asked, as they stood at the garden gate an hour later, having just watched David, Sally, Ben, and the two dogs speed away up the lane, and George take to the river with the two fishermen.

"Not this afternoon."

He took her arm.

"Nonsense. The twins are with their Nannie, Annie-Laurie and her father are in charge of the inn. Come along."

She looked up at him, met the keen glance of his tawny eyes, and knew that he knew. For a moment anger surged over her, to be followed by a most surprising sensation of peace. She met his steady look with an equally steady one of quiet acknowledgment. Once more, as on her first meeting with him, she had an absurd longing to fling herself on his chest and ask to be taken somewhere... to be free of it all.

"One of my sitters, a Catholic, told me once that a sojourn in my studio was almost as cathartic an experience as a visit to the confessional," he said, as they walked slowly together up the lovely, gracious staircase, beneath the little figure of the white deer.

"Why ever?" asked Nadine.

"I thought it was a bit far-fetched myself. Her idea was, I think, that when she saw her sins and sorrows splashed in paint upon canvas she felt somehow relieved of them."

"You've an uncanny insight, haven't you?"

"Yes, I think I have; but I combine it with discretion. And with something more. There is the seal of the confessional and the reticence of the surgery, and there is also the honour of the studio. A painter does not speak of what he reads in the faces that he paints."

Nadine did not answer. They climbed up the attic stairs and reached the door of the studio. He opened it and stood aside, and she went in. It was a large room with two dormer windows looking north over the orchard. The walls and the sloping roof had been plastered and whitewashed, but the old oak beams had been left untouched, with an oil lamp hanging from one of them. The room was wildly untidy, excepting only the corner that had been given to Ben, where his things were all in perfect order, and already looked as though John Adair had been working in it for years. Yet there was beauty here. Rich colours gleamed from the stacked canvases, a pot of flowers stood by one window, and over the screen behind the model's throne was flung a glorious strip of green velvet—mid-forest green— the background for Nadine's portrait. She looked at the portrait. It was already to her inexperienced eyes well on the way to being finished. He had not spared her at all, and the youthfulness of the blue linen dress she wore was not echoed by the face above it. The lines about her eyes, the grey in her hair, had been if anything accentuated, and now that he had spoken of them she could see "the sins and sorrows" in her face. Yet he had given her a splendid beauty—a beauty that she did not think that she possessed. She was aware of her own loveliness, but there was something there—a sort of finality of beauty—that she knew was not hers.

"It's not quite right," she said.

"No. I've got too far ahead in time. That happens sometimes even in photography, you know. At the time it is taken a photo is not a good likeness, yet two years later it is. It's odd that that should happen in such a mechanized art as photography. In a portrait it is understandable."

"Why?"

"There's a patient angel in us all—the spirit in the making. And he has two faces. He is the two things that you may be if you do this, or that. Sometimes you see the one looking out of the window, sometimes the other."

She glanced at him with tender amusement. How ridiculously childish even the cleverest of men could be at times!

"And this unattained beauty that you have given me?"

"You'll attain it. The first time I saw you, in the train, I said to myself, 'She's not at the height of it yet.' It waits, that beauty, for the denial to give the humour to the lips, the gentleness to the eyes."

"What denial?"

"You know, or you should know, what needs cutting out of your own life. Some quite trivial thing, probably—perhaps no more than some reservation of thought. But it's enough."

"Enough?"

"To keep you stewing in your own juice, pulled both ways and getting nowhere. Cut it out, that thought or whatever, and you're free, and probably others, too. We're so bound together in this complicated world that the spiritual condition of each one of us is as catching as the measles."

"Oh, words, words!" said Nadine impatiently.

"Yes. Sit down, will you, and we'll make a start."

She took her place on the throne, and for an hour, as he worked, such talk as they had was the easy, trivial gossip that befitted the warm, sleepy afternoon. She did not avail herself of the honour of the studio to tell him anything at all about herself. He had not really expected that she would; she was too proud a woman. And he loved her pride. Seeing it, as he did, as a threat to the happiness of his Sally, yet he loved it. With what dignity had she accepted the fact that he knew of her unbecoming love for David! There had been no plea to him to keep her secret, no attempt to justify herself—merely a queenly acceptance of inevitable consequence. Undoubtedly she had greatness in her, yet could she ever do it? Could so proud a woman ever admit to herself that a man who had once most deeply loved her now longed, though he might be as yet unaware of his longing, to leave her and pass on? He wished he could ease things for her, give her some sort of a prop to cling to while her pride broke beneath her. There was his own love, but it was without passion, a poor sort of exchange for the fire that her temperament had always needed. Yet such as it was she should have it. And presently there would be compassion, of which by small evidences, chief among them her attitude to that suffering girl Annie-Laurie, he knew her capable. With denial compassion would grow. That was inevitable.

He might in thought extol compassion, but he had none for his sitters. As he painted, the woman he thought he loved ceased as a woman to exist. Paint-brush in hand he was as a heathen priest before the altar of sacrifice. Rather than let the fire go out he flung in anything or anybody (except perhaps Sally, who was himself) with no compunction whatever. Nadine was almost fainting with exhaustion before he noticed it; and then only because he found her suddenly no longer paintable.

"Tired?" he asked in surprise.

"Of course not," said Nadine, putting her hand to her forehead and finding it damp. "But it's time I saw to the supper."

He looked at his watch in astonishment.

"Did we have tea?"

"We did not," said Nadine.

"Quite unnecessary," he said. "The French don't."

"I'm not French," said Nadine. "I'm half Russian; and they have it all the time."

He came to her, gave her his hand as she stepped down from the throne, and, released now by his art, saw at last how tired she was.

"I'm a brute," he said, but quite without penitence, and took her in his arms. Finding herself where she had already so absurdly desired to be, she stayed there gratefully. He tightened his grip, which was that of a lion.

"I love you, my girl," he said.

She began to laugh.

"You expect me to believe that?"

He raised her face, looked at it and kissed it.

"Yes, you're a beautiful woman, and you know it."

She went on laughing.

"And you're making love to me because of some nefarious purpose of your own. Don't I know you!"

"Well, whatever purpose I may have in expressing it the thing's genuine right enough. You're a darn beautiful woman!"

They went downstairs together laughing. He had eased her pain more than he knew.

9

– 1 –

"*THEY'RE LATE, DEAR*," said Lucilla to Margaret. "I do hope they haven't had an accident."

"It's only just half past four," said Margaret. "And, you know, David is always late."

"David must take dear Ben back again in good time. It wouldn't be good for his weak chest to be out too late in the evening."

"That will be all right, Mother. David will be obliged to take Ben back in good time. Hilary is coming to supper."

"Yes, dear, I know," said Lucilla, with a touch of asperity. "I myself invited Hilary to supper to prevent David having supper at the Herb of Grace. The evening is such an emotional time. Is that clock right, dear? If they don't come back soon I shall see very little of my dear Ben. I told David to be back by four. Are you sure there's enough for tea, dear?"

"I don't know about enough," said Margaret. "There's all there can be until the fats come tomorrow. Somehow we always seem to have someone extra to tea the day before the fats come instead of the day after. I've used the last scrap of margarine and the last scrap of sugar. I never saw anything like the way David eats. He's so spiritual-looking, too."

"It's his nerves, dear. They need feeding. What's the time now?"

"It's still half past four. Are you worried about anything, Mother?"

"I'm worried about David."

"But he's better, I think."

155

"I know. Much better; though of course he can't see it, poor darling. It's not so much his health I'm worried about."

"Then what is it, Mother?"

"Dear, dear Margaret," said Lucilla.

The density of her daughter was a continual astonishment to her. Before the war David and Nadine had lived through an emotional upheaval as shattering as an earthquake in this very house, before her very eyes, and yet she hadn't noticed anything. Well, it made her very restful to live with. Being without curiosity and purged of pride, she asked no questions and staked no claim for a place in family councils. She was just content to look after them all; with just an occasional queer outbreak, like the buying of that abominable trolley.

"Whatever should I do without you, Margaret," said Lucilla lovingly.

Margaret stretched out a hand and laid it on her mother's. Though they had their irritations, they had drawn increasingly closer to each other of late years. They had been through a good deal together by this time. Margaret did not press the subject of what it was about David that was worrying Lucilla. Indeed, she had forgotten she had asked the question. She, also, was a very tired woman, and her fatigue took the form of being unable to think about anything except food for more than two consecutive minutes.... Except, of course, the garden.... Her hand still on Lucilla's, she looked out of the window at the glory of her Michaelmas daisies, purple and mauve and white, at the loveliness of the Japanese anemones and the sturdy first-flowering of the chrysanthemums. She would have liked to have got in a little gardening before it was dark, but with Hilary extra to supper it might not be possible. These fine autumn days were so precious.... these lovely days.... What in the world could they have for breakfast?

Serve me right, thought Lucilla, for treating Nadine as I did. I wanted to get her away from David and London, and immediately David, who hasn't been near Damerosehay for months and months, has a breakdown and comes down to stay indefinitely.... Serve me right.... But George is better in health and happy at the Herb of Grace. George, my son, is happy.

"I don't think there's anything more tiring, dear, than expecting people who don't turn up, do you?" she said to Margaret.

"I think not expecting people who do turn up is worse," said Margaret. "Because then you haven't got anything to eat."

"You mustn't attach such importance to food, dear. Other things in life are more important."

"No, Mother. Without food there isn't any life."

"There they are!" said Lucilla, her face flushing rosily like a girl's, her deadly fear of an accident lifted off her.

Margaret had not heard anything, but that did not surprise her. Lucilla knew by some sixth sense when David was near. And a minute later there was the sound of the car in the drive, and then a commotion of footsteps in the hall, the dogs barking happily and Ben's voice talking to them. Then came David's clear voice, and a girl's answering, deep-toned and lovely, and their two voices chimed together in music that sent Lucilla's heart leaping up in delight; just as it did when the season of larks came round again and waking up in the hard-dark of a spring morning she knew that once more the fitting thing had come to pass in the fitting hour.

"Who's that?" she said, and found her heart was beating fast. She struggled up out of her chair. "Margaret!" she whispered urgently, "is the room looking nice? Am I tidy?"

"Why, of course, Mother," said Margaret in astonishment, stretching out a hand to steady her.

Lucilla mastered herself and stood waiting, superbly beautiful, and already in her heart she thanked God.

They came in.

"Grandmother!" cried David in astonishment, "you get lovelier every day."

And he came to her and hugged her, suddenly oblivious of everybody and everything. There wasn't anybody like her. There never would be. Other loves came and went, but hers had been steadfast since the day of his birth.

"The same thing cannot be said of your manners, David," she said.

He laughed and released her.

"This is Sally Adair, Grandmother. She's staying with Nadine."

"How nice of you to come and see an old woman, dear," said Lucilla.

This was her usual opening gambit with the young, but with Sally's clear, truthful eyes looking into hers she suddenly thought what a silly thing it was to say. Sally seemed to think so, too.

"Why?" she asked. "People get nicer and nicer as they live. And houses. And everything."

"If they're good stuff at the start," Ben warned her.

"Vintage port," said David. "To get nicer and nicer you must love the sun and give good juice when you're bruised.... This is my Aunt Margaret."

Sally's eyes had already gone to Margaret with the same sweet look of humility with which they had greeted Lucilla, a look that had touched Lucilla as deeply as though the child had knelt and kissed her hand. It was as though before the old woman's frailty and the elderly woman's weariness her own abounding health and strength did homage; as though instinctively she was grateful, as are all the lovers of life who, accepting with such joy, must give again, lest they die, to those whose need disposes them to accept the largesse of love.

"She's gold," sang Lucilla's heart. "She's the true gold."

Aloud she said, "My dear, you're very pretty."

Sally flushed scarlet and knocked over a small mahogany table. Lucilla loved her both for the flush and for the clumsiness; she disliked the hard-boiled young who took all praise as their due and steered clear of the knicks-knacks of the old as though they despised them.

"I don't think I've hurt it," said Sally, running an anxious finger round the rim of the little table, as though it were the cheek of a child. "It's lovely, with that bit of inlay in the centre. Is it very old?"

"Yes, it's old. It belonged to my great-grandmother. Sit here by me, dear, and take your coat off. It's warm in here, I know. I'm old and I have to have a fire when I expect you young people would rather be without it. David, take Sally's coat. May I call you Sally? Ben, my darling, when you've handed the tea come and sit here by me and Sally."

David and Margaret, sitting together, talked to each other desultorily and watched the three by the fire with pleasure.

"Someone fresh does Mother good," murmured Margaret.

"I thought they'd get on," he answered.

Lucilla was looking almost absurdly happy, and Sally's flush had left her face rosily lighted. David, looking at her, remembered a line in a poem that he loved. Her face had "put on the light of children praised."

Ben ate bread and honey and felt happy; he always did when he was with Grandmother or David. It was a funny thing, but though he so adored his mother, he never felt at his happiest when he was with her. He always had the feeling that he was never being quite what she wanted him to be. Mother was rather a demanding sort of person, somehow; she always seemed asking of everyone and everything just a little more than they could give. Grandmother and David never seemed to want him to be anything but what he was; they seemed to like him like that. And as for Aunt Margaret—well, she was just dear funny old Aunt Margaret. And Sally was one of the most comforting people he had ever met. He didn't like girls as a general rule, but she wasn't like a girl. He supposed she'd be dreadfully insulted, but she reminded him of the mother wolf in the Jungle Book, the one who had mothered Mowgli. He could see her with lots of little wolf cubs cuddled up to her and Mowgli asleep in the curve of her tail. He laughed suddenly, happily, at the absurdity of his vision, his face alight with ripples of delight.

"What's the joke, old chap?" asked David.

"Look at the Bastard," said Ben.

The answer was partly true, because before he had seen that sudden vision of Mowgli in the curve of Sally's tail he had been smiling inside himself at the Bastard's position. It was the Bastard's habit to lie at Lucilla's feet with his chin on her shoe, as though he were keeping her tethered to the spot where he wished to have her. Today he had taken up his usual position, but he had stretched out a furry forepaw and laid it on Sally's shoe, and his old moth-eaten ostrich-feather of a tail was beating a slow affirmation upon the floor.

"These two," he seemed to be saying, "are mine, and beloved of me, and this hearth is mine, and here they shall remain, mistresses of my heart and hearth, while I have any say in the matter. Amen."

"Caught," said David to Sally. "Tethered to Damerosehay for ever now."

"I don't mind," said Sally. "This is the House of the Perfect Eaves."

"My dear!" cried Lucilla in delight. "So you had a grandmother who read you 'The Wind in the Willows' when you were a little girl."

"My Scotch Nannie read it to me," said Sally. "I never had a grandmother. At least, I mean, not to know. Both my grandmothers died when they were quite young."

"I grieve for them, dear," said Lucilla. "I read somewhere, and it's quite true, that to know perfect happiness a woman may be a mother, but must be a grandmother."

"I've missed my grandmothers dreadfully," said Sally.

"In that case," said Lucilla, laying her hand on Sally's, "could you adopt me?"

Sally went pink again, and her eyes were so bright in the firelight that Ben would have said there were tears in them had it not been his conviction that Sally was not the watery sort.

"Aunt Margaret," said David, "I very much doubt if we are wanted. Shall I help you wash up?"

"Be careful of the trolley over the rugs, dear," said Lucilla.

Ten minutes later, when Margaret was washing the Worcester cups and saucers and David, to her secret agony, discoursing on Ibsen and drying them with insufficient attention, Ben joined them and seized a tea-towel from the rack.

"I'll dry, too," he said. "Grandmother's showing Sally the house."

"No!" ejaculated Margaret in distress. "Why did you let her, Ben? She'll be tired to death. And catch cold, too. All the upstairs windows are open."

"Grandmother never gets tired or catches cold when she's doing what she wants to do," said Ben comfortably.

"Aunt Margaret," said David, "go to the drawing-room and put your feet up and read *The Times*. Ben and I are going to finish the washing up and peel the spuds for supper. Now don't for heaven's sake go out in the garden and weed. Put your feet up and rest." He took the dish-cloth gently but firmly from her. "We'll put away the china, too. We know where it goes."

David's courteous gentleness was quite misleading. He was really as masterful as Lucilla herself. Margaret was obliged to obey, but in the drawing-room with her feet up *The Times* lay unopened on her knee while she listened anxiously for the crash of china. But Lucilla had decreed that, at whatever danger to the china, the grandsons must be trained to be good husbands. There was a crash. There! Several plates, by the sound of it. Now that the worst had happened and the strain of listening was over Margaret was able to relax a little and open *The Times*.... But she only skimmed over the headlines. Presently she got up and crept out of the room as silently as she could, and through the garden door to the garden. Here, well out of sight of the kitchen window, she did some weeding.

– 2 –

Lucilla, upstairs with Sally, heard the crash, too.

"David and Ben must be doing the washing up to help Margaret," she said equably. "Separately they're to be trusted, for they both love beautiful things, but not together. They are fond of each other and talk about things that interest them both, and of course that doesn't do if you're washing up."

"They are very alike," said Sally, as they turned to leave Lucilla's beautiful bedroom.

"Yes, dear," said Lucilla. "I have always thought so, but you are the first person to remark to me on the likeness. You must like them both to notice it."

"Yes, I do," said Sally simply. "I like you all. I like this house."

"It will be David's," said Lucilla. "I like to think of him living here with his wife and children."

As she spoke she looked a little anxiously at Sally, watching for a sign that her words might have touched some secret spring of joy in her; for she was a little fearful now lest the conviction that had come to her that Sally and David had been made for each other should not be shared by Sally and David. But the girl by her side did not smile or flush, and her face, as she said a mute good-bye to the beauty of Lucilla's room, had a sudden look of weariness, as though a secret burden that she carried were pressing more heavily than usual. Lucilla felt cold all over with a horrid apprehension. If there was one thing she hated more than another it was having to be seriously angry with David. She had hoped never to have to be angry again, for she was too old now to bear the strain of falling out with her dearest on earth.... Yet she would be if he were to hurt this child.

"We call this the Chapel room," she said, opening another door. "Ben and Tommy used to sleep here when they were little boys."

The small room looking on the garden had two striking and beautiful stained-glass windows, one showing Saint Christopher carrying the Christ Child to safety over the turbulent waters, and the other jubilant beasts running through forest, while happy birds sang in the branches above.

"'A melodious noise of birds among the branches, a running that could not be seen of skipping beasts,'" quoted Lucilla. "This house has its history, dear, and those windows are bound up with it. You must ask David to tell you the story. It was he who found it all out."

Sally was thinking that this picture was like that other picture that she had seen somewhere, and seen again in Knyghtwood.

"It is so very lovely," she said. "They both are—but specially that one of the wood. What is it about woods that—somehow—makes one a little afraid? And yet one loves them so. They pull at one like nothing else—not even the mountains."

"To me, dear, a wood is a foreshadowing of the fact of Paradise. The trees, the flowers, the birds and animals they all seem at their happiest in a wood, as though they were redeemed already. Then in a wood they have so much to say. A bird singing to you in a wood, a deer turning his head to look at you and then disappearing through the trees—they lure you on and on; you want to go always a little far-ther—to something—some clearing in the wood. It's a queer thing, dear, but when I think of the men and women of genius—artists and saints—I seem to see their figures moving always against the back-ground of a wood."

Sally laughed happily, glad of this oneness with Lucilla.

"Is that because they go always a little farther than the rest of us, follow the white deer a bit farther on? Like those men in Hassan— 'We are they who go always a little farther.'"

"In that clearing in the wood the shadows are so clear," said Lucilla. "They see the clear outlines and come back and paint them for us, and then it is easier for us to believe in the substance. 'All truth is shadow except the last truth. But all truth is substance in its own place, though it be but a shadow in another place. And the shadow is a true shadow, and the substance is a true substance.'"

"I like that," said Sally. "It leads one on and on. Who said that?"

"Isaac Pennington. How I do run on, dear! It's old age. And I want to show you the linen cupboard. And David's room."

"Won't he mind?" asked Sally shyly.

"No, dear. He's one of those rare men who can be relied on to be tidy."

In David's austere room Sally stood in a frozen stillness and looked at his few treasures: the view of the wide sea-marshes beyond the window, his books, the galloping, sea-green horse and Van Gogh's picture of the tossing lark; and Lucilla wondered anxiously what it said to her of the free spirit of this man, a thing that could not be captured and coerced by the will of another, but was very ready to accept any self-chosen discipline. She could not certainly know, yet from the very stillness and silence of the girl beside her she drew reassurance; there was pain in it, but acceptance; where Sally loved she would never seek to possess.

"Do you ever read Meredith, dear?" she asked abruptly, for the silence suddenly pressed upon her as though with Sally's own pain, and she had to end it. "But I don't suppose you do. He's of my generation, not yours."

"Daddy loves him, and he's read me bits," said Sally, and she looked from Van Gogh's picture to Lucilla and smiled. "Didn't he say that the lark expresses it for all of us—our love of earth?"

"Yes," said Lucilla.

" 'Tis love of earth that he instils
And ever winging up and up,
Our valley is his golden cup,
And he the wine which overflows
To lift us with him as he goes.
The voice of one for millions,
In whom the millions rejoice
For giving their one spirit voice."

"Well, dear, perhaps we'd better be going downstairs again. David has to take you and Ben back to the Herb of Grace, and then be home in time for supper. You'll come and see me again, Sally?"

Sally was humbly astonished at the anxiety in Lucilla's voice, astonished, too, at the sudden love that had locked them together. They were both tall women, and standing facing each other they found they were both of the same height. Impulsively they kissed each other.

"There are not many girls," said Lucilla, "who can make friends with an old woman in such a way that she does not feel that she is old."

"You aren't old," said Sally, with no flattery, merely stating a fact. "You love life."

"So do you, my dear. And so, I think, you've never been young in the crude, possessive sense. The lovers of life, they are children at heart always in their wonder and delight, but they do not grab."

– 3 –

Lucilla that evening arose from the supper table with something of an air. "Margaret and I will leave you to your wine," she said grandly to her son and grandson.

David had arrived at Damerosehay upon this visit with quite an interesting assortment of bottles in the back of the car. He had a way with bottles; he just conjured them up. It was almost like the good old days, thought Lucilla, as she rustled (she had her best petticoat on in honour of the bottles) from the dining-room with Margaret striding humbly in her wake. It was years since she had been able to leave the men to their wine, and she did so enjoy the little interval of feminine peace in the drawing-room after dinner, when one could relax and be a bit depressed if one wanted to be. Lucilla had been trained in the tradition that lays upon the woman the duty of amusing the men in their moments of leisure, and not one of her sons or her grandsons had ever known her preside at her dining-table or her fireside in other than a cheerful spirit.... But she had liked the little interval in between in which to pull herself together and take a fresh hold upon her cheerfulness, and, left to nothing more exciting than synthetic orange juice, the men were back much too soon.

"Help yourself to port, Uncle Hilary," said David.

"Where'd you get it?" asked Hilary, helping himself to a modest half-glass with a kindling eye.

Water, with a bottle of ginger-pop at Christmas, was all the liquid that ever appeared upon the Vicarage table, such was Hilary's dread of the intrusion of luxury into his personal life, but he liked a glass of port when dining out. It was different, dining out. Appreciativeness was one of the duties of a guest.

"A friend at court," said David, and filled Hilary's glass to the brim. "How are you, Uncle Hilary?"

"Very well, thanks," said Hilary cheerfully.

David doubted it. Hilary was looking very old; balder than ever, stouter than ever, with the lines of pain deeper in his face. Yet the atmosphere of peace that he always carried about with him was also deepened. Alone with Hilary, the house as stilled and quiet as the spirit of the man beside him, David suddenly relaxed. The tight band of iron that always seemed clamped about his head eased a little. His voice, which for so long had seemed the voice of a hated stranger, uttering cruelties and irritations springing from some deep cavern of the mind that had passed beyond his control, was his own again. His limbs were his, too, and not the tightly wired inanities of some marionette. He pressed his hand hard against the wood of the table and found it blessedly real. That hideous feeling of isolation, of being cut off from all real contact with anybody or anything, that of all the effects of nervous illness was almost the hardest to bear, momentarily vanished. The horrors were bound to return, of course, but the intervals of blessed peace were getting longer. They came very readily now in the presence of a selfless quietude such as Hilary's... or Sally's.... She was such a child, that Sally, and yet she had the same restfulness that had been the gift of long life to old Hilary. Neither of them made any demands. Unconsciously he let out a sigh of relief as the blessed ease encompassed him.

"It had to come, David," said Hilary.

"What?"

"A bit of a crack up on your part. I got it badly after the last war. It passes; if you can remember, while the horrors are on, that it *does* pass. You're lucky it's no worse."

"Damned luck," David agreed fervently. "Might have gone completely crackers. Anything but that."

"Anything on your mind at the moment?" asked Hilary.

David laughed. Hilary had a reputation in the family for density, owing to the fact that, as he never gave advice unless asked for it, no one knew that he had remarked that about which he kept his mouth shut. But David knew better. Not much escaped old Hilary. And his advice, if one did not ask for it, was sound with the soundness of a sweet-kernelled nut.

"Nothing personal," said David. "It's about the family at the Herb of Grace. They've got a man and girl there, doing the chores."

"Yes. I've come across them. An Irishman and his daughter."

"He isn't an Irishman and she isn't his daughter."

"You don't surprise me. Neither the accent nor the relationship seemed to me to ring true."

"A few years ago Annie-Laurie (her name is Doris something or other, I can't remember what) was tried for murder."

"Bless my soul," said Hilary. But he said it fairly calmly. It was his habit to take all things calmly until he had looked into them. Then if he found it necessary to get the wind up, he got it up; but if not, no. "And acquitted, obviously, or she wouldn't be at the Herb of Grace now.... And deservedly acquitted," he added firmly. "I like that girl."

"Those who followed the trial had their doubts," said David gloomily. "They considered that she had a very merciful jury and a very brilliant advocate."

"She pleaded not guilty, of course?"

"Yes."

"Whom was she accused of murdering?"

"Her husband.... And there she is at the Herb of Grace with

Nadine and the children.... And Sally Adair."

"And doing them nothing but good," said Hilary decidedly. "I repeat, I like that girl. I like Malony, too. Go on. Get the whole thing off your chest."

"That's just what I can't do. I only know the bare outline."

"Then give me the bare outline."

"It was just the usual three-cornered affair that you come across in every rag of an evening paper that you pick up. When she was quite young Annie-Laurie was engaged to Malony—that's not his name, of course, but it doesn't matter—but chucked him to marry some good-looking rotter whose name I can't remember either—I can't remember anything in these days: my brain seems made of wool—"

"All brains are," said Hilary comfortably. "Don't worry about it. It's merely the result of war-food. Call him Harold."

"Thanks. He gave Annie-Laurie a pretty bad time, and then took himself off to the Spanish Civil War. He was an ardent Communist. His politics were the best thing about him, one gathers. He didn't care what he suffered for his political faith. He was a plucky fellow, by all accounts. He was reported killed, and after a little while Annie-Laurie married Malony and had a child by him."

"The Enoch Arden story? It repeats itself pretty often in time of war."

"Yes," said David. "He'd been badly wounded, and came back in poor shape. Annie-Laurie went back to him, taking Malony's child with her. They had a flat in Town, and she apparently looked after him devotedly."

"And Malony?"

"He just went on with the job. He was a well-known comedian—pantomime, music-hall and radio. Annie-Laurie was in the same line of business. They'd done acts together when they were married, but they had the sense to part company when she went back to her first husband. But Annie-Laurie went on working—she had to, poor girl, she had a sick husband to look after and she needed the money—but she wasn't very successful without Malony. Then he took to seeing her again occasionally, helping her as much as she would allow him to. You can't blame him. He loved her and she had his child. But it naturally led to trouble between Annie-Laurie and her husband. Then the child died."

"Poor Annie-Laurie!" murmured Hilary.

"After that everything seems to have gone wrong between them, though she continued to look after him. He slept badly and was allowed sleeping tablets. One night she gave them to him, and the next morning he was dead. She fetched the woman from the flat below, saying that he had taken an overdose of his tablets. His own doctor was away at the time, but the neighbour insisted on fetching another. He examined the tablets, and found them to be of a strength that no doctor in his senses would have given to a man as weak as Annie-Laurie's husband. He made a fuss about it, and things looked black against Annie-Laurie. Her great friend was a chemist's wife in the next street. She was there a good deal, and very often helped the short-handed chemist in his work, for she had been a dispenser at one time. She knew where he kept everything. The night before her husband died she went there to fetch him some more tablets, which the chemist had promised to leave ready for her in the place where he always put them. It was after closing time, and there had been an air-raid warning, and the chemist and his wife had gone to the nearest shelter. She had the place to herself. She did not take the box of tablets put ready for her though it was staring her in the face in its accustomed place, but took from the chemist's private drawer the key of the cupboard where he kept his drugs, and took a box of these much stronger tablets. Her finger-prints were on both the key and the cup-board. She said, of course, that in the commotion of the air-raid she had not been able to find the right box, and so had unlocked the cupboard and taken what she thought was the same stuff. But it looked bad. Especially as she had had a row with her husband that very evening. The people in the flat below heard it. They heard her threaten him."

"A girl capable of planning a cold-blooded murder would have had more sense than to leave her finger-prints on the cupboard and the key," said Hilary.

"That was one of the points her advocate made. He was a brilliant fellow. He got her off in the end."

"Whatever made you take such a burning interest in all this?" asked Hilary. "The war was on, and you had plenty of other things to think about."

"I followed the trial in the papers," said David. "I was, as you say, burningly interested. You see, I had met her once, and as an artist she was unforgettable."

"She was good?"

"Yes. So was Malony. I saw them both on the halls and in panto-mime before their troubles. He was just an extremely clever come-dian, but she was—something very much more. She was reaching after something. Watching her, one was reminded of a leaping flame, like a hand reaching; not getting there, but jumping for it. Her voice wasn't much, but she sang with a simplicity that got right under your skin, and she never sang cheap stuff; generally old Scotch and Irish ballads, but sometimes extraordinarily arresting little songs that I sus-pect she made up herself. She could be funny, but she could be sad, too; and it was always real sadness, savage sometimes, but never senti-mental. Her dances were very simple, but she had an airy lightness, like autumn leaves blowing, and they all had a touch of originality. There was one unforgettable one, which she did in some pantomime. She danced dressed as a little Christmas tree, with Malony lumbering about in the background as an extremely comic Father Christmas. She was dressed in spangled dark green with Christmas roses in her hair and bells round her waist that chimed as she danced. I can't think where she got them from, for their chime had a special loveliness. She has them now, tied to the mast of the house-boat. When she'd finished the dance she'd sink to the floor and hold out her hands to an imaginary fire, and sing; something about bells; I don't remember the words, but the tune's in my head now."

"You've remembered everything in the most astonishing detail," said Hilary, a little dryly.

David laughed.

"Yes. It was unforgettable. There was a touch of genius there. Needless to say I don't think she was particularly successful. Her art was too delicate for the sort of work she was doing. It was Malony who pulled her through. He would have pulled her to the top with him if they'd gone on together. I wonder why they didn't start again when their troubles were over. And why in the world are they mas-querading as father and daughter instead of husband and wife?"

"Did Annie-Laurie recognize you when she saw you at the Herb of Grace?"

"I think she did. She looked stricken for the moment. But I don't think I gave myself away. I don't think she knows that I recognized her. And now what the dickens am I to do about it?"

"I don't see the necessity, as yet, for your doing anything about it," said Hilary comfortably, spinning out his glass of port as long as possible, for he did not intend to allow himself the luxury of a second glass.

"But George would have a fit," said David, "if he knew that a girl with a past like Annie-Laurie's was living in close day-by-day contact with his wife and children."

"He would indeed," agreed Hilary. "His reactions are always entirely conventional. But unless you tell him, why should he know?"

"But, Uncle Hilary, Annie-Laurie had two husbands at once, and I believe she murdered one of them."

"It wasn't her fault that she had two husbands at once, and you only suspect her of murder; you have no proof. And who are you to throw stones? There was a time when you and Nadine contemplated a relationship that was unsound, to say the least of it. You can pass no judgment without a knowledge of motive. What matters you know, is not so much what we do as why we do it. Our actions are only the letter. It's the spirit that counts."

"It works the other way round, too; at least, so Grandmother says. A systematic course of action creates the complementary spirit in the end."

"Desire is a better word there than spirit—the desire to which you do violence by a chosen course of action; and deep below them both is the motive, the spirit, the mainspring."

"'And all shall be well, and all manner of thing shall be well, by the purification of the motive in the ground of our beseeching,'" quoted David.

"The beseeching," said Hilary gently, "the crying out, like the upthrust of the green shoot from the sod, or the leap of the flame from the charred wood. So long as that cry goes up from a soul, though it be for she knows not what, she is not totally lost."

"We're wandering from the point a bit," objected David.

"No. The point is that Annie-Laurie's all right. There's the leap of the flame there. You saw it in her art, and did not forget it. I've seen it in her devotion to Nadine."

"Is she devoted to Nadine?"

"Yes. And Nadine to her. That is, if my observation is not at fault. Leave this to Nadine. It's her business—and mine, too, now you've told me. But not yours. Odd how the artistic temperament always makes the sufferer feel that every problem of the universe must be dealt with by himself. A form of arrogance, really."

"*You've* just shouldered Annie-Laurie," retorted David.

"All sin and trouble are the business of a priest. And if that sounds arrogant, too, it's not a personal arrogance. We work under orders, but not under our own steam."

Desolation swept in upon David once more. The iron band clamped down upon his head again. They seemed to have been talking for a long time, and his happy moment of relaxation was swept away completely upon the tide of exhaustion. He was lost again in the darkness of his own futility; of the apparent futility of everything that they had all of them done and suffered during these last years.

"Don't you lose heart?" he asked Hilary abruptly. "Wonder what's the good of it all in this world when whatever you do it's no use?"

"Only when I have bronchitis," said Hilary cheerfully. "The superior strength of evil is a numerical superiority, not one of quality. Outside time numbers have no meaning—only quality. We ought to go back to Mother and Margaret, I think. I enjoyed that port."

At the door he paused and subjected his nephew to a keen glance through his thick glasses.

"This sense of futility—Ben has it, too. It's nothing—merely the reverse side of aspiration—and inevitable, just as failure is inevitable. Disregard them both. What can we expect when we aspire as we do, yet remain what we are? Struggle is divine in itself, but to ask to see it crowned with success is to ask for that sign which is forbidden to those who must travel by faith alone. Each fresh leap of the flame from the charred wood lights your footsteps a little farther through the dark. Good Lord, how tedious I am! That's the sermon I preached last Sunday. They all had a good sleep, and I thanked God that I'd been able to rest them so nicely."

David heard that hateful voice that was not his own snapping out some irritated reply to words he had scarcely heard. They went into the drawing-room and played a frightful game of bridge, at which Lucilla and David were skilled, and Hilary and Margaret so inept that it was torture to partner them. But Hilary enjoyed himself, just as he had enjoyed himself drinking the port. Increasingly, as he got older, he enjoyed things. As his personal humility deepened, so did his awareness of the amazing bounty of God.... So many things.... The mellow warmth of the port, the pleasure of the game, the sight of Lucilla's lovely old face in the firelight, and David's fine hands holding the cards, his awareness of Margaret's endearing simplicity, and the contentment of the two old dogs dozing on the hearth....

One by one the small joys fell; only, to Hilary no joy was small—each had its own mystery, aflame with the glory of God. Yet when ten o'clock struck he lumbered to his feet and wished them good night. He lived as firmly by the clock as any monk. Margaret went with him to the door, and Lucilla and David were alone.

"My dear old Hilary," said Lucilla. "He'll be so happy walking home under the stars. And so happy praying for us all in that cold, draughty study of his before he goes to bed. And if his rheumatism keeps him awake most of the night he won't mind much, for it'll give him the opportunity of a few more wakeful hours in which to praise God. When I feel depressed, thinking of the sons and grandsons whom I brought into the world to be killed or maimed by these horrible wars, I think to myself, 'Well, I did at least give life to one happy man.'"

There was sadness in her voice, and he knew that she grieved because he, her dearest on earth, was ill and not happy; but he was too bewildered by his own wretchedness to be able to think of anything to say to comfort her. To help them both through the next few minutes he reached for the book on the table beside her.

"What were you reading, Grandmother?"

She regained her cheerfulness at once, deeply ashamed of its momentary loss.

"Meredith. While you and Hilary were taking such ages over your port I was trying to find that bit about the lover of life. That darling Sally whom you brought to tea with me—she's a lover."

David found what she wanted and read it to her.

"The lover of life holds life in his hand,
    Like a ring for the bride.
The lover of life is free of dread;
The lover of life holds life in his hand,
    As the hills hold the day.

"But lust after life waves life like a brand,
    For an ensign of pride.
The lust after life is life half-dead:
Yea, lust after life hugs life like a brand,
    Dreading air and the ray.

"For the sake of life,
For that life is dear,

The lust after life
Clings to it fast.
For the sake of life,
For that life is fair,
The lover of life
Flings its broadcast.

"The lover of life knows his labour divine,
    And therein is at peace.
The lust after life craves a touch and a sign
    That the life shall increase.

"The lust after life in the chills of its lust
    Claims a passport of death.
The lover of life sees the flame in our dust
    And a gift in our breath."

He scarcely took in what he read, but the rhythm of the words was restful, even as Hilary had been restful... and Sally.

"Darling, you must go to bed," said Lucilla, eyeing him anxiously.

He got up, lit their candles and put out the lamp. They went up the stairs together, his arm around her, the old dogs following after; for nowadays they had chosen to sleep in padded baskets on the mat outside Lucilla's bedroom door. They felt lonely in the night, now that they were old, and liked to be near her. In her room David took Lucilla in his arms and kissed her eyelids, her hair, her soft old cheeks, as a lover would do. He was most truly her lover. To the depth of his soul he hated himself that his wretchedness was yet another burden for her to bear. But he could not help it. Abruptly he left her, without words, lest his control break and he grieve her more than ever.

"Fool," he said to himself, lying still in the darkness of his room, stretched tautly by the fear of the pack of nightmare sensations that leaped at him like hounds at a deer through the sleepless nights. "This is just what's called a nervous breakdown. No one thinks anything of it. It passes. You don't go crackers and chuck yourself out of the window if you remember that it passes. It passed for ten minutes during dinner. It will pass again when the morning comes. Hilary went through the same thing after the last war, and now he praises God through the nights. It passes."

He tried to relax, then found himself tossing restlessly, his mind going back over the past. Nadine! Nadine! Why could she not let go?

"The lust of life clings to it fast." It had been like light to love her. They had loved as deeply as a man and woman can, and then had chosen to set it behind them and pass on. But she still looked back over her shoulder, holding him with her look. Let go. Let go. Let me go on. If I could go on there might be another dawn.

"Hillsides are dark,
And hill-tops reach the star,
And down is the lark,
And I from my mark
Am far."

The rhythm of Meredith's words was not quieting any more, but torturing, like the ticking of the wretched cuckoo clock out in the passage. He tried to wrench his mind away from their stupid repetition, to disentangle himself from the monotonous ticking of the clock, from the even more monotonous remarks of the cuckoo at each quarter of an hour, and think of Sally in the woods this morning. The light had seemed to gather about her, and the old Bastard had leaned his head against her knee. She had never seen death, nor inflicted it. While he had been with her he had looked at the world with her eyes and the light had streamed over it as from the east. His uncurtained window faced east, over the marshes. If he waited long enough the night would pass and the dark square of the window lighten to twilight grey; and then silver, and then gold.

CHAPTER

– 1 –

*C*HE TWO FISHERMEN LEFT THEM, and the weather broke. One day St. Luke seemed reigning as triumphantly as before, with the sky a lovelier blue, the woods a more glorious gold, the stillness deeper and holier than ever; but the next day, a Sunday, there was a subtle change. In the morning the sun still shone from a cloudless sky, but there was a scarcely perceptible chill in the air, a sharpening of outline, a silence of birds; by nightfall there was a grey veil over the sky and it was so cold that Malony lit a roaring wood fire in the hall, and after supper, instead of going to the drawing-room, they sat in front of it, and Ben roasted chestnuts for them all, while George and John Adair smoked their pipes and Nadine and Sally knitted for the twins.

The Eliots found it a queer sort of evening—a transition evening. Hitherto the Herb of Grace had been to them a summer home; they had known it only permeated with sun and light, flower-scented, windows and doors wide open. But now doors were shut, curtains drawn to hide the sad, grey dusk. Instead of the lap of the water against the river wall they heard the whisper of the flames, and instead of the flowers in the garden they smelt the roasting chestnuts, burning apple logs, coffee, the oil lamps, polish—all the home smells. This intimacy with the house was deepening; when winter came it would be deeper still. Nadine glanced over her shoulder at the firelight gleaming upon the dark wood of the panelling, at the shadows gathering in the corners, and marvelled to see how the old place seemed to have shrunk in size with the shutting out of the daylight. It seemed gathering them in, holding them close.

"Like an old man wrapping us round in the folds of his cloak," said Ben.

"H'm?" asked George sleepily.

"When we first came, and it was summer and we didn't so much need his shelter, he just stood there with his arms held wide, welcoming us. He didn't come very near. Tonight he's closer."

"H'm?" asked George again, and this time he sounded a little worried.

"He's talking about the look of the house from the front door, darling," explained Nadine soothingly. "It does look like that, you know. The way the stairs branch is like arms held wide."

George shot up his left cuff and glanced at his watch. "Time for the News?"

"Not quite yet," said Sally with relief.

She hated the News, though she always heard it through once a day from a painful sense of duty. It was right that one should know. It was wrong to hide one's head in the sand like an ostrich. Though not wrong, she thought, for the ten minutes that remained before Big Ben struck, to cuddle oneself up in the folds of this old man's cloak and enjoy the sense of warmth and safety that it gave. For this was no false safety. This old man's cloak was something real, a symbol of spiritual safety that one sought with one's eyes wide open to the probability, the certainty even, of material disaster. She had not forgotten Lucilla's quotation about the reality of symbols.

"When you've finished Brockis Island, Ben, you might paint his portrait," suggested John Adair. "You've not tried your hand at a portrait yet, have you? At least not a man's portrait. The white deer in the drawing-room, of course, is an excellent likeness."

"What of?" demanded George; and now he looked definitely worried, and the explanatory jerk of John Adair's pipe-stem towards the little stone deer in the alcove, glimmering up above them in the shadows, did not seem to help him at all.

"I can't paint him yet," said Ben, sitting cross-legged on the hearth, with the firelight gleaming on his absorbed face. "I don't see him quite clearly yet. At least, not his face. It's still hidden under his hood. You see, I've no clue to what he looks like."

"You've the house," said John Adair.

"That's his body. I can see that all right; the build of him, the attitude. But not the face."

"You'll see it soon, Ben," said Sally comfortingly. "Summer, the build of the body—Autumn, the feel of his cloak—Winter, his face." She looked round upon them all suddenly with wondering eyes. "Winter. Christmas at the Herb of Grace! Where shall we all have got to by the time Christmas comes?"

"George, turn on the News," said Nadine, taking pity on her poor husband. "It's time, I think."

The tolling of Big Ben filled the silence. George smiled at the comfortable familiarity of the sound, but Ben's involuntary shiver expressed the feelings of the others very accurately. Night by night now the tolling ushered in the announcement of so many ruined hopes. George, though he worried about the state of the world as much, and more, than anyone, was nevertheless one of those who get a lot of comfort out of hearing another fellow stating the facts of the case out loud. He then felt that his anxiety was justified, and the consequent self-inflation strengthened him to bear it. The News was followed by a talk upon atomic energy, and after that, unable to look each other in the eye, they seemed also unable to think of anything to say.

"Go to bed, Sally," said John Adair abruptly to his daughter. "You look fagged out."

"So she does," agreed George, eyeing her anxiously. He liked Sally. No nonsense about her, and an excellent seat on a horse. She had been out riding with David this afternoon, and it was his opinion that David took her too far. "Takes it out of her," he muttered.

"Yes," said John Adair, low and savage.

He completely detested David just at present. He was draining Sally of everything she had to give and giving nothing whatsoever in return. It was unconscious, probably. He was a sick man, and the sick batten upon the strong without knowing that they do it. Nevertheless, he hated David.

Startled but obedient, Sally rolled up her knitting and bade them good night. They watched her tall figure go slowly up the stairs. When she came home she had changed her riding things for a house-coat of peacock blue. The fine soft wool fell in long folds to her feet, and she had a gold belt round her waist. The light gleamed softly on her bright head. When she reached the white deer in the alcove she turned round and smiled at them, reluctant to leave them, then she turned to the right and the shadows folded themselves around her blue and gold. The room seemed darker. There was a short pause.

"Looks like one of those fellow's angels," said George. "That fellow—what's his name?—something to do with a bottle—know it as well as my own name."

He looked appealingly at his wife, whose post-war loss of memory was not as severe as his own.

"Botticelli?" suggested Nadine.

"That's right," said George.

"I don't always like the Botticelli faces," complained Ben. "When she turned round just then she looked more like Juliet on the balcony."

John Adair hooted derisively; but he was pleased. "Too much muscular development for Juliet."

"It was her face, saying good-bye," persisted Ben. "You know— 'Good night, good night. Parting is such sweet sorrow.' I wish David had seen her like that, on the stairs. You know, he's played Romeo about a million times."

He spoke out of his ignorance, and, leaning back against his mother's knees, wondered at the sudden tremor that went through her body; and wondered, too, at the look John Adair gave her, sorry yet somehow merciless.

"Yes, she looked fagged out," reiterated George worriedly. "Does she need a tonic, do you think?"

"I leave it in Mrs. Eliot's hands," said John Adair gently and inexorably.

Nadine could stand no more. She rolled up her knitting.

"Ben, it's past your bedtime. I'll come, too."

They went up the stairs, Nadine graceful as a willow wand, Ben, nearly as tall as she was, with his arm round his adored mother. George watched them.

"Yours," said John Adair. "Lucky man!"

George leaned forward and flung a log on the fire; his face in the sudden leap of light looked old and haggard.

"I don't make her happy," he muttered. "Can't get the hang of it somehow."

"Believe me, you will," said John Adair quietly. "You'll ask—how do I know that? Intuition, chiefly, but also a sense I have of a strong pulse of creative joy that beats in this house. That perpetual weary turning back to the past for refuge, that we are all more or less guilty of these days, is not the natural reaction to the challenge of this house. Maison Dieu. In this place we are urged creatively forward to an ending that is for each of us altogether good."

George smiled. The fellow talked like a book, and not the sort of book George cared about, either, but he was a comforting fellow, none the less.... Gave you the feeling that he had the universe well in hand.

"Botticelli—that reminds me," said his guest. "What about that bottle of whisky David brought down?"

George fetched it, and the remainder of the evening passed pleasantly.

– 2 –

In the night a wild south-wester from the sea sprang upon them. It sprang so suddenly that everyone except the twins woke up.

"Annie-Laurie!" exclaimed Nadine, hearing a faint chiming of fairy bells borne through the open window on the wind, and knowing that the house-boat must be swinging. "We ought to have moved them in before this."

"They're all right," murmured George sleepily. "Stout little craft. How you do worry about that girl! More than you do over your own children," he added jealously.

"Ben and the twins are safe inside the Herb of Grace," said Nadine. "Shut the window, George. The rain's blowing straight in."

"Horizontal weather," muttered George, shutting the window. "There must be a racket out at Damerosehay."

He went back to bed and fell asleep again, but Nadine lay awake thinking of Damerosehay. There they would be getting the full force of the wind, and the old house would be shuddering and creaking, and the trees in the oak wood would be stretching their old arms to shield it as well as they might.... David would be awake.... On just such a night as this, before the war, they had both of them lain awake and steeled their wills to give each other up. She could remember as vividly as though it were yesterday the hours of misery she had lived through that night; and in the morning she had thought the conflict won. And so it had been up to a point; she had gone back to George.

But she had not ceased to love David. The love for her husband that Lucilla had assured her would eventually be born of a way of life that assumed it had not been born; because she loved David too utterly to let go of him, to endure the thought of him married to another woman. Without him there in the background of her life, still loving her, still faithful to her, she could not live. To the thought of him still there she clung when life got too much for her, as other people clung to religion. It meant as much as that.... David waiting.... If George should die.... David waiting.... But what if he waited now against his will?

The question burnt into her brain. She lay in the noisy darkness facing it, and hating John Adair, who had brought her to this pass. For he had made her face it. Subtly, with no clear word spoken; yet he had made her face it. He demanded of her the ultimate denial, without reservation; and correlated with that the ultimate giving, without reservation. He asked of her the single mind, the Herb of Grace.

What right had he to ask it? she demanded passionately. What did he know of the kind of love that had been for years between herself and David? What he called love was just emotional enjoyment, equivalent to the feasting of a body already well nourished, not the feeding of starvation upon the bread of life. The bread of life to him was his art. What response would he make to a demand that he tear that out of his life? He did not understand the hugeness of the thing that he was asking out of his own selfishness. For what he wanted was that she set David free for his Sally.

She had faced that, too, now. In the last few weeks there had been much coming and going between Damerosehay and the Herb of Grace, and it had gradually dawned upon all the adult members of both households, as it had shone upon Lucilla in a flash of insight in the first moment, that Sally and David walking together, riding together, sailing his boat together, was a sight that somehow satisfied them with a sense of fitness. This satisfaction had not yet reached the point of being openly expressed, they were perhaps scarcely aware of it themselves, but Nadine was aware of it through every nerve of her body; and aware, too, of the depth and maturity of Sally's love for David. It was a love she could not even hope to weaken. A crude, possessive love, or even the romanticism that one would have expected to find in a young girl's first passion, she would have fought. But this she could not fight. There were no tender glances, no naïve flatteries, nothing that gave any excuse for ridicule. She was only aware of Sally's love as she was aware of the presence of spring in the world when as yet there were no green shoots or bird song, aware of it as a hidden power, sealed in with patient pain until the hour should strike. Against this she could do nothing; even if it had been possible, she could not hurt so fine a thing. Nor could she any longer dislike the girl who had proved herself capable of it, and who so quietly, though perhaps unaware of what she did, put her happiness in the hands of the older woman to make or mar as she would. For that was how it was. David, self-absorbed in his own wretchedness and clinging to the past like the rest of them, was not likely to leave the familiarity of an old allegiance, even though it had become for him now a prison, unless she herself did violence to it and set him free.

Well, she was not self-deceived now. John Adair had seen to it that she should not have the excuse of ignorance. "I leave it in Mrs. Eliot's hands," he had said quietly, as though he trusted her. The trees of Knyghtwood, tossing and complaining in the wind, cried out with many voices. How she hated the sound of a gale in the trees! There was a nightmare quality in the rush of the great wings, the queer sudden silences broken by whisper and lament, and then again the loud cry and the clamour, with every nerve in one's body stretched in sympathy with the mysterious anguish that wrung this crying from the heart of the world. Again! Again! It was just such a night as that other night at Damerosehay. The denial then had not been complete. Now it must be.

As though flying from the fact, she suddenly slipped from her bed and reached for dressing-gown and slippers. She'd start screaming if she stayed here listening to the wind any longer, with George snoring beside her. She went to the door and slipped out into the dark passage. It was quieter here, the roar of the wind seemed to come from a long way away, and the great gusts had no effect at all upon the immense strength of the house. When they smote upon this fortress there was no tremor. It was warm and safe. "Like an old man wrapping us round in the folds of his cloak." She groped her way down the passage to the foot of the attic stairs. Hardly knowing what she did, she went up them and found herself at the door of John Adair's studio. She turned the handle and went in, felt for the matches and lit the lamp. She took a cigarette from his box, lit it and sat down in a chair, one of the pieces of drapery tucked over her knees. In pre-war days she had been too fastidious to smoke, but now her overstrained nerves often drove her to it. It was quieter here in this north room than in her south bedroom, and she felt less tormented. Though even here the stricken trees seemed still present with her. John Adair had a passion for trees, and they looked out at her from several of his canvases, and from Ben's painting of Brockis Island. She had not seen Brockis Island yet, for she still had not explored farther than the fringe of Knyghtwood. She did not really care much about woods, even though it had been in a wood that David had first told her that he loved her.... David.... She pulled herself sharply away from the brink of that pain and found herself looking at her own portrait, at that extraordinarily lovely woman to whose perfected beauty she had not yet attained, set against the background of a wood, with small blue flowers growing at her feet.

A sudden bitter little exclamation broke from her, and she jumped up and went to the picture. He had altered the background without telling her, and instead of the green drapery it was the background of just such another wood as that in which David had first loved her. And the flowers about her feet, echoing the blue of her dress, were the same flowers as those on the inn signboard—the flowers of the narrow-leafed rue. How dared he! How dared he paint her unsparingly, beautiful yet with the grey in her hair and the lines upon her face, against the background of the warm love he was forcing her to deny; and with that bitter herb at her feet? She went back to her chair and smoked her cigarette furiously, to the end. Then she stubbed it out and forced herself to be more reasonable. How could he possibly know about the wood and David? He didn't know. He was merely obsessed, like everyone else in this house except herself and George, with that detestable Knyghtwood. And it was natural that at the feet of the hostess of the Herb of Grace he should paint the flowers from the inn signboard. "I'm sorry, John," she said, and helped herself to another of his cigarettes and smoked it more quietly, looking about her, reaching for the comfort of his strong presence by looking at his things.... It was odd how his steady, passionless love was supporting her these days. Angry though she was with him, yet she was leaning on him.... What a wildly untidy man he was! His books were all over the place. There was one on the floor by her chair, and she bent and picked it up. Meredith. Old-fashioned. She'd never read him. The book opened of itself at the marker of a jay's feather thrust between the pages. It marked a lyric. Startled, she read it through, hearing every word as though spoken in John Adair's voice.

"Should thy love die;
O bury it not under ice-blue eyes!
  And lips that deny,
  With a scornful surprise,
The life it once lived in thy breast when it wore no disguise.

"Should thy love die;
O bury it where the sweet wild-flowers blow!
  And breezes go by,
  With no whisper of woe;
And strange feet cannot guess of the anguish that slumbers below.

"Should thy love die;
O wander once more to the haunt of the bee!
  Where the foliaged sky
  Is most sacred to see,
And thy being first felt its wild birth like a wind-wakened tree.

"Should thy love die;
O dissemble it! smile! let the rose hide the thorn!
  While the lark sings on high,
  And no thing looks forlorn,
Bury it, bury it, bury it where it was born."

So that was it, she thought bitterly—that was why he had painted her against a background of trees. So this was what she had to do: go out into the depth of Knyghtwood, bury her past there and come back laughing.... How very easy it sounded!

Suddenly everything seemed unreal. The things in the room about her were travelling away at a great speed to a great distance. She got up hastily, turned down the lamp, groped her way to the door and down the stairs. She knew this nightmare sensation of old. It presaged moments of despair—those moments when she felt she could no longer bear to live, and yet knew herself unfit to die. She'd better be in bed before the full wretchedness surged over her. It came, she knew, chiefly from deadly fatigue, but that did not make it any easier to bear. She reached her room, still filled with the noise of the storm and George's peaceful snoring, got into bed and lay down to await her black hour.... But it did not come.... Very faintly in a lull in the storm something interposed itself between her spirit and its coming. She heard again the far-away chiming of bells.... Annie-Laurie.... What was the burden that Annie-Laurie carried, rocking through the storm in her house-boat? Whatever it was, much greater than her own. Remembering Annie-Laurie, Nadine was once more ashamed of herself. What a ridiculous fuss she was making about doing what everyone was always doing every day, every hour, every moment of their lives almost: gathering in the divided allegiance, denying it to the one thing, giving it to the other; the choice never really in doubt when to the inner beseeching of the spirit the motive is revealed. It was a process that could not end while the eventual salvation of one's soul was still a possibility, the pain of the unceasing effort merely a question of degree, but not differing moment by moment in essence. One lived, and it was so. Accept it and have done.... She went to sleep.

CHAPTER

– 1 –

ON THE MORNING THE RAIN was descending in a solid sheet. Upon awakening, the twins looked out at the weather, looked at each other, and decided simultaneously, with no word said, what they were going to do this morning. It was a wicked thing. They looked at each other and laughed delightedly. They were going to be bad today. They were going to start right off by being bad. That was always the way with the twins. One evil action planned, say, for midday, worked both retroactively and progressively; their strong histrionic sense compelled them to see to it that their behaviour throughout the day was in keeping with the culminating point.

So when Jill came to call them she found they were not in their beds. But she did not let this phenomenon disturb her. She was used to it.

"Now where are José and Jerry, I wonder?" she said aloud, rummaging in the little flower-painted chest of drawers for warm garments in keeping with the sad change in the weather. Then she listened, expecting to hear the grunting of a bear under the bed, or the roar of a lion shut up in the wardrobe. But there was no sound at all, and a search all round the nursery showed it to be completely empty; though two little pairs of pyjamas were neatly folded and placed in the fireplace. She went out into the passage, noted that the General had already gone downstairs, leaving his wife's bedroom door ajar, and raised her voice.

"Madam!" she called.

Nadine, weary and heavy-eyed, but as usual impeccably groomed, came to her bedroom door clipping on her earrings.

"Yes, Jill?"

"The twins have disappeared, Madam," said Jill in a clear, carrying voice. "Such a pity! It's their favourite breakfast. Boiled bantam's eggs and bread and honey."

Nadine knew Jill's methods with the twins, and co-operated. Whatever Jill did or suggested, she always, now, co-operated. When she had first seen Jill at Damerosehay she had felt herself caught, fearing that she would be for the rest of her life the prisoner of Jill's high standards. And her fear had been justified, for this gentle but extraordinarily tough-willed young woman now had her as firmly in hand as the twins themselves. But she was not dismayed at her bonds because she was unaware of them. Jill, also, was unaware of them. Hers was the unconscious tyranny of inexorable great expectations.

"Well, Jill," said Nadine, also in a clear, carrying voice, "they won't be able to have any breakfast, that's all. What a pity! Send the eggs into grown-up breakfast. Mr. Adair will enjoy them."

The twins disliked John Adair. Upon finding them in his studio one day squeezing oil-paints on to the floor, he had smacked them good and hard.

"Very well, Madam," said Jill, and went quietly along the passage towards the turret staircase leading to the kitchen.

As she passed the linen cupboard the door flew open and Jerry and José, stark naked, fell out upon her from the top shelf.

"Old Beaver's not to have our eggs!" they shouted as one child. "Jill! Jill! Old Beaver's not to have our eggs!"

Gently but firmly Jill seized a bare arm of each.

"Now, Jerry and José, I've told you before, and I tell you again, you are not to run about the house with no clothes on. It's not respectable."

"We had to be with no clothes on," said Jerry loudly. "We were hatching out."

"In the incubator," explained José. "Chickens are all bare when they're borned."

"They are not," said Jill, leading them firmly towards the nursery. "It's just that their feathers don't fluff out at first."

"Did Mummy lay us in an egg?" shouted Jerry.

"She did not," said Jill. "An angel brought you both and laid you one on each side of her when she was asleep. Straight from heaven you came, though no one would think it, seeing the way you behave now. And you must not shout like that about being born. It is one of those subjects which ladies and gentlemen discuss quietly." They were now in the nursery, and she led them sorrowfully to the fireplace. "And look where you've put your pyjamas. That's no place for pyjamas."

"It's a nest. We put our pyjamas there to make it all soft to lay eggs in."

Jill foresaw that it was going to be a difficult day. Without a word she put them into their woolly combinations. She had never before had to deal with children quite like these. She supposed it was the artistic temperament. Mrs. Eliot was artistic. And, on the other side of the family, Mr. David. And dear Ben, of course. Ben had been a difficult child, too, with his fancies and his asthma; but he had been loving. The first child generally was loving, Jill had noticed; the father and mother probably being a bit taken up with each other at the time, the honeymoon not worn off yet, as you might say, and the child wanted. These two were not loving; bitter at heart their mother must have been when she bore them, and not wanting them at all; though one could hardly blame her for that, poor soul, for she'd not had the strength for it, and she'd not been the same since, and likely never would be. Jill suddenly bent down and dropped a kiss on top of each dark head. Not loving yet, perhaps, but they would be by the time she'd finished with them. You could waken response in children just by giving them love, she'd found; like putting baking-powder into a cake. And she had never loved children as she did these. Coming to her as they had, with her husband dead and her hope of children of her own gone for ever (for she'd never look at another fellow after Alf, not she), they had healed her heartache and filled the void in her life and brought her a delight she had not expected to feel again. And though they were rather heartless little creatures as yet, they had a something that she had not come across in other children of their age. The word that occurred to her was intuition, though she was not very sure what the word meant. There were things that they seemed to know without benefit of experience or learning. They could not express what they knew, but a chance word dropped here and there, like a few petals of cherry blossom drifting down from branches far out of sight above the ceiling of a wood, made her aware of hidden wealth.

"Jill's loving little children," she said to them, with faith, kneeling down between them. "Jill's good little twins," she added hopefully, and her arms went out like the wings of charity and hugged them close.

The twins responded, for the moment, to the power of suggestion. They kissed her ears with enthusiasm and co-operated wholeheartedly in the subsequent arraying of their persons in the poppy-coloured jerseys that she considered suitable to the gloom of the day.

"We're not going to do any lessons this morning," said José.

"Indeed you are," said Jill.

"No," said José.

"Stow your gaff, José," said Jerry.

"That's no way to talk to your sister," said Jill severely.

"O.K.," said Jerry genially.

Then they went down the turret staircase, past the low, arched doorway to the store cupboard, to breakfast in the warm, firelit second kitchen, now the family living-room, and feasted upon bantam's eggs and bread and honey and milk, until the poppy jerseys took on a pronounced aldermanic bulge in the front and a corresponding concave curve in the back. When they had finished Jill cleared the table, gave them some jigsaw puzzles to play with until it should be time for their morning lessons, and went into the other kitchen to grill the herrings for the grown-up breakfast. The twins exchanged a glance, then bent their sleek dark heads demurely over their puzzles. Jill looked in on them before she carried the herrings and coffee through to the hall, and decided from the look of them that they were tethered for another half-hour. She'd be able to slip up and help Annie-Laurie with the beds.

As soon as she had gone the twins looked at each other again, slid from their chairs and ran through into the inner kitchen. They knew where Mother kept the key of the store-room: in the right-hand drawer of the big pitch-pine dresser. They took it out, together with a kitchen spoon, and scurried up the stairs to the little, low, arched doorway. They un-locked the door, went inside, locked themselves in, and were safe ... safe... safe... and laughed aloud out of the splendour of their joy.

It was not only because of the jam that they had come here, nor because they wanted to escape morning lessons, but because of a special feeling they had about this little room. They knew that it was the heart of the house, right deep in, just as the Place Beyond was the heart of Knyghtwood. This little room held something that the other rooms did not hold. The other rooms were each of them just one of many rooms, differing from each other only in shape and size, like the petals of a daisy, but this was one room all by itself, like the gold heart of the daisy that is a thing all by itself. You can pull away the daisy petals, and the heart is still there, unhurt glowing like a little sun; but if you tear away the heart from among the petals, then there isn't any flower any more. This they knew without knowing that they knew it. They had wanted to be here in the store-room all by themselves for a while, just as they had wanted to be alone in the Place Beyond, and had run away from Sally so that they should be.

Well, here they were, and here also was the jam. They looked about them, the tips of their tongues just showing between their parted lips. The strange little octagonal-shaped room with the three small lancet windows had changed since Auntie Rose's day, but not, the twins thought, for the better. Nadine had not admired the shining mustard-coloured paper with the chocolate lozenges like Easter eggs that they had thought so handsome, and had made Malony put a wash of cream distemper over the top of it... though they were happy to see that owing to an insufficiency of distemper the chocolate eggs still showed through a bit... and she had not admired the slatted, sagging shelves with their stains of bygone feasts; she had made George and Malony take them down and make and put up clean white deal shelves with neat little metal brackets supporting them underneath. And upon the shelves there was not quite such a glorious welter of things to eat, all higgledy-piggledy in great brown crocks; there were just neat rows of glass jars all the same size and all neatly labelled, containing the jams and jellies and chutneys Nadine and Jill had been making throughout the summer, an army in perfect formation of Kilner jars filled with bottled fruit, and tall, shining, golden pots of honey.

"Honey?" queried José.

"We had it for breakfast," said Jerry. "Strawberry jam."

He bent down, hands on knees, and José climbed on his back and reached down a jar of strawberry jam. They were not messy children—the beautiful, fastidious Nadine could never have given birth to a messy child. They had remembered to bring a spoon, so that they should not have to put their fingers in, and sitting side by side on the floor, they ate daintily, turn and turn about, until there wasn't any more. Nor were they greedy children. They did just consider going on to a pot of blackberry and apple, but after holding wordless communion upon the subject they turned the idea down. Enough is as good as a feast, and though they felt quite well after the strawberry, they thought that perhaps after the blackberry and apple they might not.

"Put the pot back where it was," commanded Jerry, who possessed both a tidy mind and the firm conviction that females had been created by God to do all menial tasks; and he bent double again, with hands on knees. In this position, with José on his back, he looked under the lowest shelf and noticed something.

"Come down," he commanded José.

She came, and they dropped upon hands and knees and gazed together at the pleasing sight.

Malony hadn't had quite enough distemper to go right down to the floor all the way round, and beneath the shelf a few inches of the lovely mustard-and-chocolate paper had been left uncovered; what was more, it had come unstuck at the juncture of the wall and the stone floor of the little room, and was curling upwards in irresistible curls like autumn leaves. Jerry seized one and pulled, and it ripped upwards, bringing the distemper with it in a shower of chalky dust. There was another paper under the egg one—green with red roses on it—and that also was coming unstuck and curling up. With a squeak of excitement José seized a curl and pulled, too; and then they both opened their mouths for their special train-going-into-a-tunnel shriek, which was torn from them in moments of extremist joy, but checked it suddenly, lest they should be heard and discovered. After that they worked in silence though now and then, remembering Ben stripping the paper from the panelling in their mother's sitting-room and Ben and Tommy pulling away the black marble surround in the drawing-room, they exclaimed softly, "For the glory of God, my hearties! Heave-ho, my hearties, for the glory of God!"

"Here's a bunny," said José; quite quietly, as though the finding of a bunny were a common occurrence.

She had cleared quite a large patch, and sure enough there was a dim form on the wall, brown against a green background, shaped just like the hind quarters of a rabbit.

"It's just one of the Easter eggs," said Jerry.

"No," said José. "It was under the Easter eggs, and under the red roses. It's an Easter bunny, but not an Easter egg."

"Scrape, scratch, scrabble and scrooge," commanded Jerry.

They did so, and found a very odd-shaped robin, and a little star-let flower on a long green stalk.

"There's a third paper under the rosy one," said Jerry.

"No," said José. "It's a picture painted on."

"Scrooge, scrabble and scratch," repeated Jerry. "For the glory of God, my hearties. For the glory of God."

– 2 –

John Adair and Ben were indifferent to the weather. Their studio to them a kingdom was, and they didn't care what happened out-side. Breakfast over, John Adair cocked his right eyebrow at Ben, and Ben, flushing with pleasure, nodded. This cocking of the eyebrow meant that the great man was in the mood for the dealing out of a lit-tle instruction. When he was not in the mood they would sometimes work together for a whole morning companionably enough, but in a silence that Ben knew better than to break even with a hasty move-ment, let alone a remark. He was aware to the depths of his humble soul of the immense honour done him. Here was he, a raw, inexperi-enced, futile dabbler in the great art, and one of the most famous painters of the century had seen fit to pick him up out of the mud, so to speak and set him upon his feet, and teach him and encourage him and make a man of him. For that was exactly what John Adair had done. He never treated Ben as a child, as George and Nadine did, and in teaching him he never talked down to him, indulged or flattered him; he treated him as a man and an equal, storming at him sometimes to such an extent that Ben's ears flapped out from the side of his head like two scarlet flags of distress, but keeping always between them the bond of two men working together at a craft that was to both of them the most precious thing in the world.

And sometimes, though the boy was not aware of this, he looked at Ben's efforts with a queer humble respect, stroked his beard, put a hand on the boy's shoulder and shook it affectionately, and then turned back to his own work with a smothered exclamation of fury. Once when Ben, scarlet to the roots of his hair, had dared to mutter, "That's grand, sir," as he stood before Nadine's portrait, John Adair had turned on him savagely. "Grand? You young fool! I know what I am, boy; a cross between a detective, a psychiatrist, and a fashion-plate artist. I'd have done better to set up my plate in Harley Street, or study dressmaking under Norman Hartnell." Then he had swung round upon Ben's crude little painting of a summer dawn stealing into the secret green recesses of Brockis Island. "How'd you get it?" he muttered. "The sound of the pipes in the air, the smell of the dew—and the trunks of the trees like liquorice sticks, and that damned rabbit jointed as no rabbit was jointed yet since the animal came out of the Ark. God knows we eat rabbit often enough in this house. Haven't you ever noticed the formation of the femur?"

"Tommy would have," Ben had chuckled. "He's going to be a surgeon. Funny to think you've not met Tommy yet."

"Hope the Pirate and I get on when the time comes," John Adair had commented dryly. "A surgeon, did you say? As detective and murderer, we'll doubtless have much in common."

Today he was in one of his brisk and critical moods.

"Come on now," he admonished Ben. "No good messing about any longer with Brockis Island. I'm sick of the sight of it. More like a pre-war advertisement for face powder every time you touch it. Chuck it in the corner and make a fresh start. Get going with that fellow. If you've not seen his face yet, you've seen the attitude—you said so last night. Get going, now. Your sense of anatomy being what it is, you'd better hang up Horace."

Ben went to a large box hidden away in a corner and produced from it a somewhat battered skeleton. It was his very own. He had had a birthday lately, and John Adair upon one of his trips to London had got it and conveyed it home, strapped up in a railway rug, as a birthday present. The presence of Horace at the Herb of Grace was not known to anyone except the two artists.

"When the holidays come, and Tommy comes home, do you think it would be wrong not to tell him I've got Horace?" asked Ben.

"Most certainly keep Horace dark," counselled John Adair. "I know these surgeon fellows. Horace will be hacked bone from bone in the twinkling of an eye."

"It seems a bit mean, somehow—"

"Not at all. We all have our reticences. They are particularly desirable in large families, where the piratical spirit is apt to batten upon the knightly. Now come on, Chevalier, get going."

"Chevalier?" queried Ben, hanging Horace on a nail.

"Sally's name for you, so I understand."

"What does she mean by that?"

"No idea. Better ask her."

"I wouldn't like to," said Ben; but he spoke dreamily, for he had already fastened a large piece of paper to his board, and chosen a piece of chalk, and the world outside the studio door was slipping away. Brockis Island had been in water-colour, but this was to be in oils, no less. But he was going to do a preliminary sketch in coloured chalks first.

"Shout when you're ready for some devastating criticism," said John Adair.

"Umm," said Ben.

The painter smiled and turned his back on the boy. That "umm" of Ben's—a contented humming sound like bees getting down to the job—meant that he had already tasted honey. "For he on honey-dew fed and drunk the milk of Paradise." Lucky young squirt! The gods were already as liberal with their gifts as the boy was quick in his response. It seemed to the painter that as vision and imagination met and fused, the light brightened in room.... Then he mocked at himself. The rain had stopped for a moment and the sun had come out.

For an hour there was complete silence, a locked and happy silence, no door in either absorbed mind left ajar for the intrusion of irrelevancies. Then a light step sounded on the stairs.

"Mother!" gasped Ben and with a swift movement of panic swung his drawing round with its face to the easel. With an equally swift movement John Adair unhooked Horace and stowed him away out of sight.

"Come in," he called.

Nadine entered.

"Are the twins here?" she asked.

"No, Mother," said Ben.

"You don't know where they are?"

"No."

"They're completely lost," said Nadine wearily, a worried frown between her brows. "Jill left them in the kitchen doing jigsaws, as good as gold, and now they've just vanished."

"Let them vanish," said John Adair callously. "A peaceful morning will then be enjoyed by all."

"With my twins perhaps drowning in the river?" asked Nadine indignantly. "Jill is hunting in Knyghtwood, and George has gone to look for them along the river-bank, and Sally went along the lane to the Hard. Why I was such a fool as to consent to George buying a house by a river I don't know. Unless the twins are actually under my eye or with Jill, I live in a state of perpetual torment."

John Adair looked at her with benign interest. She was more maternal than he had thought.

"Shall I come and help look, too, Mother?" asked Ben dutifully, but a little desperately; for he had just seen in a flash what he wanted in his picture, and if he were to stop now he'd never get hold of it; it would be gone, like a galloping white deer in the forest.

"No need," said John Adair quickly; for by Ben's tone he knew exactly where he was. "Nothing untoward ever happens to tough guys, and I never met a tougher pair than those children."

Nadine swept them both with a withering glance.

"I've also lost the key of the store-room," she said. "So there will be semolina pudding for lunch instead of jam puffs. And you won't forget, will you, that lunch is early today? I'm going to the hairdresser's, and taking the twins, too, to have their hair cut—that is, if my twins turn up."

Both the artists groaned. They both hated semolina pudding and early lunch. Nadine withdrew, outraged at the unhelpful selfishness of the artistic temperament. John Adair restored Horace to his nail, and Ben turned his drawing round again, and silence held them. After a while he let out a deep sigh. John Adair knew where he was. To the best of his ability he had captured what he'd seen.

"Your mother, of course, came in at an awkward moment," he said. "You were perhaps right, just then, to turn your board round. But, generally speaking, don't do that. Don't hide your work. What you have done you have done, and you must take the consequences."

"I hate people seeing my stuff," murmured Ben.

"Afraid of being laughed at? Well, what of it? Never hide from adverse criticism. Mockery, indifference, misunderstanding—welcome the lot. Criticism of your work is much the same as criticism of yourself, you know, your work being an extension of yourself, and there's nothing like good slashing personal criticism for begetting humility. A conceited man never yet made a good artist. How could he? Satisfied, you stick where you are."

"But even the humblest artists writhe a bit when their work is slashed," objected Ben. "It's as though there were something in it besides an extension of themselves... something else...."

"So there is, of course. Your vision, given you, nothing to do with yourself. Mockery aimed at that seems to you a form of sacrilege. But even that you must not resent, for it is not possible to mock at an artist's vision unless his presentation of it is at fault. Dress it up in ridiculous garments and it is you who are guilty of sacrilege, not the mocker."

"Yes," agreed Ben. "I wish I hadn't drawn the white deer in the picture in the drawing-room so badly."

"Yes, it was a pity. As regards technique, it's one of your worst efforts. He's the thing sent, is he?"

"Yes. The other deer are galloping after him, and the light comes from him. Without him the other deer wouldn't know what direction to take; or, if they did, they couldn't see the way."

"They, I suppose, are a man's own natural powers?"

"Yes. Did you guess that when you saw the picture?"

"It's an interpretation of your obviously allegorical work of art that occurred to me."

There was a note of amusement in his voice that made Ben's ears go red again.

"Unutterable ass I must seem to you," he murmured.

"No. If I smiled, it was as much at myself as at you. We're all of us helter-skelter after the white deer, each of us arrogantly expecting to catch up with him at last. Yet who does? To most of us he gives no more than a sense of direction. That's all."

"In this life," said a voice. But there was no sound. The man who spoke was the man in Ben's drawing.

Ben fell back a few paces and looked at the picture.

"I don't think I can do any more for a bit," he said.

"That being so," said John Adair, "I suggest that there may be some connection between the disappearance of the twins and the disappearance of the key of the store-room."

"Gosh, yes! I never thought of that. Nor did Mother." And Ben swung round.

"May I look at your work while you're away?"

"Yes, Sir, of course. But I haven't had time really to—"

"Don't make excuses," interrupted John Adair. "You've had plenty of time to make a good start. If you haven't that's your fault. And don't say 'but.' You know how I detest the word."

– 3 –

Ben took himself off, grinning. He ran lightly down the turret staircase, tried the store-room door and found it locked. He applied his ear to the key-hole. Inside he could hear squeaks and scratchings and sneezings, like little animals scrabbling and scrooging.

"Hi! Rat! Mole!" he called softly. "Badger here. Let Badger in."

There was a cessation of the scrabblings and scroogings, but not of the sneezings.

"Only Badger?"

"Yes, only Badger."

The door was unlocked and Ben was admitted.

"What on earth?" he demanded.

The floor was covered with flakes of distemper and peelings of wallpaper. The twins themselves had a powdering of white dust all over them, and their faces and hands were filthy. But they looked radiantly happy.

"Look, Badger, look!" they cried, seizing hold of him. "Under the shelf. A wood and flowers growing. And a bunny. Look!"

Ben, sneezing loudly as the white dust went up his nose, was dragged to the floor and pushed beneath the shelf. For two hours they had been scratching and scrooging, using the old iron key and their industrious little finger-nails, and they had laid bare quite a large patch of the original wall of this strange little octagonal room. The rear elevation of a rabbit was now clearly to be seen by an imaginative eye, also a small clump of starry red flowers, a robin and the root of a tree. Ben backed out from beneath the shelf, his face white with excitement. He sat back on his heels, thought for a moment in silence, and then addressed the younger brethren.

"Now, see here, Rat and Mole. I'll give you a bob each if you don't say a word to anybody yet awhile about the bunny and the flowers on the wall."

"Why not?" demanded Jerry.

"Rat and Mole," said Ben impressively, "there's a picture painted there under the wallpaper and stuff. I think it's a very old picture, perhaps hundreds of years old. I want to get much more of it uncovered before we tell everybody about it."

"*We'll* uncover it," said José. "Jerry and you and me."

"It would take us too long, and we might scratch the picture with our nails," said Ben. "It needs what they call an expert to do it properly—someone like Old Beaver."

"But it's *our* picture. *We* found it," said the twins indignantly.

"Yes, I know you did, and it was jolly clever of you. And later on I'll tell everyone how clever you were. But just for now, Rat and Mole, you must keep your mouths shut. Promise? A bob each."

The twins sneezed and looked doubtful.

"Rat and Mole, did you know Mummie was taking you into Radford this afternoon, in the car, to have your hairs cut? If you have that two bob you'll be able to buy things at Baxter's."

Jerry and José looked at each other. Baxter's had fireworks, and the 5th of November was approaching. But two bob was insufficient. There was no need for speech between them. They knew each other's minds.

"No," said Jerry. "It's *our* picture, and we won't not tell everybody about it."

Ben tried another tack.

"If I take down a pot of jam to Mummie there'll be jam-puffs for lunch, but if I don't there'll be semolina pudding."

The twins made despairing noises. They hated semolina even more passionately than did John Adair and Ben. Yet they stood firm. They were, as John Adair had remarked, tough guys.

"No," said José.

"Half-a-crown between the two of you."

"No," said Jerry."

"Three bob."

"No," said José. "More."

Ben felt desperate. He possessed only three and sixpence half-penny.

"Mercenary little beasts," he said. "Three and sixpence half-penny."

"Five bob between the two of us," said Jerry. "And a pot of raspberry jam for the puffs."

"O.K.," said Ben bitterly. "Now come along up to the bathroom and get clean, and if you make a single sound while I'm washing you I'll smack you as hard as Old Beaver did when you squeezed his paints on the floor. O.K.?"

"O.K.," said the twins.

Ben seized a pot of raspberry jam from the shelf and pulled them out of the store-room, locking the door behind him and slipping the key in his pocket. They sped noiselessly up the turret stairs and along to the bathroom, where Ben brushed the white dust out of the twins' hair and off their jumpers, and scrubbed their hands and faces till they squeaked; but very softly, for they were children of their word. Then, leaving them drying themselves, he raced up the attic stairs to the studio. John Adair, standing still and attentive before Ben's drawing, looked round in surprise.

"House on fire?" he asked.

"No, Sir. Could you lend me one and fivepence halfpenny? I wouldn't ask such a thing, but it's pretty desperate. And, Sir, please may I use the telephone in your room? If I use the house one downstairs everyone hears what I say, and I don't want them to."

"Putting something on a horse?" enquired John Adair, counting out one and fivepence halfpenny from a handful of loose change with maddening slowness. "Buying a ring for your best girl? I'm not an inquisitive man, of course; but before parting with such a vast sum as one and fivepence halfpenny—"

"I'll tell you later, Sir," said Ben, grabbed the cash and fled back to the bathroom, seized the twins and the jam and descended to the hall. "Hoy!" he yelled. "Found!"

Nadine appeared from the drawing-room.

"Jerry! José! Where *have* you been? You've frightened Mummie to death, and poor Jill is getting all wet looking for you outside. And Daddie and Sally, too."

"They'll dry," said Jerry.

"They were playing in the store-room, Mother," said Ben. "They didn't do any harm there. I've locked it up again. And here's a pot of raspberry jam, Mother, for the puffs."

"They're sure to have done some harm there," said Nadine. "How much jam have they eaten?"

"One pot of strawberry," said José.

"Pigs," said Nadine. "Give me the store-room key, Ben, and ring the dinner bell at the front door. I told the others I would if they turned up safely."

"No, me!" shrieked Jerry, and seized the bell as Ben fled upstairs, his hand still clasping the key in his pocket.

In John Adair's bedroom he sat breathlessly at the writing-table and rang up Damerosehay. By the mercy of heaven it was David himself who answered.

"Yes?" he enquired in a cold, bored, non-committal voice.

But Ben was too excited today to be chilled by the extraordinary way in which people you love speak to you on the phone when they haven't the ghost of a notion who you are.

"David! 'Smee!"

"Who?"

"'Smee. Ben. David, there's a fresco on the store-room wall!"

"A what on the store-room wall? Don't pant so, old boy, I can't hear a word."

"A *fresco*. F for Freddy, R for Reginald, E for Ernest, S for Sydney—"

"Oh, *fresco*." David's voice became suddenly interested. "How did you find it?"

"The twins found it. They stripped a bit of the paper off. David, Mother and the twins are going to Radford this afternoon, and Father's taking Sally to see the Abbey, if it clears—and you can see it's going to—and Malony and Annie-Laurie will be busy moving into the flat over the garage (they got nearly blown away in the houseboat last night), so come over this afternoon, and you and I and Old Beaver will work at it in peace and quiet."

"Don't the family at large know about it?"

"No! I couldn't bear them to—not yet. It seems sort of—private—I can't explain. It must be just you and I and Beaver."

"What's to be seen so far?"

"A rabbit and flowers."

"Sounds to me like an illustration for some child's picture book, pasted on by Auntie Rose's mother-in-law."

"No!" yelled Ben furiously. "It's not *that* sort of rabbit!"

"You mean not a sentimental rabbit? Apocryphal, perhaps."

"*No.* There's nothing apocryphal about it. It's *real.* It's *alive* there on the wall... just the hind part," he added weakly.

"Keep calm, old boy. I'll come along," said David, suddenly as serious as could be wished. "And thank you very much for letting me in on this."

There was a click and he had gone. Ben replaced the receiver, and with his short, stiff, dark hair standing up in peaks all over his head, and his eyes shining, he rushed back to the studio and poured it all out to Old Beaver, where he still stood thoughtfully before Ben's easel.

John Adair's reception of the news, though not as enthusiastic as could have been wished, was not unsatisfactory.

"Quite possible," he conceded. "The room's octagonal, you say, with lancet windows? And this is a Pilgrim Inn. It might have been the Chapel."

"Would they have had a Chapel in a Pilgrim Inn?"

"If, as you seem to think, Mine Host was a monk, put here to look after the pilgrims coming to the Abbey." And he indicated the drawing before which he stood.

Ben looked at his chalk drawing, which half an hour ago had been his very life, but which for the last twenty minutes he had completely forgotten.

"I didn't think of him as being a monk." he said, puzzled. "Just as being wrapped in a dark cloak, because of the dark panelling and the stairs. Besides, he's too burly-looking for a monk, surely."

"The Cistercians were fine farmers," said John Adair. "Great fellows for tilling the land and raising stock. The chap you've drawn is a Cistercian lay brother. I like the look of the fellow so far; though I'd be glad to see him with a face. And where the dickens is the light coming from? The only place it can come from, if you're standing in the entrance to the inn, is the open front door behind you; but in your picture it is coming from behind the figure."

His tone was severe, and Ben's ears went scarlet. He had drawn a large, sturdy man standing on the stairs of the inn with arms held wide. The figure was superimposed upon the cruciform structure of the branching staircase as the Figure is fastened to the Cross, appearing one with it. But except for a willed strength in the attitude, as though the man braced himself against the wood of the cross, an immense patience in the sturdily planted feet, the figure did not suggest suffering. The outspread arms suggested a huge welcome, the fold of the habit had winged protectiveness, and the cowled head was held high, as though the man laughed. The lighting came from behind the head, giving a clear outline to both head and shoulders, in striking contrast to the rest of the figure, where the falling folds of the habit were scarcely distinguishable from the dark wood of the stairs.

"The light comes from the alcove behind him," said Ben suddenly. "The alcove where the white deer is. You can't see the deer, but he must be there, shining like a lamp."

"Did you think of that while you were working?"

"No. I just felt one ought to see his head and shoulders clearly."

"It's better, of course," said John Adair slowly, "to have a good reason for what you do before you start, rather than manufacture one to fit the facts of the case afterwards."

He spoke hesitantly, for the power and beauty of the boy's drawing had touched him so deeply that he was at a loss as to what to say. He was afraid to praise too much, lest Ben became self-satisfied, afraid to criticize too severely lest he grow discouraged. Above all, he was at a loss as to how to advise him to go on with his picture; afraid that the delicate beauty of it, caught now in a few sure lines, a few fine contrasts of light and shade, be lost in the over-elaboration of detail with which Ben in the late stages of his work unconsciously tried to hide the faultiness of his technique. He felt in the same sort of fix as a man watching a butterfly fluttering against a window-pane, anxious to guide the creature the right way out, but afraid to handle lest he injure its fragile wings. He decided, this time, to let the boy and his picture severely alone. To Ben's tentative, "Is it all right, Sir, so far?" he replied briefly, "Yes. Don't attempt the face until you see it clearly, and keep the whole thing as simple as possible."

"I'll put it away, I think," said Ben. "I won't go on with it until we've uncovered the fresco."

The dinner bell sounded, and they went downstairs to devour shepherd's pie and jam puffs.

CHAPTER

– 1 –

AFTER LUNCH EVERYTHING FAVOURED THEM. The rain stopped and the sun broke through. Nadine, Jill and the twins went off in the car to Radford, George and Sally to the Abbey, and Malony and Annie-Laurie to the business of moving house. When John Adair and Ben sat down at the open front door in the sunshine to wait for David they had an empty house behind them.

"Well, here we are," said John Adair. "Rat and Mole out. Beaver and Badger at home. What's David?"

Ben had been unaware that the painter's nickname was known to him. His ears flew their usual flag of distress. "I—we hadn't thought of a name for David."

"Placidus," suggested John Adair.

"Placidus?"

"He's in the National Gallery, painted centuries ago by Pisanello. Placidus and your cousin—they've the same face. Queer. Wood, in tempera. Riding through a forest. You must know the thing as well as I do."

"I've not been to the National Gallery," said Ben with shame. "You see, in the war the pictures were taken away, and then David said he wanted to take me. And then he was busy and kept forgetting. And I didn't like to go without him."

"Great Scott!" said John Adair. "Has it been reserved for this un-worthy dauber to take William Blake the Second for a personally conducted tour of the great masters?"

Ben grinned and hugged his knees. He liked Old Beaver in a bantering mood. It was the invariable cloak of his affection, that gripped beneath it with a sureness of touch that left one in no doubt that he liked one. It struck him suddenly that he had never seen Beaver tease David.

"Do you like him?" he suddenly demanded. He hated people he liked not to like each other.

"Who? Placidus? As an artist I take off my hat to him, as a man I am at present reserving judgment. At the moment there is a certain dilatoriness about him that is just about getting my goat."

"It mustn't," said Ben quickly. "I can hear the car now."

A moment later David was coming slowly up the steps and taking his time over the latch of the blue gate.

"Don't hurry," said John Adair sharply.

David looked up and smiled, wincing a little at the hard tone, exactly as Ben would have done.

"Am I late? I'm sorry."

He spoke gently, as Ben would have spoken, with that same willingness to be criticized that so enriched the genius of both of them. The likeness between the two suddenly presented David to John Adair from a new angle; he saw him linked to Ben and not to Sally, and, Sally out of the picture, he looked a different man, and the artist hated himself for his bitterness. David looked, still, a very sick man, and a bewildered man, as though he had lost his bearings in this brave new world that was, and yet so hideously was not, that for which he and his contemporaries had fought. John Adair had understood him well enough, though impersonally, when he had sketched him that day in the theatre. It was only now, when the man's sickness of body and mind had touched him to his own hurt, that his understanding failed. Merely impersonal understanding might make a fine painter, but it does not make a humane man. He hated himself. David needed every ounce of energy he possessed, or could get from those about him, for keeping his end up; ridiculous to expect of him anything else for the present. Nature knew what she was doing when she kept her new-born creatures with blind eyes while they gathered their strength; and this was a man who was passing through a painful period of re-birth. And Sally knew what she was doing when she gave all she had and asked for nothing. It was only he, John Adair, who was a crass old dotard.... Suddenly, with a flash of insight, he knew the man.... He jumped up, went to meet David with outstretched hand, faced him squarely with his tawny eyes alight.

"Forgive the impatience of these two musketeers, waiting for the third."

The extraordinary warmth of the tone astonished David, the almost blazing kindness in the eyes, the strong grasp of the hand that seemed apologizing for he did not know what. And Old Beaver's likeness to Sally was suddenly staggering. He had not before noticed more than the superficial likeness of colouring and haphazard features, but now the glowing comfort of the man's presence, his strength and generosity, were so like Sally's that she seemed actually here with them. Seeing her there in her father, trying to come near to him in the person of her father as she had never tried to do in her own person, he felt suddenly closer to her than he had ever felt; closer than he had been able to feel to anyone for what seemed like a century, delivered at last from the hideous sense of isolation. Perhaps now he would be able to give as well as take; that had been the worst thing of all, the endless taking.... The release of the moment was so sudden that it stunned him, and he stood speechless with relief.... And all this because Old Beaver had suddenly turned friendly.

John Adair came to the rescue. He slipped his hand into his son's arm and propelled him up the path towards Ben, dancing with impatience on the doorstep. Yes, his son. Even if David remained in bondage to Nadine, never loved Sally, never married her, yet he was spiritually his son by virtue of that flash of insight that had come to him that day in the theatre, when he had seen him as the prototype of many and drawn his face with love and understanding; and even more because of this second moment of deep personal knowledge. This was what men craved for when they craved a son.

"Come on," implored poor Ben. "Oh *do* come *on!*"

– 2 –

Entirely unaware that in revealing David to Old Beaver as being made of the same stuff as himself he had precipitated a crisis, Ben conducted his elders to the store-room.

"There!" he said. "Illustration from some child's picture-book, my foot!"

Pausing to pull up the knees of his trousers, and nearly driving Ben mad by this sartorial caution, David folded himself up beneath the shelf to examine the phenomenon beneath it. John Adair, who suffered from rheumatism in his knees, waited for his verdict before deliberately courting unnecessary suffering.

"Might be worth investigating, I think," said David.

The coolness of his report infuriated Ben.

"*Might be!* Can't you see the rabbit?"

"Well, yes. Now you mention it there's something here that might be a rabbit."

John Adair sighed, and with loudly cracking joints crawled beneath the shelf. His reaction was far more satisfactory than David's. After a few muttered exclamations he exploded into sudden enthusiasm.

"By my beard, I believe the boy is right! But the darned shelf is in the way. Get the tool-box, Ben. Look lively!"

Ben dashed off for the tool-box, returning with it to find both men with their coats off, clearing the shelf of Nadine's jams and chutneys. For three hours they worked feverishly. They took all the bottles down to the kitchen, unfortunately breaking a few in the process, and removed the shelves from the wall; groaning as they got out the nails that had pierced right through the wallpaper to whatever was beneath it. "Sacrilege!" exclaimed John Adair. "Bloody sacrilege!" Then they set to work to remove what they could of the distemper and paper. It was easier than they had expected. The little room was damp, the distemper was already peeling off and the two layers of paper came away in solid strips. Beneath them damp stains and patches of paste spread a dingy film over what was below; but there was no doubt about it that what was below was buried treasure.

"Let it alone!" John Adair shouted at Ben, who was trying to peel off a patch of paste with his fingers. "Don't touch it, you young vandal! This filth must be got off with the proper stuff, if you don't want to harm the fresco. That's all we can do for now; but, by gad, we've done a good day's work. Look at it, you chaps. Look at it! Sixteenth century, at a rough guess. Floor to ceiling the whole way round. Look at that bit of colour there—the blue and the green. When we get that cleaned it will be as fresh as the day it was painted. I should say it's a wood or a garden. Now praised be God who has matched me with this hour."

"Is that shape there a chap on a horse?" asked David. "Gosh, what a find!"

"And look there!" cried Ben. "There's a cross there!"

"Bless the boy! Where?"

"There! On the east wall. That's where the altar would have been. This *was* a chapel."

They sat down on the pile of shelves, got their breath and stared incredulously. Until they could get the walls properly cleaned they would not know the full glory of their find; but that there was glory there they knew. They were like men staring at the shifting mists obscuring a heavenly landscape, seeing through it no more than shreds of colour, hints of celestial shape, yet aware the longer they looked that to see the whole was worth any price whatever that could be paid.

"And God knows there's enough here already." said John Adair gently. "Enough, in all conscience, to make a man glad he lived to see it."

"The more you look the more you see," said David. "Surely that's a man on a horse. A white horse, I think—or will be when he's clean. Dogs round him, perhaps? And I should say he's a dressy fellow. That red and blue is where his coat would be."

Ben gave a sudden shout.

"It's the white deer! The one in the alcove! The white deer holding up the cross in his antlers!"

"Where?" demanded David.

"There! Behind the altar!"

"The wish is father to the thought," murmured John Adair.

"No, Sir. Look there. You can see his neck, his pointy face. He's turned his head to look at the man, and the man has reined in his horse to look at the deer. The horse was galloping a minute ago. Look at his legs. He's been halted suddenly, and his hoofs are slipping on the wet grass of the wood. The animals and birds, they're just going about their business in the wood, not taking any notice. No, look at that old dog! He's bowed his head. He's worshipping. So's the man, I think, though his head's high. No, he's not looking at the deer; he's looking at the cross."

His elders, looking intently, could make out little of all this.

"Since you say so," murmured John Adair. "I've not my glasses."

"I think he's right," said David slowly.

"I don't doubt it. His long-distance vision is extremely good."
From somewhere far away in the house there came a faint hail. "I
suppose we now let the family in on this?"

"No!" said Ben sharply.

He couldn't bear the thought of everybody knowing about this
place. If Father or Mother, or Malony, or someone, were to call the
walls a dirty mess he would murder them.

"No help for it," said David. "What's your mother going to say
when she comes home and finds jam-pots all over the kitchen floor?"

"Oh, gosh, if it just didn't happen to be the store-room!" groaned
Ben.

David got up quietly, and went out of the room. The hail had
been George's, but he thought he had heard Sally's voice, too. He
ran down the turret stairs and went through the kitchen to the hall.
George was stretched in a chair puffing at his pipe, relaxed and
happy after a very pleasant bout of physical exercise in the company
of a pretty and appreciative girl. That Sally liked him, and had no
hesitation in showing that she did, was a source of satisfaction to
him. He could not, he thought, be quite such a dull bore as Nadine's
patient tolerance always made him feel that he was. Sally in her
golden-brown tweeds had an armful of spindleberries that she was
just going to arrange in a blue pot. She had not known that David
was coming today, and, taken by surprise, she took a few quick steps
towards him before she could stop herself, the joy blazing out in her
eyes, her cheeks as pink as the berries, her eagerness like that of her
father three hours ago. Had she always lit up like this for him, and
he had not noticed it, David wondered, or had his moment of liberation set her free, too? Had she always loved him, and he had not
known it until her father's huge kindness had brought her so close?
He was a blind, self-centred fool. Regardless of George, he went to
her and took the lapels of her coat between his hands. He had to do
something with his hands to keep his arms from going round her in
gratitude and compunction: gratitude for the sound normality of
her, the healthiness, the child-likeness, that had companioned him
through these past horrible weeks of isolation and brought him to
that final moment of release out there in the garden; compunction
that he had not seen until this moment what she was, what she had
done and what she gave. Could he give, too? He didn't know. She
made no demand as she stood there smiling at him; she did not

understand the meaning of the word investment; that was the glory of her. He had always thought that there was no more odious position for a man than to be loved by a woman whom he could not love in return; and bound to Nadine as he had been for so long, and afflicted with the curse of his good looks, he had several times found himself in that position; yet with Sally it was somehow not odious. He could love the gift of her love just as he would have loved any other gift of hers, because it was a free gift and rebounded back upon her, to her own enrichment. Yet a wrench of pain went through him because of her pain; if he could not now get free and come alive and whole for Sally, he would hate himself until he died.

"We've something to show you," he said quickly. "We've found something—your father and Ben and I. Come along and see it. You, too, Uncle George. Glad it's you and Sally to see it first."

George heaved himself to his feet. Shrouded in tobacco smoke, he had noticed nothing. David put his hand into Sally's arm and hurried her along. She came laughing. She did not quite know what had happened; except that David was suddenly nearer than he had ever been, and that the whole world shone with clear light. They ran up the turret stairs, George lumbering after.

"There!" said David, at the store-room door, and took his hand from her arm.

While the others gazed not at the frescoes but at her, she stood in the centre of the little room unaware of them, still pink-cheeked and bright-eyed, still unconsciously holding the armful of spindleberries, and gazed about her with adoring wonder; not amazed exactly, because that supreme joy of childhood, the expectation of gloriously unlikely things likely to happen at any moment, was still hers, but yet at the same time deliciously surprised to find the expected unlikeliness quite so unlikely as all this.

"There's the Chevalier on his horse, riding through Knyghtwood," she said. "It's rather like the picture I told you about, David—the one I saw somewhere, but couldn't remember. I used to see the wood behind Ben, and then I saw it behind you, that day in Knyghtwood. You were looking at a kingfisher. What's he looking at? Could it be the twins' Fairy Person with the Horns?"

The voice of George made itself heard.

"What on earth are you talking about, Sally, and what the dickens is Nadine going to say to all this mess?"

"All this mess, General, is, I believe, a most priceless sixteenth-century fresco," said John Adair, still sitting upon the pile of shelves, and now smoking a pipe to calm himself. "Of course we'll need to get the thing cleaned up before we can be certain about it, but I shall be very much surprised to find myself mistaken. And, Sally, I'm ashamed of you. You have visited the National Gallery with me from infancy up—in smocks, in pigtails, in your first fur coat, as child, girl and woman—and gazed twenty times, if once, at Pisanello's Placidus, and yet for all you apparently remember of the thing you might never have set eyes on it. This fresco portrays the same story as Pisanello's masterpiece. It was a very popular subject for artists in the Middle Ages. You should all of you have seen that at once. The ignorance of all so-called educated people appals me."

"When did *you* see it, Sir?" grinned Ben. "A sort of gleam came into your eye when Sally said about having seen David as Placidus, and that was only two minutes ago."

"Hold your tongue, boy. Sit down, General. It isn't as uncomfortable as it looks. These were once the store-room shelves."

"So I see," said George heavily.

It was the only thing he did see. It had taken him and Malony a long time to put those shelves up. The walls looked just a mess to him, and of what they were all talking about he had no idea.

"Who *was* Placidus, by the way?" enquired David.

"It was a pity you neglected to conduct Ben round the National Gallery. If you had, you might have noticed him. But then, again, you might not." John Adair, puffing out spirals of smoke, was enjoying himself. "None of your generation seems to notice anything unless it explodes. You've probably been to Wells Cathedral and taken no note of the carved figures of the saints upon the west front, and to Chartres Cathedral and retained no memory of its windows, and to Abbeville and not even noticed that there were any windows, and to the Church of St. Eustace in Paris—"

"Eustace!" interrupted David. "Pisanello's Vision of St. Eustace. You put me off the scent by calling him Placidus."

"His mother gave him the excellent name of Placidus. He only called himself Eustace when he took religion. Just another example of that deplorable loss of aesthetic taste which so often unfortunately accompanies conversion. Eustace—dreadful name! One thinks at once of a parson's dog-collar. Now I'll tell you about Placidus—"

"You will not," interrupted Sally firmly, sitting down suddenly on the floor. "No one tells a story worse than you do. It's coming back to me, and I'll tell it. I don't remember it all, but I remember what matters."

"Go on," said Ben, and slid to the floor beside her.

David joined George and John Adair on the pile of shelves and watched the two of them together. Sitting there on the floor, there did not seem much difference in their ages; they were the child who tells a story and the child who listens, all down the ages. The light was fading now, and in the dimness it seemed to him that all things flowed together: past and present, love and agony, life and death became fused into one timeless moment of longing—the longing that linked together so many journeys, quests, martyrdoms, making them all one, the oneness the object of them, the goal, the crown.

– 3 –

"He lived in Italy," said Sally the child, telling a tale to Ben the child. "He was a Roman noble, a great huntsman, a rich fairy-tale knight, riding out from the pages of an illuminated missal on his great white horse with its gay trappings, his spurs on his heels, his hunting-horn slung over his shoulder, his hunting-knife in his belt and his spear in his hand, his garments all bright and gay and richly furred, his dogs bounding about him. And one day, in this beauty and this pomp, he went hunting in the forest outside Rome—the dark forest where there were wild beasts in plenty for a brave man to slay, boars and bears as well as the deer and the swift hares. But it was not only because of the good hunting that Placidus rode through the Roman forest: he rode in pursuit of something else besides excitement and danger, something unknown, to which his tongue could give no name and of which his imagination could form no image. And he rode alone because the huntsman of the unknown must follow a path narrow as the confines of his own body, lonely as his own pain, dark as his own ignorance, and his way is his own way, and cannot be shared with another. But though the forest was dark and dangerous, and the path narrow, it was full of gleams and flashes of beauty that were as candles lit along the way, beckoning Placidus on and on to that something beyond of whose existence he had no proof except the fact of his own journeying, but which he knew he would surely recognize under whatever guise his quarry would choose to show itself to him at his journey's end.

"And so he rode, and was glad of the flowers that were singing-bright beneath the forest trees, of the melodious birds in the branches, of the streams and the pale stretches of still water; and of the running that could not be seen of skipping beasts. The day wore on, and still Placidus rode he did not know where, after he knew not what. And then, at last, he saw it: a white deer, the most perfect creature he had ever seen, with great branching antlers, the magnificent head reared proudly, the splendid body poised for flight. For a moment the flashing eyes met his, commanding him, and then the creature was off, silver hoofs spurning the ground, the perfect body a white flash of speed, the antlers swaying this way and that, yet never entangled in the branches, beckoning, challenging, defying. One clear call did Placidus sound upon his horn, and then he, too, was off, his dogs after him, his horse stretched out to full gallop, with great hoofs pounding on the forest floor. Placidus bent low in the saddle, whispering threats and cajolements, reckless of time or place, life or death, knowing only that he must follow that deer until the end. And so the wild chase went on. But he could not catch up with the creature; it was always a little ahead. The horse was near foundering, his own breath came in gasps, some of the dogs had fallen behind, but still he went on. And then the ground rose steeply and the rocks of a mighty mountain towered up before the failing sight of horse and rider. The deer bounded up it, swift yet unhurried, as though winged. But Placidus could not follow. He reined in his horse, lest it dash itself to death against the rocks, and bowed his head in shame. He, the unconquerable huntsman, was beaten at last.

"And at that moment of his shame the miracle happened. The deer stopped and swung round to face him, lifting its proud head, and the antlers formed themselves into a gleaming cross, with a crucified Figure upon it—that strange symbol of the Christians which he had seen many times, and sondered at for a moment or two; and then had turned aside and gone on his way, thinking no more about it. But now he could not turn aside, for the deer, the vision sent to him, had led him directly to this end. His way was blocked by this impassable mountain and the challenge of this cross. There was only one thing he could do, and he did it. He leaped from his horse and fell upon his knees. And a voice cried out loudly, echoing through the forest, 'Placidus, why dost thou attempt to injure me? I am Jesus Christ whom thou hast long served in ignorance. Dost thou believe in Me?' And Placidus answered, 'Lord, I believe.' The voice came again, the words spoken this time very low in his own soul, as though in warning, 'Many sorrows shalt thou endure for My sake, many temptations will assail thee; but be of good courage, I will always be with thee.' A thrill of dismay went through Placidus, yet he did not hesitate, for he knew that he was not yet at his journey's end; as he had followed the vision of the deer to the vision of the cross, so he must follow the vision of the cross to something beyond again. What it was he still did not know, but, in spite of the fear, he did know that to attain at last he would give all that he had, down to the last drop of his blood. 'Lord, I am content,' he said. 'Only give me patience to endure all things for Thee.' When at last he looked up again, the deer with the crucifix between its antlers had disappeared and night was falling in the forest."

"Not so bad, Sally," said her father as she paused. "Though I dare say I could have done better."

"It sounds like St. Paul on the Damascus road," said Ben. "Go on, please, Sally. What happened after?"

"Very much like St. Paul. Just the same pattern—it's always the same pattern. He did give all that he had. He lost his wealth and his great position, and in the end was burned to death in Rome by order of the Emperor Hadrian. There are lots of stories about his life as a Christian, but I don't remember them very well. It's the first bit that came back so vividly, all in a rush, because of this place."

"Funny thing, memory," said David. "Like a store-room full of cupboards. Something makes one of the doors fly open, and out falls a lot of stuff you didn't even know you had."

"I know perfectly well," said a clear and beautiful but icy voice, "that I had more in this store-room than is now upon the kitchen floor. There are four pots missing. Have you smashed them?"

It was Nadine standing in the doorway, her hands in the pockets of the long cherry-red coat that suited her better than any other garment she had. She was hatless, her dark head held proudly, her face white with weariness and anger. She looked beautiful, but lonely and desolate. All his old love for her, all that had been between them for so long, seemed to surge over David in a wave of anguish. How long had he known Sally? Just a few weeks. And Nadine had been to him the only woman in the world for as many years. He jumped up and went to her.

"Nadine, do forgive us. We'd no right to pull the place to pieces like this while you were out. It was insufferable."

This was an aspect of the affair that had not hitherto occurred to anyone else; except George. Now they saw, to their shame, that there was something in it, and gathered round her full of explanation and apology. They were dreadfully sorry. They might at least have waited for her. But they had been so excited. They knew there was a frightful mess. But didn't she think it was worth it? Had she ever seen anything lovelier than these painted walls?

Nadine, glancing round the walls, saw nothing but a vague mess. Her eyes met her husband's, and saw them hot with anger. For her sake against these others.... She smiled a little; at George only, feeling queerly close to him.

"Well, there it is," she said, with a hard control that deflated the sinners far more completely than if she had lost her temper. "What's done is done, and I expect what you have found will turn out very interesting. It's past five o'clock, and you must all be dying for tea. Annie-Laurie is just taking it to the drawing-room. I'll ring for her to bring me mine in my sitting-room. I've got a bit of a headache."

And she turned and left them, her slim, bright figure mounting up the turret staircase like a tall angel going away into heaven and leaving the earthbound to their doom.

– 4 –

She went into her sitting-room and shut the door, but she did not sit down. With her hands still in her pockets she stood looking out of the window. The brief spell of sunshine was over, and a mist had blown in from the sea. She shivered, looking out at the cold, opaque greyness. She felt as though she were looking at some dismal grey stone mountain. She had come to a dead end. There was a light step outside and a tap on the door. She thought it was Ben, come to apologize yet once more. She wanted only to be alone, but her past carelessness over Ben was still a reproach to her, and in these days she could deny him nothing.

"Come in," she called.

But it was David who came in, almost the David of seven years ago, glowing with sudden re-born love for her, his usually ready tongue unable to give the form of words to the shamed turmoil of his thoughts.

"Nadine—Nadine—I'm so sorry—"

It was in her hands. This was her chance. He was in a mood of reaction. She could bind him to her all over again, or she could set him free. It was not so difficult, for her choice had been made last night. Step by step she had come to this; it was only the last step of many. She moved back, her hands still in her pockets.

"There's no need to apologize, David," she said coldly.

"There's every need. To make a mess of your house without your knowledge, in your absence, was an unpardonable thing to do. And it was my fault. Ben and Old Beaver were blind with enthusiasm. It was I who should have called a halt. I've behaved like a cad to you, Nadine."

And in more ways than one, said his shamed and loving look.

"Nonsense," she said curtly. "What a child you are, David! You look like a naughty little boy caught by his mother stealing sweets from the cupboard. I was only annoyed for the moment about those smashed jam-pots." She stifled a yawn. "I'm dead beat, that's all. Being shampooed always tires me to death. Tomorrow I shall be as keen about the frescoes as you and Ben, and glad that both of you have the interest of them. Tommy will be excited, too, when he comes."

She classed him with her children; then she turned to her mirror, taking her hands from her pockets and giving her beautiful hair a few deft touches. He saw her face in the mirror, apparently absorbed in the result of the shampoo, with a little twist about the mouth that his humiliation read as contempt. A major operation, even though one may have desired it, is never pleasant, and he went rigid with pain. She, too, saw him in the mirror, and it was all she could do not to turn round and hold out her arms to him. Instead she turned away and took off her coat.

"It's all right, my dear," she said, in a tone of voice that relegated him now to the status of the twins. "Such a fuss about nothing!" She yawned again. "I'm dying for a cup of tea. If Annie-Laurie isn't available yet, send my dear old George along with one, will you?"

Without a word he went away and left her. She groped her way to the little arm-chair and sat down. It was done. She had denied. It was over.... No, it wasn't.... That was where she had gone wrong before. There was never a last step, but only one more step. Nothing is ever over, it is all a continuing process. Lying back in her arm-chair, she shut her eyes and made her submission to the process; it seemed somehow a personal submission to a personal power, a reorientation of herself.... Yes, she said.... Well, what next?... That hateful poem she had read in John Adair's room came to her mind. She had denied. Now she had to go out into that detestable wood and learn to laugh.

13

– 1 –

*C*HE WINTER WAS UPON THEM, with gales and rain and driving mists from the sea, with now and again a calm, still day just touched with frost, when the blue egg-shell sky, the last gold on the trees and the green of the rain-washed grass seemed, in spite of their brilliance, to be without substance, lovely, but transitory as the spiders' webs that in the early mornings stretched their sparkling filaments from branch to branch in the bare apple orchard.

Knyghtwood, though the gales had stripped away most of its leaves, had not lost its fascination for Ben and the twins. Indeed, its spell seemed deeper than before. The trees all had faces now, the twins said, and fingers and toes. They dug their toes in hard when the wind blew, and stretched up their arms to the sky, and pulled down the clouds with their long, grey fingers, and made purple cloaks out of them that they wrapped about their bare limbs when the night fell coldly.

An old white owl had taken up his residence just inside the wood, and at dusk he would sit on top of the green gate and stare benignly at the Herb of Grace, as though through the night he intended to have it in his special care. In flight he was like a great moth, heavy and lumbering, as though his wings were burdened with the weight of dreams, yet his glimmering body made no sound in the air. The small birds were silent now, except for gurgling conversations beneath the bushes, but the owl, when he blundered about the house in the night, had a very reassuring kind of hoot, like a watchman's cry of "All's Well," and the gulls were vociferous as they drifted and tossed over the river. When the house-boat was packed up for the winter Annie-Laurie had taken her bells from the top of the mast, lest they should tarnish in the salt winds, but the place of their chiming was taken by the rustle of the dry sedges. There was always music about the Herb of Grace, and always a drifting beauty. The holiday season was over, and not many strangers came to the inn. There would be an influx of visitors again in the spring, but for the present it was quiet. Those who lived there felt that for the time being they had strangely lost touch with the outside world and all its terror and pain. Their present concern was with the house and with each other. They had some pattern to make here in this place, and they must weave together their hopes and fears, their loves and joys, about the central of the Chapel in the heart of the house.

The Chapel was the important thing just now. A friend of John Adair's, an expert, had been down to see the frescoes and had shown them what to do, and now John Adair and David, Ben and Sally, worked increasingly at the restoration of the walls, removing the dirt of ages from the glowing colours below. The frescoes were incredibly lovely. The background of the wood had been painted with a lavishness and eagerness that were astonishing, but, to Ben's delight, the artist's perspective and anatomy were as poor as his own, and he had bothered no more than a child would have done about any kind of likelihood. He had had no hesitation whatever in expressing his passionate love of trees, birds, animals, butterflies and flowers in such a welter of them as took the breath away. He had splashed the trees of Knyghtwood on to the walls in all the splendour of their summer foliage, the knotted strength of their roots holding firmly to a green, mossy earth sown thickly with all his favourite flowers, bees and butterflies hovering over them and sipping their honey, regardless of season or soil or habitat or anything whatever, except a desire to paint, for the glory of God, every flower and insect that God had made that he could manage to get into the space at his disposal.

It was Ben's guess that he had started with the flowers and butterflies, and then found himself left with no space on the floor of the wood for the birds and animals. But he had not let this worry him. Up above, in every small break in the foliage of the trees, where one expected to see a patch of sky, one saw instead a little leaf-framed picture of an animal or bird enjoying itself. One showed a gull in flight, another a swan sailing on a patch of blue water. There was a deer feeding, a little doe fast asleep, a kingfisher diving for a fish, a robin building a nest, an owl in contemplation, a badger's holt with the back view of the badger going in, a rabbit's burrow with the front view of the rabbit coming out, a squirrel eating nuts, a field mouse sitting up on its hind legs and washing its ears, and as many others as there were frames in the trees in which to put them. There was no sky anywhere, because there was no space in which to put it; but the whole scene shone with so clear and lovely a light, so tranquil and yet so glowing, that one knew that the hot blue of a midsummer day was passing to golden sunset, with a breath of coolness stirring in the wood and the birds' voices rising in a paean of praise.

Through the wood rode Placidus on his white horse with its golden trappings, Placidus in his poppy-red jerkin and blue cloak, with his dogs about him. Any danger that the brilliance of the wood might have dwarfed the splendour of Placidus was got over by making the man, the horse and the dogs bigger than life-size in comparison with the wood. And there was another striking contrast between the figures of the story and the background against which they moved. The flowers and all the little creatures up in the trees had a strange stillness. They weren't going anywhere. They had reached their moment of completion and stopped there. But the dogs were stretched out in full chase, the horse, suddenly reined in from the gallop, was pawing the ground; Placidus, though for the moment still in awe and wonder, was taut as a bent bow; the whole group was vibrant with eagerness and urgency, a complete contrast both to the stillness of the wood and the stillness of the images upon the east wall.

It was a shock to turn from the jostling brilliance of the wood to the austere splendour of the east wall. The great immobile figure of the deer, white and shining, holding the crucifix aloft between its antlers, had behind it no flowery background, but the bare slope of a purple mountain. Though it was still day in the wood, night was falling on the mountain; darkness veiled it, and far up beyond the topmost peak a few stars shone. But they gave little light. The stag glowed by virtue of the light that shone from the Figure on the cross, a radiance so bright that the actual outline of the Figure was lost in it. The stillness of those images was quite different in quality from the stillness of the wood. It was the stillness not of completion, but of depth. Looking at them was like looking over the edge of a boat down into a calm sea; one knew that far beyond the limit of one's vision were unimaginable things.

And all this had been hidden for years beneath layers of dirty wallpaper. Their awe deepened the longer they worked, and their happiness, too. The thought of this glory, waiting here for so long for rebirth, hidden but safe, was invigorating in these days of anxiety and fear. It was a prophecy, and as such they hugged it to them. Everyone seemed to feel the same. Lucilla and Margaret and Hilary were constantly jolting over in the Ford to see how they were getting on and to gloat over a clump of primroses freshly disinterred, or a butterfly sunning itself upon a clump of pansies. Malony and Annie-Laurie, though they said little and visited the Chapel seldom, looked at it when they did come with a queer sort of frustrated hunger, as though it were offering them something that they did not yet know how to take. The twins were perpetually underfoot and a terrible nuisance, and Jill, summoned to fetch them away, marvelled afresh every time that Auntie Rose's mother-in-law's mother-in-law, who was suspected of having pasted up the first wallpaper, should not have realized that the dirty walls held this wealth beneath the dirt. George and Nadine put in no work upon the walls, and of all the household were the most detached in their attitude towards the frescoes; George because he and Malony had worked damned hard making and putting up the shelves, and he could not help feeling that in their usefulness and fitness for their purpose they had been just as good a thing as those uncanny pictures; and Nadine because she was living now in a queer, exhausted, detached state, her chief emotion a quite unreasonable hatred of woods.

– 2 –

It was on the day when a telephone message had summoned Lucilla, Margaret and Hilary to come and inspect the latest discovery—a green toad with a jewel in his head sitting on a mossy stone and laughing—that Hilary decided to call on Malony and Annie-Laurie in their new establishment. It was, he knew, their half-day, but he hoped that the business of settling in would have kept them from going out. He had the feeling that Malony and Annie-Laurie, George and Nadine, were just at present loose ends at the Herb of Grace; they weren't as yet getting properly woven into the pattern. John Adair and Ben, David and Sally were, he felt, unconsciously working out a satisfactory relationship with each other as they worked at the walls, but the other four, not working at the walls, were not. He was too scared of Nadine to attempt any weaving in where she was concerned, even had he known certainly what was the matter with her, and he did not, though he was prepared to hazard a shrewd guess; and George, he felt, would get automatically tucked in if she was. But Malony and Annie-Laurie did not scare him in the least. The likes of Malony he had known in and out and through and through during the First World War, and Annie-Laurie he had sized up in the first five minutes of their acquaintance as just a gallant girl in a bad mess. He was deeply attracted by gallantry, and a mess was a thing that he always snuffed from afar, as an old war-horse snuffs the scent of powder.

Having duly admired the jewelled and laughing toad, he quietly absented himself from the company in the Chapel and hobbled down the turret stairs to the kitchen. The two old dogs, Pooh-Bah and the Bastard, had accompanied the party from Damerosehay. Pooh-Bah remained with Lucilla, so that the consideration and loving care that always enveloped her should envelope him also; but the Bastard, although he was feeling his age today, wheezed down the stairs after Hilary. He felt purpose in Hilary's movements, and he always liked to go with his family whenever they were doing anything important. He had an obscure feeling that if he didn't they might make some mistake.

Jill was in the kitchen ironing, with the twins in a couple of large cardboard boxes under the table. Hilary smiled at her, with immense pleasure in the sight of her, for it was his opinion that she was as near to God as any woman of his acquaintance except Lucilla. She smiled back with simple friendliness, for she thought the Reverend Hilary was a dear old soul; though how he could be the son of Lady Eliot, so stout and homely looking as he was, beat her.

"Ironing," said Hilary, sniffing appreciatively. "Best smell in the world, barring fried sausages—pre-war."

"Yes, Sir," smiled Jill. "How's your rheumatism today?"

"It's lumbago," said Hilary. "It switched over in the night. I like variety. It keeps one young."

"Try salt, Sir," said Jill—"kitchen salt warmed in the oven, folded in warm flannel and then applied to the afflicted part. My Auntie Rose always did that for my uncle. He was a great sufferer before the end."

"Was he?" said Hilary, and, seeing Jill disposed for conversation, he propped himself up against the dresser and lit his pipe. Malony and Annie-Laurie could wait for five minutes. An ability to let things wait for five minutes was part of the general peacefulness of his state, and if it irritated his family, it commended itself very highly to his gossip-loving country parishioners. "Poor chap! What was it at the end?"

"The *doctor* called it peritonitis," said Jill.

"And what was it really?" asked Hilary, aware of the strong conviction of the country mind that it always knows better than the doctor.

"Blackberry tart. He would have it."

"After Michaelmas?"

"Yes. After Michaelmas."

Hilary shook his head sadly. The devil, as is well known, overlooks blackberries at Michaelmas.

"A pity," he said. "A nice chap. I met him once. I was sorry when he died."

"It had to be," said Jill philosophically.

"I hope your aunt is happy with her daughter-in-law?" asked Hilary.

"No, Sir. She don't get on with her like she thought she would. Edith, she's more managing than what Auntie thought she was. And she's a poor cook, too, and won't be taught. And it just about gets Auntie down to see Sydney (that's her son, Edith's husband) not fed as he should be. And he takes Edith's part, of course. And then Auntie thought she'd enjoy taking it easy after working so hard all her life; but she don't."

"Why doesn't she come back here and take on the cooking?" enquired Hilary. "It's far too much for Mrs. Eliot."

Jill placed her iron carefully on the stand and her beautiful grey-green eyes fixed themselves in astonished delight upon Hilary's face.

"Well, there now, Sir! I never thought of it!"

Hilary suddenly fell into a panic. He had spoken on impulse. Would Nadine and Auntie Rose, as past and present mistress of the Herb of Grace, get on?

"It's not as though Auntie Rose had ever cared much about the place," said Jill, following the drift of his thought. "She never did, apart from the kitchen. She would have, I expect, for everyone loves the Herb of Grace, but you see, Sir, for the first twenty years of her married life her mother-in-law lived here with her, and that got her to feel somehow that her home was never rightly hers."

"Allergic to in-laws," murmured Hilary.

"Give her a free hand in the kitchen, and one of the big attics where she could put her suite and the brass bedstead, and she'd be happy as a queen, and come to love the place as much as the rest of us. Mrs. Eliot would give her a free hand in the kitchen. Mrs Eliot is like that, Sir. She never interferes."

And Jill's eyes left Hilary's face and glanced lovingly downwards. Nadine left the twins as completely in her care as though they were her own. Following Jill's glance, Hilary became aware for the first time of the completely silent, immobile occupants of the cardboard boxes.

"What are they?" he asked with interest.

"I'm not quite sure, Sir," said Jill. "Whatever it is, it's nice and quiet so far."

The grandfather clock struck three, there was a piercing shriek, and the two cardboard boxes ricocheted from beneath the table and sped around the room, roaring, whistling and screaming as they went. The cat Smith, asleep on the hearth, leaped to the window-seat for safety, and Mary, also present, fled beneath the dresser. The Bastard, lying near the open door to the porch, gave a half-turn over, like a porpoise, and rolled through it into safety.

"The three o'clock express from Paddington," hazarded Hilary.

He lingered a moment or two, astonished beyond measure at the way the twins, merely by the oscillation of their small bodies within them, kept the cardboard boxes in motion. Then, further conversation being impossible, he smiled at Jill and went out into the stable yard.

– 3 –

"Grand old place," he thought, pausing to look about him.

It was a fine, still day, with the sky faintly veiled in mist, so that the suffused sunlight fell silverly. The cushions of moss were emerald between the cobbles, and the garnet-coloured walls and the steep, crinkled, amber roofs of the outbuildings glowed with a heartening warmth. Beyond the silver trunks of the old apple-tree there was a violet haze of shadow behind the bronze and gold of a few late chrysanthemums. There was a bonfire burning somewhere, its pungent scent mixing with the smell of the wet chrysanthemums, the scent of ironing from the kitchen, and the smell of a baking cake drifting down from the open door up there—the door that opened on the Malonys' balcony.

Hilary crossed the stable yard with as much alacrity as his lumbago permitted, the Bastard lumbering after him. He had lunched early and inadequately upon powdered egg, tough bacon and cheese that in pre-war days would have been relegated to the mouse-trap. He had a most faithful and devoted housekeeper, but she was too old to be able to think of anything to eat except powdered egg and bacon and cheese, once the microscopic weekly joint was finished; and then just powdered egg and cheese when the bacon was finished, and then, when the cheese was finished, just powdered egg. The Vicarage cakes were bought from the baker, and fell into chalk while you looked at them. Hilary, with the Bastard lumbering slowly after him, laid a hand upon the beautiful wrought-iron hand-rail and pulled himself up the old worn stone steps with lips compressed by pain, and nostrils twitching with the titillation of the aroma that floated down to him from above. Half-way up he paused to get his breath, prayed God to forgive him for the greediness that he was not at all sure was not growing upon him with age, prayed for guidance in the task that lay before him, prayed that he might get up the rest of these darned steps without disaster, mopped his face, and went on again with one hand on the rail and the other unconsciously clutching his back. The Bastard, faint but persevering, followed.

He was in poor shape by the time he got to the open front door of the Malony flat and found himself confronting a coldly furious Annie-Laurie. Visitors at her winter quarters were as unwelcome as they had been on the house-boat. Entrenched in her home, wherever it might be, she was like a lion in its den. She must feel safe there, or she just could not bear it.

Hilary understood this, after a glance at her face. Naturally, that was how she would feel, and he had been an old fool, he told himself, not to have thought of that before.

"Forgive me, Annie-Laurie," he panted. "I thought I'd like to come and pay a call on you and Malony, and it never occurred to me that I ought to have waited for an invitation." He paused to get his breath again. "The fact of the matter is, you know, that when you've been Vicar of the same country parish for half a lifetime, as I have, your parishioners get used to you blundering in and out uninvited, like an old dog, and they don't let it put them out at all."

He paused again, looking at her comically and apologetically.

"And I won't let it put me out either," said Annie-Laurie, with sudden generosity. Really, he did look like an old dog, panting there upon her doorstep; they were a couple, he and the old grey, woolly creature wheezing at his heels. And they were both in a bad way after the climb. Ridiculous of them both to have attempted it, but since they had, there was nothing she could do except let them in to sit down a bit before they climbed down again. "Come in, both of you," she said, standing away from the door.

"Both?" enquired Hilary, and, his own shortness of breath having now subsided somewhat, he became aware of the noise like a steam-engine that the Bastard was making behind him. "Poor old Bastard! I'd no idea he'd come, too. Now, what induced him to come up all this way after me? He's no idea what he can do, or can't do, at his age. Must be deeply attached to you, Annie-Laurie."

"I'll give him a drink of water," said Annie-Laurie. "Yes, he likes me. I love dogs, and they know it. This one's a dear old mix-up, isn't he? Mostly Welsh sheep-dog, I think."

Hilary thought the wish must be father to the thought. He himself had seen no signs of Welsh ancestry in the Bastard. He lowered himself thankfully into the nearest chair and watched her as she filled a blue bowl with water for the Bastard. When he had finished she spread a little red rug before the fire and settled him there, sitting on her heels beside him and rubbing him gently behind the ears. He let out a gusty sigh of contentment and dropped his head against her knee. Hilary perceived that the Bastard must have known what he was doing when he came along, too. His presence was undoubtedly having a very softening effect upon Annie-Laurie.

Hilary looked about him. The genius of Malony had made a delightful flat out of the old place. The kitchen-sitting-room was in the middle, and the two bedrooms opened out of it to either side. The wood partitions were only plain deal boards, but they and the plain, rough doors had been painted the same colour as the fine old raftered roof overhead, and they did not look incongruous. An old outhouse that had fallen into ruin had provided Malony with enough beautiful garnet-coloured bricks to build a fireplace, where a log fire was burning. To one side was a basket full of logs, and on the other side a home-made bookcase with a few books in it. There was a pretty old gate-legged table, a few old chairs, a Welsh dresser with flowered china upon it, an oil cooking-stove, gay curtains at the windows and cushions on the window-seats. The floor had been stained to match the rafters and was bare except for two cherry-coloured rugs.

"It's a pretty room, Annie-Laurie," said Hilary gently.

Annie-Laurie smiled at him.

"Yes. The furniture in the house-boat is all part of it, fastened in, so Mrs. Eliot gave us the table and chairs and the dresser and stove. And the furniture in our rooms, too. It's all old. She got it at some place she knows of in London. Mrs. Eliot has been very good to me."

"She's very fond of you, Annie-Laurie—like everyone else."

Annie-Laurie gently lifted the Bastard's head from her knee and got to her feet. Her face, relaxed and girlishly happy as she petted the Bastard, looked suddenly old again. She moved restlessly to the dresser and began to take down cups and saucers and plates.

"You'd like a cup of tea," she said.

"Oughtn't we to wait for Malony?" enquired Hilary.

"He's gone to Radford. He said he wouldn't be back till late. I don't know what he's doing."

She had her back to Hilary, but from the curtness of her tone he judged that Malony had not betaken himself to Radford with her approval.

"Had you put that cake in the oven a bit earlier he wouldn't have gone," he said.

"It's just about done." She looked back at him over her shoulder, smiling a little anxiously. "But it'll be all spongy and hot."

"Elderly though I am, and much afflicted with various infirmities, I thank Heaven that they do not include digestive weakness," said Hilary fervently. "I am happy to tell you, Annie-Laurie, that no cake is ever too spongy or too hot for me."

Annie-Laurie laughed outright. He really was the most comical old cove. It was just a gossip that he wanted—a gossip and a bit of cake; and perhaps to get away from the somewhat rarified atmosphere that existed inside the Herb of Grace these days, with everyone except the General and Mrs. Eliot gone mad over those painted walls. Now that she had ascertained what he wanted she was suddenly happy and at ease with him. Comic though he was, he was pleasant to be with. One felt that, whatever his past troubles, he had come through them. He had the peacefulness of a ship drawing near to the harbour and entering it gently with slight headway on.

While she boiled the kettle, cut bread and butter, took the cake out of the oven and laid the table, Hilary chatted amiably about dogs, but behind his thick glasses his short-sighted, steady grey eyes did not miss the personal details of this room. There was a bunch of prettily shaped brass bells hanging from the central beam. There were pots of beautifully arranged autumn berries on the window-sills. The books in the bookcase included the poems of Yeats, several of the dramatic works of Ibsen, Barrie, J. M. Synge and Sean O' Casey, the poems and most of the novels of Mary Webb.

"Tea's ready," said Annie-Laurie.

Hilary enjoyed his tea. He ate slowly, talking easily and amusingly meanwhile, telling Annie-Laurie tales of the country folk in his parish, repeating bits of folk-lore, telling her things about the birds and beasts. He was rewarded by seeing her cheeks glow and her eyes shine softly as his apparently casual talk reached down to what, from David's talk of her, he had guessed to be the roots of her being. She began to talk a little, too, not saying much, but revealing here and there by a knowledgeable word that he had guessed right, and that she was countrybred.

"The hills of Shropshire?" he asked her gently. "The hills that look towards Wales? Were you brought up there?"

She looked up, startled. "Why—yes—?"

"You look mountain born," he told her, smiling. "You like Welsh sheep-dogs, and I see from your books that you like Mary Webb."

"Actually, I'm Welsh," said Annie-Laurie.

Hilary nodded. He had thought so. Something in her voice. And she was a typical Celt.

"Walking tours were my favourite holidays in my young days," said Hilary. "Not that you'd think it to look at me now. I tramped all over Shropshire; it was my favourite English county. I saw a lot of Wales, too."

He went on talking, speaking of this place and that, watching her eyes light up when he mentioned a place she particularly loved. Gradually she began to drop a few scraps of information. She had been born on a farm, and had spent her childhood in the hills, the only girl in a family of boys, having fun with their dogs and animals. She especially loved the sheep, and their old shepherd used to let her help him at the lambing season. He gave her a bunch of little bells—Morris dancer's bells that had been in his family for generations, and sometimes for fun she used to fasten them round the necks of the lambs. She was very happy while she was still a child; not so happy when she grew older and realized how hard a man her father was, and how her mother feared him. After her mother had died she had not been happy at home any more, and had fought hard to get away.

"Win a scholarship?" asked Hilary.

"Yes.... Will you have another cup of tea?"

"Thank you," said Hilary.

It was his third, and he didn't want it, but anything to delay the moment of his departure. The threads were gradually coming into his hands, he felt, but it was difficult going. At the last "yes" she had shut up like a clam. So she'd won a scholarship. Gone to a good school. Had a good education. Among other girls, away from teasing brothers, she'd discovered her gifts—her singing voice, her beauty, her dramatic talent. Restless, fiery, ambitious, feeding on the Celtic poets and dramatists, she would have aimed high, but, as a farmer's daughter, would have known the value of hard work. She had worked as a dispenser, David had told him. That must have come after school, but it wouldn't have contented her for long; but she would have slaved at it, saving money to help with her dramatic training. The evidence of her books made the next step obvious.

"Was it repertory after that?" he asked gently.

He'd gone too far. She was too courteous a hostess to protest at his questions, but she was not going to answer them. She put the tea-pot carefully and slowly back on its stand, then she clasped her hands on her lap. She did not look at him, but he felt her anger and her fear. There was nothing for it now but to give up or to take the bull by the horns. If he gave up he would have done her more harm than good; made her angry and afraid and nothing else. Nothing for it now but to go on.

"Annie-Laurie," he said, stirring his tea with deliberation and speaking slowly and softly, almost as though to himself, "you must try to forgive the curiosity of an old country clod like myself. It's always seemed odd to me that I should be such a dull fellow when others of my family are so artistically gifted. I have always so loved their gifts— almost worshipped them—my mother's beauty, David's art. All artists, all creators of beauty, have my astounded reverence.... You have it.... I like talking to artists—hearing them tell about their early struggles, finding out by what steps they won their place in their world; that makes me too curious, perhaps. You must forgive me. I never saw you on the stage. I wish I had. But I have heard how lovely you were." He looked up at the bunch of bells hanging from the beam over their heads. "Were those the bells you wore when you danced the Christmas-tree dance and sang the bell song? That was the loveliest thing you did, wasn't it? The thing that no one who saw or heard you ever forgot."

She got up abruptly and went to the window and stood there with her back to him. Her anguish seemed beating in waves through the room. Hilary went on calmly talking.

"You made good use of your mountain upbringing; got the freshness and simplicity of it into your work. You'd a lot to give. What I can't understand, Annie-Laurie, is why you did not go back to the stage when all that unhappy business was behind you. Didn't you want to go on with the job?"

Annie-Laurie, in control of herself at last, turned round. He thought that she looked like an old woman.

"So David Eliot *did* recognize me," she said in a flat, unemotional voice. "And gave me away."

"How could he help recognizing you? He had seen you on the stage, and you won him then. It was he who used the word 'unforgettable' of the loveliness of your art."

"It's always the same," said Annie-Laurie. "Wherever I go it follows me. We can't get away from it, Jim and I. To get away from it, and to feel safe, that's all I want. They didn't know here—at least, I had to tell Mrs. Eliot a little—that was only fair—but I didn't tell her much. You see, I wanted to stay here. So did Jim. One feels so safe here. And I like Mrs. Eliot—I thought we should be able to stay—"

Her voice trailed away dully, in incoherent sentences.

"Why can't you stay?" asked Hilary. "They all want you to stay. Have any of them behaved at all differently to you since my nephew recognized you?"

She looked at him, thinking over what he had said, and as the implication of it dawned upon her a transformation passed over her face that tore at his heart. She grew slowly young again. It was like the rising of the sun. Watching her, he realized a little of the agony she must have gone through, fine creature that she was, dragging that story with her wherever she went, smirched and imprisoned by it, like a crippled seagull stuck in the mud. And now this joy. People of honourable and cleanly living, people to whom she was essentially akin and with whom she was happy, knew her story and discounted it, accepting her for what she actually was, and not for what she appeared to be when the shadow of it fell upon her. He wondered for how many years she had waited for this, and to what extent her mind had been poisoned by the apparent hopelessness of her hope.

Then shame fell upon Hilary. He had made what he considered his worst blunder yet. And it was a sinful blunder. He had lied; not in actual words, but in implication; he had made her believe that the whole family, and not only David and himself, knew her story. Yet, seeing her joy, he knew he could not go back and correct the blunder, for his unintentional lie had drawn out one of the envenomed stings that were poisoning her mind. All he could do now was to take it into the pattern of things and try to build good upon it. That's the only use we can make of our sins and mistakes, he thought, we poor human sinners and fools.

"Then Jim and I can stay," said Annie-Laurie at last, on a long breath of relief. "We can stay. And they won't talk to me about it. It's been good of them; to know and not talk to me about it. I—can't talk about it."

"No, they won't talk to you about it," Hilary was able to assure her with complete conviction. "And I won't either, after today."

Annie-Laurie slid to the window-seat and sat with her hands folded in her lap, smiling at him.

"I'm glad *you* did, today, because otherwise I shouldn't have known—"

"That you can stay here, *safe*, for as long as you like."

He stopped, for he did not know how to go on. Her fear was the worst poison. She was obsessed by it. He was pitifully aware of the obvious fears through which she already must have passed—the fear of death, of shame, of publicity—but without the full confidence which she evidently was not going to give him he could not know what fear it was that haunted her now, whether it was of some objective disaster or of something in herself; he had known cases where unacknowledged sins had given to unhardened sinners such a horror of themselves that they had become mentally ill. Annie-Laurie, he could see, was nervously unbalanced as well as physically frail. But his ignorance made him powerless to help her further. Shame surged over him again. Beyond entangling himself in a whopping if unintentional lie, he didn't seem to have done much. Old fool! His shamed eyes on his knotted, rheumatic hands lying on his knees, his mind searched back over their conversation to find some word, some sentence, that should serve him as a signpost to the next step. It shone out suddenly. "I like Mrs. Eliot." The quiet words had expressed much more than liking. Nadine meant more to this girl than all the rest of them put together. He had been right when he said to David that this was Nadine's business. The next step was obviously to go to Nadine, of whom he was so ridiculously terrified, and make a clean breast of the whole thing. It would be a help that she already knew a little of the story, but even so he could not imagine what her reaction would be, he knew her so slightly.

"Thank you, Annie-Laurie, for the best tea I've ever eaten." He got up to go, and she came to him, smiling, and he took her hand. "You know, of course, of what any man or woman possessed of any insight whatever is convinced the minute they set eyes on you, and that is that the verdict of 'not guilty' was a true verdict."

It was the worst thing he could possibly have said. Her blue eyes looked suddenly black in her blanched face. For perhaps ten minutes he had brought her back her youth and given her happiness, and now with that one sentence he had shattered his gift so cruelly that he thought it would have been better if he had never brought it to her. Yet somehow he kept steady. He kept his eyes on hers, in spite of what he had seen in them, and there was no change in the kindness of his smile. He said what a good cake it had been, and left a suitable message for Malony. He told her again what a pretty room it was, and whistled to the Bastard. As he went down the steps he called back a few cheery remarks about the weather, and in the yard, though she had shut her door, he turned and waved, in case she should be looking out of the window. It was not until he was safely within the shadow of the porch that his legs gave way beneath him and he sat down suddenly on the seat. The Bastard, his legs also giving way in sympathy, sat down suddenly, too, and laid his chin on Hilary's boot. After ten minutes of misery Hilary suddenly lifted his head and took a deep breath, as though a load had been lifted.

"Nevertheless," he said, "though she did it, yet she's innocent."

– 4 –

The ironing had been cleared away, and Jill and the twins were having nursery tea. They were a pleasant sight. The twins had blue bibs with rabbits on them, and a shaft of sunlight was coaxing unexpected gleams of gold from Jill's pale hair. There was honey for tea, and sponge fingers. The twins, with their heads tipped back and mugs of milk obliterating their noses, took no notice of their uncle, but Jill looked up with a smile. She had a writing-pad beside her plate and a pencil in her hand, and was writing as she ate bread and honey.

"Just a line to Auntie Rose to catch the post," she explained to Hilary. "Before I mention it to Mrs. Eliot I thought I'd just sound Auntie."

"Yes, do, Jill," implored Hilary. "I should hate anything to be done hastily because of a chance remark of mine."

"There's many a good thing comes to pass just by chance," said Jill. "Jerry, drink your milk quietly. There's no need to make that rude noise."

Jerry continued to make a loud wet noise inside his mug.

"Jerry, dear, did you hear what I said?"

Jerry lowered his mug slightly, so that his bright eyes sparkled at Jill over its rim, but the noise he made was louder than ever.

José put her now empty mug down on the table, panted from the exertion of absorption, wiped away a milk moustache with her bib, and explained:

"He's ducks quacking."

"He is not," said Jill. "He is a very disobedient boy making a very rude noise. Jerry, stop that noise at once."

She did not raise her voice. She looked at Jerry, and he looked at her. He quacked louder. Jill stretched out a hand and removed the mug with a quick, deft movement that spilled no milk and expressed no irritation, merely calm, unhurried resolution. Jerry made a noise like a turkey gobbling, and José hee-hawed like a donkey. Jill picked up the honey-pot and put it out of reach on the dresser.

"I told you yesterday," she reminded them, "that if you were noisy at tea again you should have no honey."

Her charges burst all at once into the most appalling roars. Their faces went as scarlet and crumpled as opening poppy buds, but no tears appeared. Either their eyelids were too tightly screwed up to allow the passage of any moisture, or else the *tour de force* was not an expression of grief, but merely of frustration. Whichever it was, Hilary decided that nursery tea was not such a pleasant sight as he had thought. He smiled at Jill and, followed by the Bastard, beat a hasty retreat to the turret stairs. Looking back, he saw that the twins' faces were now fuchsia coloured, and feared for the blood-vessels in their heads. Jill, however, seemed to have no such fears. She was going placidly on with her letter.

Hilary went up the stairs to the Chapel and, to his astonishment, found it empty of everyone except Nadine. His heart missed a beat. Though he had decided to talk to Nadine as soon as possible, he had had a lingering hope that today might have proved impossible; tomorrow, he thought, would have been better. But there it was. He had noticed before that, a resolve taken, God tends to put one to the test with humorous suddenness that is slightly disconcerting.

"Could I talk to you, Nadine?" he asked abruptly, giving his courage no time to ebb out at his boots.

Then he abruptly forgot himself as he looked at his sister-in-law. In her plain dark dress, standing there remote and still, she did not seem the Nadine whom he knew. He had come upon her at a moment when she had believed herself alone, and though she had turned round to him when he spoke to her, it had been with the slow movement of a half-awakened dreamer who does not know yet who has disturbed him. Facing him, she was still again, and her face looked pathetically young, like that of a frightened little girl emerging from a sleep in which she had forgotten that today it is the dentist. Suddenly Hilary knew that he had never known Nadine at all. A woman of the world he had called her, and been afraid of her, and yet had never really thought out what he meant by the cliché. The term, examined, was meaningless, like most clichés, and in using it he had been guilty of the intellectual laziness of all cliché users. If she was a woman of the world, he was just as much a man of the world, but both of them only in their outward seeming. Their intrinsic selves were in the world, but not of it; what was of it was the mask that each of them wore—masks made for them by the way of life that each had to follow, hers a mask of sophistication, and his of austerity. But only masks. They looked at each other, both of them, and, with a flash of astonishment, saw each in the other the frightened, ignorant, simple children that they were. They smiled, then moved towards each other, assuming each their familiar relationship; with a difference.

"I was just thinking about you," said Nadine.

A low wooden table had been brought in to hold the paraphernalia needed for cleaning the walls. She sat down on the edge of it and cleared a space for Hilary to sit beside her. She was not afraid of him any more. The challenge in him that had always scared her, the challenge of a man who had done what she dared not do, was no longer there.

"About me?" asked the astonished Hilary.

"Wishing I could be happy like you. And like the man who painted these walls."

"Yes, he obviously enjoyed himself," said Hilary, looking about him. "Not that it matters."

"You mean—not being happy doesn't matter?"

"No. Why should it? At least, not the sort that I think you're thinking of; personal enjoyment. That is largely a matter of temperament and health, I think—things over which you've only the control of your common sense, not your choice."

"But there's another sort, a matter of choice?"

"Yes. Best described by saying it's how you choose to use your unhappiness. That sounds a very negative sort of thing. But it isn't really."

"I know what you mean," said Nadine. "Compassion isn't at all negative."

"And those who are happy in the first way never seem capable of it. Which brings me to what I wanted to talk to you about. Annie-Laurie. Now, there's a child in a thoroughly bad emotional and mental state, in pretty desperate need of compassionate help."

"You've been talking to her?" asked Nadine.

"Yes, and I could scarcely have made a worse mess of things. It's your job, Nadine, not mine."

"It's difficult," said Nadine. "She's not the child she looks, and she's only been open with me up to a point."

"I've collected some scraps of information that might be useful to you. Not a very pleasant story."

"Never mind. Tell it to me."

He told her the story David had told him, his conversation with Annie-Laurie and his own conclusion.

"My poor Annie-Laurie!" murmured Nadine, and she shivered a little. Those two men! Annie-Laurie must have been torn to pieces between their conflicting demands. And the child. And the death of the child. She thought in silence for a few moments. "If it's as you say, and she's guilty, and yet somehow justified, it will have been because of the child. The child will have been the crux of it."

"She's maternal?"

"In her way, as deeply so as Sally. Seeing them with the twins, I've envied them both. I'm not, you know. It's one of the lacks in me that has made my life with George difficult. And I've noticed that Annie-Laurie has hard work not to dislike Sally."

"I can't see that that's a proof of deep maternal feeling," said Hilary dryly.

"Yes. It must be obvious to Annie-Laurie that Sally has been born into a social class where the chances are that she will be loved with honour, and bear children who will have a reasonable hope of happiness. For Sally nothing will ever be squalid."

"Yes, I see," said Hilary slowly. "Poor Annie-Laurie! Jealousy is one of the worst of the pains. It's a point gained, I think, even though I gained it by a shocking lie, that she thinks you have known for some while more of her story than she actually told you."

"Yes, that's a great point. It will make her really talk to me, I hope. There's not much I can do until she does.... Hilary, can you see any connection between woods and laughter?"

He started at the abrupt change of subject. Then he was grateful for it. It was one of Nadine's social gifts that when a subject of conversation was finished with she would never allow the issue to be confused by too much talk.

"That man, now," said Nadine, glancing around the walls. "He painted a wood, and you can almost hear him laughing. And my family always come home laughing from the woods. And I read a lyric of Meredith's the other day that seemed to take it for granted that there's no whisper of woe under 'foliaged sky.'"

"'Where the foliaged sky is most sacred to see,'" quoted Hilary. "To many people a wood is a symbol of Paradise, I think, and it's the accepted belief that you laugh a good deal in Paradise.... Where are all the others, by the way?"

"In the drawing-room. I was on my way upstairs to fetch the twins' new winter coats to show Grandmother, and then I slipped in here for a minute."

"And then I wasted your time like this," said Hilary, getting up. "You go on and fetch the coats, and I'll go to the drawing-room and make our apologies."

Nadine got up, too, and stood smiling at him.

"Not waste of time. A very profitable twenty minutes. Thank you, Hilary. I seem to have got to know you better these last few minutes than in all the years before. I used to be scared of you."

"Of *me?*" ejaculated Hilary in astonishment. "I didn't know you were ever scared of anybody."

"I'm not as bold as I look," said Nadine.

"We none of us are," mused Hilary. "And doesn't it strike you as strangely ridiculous that human creatures, scared rabbits as we all are at heart, should ever be afraid of each other?"

"Especially nowadays," said Nadine. "Don't you feel sometimes, with such doom seeming to hang over the world, as though we were all rabbits at harvest time, bolting farther and farther into the middle of the field where the corn still stands, with that awful machine coming nearer and nearer?" They were standing at the door of the Chapel, and she laid her hand on the strong stone wall beside her, as once she had laid it on the warm panelling in her sitting-room, seeking reassurance. "This old inn is like the standing corn."

"It's a good symbol, this house, like a fortress," said Hilary, and turned to go down the turret stairs.

Nadine heard him murmuring to himself as he went: "I will say of the Lord, He is my refuge and my fortress, my God, in Whom I trust!"

Though Nadine thought she never prayed, she found herself going on with the psalm as she went upstairs. "He shall cover thee with His pinions, and under His wings shalt thou take refuge.... The Most High, thy habitation.... Thou shalt not be afraid." A flashing moment of happiness came to her. Somehow, beyond the doom, it was all right. The fortress was not static, like the standing corn. It was an ark that carried you through.

– 5 –

Tea over, David had slipped away into Knyghtwood to avoid being alone with Sally. It was odd to find himself avoiding Sally, when for weeks he had been clinging to her like a drowning man to a strong swimmer. But, then, during the past weeks his clinging had been unconscious. Now he was conscious of it, and had abruptly let go, lest he drown her as well as himself in his wretchedness. He was fighting his way back to physical and mental health, but he had not got there yet; the moment he thought himself cured he was plunged back into hopelessness again; and the blackest moments now were those against which Hilary had warned him, when he could not believe the night would ever pass. One of them was upon him now. He did not believe he would ever be able to work again and if he couldn't, what then? There seemed no answer.

On the day when they had discovered the frescoes the terrible sense of isolation had taken itself off for ever. At the time that had seemed a blessing, but now he was not so sure, for he was now so painfully conscious of the emotions of other people. Before, the people about him had seemed to move like figures in a dream, and he had fought to come near them, and could not do it; but now it was the other way round—they pressed in upon him, and all that they felt he felt, too, almost to the point of suffocation. Above all did he feel now, almost unbearably—the weight of Sally's sorrow in her love for him. He had hoped he would get free, come alive again and love her, give even as she gave. Well, he couldn't. Nadine had set him free—brutally, he thought, for he was still staggering from the shock of it—yet he remained numbed and powerless. He had nothing whatever to give Sally. Nothing whatever except the burden of himself.

Yet how desperately he longed for her, and how much he missed her! They were together, of course, while they were working at the walls, but that was a companionship without intimacy, for her father and Ben were there, too, and the work absorbed them. He ought to have been thankful for that, for it had made it possible to drop their walks and rides together naturally and inevitably. But he wasn't thankful. He wanted her to himself again, this girl whom he did not love.... It was odd.

Mere selfishness, of course. He had said to himself, on that day when he had first met her in London, that there was no way that he knew of to recapture the vision and strength of a child. Yet with Sally during the weeks that they had been together he had thought that there was; the way was to be with a strong and visionary child and share the vision and the strength. He had done that with Sally... almost.... He might have done it altogether if he had not cut himself off from her.

Long ago, at Damerosehay, walking for the first time along the road of denial and pain, he had discovered something: that it *was* a road, not a quagmire—a real road, strong and hard, leading somewhere. He had discovered the reality of the way and the end, and though he had passed through several different kinds of hell since then, his faith in that reality had never quite failed. That had been a sort of re-birth. "That which is born of the flesh is flesh, and that which is born of the spirit is spirit." Those words were the signpost. He had ground down his flesh then, and discovered his spirit.... He would never forget that day. He had stood in the wild garden at Damerosehay, with the blue bird in his hand, and it had flown up from his hands, singing.

And now he was once again at the cross-roads, but he was not alive and vibrant, as he had been before: he was like a man blind and paralysed. If he had been able to see which road to follow, it would have done him no good because he would not have been able to follow it. Nothing to be done about it but carry on from day to day, bearing as best he could the wretchedness of uncertainty and inaction, trying to let the burden of himself weigh upon himself only; and deny himself Sally. That was all he could do.

In even the smallest of selfless decisions there is a liberation from self, and David suddenly found himself noticing the wood. No wood in the world would ever mean as much to him as that scrap of an oak-wood at Damerosehay; but this was an excellent wood, all the same, and extraordinarily beautiful on this still day of early winter. He walked very slowly, aware of the immense age of this wood. It was the same wood that the artist had painted on the Chapel walls centuries ago.... The same wood.... Centuries ago, and it still patiently endured "the heat of the sun, the furious winter rages, the lightning flash, the dreaded thunder stone." Shakespeare meant so much to him that half the time he thought in the words of Shakespeare without knowing that he was doing it. "What freezings have I felt, what dark days seen! What old December's bareness everywhere!" The old wood seemed talking to him now, telling of its immensity of patience. Patience. The last lines of the sonnet of patience slipped into his mind.

> "Till whatsoever star that guides my moving
> Points on me graciously with fair aspect,
> And puts apparel on my tattered loving,
> To show me worthy of thy sweet respect:
> Then may I dare to boast how I do love thee;
> Till then not show my head where thou mayst prove me."

Tattered loving. That exactly described his feeling for Sally. Not a proper loving; nothing, yet, worth giving her. He could not, yet, shake off the yoke of inauspicious stars. He must wait. Patience. It was all about him in the still old wood, smiling at grief, waiting once more for spring, as the painted wood within the Herb of Grace had waited for so many years for its re-birth.

CHAPTER

– 1 –

𝒞AROLINE SAT ON THE EDGE of the railway-carriage seat, breath-less with joy and excitement. The most absolutely glorious thing had happened. She'd had measles at school, had been consid-ered unfit for the end of-term festivities and examinations and been sent home a fortnight early. It was only the beginning of December. The Christmas holidays were lengthened by two whole weeks. She was going home a whole two weeks or more before Tommy. She was going home to Mother and Daddy, to Ben, Jill and the twins, to Grandmother and Aunt Margaret and Uncle Hilary, to David, Malony and Annie-Laurie a whole fortnight early.... Home to the Herb of Grace.... Home.... The grinding train wheels beat out the glorious words.... Home.... Home.... Their first Christmas at the Herb of Grace.... Home.... the Herb of Grace.... It was their first real home. She had not liked the Chelsea house at all. It had seemed small and dark, and there had not been a garden. And it hadn't had a welcoming feel about it. Always it had seemed to draw back a little, as though afraid of getting its smart polish scratched. And it was con-nected in her mind with air raids and not feeling safe. Caroline was secretly afraid of many things, but at the Herb of Grace she always felt safe. It was like a strong stone fortress, and it welcomed you with a mighty laugh. How it would laugh at Christmas! She could just see and hear it laughing, with a lighted Christmas-tree in the hall and holly everywhere, and log fires roaring, and everyone singing carols at the tops of their voices.

She opened her eyes, that she had shut to see the Herb of Grace laughing at Christmas, and looked joyously out of the window. She was alone in the carriage, for this was only a branch line, and not many people travelled by it. She had been escorted to the last junction by Matron, and then, to her joy, left in charge of the guard to do this last bit alone. She was glad, for this was the first time she had done the journey from school to the Herb of Grace, and she wanted to be alone so as to get the landmarks well into her mind. That was one of the chief joys of home-comings: watching for the familiar landmarks and greeting them one by one as they came trooping to meet you. Caroline didn't really care very much about school. Victorian child that she was, strayed into the twentieth century by some peculiar mistake, it was her opinion that woman's place is in the home… especially when home was the Herb of Grace.

She glanced from the window to her little wrist watch. They were due at Radford in ten minutes. Who would meet her? Mother had said that somebody would come with the car, but not who it would be. It might be Mother herself in her fur coat, smelling of violets; and that would be lovely. Or it might be Malony, which would be very nice. Or it might—perhaps—be Daddie in his rough tweed overcoat that smelt of tobacco and wood smoke. At the thought that it might be Daddie—alone—her ecstasy was so great that she could hardly bear it. She had to go back to watching the landmarks again, or she would have burst. It was almost sunset now, still and cold and beautiful. She saw a group of pines outlined starkly against a lemon-coloured sky, a farmhouse with higgledy-piggledy roof and lights in the windows, a white wooden bridge crossing a stream, and knew that she would not forget them as long as she lived.

A lighted signal-box slipped by the windows, and there was a row of houses beyond the line. Goodness, they were nearly there! She jumped to her feet, and wondered if she'd got everything. Her box had been sent on in advance, but she had a little blue suitcase in the rack, and a paper bag holding some sandwiches which she had been too excited to eat, but had treasured for Mary. And she had a second much-battered suitcase that Matron had lent her, containing her Christmas presents for the family. There was a pochette for Mother, a cigarette case for Father, a wooden box to hold paint-brushes for Ben, a slightly larger box to hold bones for Tommy, a needle-case for Jill, two woolly rabbits for the twins, an egg cosy for Grandmother, a pincushion for Aunt Margaret, a holy book-marker (holy because it was purple and had a cross embroidered on it) for Uncle Hilary, a little bunch of felt flowers for Annie-Laurie and a pen-wiper for Malony. She had made all these things herself in the handicraft class, and had not dared trust them in her box lest it be lost, sent on in advance as it was and there wasn't room for them in her own suitcase, so she had had to borrow one of Matron's. Though she had not got a clever brain, she had clever fingers, and she loved making things. She should have lived in the era of bazaars. They would have been the breath of life to her. One, two, three. Yes, she'd got everything. Was she tidy? Mother might meet her, and Mother liked her to be tidy. There wasn't a glass in the carriage, but she shook herself, brushing smuts off her grey school overcoat, pulling her long grey woollen stockings straight, settling her grey felt hat more firmly on her shining, smooth gold head. Then she let down the window and hung out. She could see the platform now, with the lights, and the lovely blue dusk behind them, and figures moving about. There was one rather outsize figure, very upright. Was it? It was! She shrieked with delight. It was Daddie in his thick brown overcoat, his hands deep in his pockets, the yellow scarf that she had knitted for his birthday wound round his neck. His felt hat was set jauntily at an angle, as she liked him to wear it, and as he always wore it when she was about just to please her, and his eyes were scanning each carriage window as it passed him with an eagerness that almost matched her own.

"Daddie!" she shouted, but he couldn't hear her above the noise of the train.

She opened the carriage door and yelled again, and this time he did hear. He raised his hat, then strode towards her and held out his arms, and she fell into them as the train glided past.

"Hullo, my Elf! Hullo, my little Elf! Lord, how you've grown!"

He hugged her and, laughing, she wound her arms round his neck and hid her face in his coat and sniffed the familiar scent of tobacco, and the smoky smell that was the smell of the tweed. He set her down and held her away from him and saw her usually pale little face rosy with joy, and her grey eyes shining, as she danced up and down in his grip. It was only in these homecomings, and then only if they were alone together, that she was so wildly loving and abandoned in her joy. By the time they got home her happiness, though sweet to see, would be demure and quiet—not this flaming thing. He doubted if anyone but himself knew that she could be like this. It was something that she seemed able to show only to him; just as he dared show only to her the full depth of his tenderness. She knew he wouldn't laugh at her, he knew she wouldn't suspect him of emotionalism. There was a strain of mockery in Nadine and Tommy, a touch of austerity in Ben, that forbade exhibitions of sentiment; but with each other George and his daughter could express their feelings and be the better for it.

"My things!" cried Caroline, and dived back into the carriage to retrieve them.

"I'll take 'em," said George, and relieved her of the suitcases. He always treated her like a grown-up lady, raising his hat to her and carrying her things.

Clasping the packet of sandwiches for Mary, she danced beside him to the waiting car. He tucked her up tenderly in the seat beside him, and they slid slowly down the main street of Radford. The lights were lighted now, and in some of the shop windows there were already a few festoons of coloured paper, calendars and Christmas cards, and attractive cardboard cartons that hadn't anything in them.

Caroline could hardly remember the gay illuminations of the pre-war days, and this extremely modest display filled her with excitement.

"It's lovely!" she cried. "Oh, Daddy, it's lovely. And there are Christmas presents in the windows." She lowered her voice to a very secret whisper. "Daddy, there are presents in that little brown case. Things I've made!"

George knew what was expected of him, and drew up instantly beneath a lamp-post.

"Show me," he commanded.

Caroline knelt up in her seat, reached into the back seat for the case, opened it, extracted her father's cigarette case and carefully stowed it away in her pocket, keeping an anxious eye on him, lest he should see. But George had become extraordinarily interested in something on the other side of the street, and the dangerous moment passed over quite safely.

"There!" said Caroline, sitting down again triumphantly with the open case on her lap. "I made them. That's for Mother. Do you think she'll like it?"

"Great Scott!" exclaimed George. "You made all those, Elf? Good heavens, dearest! I'd no idea you could do that sort of thing. That for Mother? Never saw such a pretty thing. Fit for a dinner party. That for Grandmother? She'll love it. I'm proud of you, Elf, I am indeed. Didn't know you had it in you."

His astonished admiration was genuine. He was one of those parents who are completely bowled over by capability in their offspring. It was to him incredible that the creature who once had been just a small white bundle held between his hands could develop into this paragon of beauty and brilliance.... For he was also one of those parents who think their children beautiful, no matter how plain.... Nadine had been born the other kind of parent, setting for her children, because they were hers and she loved them, an intensely high standard that in future years would help them immensely in achievement, but was a sore trial to them now.... And she did not think them beautiful if they were not.... She and George combined made a very good aggregate of parenthood.

Caroline was not a vain child. She was not puffed up by her father's admiration, only sweetly warmed and comforted by the unconscious knowledge that to one human being on this earth she mattered supremely. She closed the case and smiled at George, sharing to the full his profound wonder at the miracle of achievement. It surprised her as much as it did him. Two years ago she could only make cross-stitch kettle-holders.

"So you've got her back again? Good!"

With an effort George and his daughter wrested their attention from each other and blinked at the figure beyond the window. It was Hilary, planted squarely in the gutter and beaming at them through his thick glasses, his hat planted unbecomingly on the back of his head, and the collar of his disgracefully shabby overcoat turned up to meet his cold, pink ears. They smiled at him. They were both very fond of him. He was a simple person, like themselves. He was made supremely happy by the sight of their reunion, and did not mind letting them see that he was.

"Give you a lift?" asked George.

"No, thanks. I've some business to do, and I've got my old Ford at the garage." He lowered his voice. "Malony back?"

"No," said George.

"H'm," murmured Hilary. Then he raised his voice again. "Glad to see you back, Caroline. We miss you."

He raised his hat to her (he, too, always treated her like a grown-up) and stepped back on to the pavement. They called good-byes and slid off down the street.

"Is Malony away?" asked Caroline.

"Just for a day or two," said George. "Now we'll soon be home. Warm enough?"

"Umm," murmured Caroline, in utter joy, and nestled as close to him as she could.

It was wonderful driving home, with the last glow of the sunset lingering in the west, and the hedges black and mysterious on either side. There were lights in the cottage windows, and sometimes they had forgotten to draw the curtains, and one saw the flicker of firelight, the bright heads of children sitting round a table, munching their "cooked tea," a man reading a paper with a pipe in his mouth, or a woman with head bent over her darning. This, too, was new to Caroline, used to the years of black-out. It was lovely and most magical—like turning the pages of a story-book, each fresh window a fresh story.

"The Hard," murmured George, and she sat bolt upright and saw the uneven roofs of the old cottages black against the still-glowing sky, and the rosy light from red-curtained windows lying obliquely across the grass verges of the street that sloped steeply to the pale gleam of the river beyond.

There was a dance of light upon the water, shed from an unseen lantern, and as the car slowed down before the gate that led to their own special lane she heard a faint chiming of heavenly music. Perhaps it was only a wireless in one of the cottages, but it was so unearthly that she half expected to see Ben's herd of red deer galloping up the street, with the one white deer among them. They were in their own lane now, and the car's headlights showed her the steep banks covered with gorse-bushes, with the oak-trees arching overhead. They turned the corner, and the lights lit just a little of the mystery of Knyghtwood upon the one side and the old orchard upon the other. An owl hooted softly from the depth of the wood, and at the bottom of this lane, too, light danced upon the water, shining from the lanterns set out in welcome upon the river wall. They stopped at the foot of the stone steps leading up to the blue gate, and the front door was wide open, and from it light streamed out, and Mother was coming quickly down the garden path, wearing her fur coat because it was so cold, treading the broad band of light that shone from the front door as though it were cloth of gold spread for her queenly feet. And after her came the twins, shouting at the tops of their voices, and Mary barking wildly, and Jill and Annie-Laurie. After that she scarcely knew what happened. She was in Mother's arms, cuddled against soft fur, sniffing the lovely violet smell, feeling Mother's smooth, cool cheek against hers. She was hugging the twins, nearly deafened by their yells. She was hugging Mary and having her face licked all over. She was hugging Jill and kissing Annie-Laurie. She was inside the Herb of Grace, with the door shut and the firelight gleaming on the panelled walls, and it was warm and safe inside, and she was home.

– 2 –

Hilary, however, was not, though he wished most sincerely that he was. The cold weather touched up his rheumatism, and he disliked being out in it quite intensely. And what good did he think he was doing, he asked himself, wandering round Radford and poking his head in at all the pubs? He couldn't run Malony to earth in any of them, though enquiries made of the landlords elicited the fact that he seemed to have been in most of them in the course of the previous afternoon. Pub-crawling. This was the second time. There had been the time when he had been to see Annie-Laurie and found Malony absent; George had told him later that Malony had arrived home at midnight that night, very wretched and much the worse for wear. But this time it was more worrying, for he had been missing since the afternoon of the day before. Hilary had had lunch at the Herb of Grace, and had found them all in a great flap, Malony's absence having revealed to them, not only that they were fonder of him than they had realized, but that his efficiency, humour and unselfishness were the mainstay of the place. Without him everything seemed immediately to fall to pieces.

Hilary had always known himself possessed of a deep regard for the gallant little man. He found these outbreaks of Malony's difficult to reconcile with his character as he knew it, for there was a whipcord strength about Malony that seemed totally opposed to weaknesses of the flesh. He supposed that Malony's rare outbreaks were much on a par with Margaret's, when she bought the trolley and wheeled it home through the lanes and made herself those terrible unbecoming jumpers. Those whose selflessness, through a happy accident of temperament or through long discipline, is instinctive are as unaware of it as those who trade upon it. As a matter of course, without comment, like a table of well-seasoned wood that does not creak, they accept the burdens laid upon them, and as a matter of course the burdens pile up. Yet a drop of self-seeking lingers somewhere, seeking a vent, and, like the flame within the volcano, it must have it. The brilliant colours of Margaret's jumpers, her rare grabbings of some coveted possession, were typical of her sex and class, thought Hilary, with its emphasis upon the importance of beauty and property. The longings of Malony's class (for Malony, he suspected, unlike Annie-Laurie, had his roots among the very poor) were born of insecurity and hardship; they were for forgetfulness, warmth, shelter. Different in quality, but the same in essence, the result of that ridiculous illusion, so hard to mortify, that personal enjoyment is important.

Hilary's cogitations brought him to the end of his fruitless round of visits, and he limped back to the garage. How idiotic he had been! If he had found Malony it would have annoyed the fellow intensely. He had merely wasted his time and made his rheumatism worse. So much of the work of a parish priest appeared sheer waste of time. Not that he let that worry him. He merely accepted it as one of the facts of the case, and put no reliance upon appearances. The older he became the more convinced he was that everything was more or less illusory, excepting only that flame, that motive in the soul of which he and David had talked. The rest was just smoke.

He disinterred his decrepit Ford, climbed into it and chugged home, only to find it was his old housekeeper's half-day and that his study fire had gone out. It was his own fault. He had told her he would be back for tea, and then, instead of returning, he had set out on the idiotic search for Malony. His old Mary, he knew, was going to spend the evening at the Women's Institute dramatic show, and would not be back till late. But she had done what she could for his comfort before leaving. His tea—the heel of a sawdust cake and three thick pieces of bread and marge—had been set ready by the now extinct study fire, and his supper—bread and mouse-trap cheese and a couple of sodden sausage rolls—had been put ready on the dining-room table, with a box of matches beside his plate with which to light the dining-room gas fire. Hilary's was one of those vast pitch-pine vicarages that face north and have no proper damp course, though he seldom noticed it. But tonight, somehow, he did notice it. The cold of the place struck him like a blow and made him feel oddly depressed—a sensation to which he was not accustomed. And when he carried the sodden sausage and the mouse-trap cheese in from the dining-room and set them beside the sawdust cake, it being his intention to combine tea and supper and make one meal of them, he was conscious of a sudden sensation of nausea in his stomach. And this sensation also was unfamiliar, for, as he had told Annie-Laurie, he had as a general rule the digestion of an ostrich.... For which blessing he daily thanked God; for few things are more inimical to prayer than indigestion.... It was the cold, he decided, and not the sausage, and lowering himself cautiously to his rheumatic knees, he set about relighting the fire.

But Hilary was not a practical man. Twenty minutes later he was still relighting the fire. The bell rang. He heaved himself to his feet, dusted his dirty hands and went to the front door. On the doorstep, hunched up in a shabby overcoat and shivering in the cold, stood Malony, speechless, looking exactly like a sick monkey.

"Come in at once, man," said Hilary cheerfully. "Forgive the mess I'm in. My housekeeper is out, and I can't get my study fire to go."

If Malony had seemed to hang back, the plight of Hilary's study fire made him instantly change his mind. He stepped in briskly and shut the door behind him. Glancing at him, Hilary saw that the outbreak was over; he was dead sober, though obviously in the grip of the exhaustion and depression of the day after. Spiritually, too, he was back in his usual state, shouldering with alacrity the burden of Hilary's study fire. He was in the study almost in a flash, and almost in a flash he had it blazing.

"Malony," said Hilary, "you are the most efficient man of my acquaintance."

Malony rose and eyed the food upon the table with contempt.

"Were you thinking of having a meal, Sir?"

"If you'll share it with me."

"With your permission, Sir, I'll take these out to the kitchen and dish up something hot," said Malony, and swept the unappetizing morsels together on the tea-tray. Then, lifting the tray with one hand, he pulled Hilary's battered old armchair to the fire with the other. "You look as though you needed a rest, Sir.... All well at the Herb of Grace, Sir?"

Hilary sank gratefully into his chair.

"Yes, very well, I think. They've just got Caroline home."

"I asked, Sir, because my pal, the landlord of the Crown, said you'd been asking for me when I popped in there just now." His sad, dark eyes were anxious in his puckered monkey face. "So I just called in to ask you—"

"Yes, they're all right. It's you we've been anxious about.

"You were looking for *me*, Sir?" asked Malony incredulously.

"You're part of the family, you know, Malony; you can't go off like that and not have us all in what the children call a flap." He stretched out his hand to the telephone on his desk. "Now you go and dish us up something in the kitchen and I'll ring up and tell 'em you're safe. Second door on the right. Hot coffee might be a good idea, only I don't know where Mary keeps it."

"I'll find it, Sir," said Malony gently, and immediately disappeared with that slick, deft noiselessness that was part of his stage training.

Hilary got George on the phone, told him to expect Malony when he saw him, and then lay back in his chair and stretched his feet luxuriously to the blaze. The room was becoming gloriously warm, and already the scent of coffee was creeping in, and the delicious smell of something frying. Hilary sniffed with appreciation, and just for the moment yielded to the pleasurable idea that he was one of those old coves who before the war used to live in luxurious chambers in Town, waited on hand and foot by a faithful manservant. Then he thrust the notion from him in horror and remembered that he hadn't said Evensong. He pulled his office book from his pocket, recollected himself and made a start, but the increasingly appetizing smells from the kitchen kept insinuating themselves between him and his God, and he put the book back in his pocket and gave it up as a bad job. He was deeply humiliated. He had thought in his younger days that increasing age would mean increasing freedom from the weaknesses of the flesh, and yet here he was with his soul apparently at the beck and call of a frying-pan. However, the humiliation was salutary. That was the best thing about old age; it didn't leave you with much upon which to congratulate yourself.

Malony came back with a loaded tray. He had brought a second plate, but set it rather tentatively upon the table.

"You said, Sir—?"

Hilary got up and pulled another chair forward.

"Of course I did. And drop the Sir, will you, just as you've dropped your Irish accent? Chuck all the disguises for a little while. It'll rest you. You do me a great honour. It's not every day that I entertain a famous comedian to supper, still less have him waiting on me hand and foot. Gosh! What a superb fry! What on earth did you put in it?"

He bent boyishly over the dish before him. Malony had fried spoonfuls of powdered egg to crisp little fritters, had added the sausages, disinterred from their coffins of sodden pastry, onion, parsley and potato, and had made of the dish a work of art. He had made crisp toast, too, and superb coffee. Hilary's thick glasses were misted by the steam from the hot dish, and he took them off to wipe them, smiling across at Malony as he did so. The man opposite, divided between anger and relief at the stripping away of his defences, his nerves jangling, was taken utterly aback by the extraordinary beauty of Hilary's eyes without their glasses, by their keen, straight glance, by the enveloping warmth of his utterly happy yet rather deprecating smile. The immense power of his goodwill, together with his personal humility, made a sudden unexpected appeal that got right under Malony's guard before he knew where he was. He wasn't out to do you good, this chap—he didn't think enough of himself for that—he was simply out to jog along beside you for a little, and pass the time of day, knowing you were down on your luck, and thinking a bit of companionship might not come amiss. And he was straight. He didn't say what he didn't mean. When he'd said that about an honour, he'd meant it. He'd got sense, too. Anything you told him would be in wise keeping.

"I don't say it's not a bit of a relief to be Jim Harris for a bit," he said suddenly, helping himself to fry. "Though, mind you, I've worn so many disguises in my time that I slip 'em on and off like suits of clothes. And as for the Sir, that comes naturally—I'm not like Annie-Laurie, who comes of good yeoman stock. I was born in a back street in Clerkenwell. My father kept a pub there. That's where I got the taste for drink that's been a curse to me all my life."

Hilary readjusted his glasses and attacked his supper.

"Goes with you like a dead hen tied round a terrier's neck," he said sympathetically. "Trips you up when you're down in the mouth about something, or so dog-tired you don't know how to drag along another step. Don't I know. With me it's a sort of luxuriating in the detestableness of myself—inverted pride. I take to it, as you to drink, when my faith fails me."

"Failure of faith," said Malony. "That's a queer thing, surely, for a man like you to suffer from. I thought faith was what a parson lived by."

"So it is," said Hilary. "It's what every man lives by. But you know how in the black moments it's always the apparent failure of what you live by that gets you down. Only apparent, of course, for the mere fact that you're wretched because you think your faith's gone really means that you've got hold of it pretty firmly. If you had no faith you wouldn't care one way or the other, would you?"

"I wouldn't know," said Malony, with gloomy self-satisfaction. "I've no faith myself."

"You've all the marks of it. About the most selfless chap I ever met. Without faith in the possibility of something divine existing in humanity it beats me how you can slave for it as you do. What made you first take to the drink in Clerkenwell?"

"General ugliness of things. I was a romantic youngster. Thought life ought to be a lot different from what it was. Then a pal of mine let me down."

"There you are, then," said Hilary comfortably. "You believed in beauty, in loyalty. Drunk, you still believed in them. If you hadn't you wouldn't have been drunk. Have some more coffee. And push the fry this way."

Malony suddenly laughed delightedly. He had been so desperately cold, but now, with the coffee and the fire, he was warm. And he had been so utterly wretched—beyond the reach, he thought, of any laughter—but the droll appearance of Hilary, scanty grey hair rumpled, glasses misted by steam, elbows squarely out as he frankly and joyously attacked his meal, tickled his comedian's sense. Not that he was laughing *at* the fellow; that he would never do, after that glimpse of the man's essential quality that had been his when Hilary took off his glasses; but he unexpectedly found himself laughing with him at the absurd pomposities of human nature. Of course faith and life were synonymous, and Hilary had been right to explode his conceited assertion that he could possess one without the other, even as he was delightfully right in making no secret whatever of the fact that a man of God can enjoy his food. Reserve, though life had forced it upon him of late years, was not natural to Malony. It ebbed from him as he helped himself to more coffee, stretched his boots to the fire and leaned back in his chair with a movement of exquisite relief; almost the relief of a man released from pain. Hilary, reaching for the coffee-pot and praying for guidance, recognized the signs. He was about to be told the story of Malony's life, and from the recitation of bare facts he must build up the framework, and out of his own experience and insight clothe it with the flesh and blood of the living man; or else fail to help the man. He did not eat any more, and he poured his coffee black.

– 3 –

Malony's father had been a Cockney born and bred, his mother the daughter of an Italian owner of a delicatessen shop. He'd loved his mother. She'd been gay and charming. But she'd not lived long. Her husband had knocked her about too much, and she had felt things, both happy and sad, with too great an intensity. But she had not left her son undowered. She gave him the gift of song, the gift of gaiety, and a reverence for her sex unusual in Clerkenwell.

The pal who had let him down had been the starting-point, the spring-board, so to speak, from which he had leaped out of Clerkenwell. It had been an atrocious failure of friendship, and at the time friendship had been the basket into which Malony had flung all his eggs, after the flaming, smoky skies over the roofs of Clerkenwell had brought no fulfilment of their promises; and he had drowned his sorrows in drink to such an extent that the plumber who employed him had given him the sack. He'd had a little money, and, loathing the wet pavements that reflected the traitor skies, shrinking from every figure beneath a lamp-post, lest it turn itself about and reveal the face of his friend, hating the very intonation of the voices about him, reminding him of his friend's voice, he had taken the train and gone north, where the skies were nearly always clouded, where men use broader vowels in their speech, were less ready with their friendship, but more steadfast in it once it was given. He might have done well in the engineering shops. He was a clever workman, and his wit, his gift of repartee, his unfailing repertoire of catchy songs, made him popular wherever he was. Yet he couldn't seem to get on. Somebody or something was always letting him down, and then he'd drink, and then the positions of trust that might have been his were withheld. And industry was too impersonal and rigid a thing to satisfy him. He felt starved and frustrated in its service and, perpetually disillusioned, he perpetually moved on somewhere else. And so at last he found himself the electrician, scene-shifter and jack-of-all trades of a little repertory company in Wales. And then his talent was discovered and he was promoted to the playing of small comedy parts. And then, at last, he was happy. The intimate friendliness of the little company, the appreciativeness of the small audiences that roared with laughter at him and took him to their heart with Celtic warmth, gave him at last nearly all of what he wanted. He could give all that he had of talent, joyously, and have it accepted joyously, and receive back again in full measure that affection without which he could not live. But neither this giving nor this affection went quite deep enough. Though happy, he was not quite satisfied. And then Annie-Laurie joined the company.

He fell in love desperately and at once. Though his charming Italian mother had predisposed him for the idolization of women, he had never yet admitted any woman to more than the outskirts of his life; after his mother, none of those he had come across had satisfied him. But Annie-Laurie filled the bill. There was nothing in him that was not satisfied by the fact of her. What is given to only one man or woman in a thousand was given to him—a single-minded devotion to one human being of such power that it was beyond the possibility of change until the end of time. Hilary had come across this love a few times in his life, and he knew it for a terrifying thing, holding a possibility of pain as great as any a human being could be called upon to bear. In a lesser degree, consonant with the lesser intensity of his nature, poor old George had it for Nadine.... Sally, he rather feared, had it for the apparently ungrateful and unwitting David.... And this passion could at times be as merciless to the object of it as to the subject. Its impact had been too much for the young and inexperienced Annie-Laurie. It had swept her right off her feet, and before she knew where she was she was engaged to Malony.

She did not know that she was cheating him, for her unconscious awareness of the enduring strength of his love gave her a sense of security that made her very happy. She did not know herself. Though she knew her mother had feared her father, she did not know yet that fear was woven into her nature, and that all her life long she would crave for safety as she craved for nothing else. She thought her happiness was love. She glowed with it, expanded like a flower, and in a very short time she was a fine actress and playing leading parts in the Company's plays. She loved her art, she thought she loved Malony, and she thought she had nothing further to wish for.

But she had the fire of her race, and it did not spare her. That spring a new and striking play was to be tried out by the Company, with a part in it that suited her as no part had suited her yet, but there was no one in the Company quite suitable to play the part of her lover. Their producer was ambitious for this play, and he summoned from London a friend of his—Luke Redmayne, a very fine actor and a startlingly attractive man. He and Annie-Laurie played together with a strange and touching perfection, every word and movement close-knit in burning sincerity, the love they portrayed so illumined by the reality behind it that it dazzled like coloured glass with the sun beyond. The play went to London, they with it, Annie-Laurie's engagement to Malony broken, and in a short while they were married.

Malony was just, as well as passionate, and he made no attempt to belittle the man who had taken Annie-Laurie away from him. He was a gentleman and well educated, with just that advantage in breeding and knowledge that made Annie-Laurie feel as honoured by his choice as Malony had been by hers. But he was a man made without mercy, either to himself or others. It was, Malony admitted, a part of his charm. He was like a fine rapier, flashing, delicate, beautiful, but of the ice-brook's temper, and with a keen edge to draw blood. And he had a lust for power that gave him no rest. It was the longing for power that had made him an actor, a passionate but cruel and most inconstant lover, and a fanatical Communist. His politics were his religion. He saw in Communism a possibility of world domination by an idea that dazzled and intoxicated him. He was a born tyrant. Malony thought that he was not completely sane. Yet sincere as they are made. He flung a promising career to the winds, he left a charming wife, to fight for his faith in Spain.

Malony said little about the period of his life when Annie-Laurie left him for Luke. Hilary gathered that he had gone through hell, that he had taken to drink again, that he had been discharged from the Company and had gone back to London. He had no intention of making himself a nuisance to Annie-Laurie, he made no attempt to see her; but at least he could be in the same town where she was and watch her now and then on the stage. That was something. But to do this he had to live, and he pulled himself together and set to work to find a job. He had discovered himself to be happier as a comedian than as an engineer. He turned to music-hall and pan-

tomime, and after a hard but comparatively short struggle he succeeded with a brilliance that without Annie-Laurie meant nothing
to him whatever.

Annie-Laurie's career was successful only while Luke was with her.
Though she was so fine an artist, she did not realize her own genius.
She lacked self-confidence, the power to stand alone. Without Luke's
strength and encouragement her fears overwhelmed her—the fear
of failure, the fear of pushing herself, her anxiety and fear for Luke.
The fear tarnished her genius, and she could not hold the place she
had gained. Neither he nor she had saved any money. She had a difficult time until the report of Luke's death brought Malony back
into her life. She would take no money from him, but she consented
to act with him, and, her self-confidence restored by his faith in her,
the genius shone out again, and her success equalled his. But she
would not marry him until two years had gone by since she had
heard that Luke was dead. She had loved Luke, and his cruelty and
inconstancy had never quite killed her love. She did not love Malony, but she knew how desperate was his need of her, and she was
very fond of him; also his unshakeable faith in her, and faithfulness
to her, still gave her that sense of safety that was her deepest need.
Then they had a child, a girl, and she discovered herself to be one of
those women to whom motherhood comes naturally and with joy.
Malony was beside himself with delight in his child, and for a little
while they were completely happy.

Then Luke came home, a sick man. He had been seriously
wounded in the head and back, and for a long time he had been
hidden in the Spanish mountains, cared for by peasants, and too ill
to know who or where he was. He did not demand that Annie-Laurie
should go back to him, he offered to let her divorce him; but he
wanted her, he was too ill to work for himself, and had nothing to
live on apart from her, and she felt his need of her was even greater
than Malony's, and she went back to him.

"At that time I couldn't see it," said Malony to Hilary. "I thought
she owed the greater duty to me, for I'd been a faithful husband to
her, and he hadn't.... And we had the child.... It seemed damned
hard to lose them both."

"You could have kept the child," said Hilary.

Malony shook his head.

"No. She adored Midge."

"So did you."

"Yes, but I hadn't borne her. Annie-Laurie had a bad time when the little thing came. And Midge needed her. She was a delicate little thing. We called her Midge because she was so small. But always happy. She had that bunch of Morris-bells of Annie-Laurie's tied to the cot, and she'd laugh at them by the hour together. And if you wanted to hear her crow you'd only to swing the bells and make them ring."

He broke off abruptly. They had finished supper now and were smoking. Hilary puffed at his pipe and said nothing.

"Midge died of bronchitis," went on Malony. "I thought if Annie-Laurie had let me help a bit more it wouldn't have happened. If they'd had a more comfortable home, Midge might not have caught the cold that started it. But Annie-Laurie would take next to nothing from me after she went back to Luke—just a little for Midge, and that was all. She had a hard struggle again, for she wouldn't act with me any more; and she was too tired and discouraged to do well alone. I didn't know till afterwards how hard the struggle was, for she didn't tell me at the time. I scarcely ever saw her. I couldn't go to the flat, for Luke, poor chap, was damned jealous. Now and then we'd arrange to meet in the park or somewhere, when she was wheeling Midge out in the pram, so that I could see the kid. That was all. But she wouldn't talk much—seemed to think it would be disloyal to Luke. It was a hell of a situation all round. Then Midge died, and after the funeral was over Annie-Laurie refused to see me again. Somewhere in the middle of all this the war had broken out. I tried to enlist, but they wouldn't have me. Weak heart or some such nonsense. I entertained the troops with my tomfoolery. It was all I was good for. Annie-Laurie never wrote to me. I could only guess at her misery over Midge, and it was from other folk, not her that I heard things weren't going well between her and Luke.... She never even wrote."

"She would have thought that too disloyal, I dare say," said Hilary gently. "If I understood Annie-Laurie aright, she's best described by the old-fashioned word 'upright.' It's a good word; comprises a good many things—all the straight qualities, loyalty, truthfulness, the right sort of pride."

"She's proud all right," said poor Malony lugubriously. "Proud as Lucifer. And truthful. I believe that girl would die sooner than tell even the ghost of a harmless white lie even to save her life. Nearly scared out of her wits as she was at that damnable trial—and though you wouldn't think it to look at her, fear has always been a thing Annie-Laurie has had to fight hard against—she never contradicted herself under cross-examination, never prevaricated: just made always the same simple, truthful, inadequate statements. Her counsel had the devil of a time getting her off. She wouldn't confide in him. The few things she felt she could truthfully say, she said, but not one word more. It seemed she couldn't tell the whole truth, and she wouldn't fill up the gaps with lies, not even to save her life."

"She told the whole truth to you, of course."

"No. To this day she has never said more to me than she said at the trial."

"How did she explain giving her husband the wrong sleeping draught?"

"She said it was just a mistake. Though the right box had been put there ready for her, she didn't see it. She thought the chemist had forgotten to put it ready, and so she unlocked his cupboard and took what she thought was the right stuff."

"It was said at the trial, wasn't it, that the right box had been put where she was accustomed to find it, and where it would have been difficult for her not to see it?"

"Yes, but the siren had gone and an air-raid had begun. She was terrified of raids, though she had such grit that she never let a soul see it; never, if you know what I mean, let herself see it. She never gave way at all, even alone. A bit dangerous, that is. Means you're always taut, and then in a crisis the nerves are too weakened to register the usual sense impressions of touch and sight correctly. You're bewildered, numbed. And then Annie-Laurie hates noise. The racket of an air-raid always knocked her silly. Knowing her, I know that she could have had that box between her fingers and under her eyes and not known it. When she said she just didn't see the box, she spoke the simple truth."

"And you think that's all there is to it?"

"No. There's a bit more that Annie-Laurie's never told a soul. You can see for yourself that she's a wretchedly unhappy and unbalanced woman. There are times when I think that if she can't get it off her chest she'll soon not be a sane woman."

"You've asked her to tell you?"

"No. That would be the way to strike her dumb for the rest of her life. You don't know Annie-Laurie. She's darned obstinate. Hates being forced. Flies in the opposite direction if you try it on. She'll tell me when she can. I just wait. She knows I don't care what she's done or not done. Whatever she did, she did in accordance with what she is, and it's what she is that matters to me, so what's the odds? She knows I believe in her—like the sun. No warmth or light, no life even, without her."

"She wears no wedding ring, I notice."

"Thinks she's got no right to it. She's got a bee in her bonnet about marriage. Wife to two men at once, she feels now that she was married to neither."

"Why in the world didn't you re-marry after Luke's death?" demanded Hilary.

"One night when he had a bad turn and thought he was dying he made her promise never to be my wife again."

"The brute!" said Hilary violently.

"He was insanely jealous. A bit touched, poor chap."

"In my opinion," said Hilary, "a death-bed promise like that is not binding. It was a promise he had no right to ask and she no right to give."

"To Annie-Laurie a promise is a promise."

"What about the promise she made when she married you? Luke dead, that was once more something that must be fulfilled, surely."

"Her first marriage vow was to Luke. The one to me was wiped out by his return, she felt."

"That's one way of looking at it. Poor girl. What a tangle! Yet I can't understand her. Upright as she is I should have thought that breaking her promise to Luke would have seemed to her less reprehensible than living with you without being married to you."

"We don't live together," said Malony gloomily.

Hilary's jaw dropped, and his precious pipe slipped out of his fingers into the grate.

"You mean to say—what?"

"What I say," said Malony, with increasing gloom. "Women—they don't understand how hard it is on a man. I've never looked at another woman since I met Annie-Laurie. But I drink at times."

"Now I've smashed my pipe," said Hilary. "Well, I'm glad to know you. I've met a good many fine men in my time, but there's not one whom I should dare to say was your equal. I've a feeling that you're getting to the end of it. You're waiting, you said. Wait just a bit longer. You're getting to the end of it."

"We never seem to get to the end of it," said Malony wretchedly. "We ought to go back to the stage. That's our job—what we're both good at, what we both love. But they know all about us there, and Annie-Laurie can't face up to it. She's afraid, poor girl. She's not self-ish about it; she's begged me to leave her and go back alone. I would leave her if I thought it would be the best thing for her, but it wouldn't. She's still a sick woman, in body and mind, and she feels safe with me. That's what she chiefly needs, to feel safe. And so we just carry on with one crazy stunt after another. That house-boat business, I thought that would be peaceful—keep her out in the air through the summer, rest her nerves. It did, too. And it was a bit of a joke. She laughed a lot on the house-boat. I enjoyed it, too. I could feel myself an actor again, playing the fool on that house-boat." He smiled at a sudden memory. "Ben called me a troubadour that day we turned up at the Herb of Grace. I loved him for it. Without knowing that he did it, he saw straight through to the actor in me."

"And to more than that," thought Hilary to himself.

Malony probably did not know that some of the early troubadours were something much more than wandering minstrels. As they travelled from one land to another, from court to court and castle to castle, they linked together the adherents of a secret society of mystic teaching. The words of their songs were symbolical; the initiated understood. Discovery meant death, but these troubadours accepted that as all in the day's work. Malony was that sort of troubadour, Hilary thought. He belonged to the secret brotherhood of the Herb of Grace.

– 1 –

I T WAS TOMMY'S TURN, THIS TIME, to be returning home. He was thrilled, but not quite so thrilled as Caroline had been; so much less so, in fact, that he had felt he could bear to delay his return for a couple of days in order to spend the week-end with a friend and possess himself of a second-hand motor-bicycle, no longer required by the friend's elder brother. A motor-bike of his own had always been the chief desire of Tommy's life, for he had a passion for the internal-combustion engine that was the equal of that of his namesake Toad, but requests to his parents to give him one had hitherto been met by a steady refusal. George had said he could not afford to provide his sons with motor-bikes at present. Nadine had said motor-bikes were dangerous things and that even if they had been able to afford it she'd never have a happy moment when Tommy was out of her sight on the horror. After several refusals they had considered the subject closed. Tommy had not. Spending a week of the summer holidays with the same friend, he had secretly learned to ride it. Now it was his. There was, of course, the little matter of paying for it, but that could be seen to later. From school he had sent a postcard to his mother:

"Home Wednesday. Sent box in advance. You can unpack it if you want to. Bringing my Christmas present from you and father, so if you've got anything else for me you can keep it till my birthday. Glad you've got Auntie Rose for cook now. What about tipsy trifle for supper? And we might have wild duck, if Father can shoot one, with water-cress. And toasted cheese to follow. Love, Tommy."

And now in the crisp winter dawn he stood in the stable yard of his friend's home, attired in overalls far too large for him, thrown in gratis along with the bike, and adjusted his goggles, also thrown in gratis, and looked up at the sky and grinned. They'd expect him by the usual evening train, of course, but he was going to surprise them. Leaving so early, avoiding the cross-country journey, he'd be home by lunch-time. Give them all the shock of their lives. They'd get five more hours of him than they'd expected to. Jolly for them. He pulled on his leather gauntlets, bestrode his precious bike and with a terrifying volley of back-firing and a fearful stench (the machine was exceedingly ancient) went roaring out of the yard and down the quiet country road beyond.

"'Poop-poop!'" he yelled joyously, quoting Toad the terror, the traffic-queller, the lord of the lone trail. "'Poop-poop! The poetry of motion! The *real* way to travel! The *only* way to travel! Here today—in next week tomorrow! Villages skipped, towns and cities jumped—always somebody else's horizon. O bliss! O poop-poop! O my! O my!'"

The thought of Toad made him think joyously of home. He was going home. Home to the Herb of Grace. Home to that jolly old house where the river lapped against the garden wall and where one could mess about in boats all day long. It was winter now. There'd be log fires burning in the old rooms. He'd go shooting with Father. And there'd be hunting. He'd get a horse from somewhere and go. And there was the blessed bike. Boanerges. All day and every day he would tear round the lanes on Boanerges. There was the question of petrol, of course, but Father need not use the car much during the holidays. Do him good to walk a bit more. Life was good in the country. Much better than in the town. Jolly good thing they'd bought the Herb of Grace. Jolly old place. The Herb of Grace. Home. He'd already commanded a Christmas-tree. They hadn't had one in the Chelsea house; there hadn't been room. Now there would be. A big one in the hall. It would look jolly. Presents for everyone on it. Pity he hadn't got any presents for the family. He'd meant to get them all something, but it had been an expensive term, and he was now financially ruined. It didn't matter. He'd explain, and they wouldn't mind. They'd have him. Lovely for them to have him five hours earlier than they'd expected. He laughed again, picturing their joy. He liked giving pleasure. Then, as the white ribbon of the road sped away behind him, he shouted for joy and gave his famous imitation of ducks quacking. Good old Boanerges! She might be old, she might make the hell of a stench and the devil of a row, but she was a good goer. At this rate he'd be home even earlier than he'd thought.

It was a grand morning. The last fortnight had been cold, but now it was perfect open weather—almost like spring. It would be a green Christmas. Overhead one great planet still burned in the blue-green of the sky, with a small satellite star kneeling at its feet. Ben would have known its name. Tommy didn't. But he liked it, and the little star sort of worshipping it. The trees were motionless and black against that clear, pure sky. The mist was knee-deep in the quiet fields. Beyond the row that Boanerges was making Tommy was aware of a great silence holding the world, and he knew that if it hadn't been for Boanerges he would have smelt the faint, clean smell of wet grass. But he was not aware of any sense of deprivation. The sound and the smell of Boanerges were as music and incense in his ears and nostrils. Bending low over his handle-bars, he worshipped his machine, as the star the planet. To his mind there was nothing so grand in all the world as mechanism, whether it was the mechanism of the human body or the mechanism that the human body made. He began to sing to Boanerges, and Boanerges sang to him. They were utterly happy.

The dawn came—not the flaming sky that promises storm, but a golden dawn of infinite promise. The birds came flying up out of the east in wedge-shaped formation, and the mist lifted in soft wreaths of sun-shot silver. Colour came back to the world. The grass glowed with a green so vivid that it seemed pulsing, like flame, from some hidden fire in the earth, the distant woods took on all the amazing deep crimsons and purples of their winter colouring, the banks were studded with their jewels of lichens and bright moss, and above the wet hedges shone with sun-shot orbs of light.

"It can be gay in the country in the winter," thought Tommy. "It will be gay at the Herb of Grace. The river will be sparkly, and when the sun sets behind Knyghtwood it will be all lit up with candle-light, like that first evening."

Though an hour after starting he was hungry as a hunter he did not stop for anything to eat. Once started, Boanerges went like the wind, but there was the danger that once stopped she would not go again. There was no doubt that she was temperamental in her old age. Also he did not want to waste a minute, for he had conceived the idea that if he were to be home by, say, eleven-thirty, he would be able to give a few commands about lunch. It would be appalling to come home to boiled cod and macaroni pudding. The sun rose high in the glorious sky and the miles sped away behind him. The exhilaration of his speed made him feel almost intoxicated with delight. As always when one is out of doors for any length of time, the sun and the wind ceased to be impersonal elements and became his friends. The wind laughed in his ear and the touch of the sun on his cheek was like a personal caress; like the touch of his mother's delicate hand.... That was always the way she greeted him when he got home, with that gentle touch of her hand on his cheek, as though she felt him to make certain he was really there.... As the exceedingly sentimental comparison slipped unbidden into his mind he blushed hotly. Then laughed in delight. Mother! He'd see her in another hour. She was a good sort. If he stepped on the gas he might see her in forty minutes. Father too. He wasn't a bad old chump either. Neither was Ben, though of course completely crackers. Caroline and the twins weren't bad kids as kids go. As regards family it was his opinion that he might have done worse. He was going too fast, he knew, but there was little traffic about. But he'd slow down when he saw signs of human habitation, for he didn't want to run into the arms of the law. He hadn't got a licence.

Luck was with him. An absence of obstruction and the law aided by a miracle of speed, got him to the Hard at eleven-ten, and by a further stroke of good fortune the gate leading to their lane was open. The last mile of his blissful journey had been somewhat clouded by the fear that if he had to stop Boanerges to open the gate he'd not get her going again, and arrive home wheeling the creature, which would not be at all the sort of arrival he had planned. But some good soul had left the gate open, and without stopping he jolted joyously down their lane. *Their* lane. Home. He found, to his surprise, that he remembered the different shapes of the old oak-trees as though they were the shapes of people whom he knew. He turned the corner, and with a lift of the heart greeted Knyghtwood upon his right and the orchard upon his left, and the bright gleam of the river down at the bottom of the lane. Then he accelerated and went roaring down the hill at a pace that threatened to land him straight in the river. But he managed to rock to a vociferous, odoriferous standstill at the foot of the garden steps.

"Poop-poop!" he yelled. "Toad's home! Toad's home!"

And then he did his imitation of ducks quacking.

Summoned by the stench, the tumult and the shouting, the household came pouring out of the Herb of Grace; George first, with the twins close at his heels, screaming like an express train; then Jill and Caroline, Annie-Laurie and Malony; but not Nadine. Was Mother ill? For a brief moment Tommy felt suddenly and unaccountably sick.... Must be the motion or something.... He pulled off his goggles and lifted a suddenly rather mature face as his father came striding down to him with long, eager strides. George forestalled the question on his parted lips.

"Mother's all right. Gone to look for that water-cress you commanded for supper. I shot a wild duck the day before yesterday. It's hanging." His hand descended to his son's shoulder and gripped it hard. Their eyes met and they smiled. Tommy looked a boy again. "Ben's all right. Somewhere about," said George.

But Tommy had been at ease before receiving the assurance of Ben's well-being. It is possible that in the last resort he and George would have consigned the entire world to the bottom of the sea rather than allow a hair of Nadine's head to being injured.

"What the dickens?" asked George, eyeing Boanerges.

"Didn't Mother show you my postcard?" asked Tommy. "It's your Christmas present to me, yours and Mother's. Second-hand. I told Clive you'd send a cheque. Wizard, isn't it?... Jerry, you young fool, let that alone! José! Mole! Rat! If either of you two so much as touch Boanerges without my permission I'll flay you alive! Caroline! Jill! Pull 'em off! Jerry, you young devil! Malony, cuff his ear!"

Pandemonium had broken out as the twins, shouting, swarmed over Boanerges. George, making a remark, was unheard. He rubbed his ear, then slowly grinned, visited by the pleasing thought that he need have no anxiety as to the worldly success in life of this son of his. George's paternal anxiety did not stretch to more than the material welfare of his children; he'd not the strength for more. He left it to Lucilla to worry about their spiritual welfare; it was all he could do to get their school bills paid.

Malony competently detached the twins and handed them over to Jill, who removed them, yelling, indoors.

"Grand machine, Sir," he said to Tommy. "I'll wheel her round to the yard and give her a clean right away."

Tommy found himself quite glad to dismount. He was, he found, slightly staggery about the legs, and did not disdain his father's hand beneath his elbow as they went up the garden path, Caroline dancing joyously backwards in front of them.

Annie-Laurie, who had run back into the house, came running out again with her tweed coat on, her eyes shining.

"I'm going to find Mrs. Eliot and tell her Tommy's come," she said.

Tommy grinned at her as she ran past them. She looked different, he thought. Not like a maid any longer. More like a sister.

"Better have a sherry and something to eat right away," said George. "Caroline, there are biscuits in that box. Fetch 'em out while I find the sherry. Here we are."

They were inside the Herb of Grace, and, as Tommy had foreseen, there was a gorgeous log fire burning on the hearth, its light reflected warmly in the panelling. The gracious old branching staircase stood there before him, and seemed to hold out its arms in welcome, almost as though it were a person, and the little white deer in the alcove shone in the firelight like a lighted lamp.

His father let go of his elbow and put an arm round his shoulder. "Grand to have you home," he said. "Now for the sherry."

Tommy passed his forearm over his forehead and tousled curly hair with a gesture of relief. He let out a sigh. He was home.

– 2 –

Twenty minutes later, entirely himself again, having devoured half the month's biscuit ration and drunk to the last drop the small allowance of sherry that was all George would permit, he was striding towards the kitchen. He flung open the door and entered masterfully. Auntie Rose was there, at work at the kitchen table, and a delicious alcoholic fragrance fought almost successfully with the smell of uncooked cod. She was making the commanded tipsy trifle for supper. Tommy had seen her only once before, but she had remained vividly in his memory as a woman after his own heart; no nonsense about her, brisk, pretty and a good cook. She had seemed to him then an integral part of the Herb of Grace, and her absence last holidays had made him feel there was something missing. Also he had hated to see his mother slaving in the kitchen. It had seemed all wrong, somehow. She wasn't the sort of woman who ought to get her hands stained; also just now and then she was inclined to be a bit stingy and to talk about rations and bills in a way that affronted his own lavish instincts. But now here was Auntie Rose back in her proper place, gay and delightful, with her rosy cheeks, blue eyes and white hair done up in that enchanting bun at the top of her head. She wore a purple apron with yellow sunflowers on it, and she sang as she planted out crystallized cherries on top of the trifle with the superb generosity of one who has not paid for them. He took two steps towards her, flung his arms about her and gave her a smacking kiss upon each of her rosy cheeks.

"Now the place is itself again," he said. "What's in that trifle? Rum?"

She laughed delightedly, and fetched from the dresser a brilliant geranium-coloured fluted tin with a picture of Queen Victoria on it, that had travelled through life with her ever since the Diamond Jubilee. Inside was a cake literally stuffed with fruit. Tommy's eyes sparkled at sight of it; he hadn't seen such a cake since his childhood.

"There, ducks," said Auntie Rose, cutting a large slice and setting the tin beside him as he sat upon the kitchen table swinging his legs. "Early home, aren't you? Come on a motor-bike? Thought I heard you. Starved, you must be. I'll heat you up a cup of coffee. Eat what you like of that cake, love. We've plenty of fruit. I've a nephew in the grocery business. Yes, dear, it's rum in the trifle. Fred—that's me nephew—got me a few little extras for Christmas."

"Auntie Rose, did you scrap with your daughter-in-law, that you've come back?" asked Tommy, munching cake.

"You mind your own business, young man," said Auntie Rose, with twinkling eyes, placing a large cup of coffee and a brimming sugar-bowl beside him. "I'm here to help your Mother over Christmas. After that, what's to be will be. Now you get down off me table and let me get at me pastry-board. I've a macaroni pudding for lunch, but with you extra I'll maybe have time to knock up a few apple dumplings to go with it."

"Brown sugar and raisins inside?" coaxed Tommy, his head on one side. "Auntie Rose, this cake is wizard. Auntie Rose, I love you."

He slid off the table, turned his head in the direction of the cod and sniffed a slightly questioning sniff.

"With a tartare sauce, ducks," said Auntie Rose. "I'd thought of a plain sauce, me being pressed for time, but as you're home we'll make it tartare."

Tommy finished his cake and his coffee, peeled the apples for Auntie Rose and ate the uncooked pastry trimmings with relish. As he peeled and ate he told her all about himself—about his bike, his rugger colours, the boil he'd had at the back of his neck and the rotten food they had at school.

Auntie Rose inspected the place where the boil had been, noticed that two of his finger-nails were splitting and fancied that she saw dark shadows beneath his eyes.... Undernourished.... She made a sudden decision. She'd stay on at the Herb of Grace. Thankful though she had been to get away from her daughter-in-law and the boredom of the rest she thought she'd enjoy but hadn't, she'd not been quite sure that her subservient position at the Herb of Grace had been altogether to her liking. She had lost her heart to the General and Ben, and Mrs. Eliot had been tact itself, trusting her completely and never interfering, and with her suite and the brass bedstead she'd made a lovely bed-sitting-room for herself upstairs; but yet she'd not been quite sure if she wanted to stay. Tommy decided her. Not only did he need nourishment in the holidays, but he appreciated it. Ben never seemed altogether aware of what he was eating, and the General—poor, dear man—had a weak digestion and could only eat sparingly, but Tommy would be the perfect justification of her art.

"Now you get along with you," she said, her decision made. "I've the Christmas mincemeat to see to and scones for tea. If you haven't seen Master Ben yet, he's upstairs in the studio with Mr. Adair."

"What, Old Beaver? Gosh! I want to take a look at him," said Tommy, and went bounding off up the turret stairs as lightly as though he had partaken of no nourishment at all that day.

Out of the corner of his eye, as he bounded, he saw the closed door of the Chapel, but he let that wait. Auntie Rose as cook, John Adair and the Chapel were all additions to the Herb of Grace since last holidays, and he was taking them in the order in which they interested him—food, fame, religion; he was a hedonist, and the latter interested him scarcely at all as yet.

He knocked on the studio door, but entered at once without waiting for an answer.

"Hullo," he said, and stood looking round him, his bright dark eyes taking in the essential details of the scene in one quick glance: the two artists, the stacked canvases, his mother's portrait, some sort of a brown mess of a picture that Ben was working at, and—Horace.

"Gosh!" he whispered, and then there was silence, a silence of such ecstasy that he might have been Dante seeing Beatrice for the first time, or Cortez upon the peak in Darien.

But John Adair got there first. In two strides he was across the room and had unhooked Horace.

"Like him?" he asked, holding the skeleton at arm's length for inspection. "My especial property. Name of Horace. Not to be removed from this room without my permission, but may be examined under my eye in the interests of science whenever you like. Tommy, I presume?"

And he held out his free hand.

"Yes, Sir," said Tommy, gripping it cordially and with his most disarming grin—a grin into which he could instil when necessary a certain pathos. "Thank you. I'm going to be a surgeon, you know, Sir."

"Certainly," said John Adair heartily. "Whenever you like. But under my eye."

"Of course, Sir. Hullo, Ben!"

The brothers smiled at each other with careful moderation, each surprised to find how glad he was to see the other, and each mortally afraid of showing it.

"Hullo," said Ben. "Got your bike, haven't you? Thought from your postcard you'd got hold of one somehow. Was the gate still open?"

"You opened the gate?" asked Tommy.

Ben nodded. Tommy swung round and stood shoulder to shoulder with him before his easel, contemplating the brown mess.

"Jolly," he said.

He didn't think it was. He thought it was a mess. But it had been decent of Ben to open the gate. But as he looked comprehension dawned.

"Why, it's the staircase!" he said. "It looked just like that when I came home just now—like a man—I hadn't noticed it before." He gazed a bit longer, out of gratitude for the gate. "I like his face. Looks like Pickwick. Or Punch on the Christmas number. Or Johnny Walker. One of those jolly, beery fellows."

John Adair moved forward and stood behind the two boys, looking over their shoulders at the picture. It was now no longer a chalk sketch, but a fair-sized affair in oils. It was only during this last week that Ben had really got going on the face, and his inspection had not yet been invited. But Tommy having so to speak unveiled it, he could now take a look. He was pleased with Ben. He had not swung the picture round, as on the day when Nadine had come in unexpectedly; though he could see by Ben's taut expression that the comparison with beery fellows was odious to him; but, obeying instructions, he was abiding by the consequences of what he had done. He even laughed.

"Got the nose too red," he said humbly. "And the smile too fatuous."

"I don't think so," said John Adair quietly behind them. "That's not the complexion of inebriation, but of a healthy middle-aged man who's just come in from a tramp in the frosty woods. And the smile—it's intoxicated, certainly, but not with beer, merely with the glory of what his artist's eye has seen in the woods. It's not fatuous. Glory doesn't so much knock you silly as exuberant. What you do when you're filled up with it and spilling it out again may look a bit silly at first sight, like those arms stretched out, like those vignettes of animals shoved in among the tree-tops in the Chapel frescoes; but on a second glance, no. Take another look, Tommy."

Tommy took another look. The man's eyes were brown and very bright, with a penetrating look in them as though they saw a good deal, with the same sort of puckers about them that the eyes of sailors and countrymen have, who watch the weather and find hidden meanings in the bending of the grass and the massing of the clouds. He had a comic brown beard that jutted forward in an eager sort of way. He was not actually laughing, but the humour that touched the eyes and lips made one feel that a great burst of kindly laughter was on the way, and gave his face that look of joviality that Tommy was accustomed to associate with Pickwick and Johnny Walker. But his surgeon's eye noted now the width of the face from temple to temple, giving a look of peace, and the rugged strength of the cheek-bones and jaw. And between the man's bushy brown eyebrows there was a frown of deep concentration. Tommy felt respect for Ben as an artist. Now, if he'd painted a frown it would have looked bad-tempered, but this frown was the frown of a chap who attended with his entire self to one thing at a time. He knew suddenly that this fellow hadn't had his cheerfulness bestowed upon him at birth, like Johnny Walker; he'd fought for it and won it. No, joviality was all wrong. It was—

"Goodwill," murmured John Adair. "No one ever stops to think what that means. Not an easy thing. Unregenerate man, had he the courage to enquire into what he is really willing right down below the surface, would get a very nasty shock. Very rare—as rare as peace. When a man has both, the angels make quite a song and dance about it. Was it not prophesied, Ben, that Christmas would show you the face of this man?"

"Christmas and the Chapel walls," said Ben. "He put his whole heart into the frescoes." He paused, looking anxiously at the artist. "Is it all right?"

"Yes, it's all right. That's Mine Host of a Pilgrim Inn and the painter as revealed in his work. The colour needs toning down a bit here and there. Here, for instance—"

The conversation became technical, and Tommy left them, to continue his home-coming tour of inspection. He ran down the turret stairs, opened the door of what had once been the store-room and went in.

"Gosh!" he exclaimed in astonishment.

The walls were finished now, and the little room was furnished as a Chapel—though very simply, so as not to detract from the glory of the frescoes; merely with a plain old oak table beneath the painting on the east wall, and a few benches. A couple of beautiful old wrought-iron branched candlesticks stood upon the table, and a pot of winter greenery, in whose perfect arrangement Tommy thought he detected his mother's hand. He looked about the walls in amazement, laughing at the comic birds and animals, the extravagance of the flowers, yet awed by the beauty of what he saw, and the mystery of the picture of the knight on horseback, and the deer holding up the crucifix. He wondered so much what it was all about that he sat down on one of the benches to wonder in greater comfort. That deer and the one in the alcove, Ben's painting and the stairs, what the dickens did it all mean? He didn't know, but the value of his home was greatly enhanced for him by the sense of depth that he was now conscious of in the Herb of Grace. It was as though he had had a friend but hadn't known him very well, and now the man had suddenly shown him his heart. The man—the staircase—had put his heart into these frescoes, Ben had said. And this Chapel was the heart of the house as the place where the stag stood was the heart of the painted wood, that was so like Knyghtwood. He suddenly jumped up. Mother was in Knyghtwood, looking for water-cress to garnish the wild duck he had demanded for supper. He'd go and find her.

– 3 –

Nadine had woken up that morning feeling astonishingly light-hearted. Tommy was coming home today, and then she would have all her children gathered under her wing. She had always been glad to have them home, of course, but she had never before felt so quite passionately hen-like as she did this morning. Was she at last becoming properly maternal? She wondered why. The final agonizing break with David might have something to do with it. Letting go of David she had let go of her youth, too, recognized herself for what she now was—a middle-aged woman in whom love out of wedlock was just painfully silly but love within it profoundly sensible. Age meant deeper roots, and therefore more circumscribed affections. And then her roots were now in a house that had gradually become to her the best home she had ever known; more of a home than the one at Chelsea, which it had nearly broken her heart to leave; a house whose essential quality of protectiveness had no doubt fostered this imitative hen-like attitude in herself. But most of all she thought her deepening maternity had something to do with Annie-Laurie. It was odd that another woman's child had been able to do for her something that her own children had not been able to do. Perhaps Annie-Laurie's need of her had been greater than she knew; greater than her own children's present need. Perhaps there was some bond between them that she did not know of yet.

As she dressed she stopped thinking of herself and thought only of Annie-Laurie. Hilary had come over a few days ago to inspect the finished Chapel, had sought her out and, deprecatingly rubbing his nose, had humbly hoped that she would soon find some way of winning Annie-Laurie's complete confidence.

"You can't force it, I know," he said. "That would be fatal. But if you could find some way—I've been talking to Malony, and I can see he's anxious about her."

"Would it be betraying his confidence to tell me what he told you?" she asked, and then, seeing his hesitation, "I'm trustworthy, you know."

His charming smile flashed out at her.

"I know. And I must certainly tell you the facts, for you'll need them. But they won't get you very far, for the thing that's getting Annie-Laurie down is something that she's not told Malony."

He told her the facts, and she listened attentively.

"I'll do my best," she said.

But since then she'd had no chance to be alone with Annie-Laurie, and this morning she must go and find some water-cress for Tommy. A couple of days ago Sally had told her that there was a stream in Knyghtwood, beyond Ben's Brockis Island, and that she had a sort of feeling she'd seen water-cress growing there. She had offered to go and see, but she had been busy packing for a few days' visit to London to buy Christmas presents, and Nadine had told her not to bother, she'd go herself; with Auntie Rose to do the cooking she was so much less tired and she had more time. She had never yet penetrated the depths of Knyghtwood, and she knew it was incumbent upon her to do so; not only was she haunted by that lyric of Meredith's, but now that Knyghtwood had appeared in the house it was somehow a part of the house, and she must know her house through and through.

When she had put her household into order she put on thick shoes and her cherry-coloured coat, took a basket and prepared to sally forth.

"Shall I come too?" asked George a little wistfully.

She felt a brute at refusing him, but she knew she must go to Knyghtwood alone.

"No, George. It'll be damp, and you'll only get your asthma. I can't have you with asthma over Christmas."

"Let *me* come, Mummie," implored Caroline. "You don't know what water-cress looks like."

"Yes, I do. I've bought it in the shops."

"It looks quite different growing from what it does in the shops."

"My poppet, I've more intelligence than you give me credit for. I'm going quite alone."

"Not even Mary?"

"Oh yes, Mary, of course."

From the front door George and Caroline watched her beautiful gay figure mount the steps to the green gate and enter the wood, Mary, her nose in the air, bouncing at her heels.

"I don't *like* Mary," said Caroline with a violence unusual to her gentleness.

George laughed and slipped an arm round his daughter's shoulders.

"Your mother is rather a reticent sort of person, Elf, and the excel-

Elizabeth Goudge

lent thing about dogs is that they keep you company without asking questions, and afterwards they keep your counsel."

"Are you reticent, Daddy?" asked Caroline. "Am I?"

"We've neither of us much to be reticent about," said George, with a touch of gloom. "Simple sort of folk, you and I, Elf. That's why we suit each other. Get your coat and come up to the Hard with me to see Hitchcock about the manure."

Caroline departed singing to find her coat. She would enjoy herself much more, really, going with Daddy to see about the manure than with Mother to find water-cress. She understood neither Mother nor Knyghtwood very well; they both scared her a little.

Nadine went swiftly through the wood, Mary now bounding delightedly ahead of her. The ground that had been so hard with the frost had now a delicious elastic softness beneath her feet, and the sun striking through the bare branches warmed her lifted face.

"Something to be said for a climate that can jewel midwinter with days like these," she thought. "It's Christmas, yet in this wood you'd never know it."

It struck her as she walked that the artist who had painted the Chapel walls had not gone far astray when he set the flowers of all the seasons blooming together in his wood, for in this one today the colours were so gay and varied that spring and summer and autumn seemed all of them blooming in winter's lap. The lichens about the tree-roots might have been primroses, the deep azure shadows bluebell pools. The willow shoots were the colour of a robin's breast, and there were a few scarlet berries on the holly trees. As she passed beyond the fringe of the wood that she knew, and came to a part that was new to her, she was astonished to find individual blossoms coming out all at the wrong season—the delicate stars of strawberry flowers, periwinkles, a few celandines, dog mercury and one pale primrose. She saw, too, a plant of hellebore in full blossom, though it ought not to have been out until February. It reminded her of Christmas roses, and she stopped to look at it. She remembered that Ben had told her that hellebore is for the healing of mental illness. He had quoted "The Anatomy of Melancholy."

"Sovereign plants to purge the veins
Of melancholy, and cheer the heart
Of those black fumes which make it smart."

She looked at the flowers with elation; their winter flowering, though it was so sparse and fragile, was so triumphant. To her left a kingfisher flashed against the dazzle of the river, and she could have laughed aloud. She had shrunk from this wood, and now she found, to her surprise, that she was enjoying it. Until today she did not think that she would have done so, but her new lightness of heart was in tune with its gaiety. She was glad that her coat matched the holly berries, that Mary was such a flowery-looking little creature and that her brown suede shoes were the colour of the kindly earth, whose elasticity seemed swinging her along as though it helped her journey. She was not a countrywoman, and she had not before felt quite this sense of comradeship with the earth. It made her very happy.

When she came to the oak-tree, with the leaves of the herb of grace growing around it, and recognized the background that John Adair had chosen for her portrait, she felt, after the first moment of shock, a curious sense of home-coming. She stood still, her heart beating fast. She had caught up, now, with that woman in the picture. She had reached one of her milestones. She covered her face with her hands for a moment tried to capture the flashing vision that had come to her of life as a series of deaths and rebirths, each predestined, so that when you reached it you recognized it as something that had been waiting for you, and yet each at the same time a matter of choice, so that you came to it with a joy or pain of your own making; a paradox whose mystery baffled the mind, but whose truth the heart recognized. She remembered how the old masters in their paintings would sometimes represent the soul as a tiny child. Somewhere she had seen a picture by, she thought, Fra Angelico, of God standing behind a bier with a smiling baby in His arms. The old masters had known their business. They had had the boldness to express the inexpressible in terms of humanity; after the example of God Himself at Christmas. She took her hands from her eyes, bent down, picked a few leaves of the herb of grace and put them in the lapel of her coat. Sally, once, had done the same thing; but Sally had acted without thought, mechanically taking to herself something that was hers already, as a woman might take a trinket from her dressing-table; but Nadine picked the leaves deliberately, as an act of dedication. As she walked forward again she left behind her something buried, fallen into dust with the failing breath, and carried with her something born. "Should thy love die." The old lusting love *had* died, and was buried under the foliaged sky. It was life that she would love now with this new love, life as it was held within the walls of her home. "The lover of life sees the flame in our dust and a gift in our breath." She smiled as she walked, even as the baby in the picture had been smiling.

She went on until she came to Brockis Island, with the wild fruit-trees and the badger's holt, that was the heart of the wood to Ben because his painting of it had been the first he had done with John Adair's encouragement, the first with full knowledge that it was to this art that he had given himself, and she marvelled at its beauty, but it did not touch her as had the old tree trunk where the herb of grace grew. A second little bridge had now been placed by Ben from the island to the farther bank, and she and Mary crossed by it and walked on and came to the stream in the clearing that was the heart of the wood to Sally, because here she had met David again, but though Nadine once more marvelled at the beauty it did not touch her deeply, for the heart of the wood, the place of the vision and dedication, the white deer and the crucifix, was still for her the beech-tree.... The Place Beyond, that was the heart of the wood to the twins, no one had been to except the twins.... Nadine, unaware that it even existed, walked no further, but turned and moved slowly up-stream looking for water-cress.

– 4 –

Annie-Laurie ran light-footed through the wood. She had already been a certain way into Knyghtwood, and she loved it, but she did not linger today, because she wanted to get to Nadine as soon as possible with the joyous news of Tommy's early arrival. She knew that he was Nadine's favourite child, and her eyes were bright with happiness as she ran, because she was bringing joy to Nadine. She loved Nadine with a happiness with which she had never yet loved anyone; except, long ago, her mother, and, not so long ago, her child. Her passion for Luke, that had changed for a while, without her wish and past her control, to such dreadful hatred, the mingled reliance and gratitude of her affection for Malony, had brought pain and humiliation. She had not been so happy in the relationship of sex as she had been in the relationship of daughter and mother. The first she had recaptured again in her love for Nadine, the second she believed must be always a thing she would long for with unsatisfied anguish because of her promise to Luke.

She passed the beech-tree, and her countrywoman's eyes noted the narrow-leaved rue painted upon the inn signboard and about Nadine's feet in her portrait; she came to the island and recognized it as the inspiration of one of Ben's pictures; she ran through the wood beyond and came to the clearing, and found herself unexpectedly thinking of Sally. And then she saw something that stabbed her with almost unbearable pain, something personal to herself and to no one else. To her left the stream ran into the river, bog myrtle bushes arching overhead, and enclosed within their branches, as in a frame, she saw a white swan floating on the silver, sunlit river. Her baby's favourite toy had been a celluloid swan that accompanied her into the bath, to bed, out in the pram—everywhere. The creature had started life almost as perfect in shape and as snowy-feathered as that swan out there on the river, but the passing of time and the squeez-ings of affection had made it so dented and discoloured that at the end it was unrecognizable as a swan at all. But Midge had not cared. Her love was not time's fool. She had even been unaware, Annie-Laurie thought, that her swan had lost his first loveliness. He had been in her cot with her when she died, and Annie-Laurie had put him into her little coffin.

Annie-Laurie knew suddenly that she must sit down. Her head was swimming. It was all coming over her again, the nightmare and the madness, just when she had hoped she was getting better. The grief, and then the shock of discovery that had followed, and then the awful thing that she had done because of the grief and shock.... And then the fear.... It was all years ago now. Why couldn't she forget? She would think she was forgetting, and then some unexpected sight or sound would bring it all back again, and she'd be as bad as ever. She pushed her way through the bog-myrtle bushes, out into the sil-ver dazzle of the sunshine, and sat down on the river bank, her head down on her knees. She did not cry, for it was one of her misfortunes that she could scarcely ever cry, but a familiar icy coldness slid over her body, and pain throbbed in her temples. She was in for it again. There'd be sleepless nights again, and that awful nervous desperation that was harder to bear than any pain, and she'd snap and snarl at poor Malony, and for a week or so life would be hell for them both.

An arm slipped round her shoulders, and she looked up. Nadine in her cherry-red coat was sitting on the bank beside her, a basket of greenstuff at her feet. She looked glowing and lovely, and her face as she smiled had a new motherliness. Annie-Laurie let out an unconscious sigh of relief, as a shivering body will when it comes near a glowing fire, but her pride caused her unconsciously to stiffen a little under the encircling arm, and Nadine withdrew it. They were neither of them women who cared much for endearments.

"I was coming to find you," said Annie-Laurie. "Tommy has come home earlier than you expected him.... He's all right," she added quickly. "He's splendid. I only came because I thought you wouldn't want to lose a moment."

Nadine laughed.

"That was understanding of you. But I don't mind losing a few moments. I'm not used to tramping about in woods, and I'd be glad to sit and rest for a bit. You're not in a hurry, are you?"

"There's the laundry—"

"That can wait. You're a dear, Annie-Laurie, coming all this way to tell me about Tommy. But of course you would. Mothers understand mothers." The girl beside her shivered, but, like a good surgeon, she went inexorably on with the job. "Were you thinking about your little girl just now?"

"She had a toy swan," said Annie-Laurie, her eyes fixed now on the beautiful creature on the water in front of her. "She took it everywhere. It got awfully battered."

"Had she? Caroline had a frightful rag doll with a patch on its nose. She wouldn't look at anything else. I believe she's got it still. I've never lost a child, but I can imagine how all the little things would stab one till the end of time."

"Especially when it's your fault," said Annie-Laurie.

"You mean you blame yourself because your baby died?"

"Yes. She had bronchitis. I went out one night to do my work—I thought I ought to—I'd our living to get; for Luke, my husband, was too ill to work at that time. He said he'd look after her. But I ought not to have gone. She wasn't fit to be left. It was a cold night, and he opened the window bang on her."

There was a pause, and then Nadine quietly asked a question:

"Deliberately?"

"Yes."

For two days Nadine had been thinking over the story that Hilary had told her, wondering about many things, but in particular what it was that had turned Annie-Laurie's love for Luke to hatred. Something, of course, to do with the baby. She had guessed before this that the child was the crux of it all. She looked round, and saw Annie-Laurie's eyes fixed on hers with blank horror. That brief yes had been surprised out of her by Nadine's quietness. She would have given the earth to have withdrawn it.

"Annie-Laurie, now that you've told me that much I think it would help you if you told me everything. Was your husband very ill? If so perhaps he was not in a normal state of mind when he opened the window."

"No, he wasn't. And he was insanely jealous, too—of my baby's father—of Jim. And of Midge because she was Jim's child. We'd longed for a baby, Luke and I, but we had not had one."

"Try to tell me everything, Annie-Laurie, as you would have told your mother. Try not to leave anything out. It is never fair to anyone to tell a half-truth. It is a form of lying, and it confuses judgment."

If Annie-Laurie had hesitated, she did not after that. All her life she had taken her stand upon truth. Bit by bit, bravely, she told it all, while Nadine listened patiently, fitting among the facts she already knew those that until now Annie-Laurie had told no one. Given those facts there was no more confusion in the story.

Though Annie-Laurie had been in an anguish of fury over the open window, though she had bitterly reproached Luke for it, she had not suspected him of more than gross carelessness until the evening of his death, when he had himself told her that he had exposed Midge deliberately. They had had a row over Malony, and he had not cared what he said if only he could hurt her enough.

"He had suffered so much that he was not sane," she kept saying to Nadine. "He was not to blame. He did not know what he did or said. And it had been an awful shock to him, after we had loved each other so much, to come back and find me married to another man. I could not make him understand how I felt about Jim. I never loved him as I loved Luke—I never shall—but I felt safe with him. I was grateful to him, and he needed me. It was awful, that evening he told me he had—almost—murdered Midge. It threw me right off my balance. After that, I was hardly sane either. I cried out, 'I hate you, Luke. I hate you so much I'd like to kill you,' and I cried out so loudly that the people in the next flat heard me."

But she had not meant to bring back the wrong tablets from the chemist. Malony's explanation of her conduct then had been the right one. It was not until Luke was actually taking the first one that she saw her mistake and then, deliberately—as deliberately as Luke himself when he opened the window upon Midge—she held her peace and let him take the second. She had not known, of course, what it was that he was taking; for all she knew it was something harmless. But she had not bothered to find out. When she had found him deeply asleep, she still had not bothered.

"It was as though what he had told me had been a blow on the head," she said to Nadine, "I was stunned. I didn't come to myself till the next morning. So, you see, that verdict of not guilty was a wrong one. I killed Luke."

She had told it at last, the thing that had poisoned her life and nearly disordered her reason. Her straight back sagged, and she seemed to shrink in upon herself, as though she had no more strength left in her.

"I'm sure I'd have done the same," said Nadine quickly. "I believe any mother would."

After that she sat quietly beside Annie-Laurie, not touching her, but willing that the warmth of her understanding might reach to her. "Defend us from all adversities which may happen to the body and from all evil thoughts which may assault and hurt the soul," she had prayed once in her room at the Herb of Grace, that first time Annie-Laurie had talked to her. The old inn gave one a very comforting feeling of physical protection, but this wood gave one more than that: a sense of spiritual safety, of release from the burden of tormenting thought.... There grew in it the hellebore, that was for the healing of mental sickness.... After a while Annie-Laurie straightened herself, and with both hands pushed the hair back from her forehead with a gesture of such unutterable relief that Nadine knew she was released. She had told at last.

"I ought to have told at the trial," said Annie-Laurie. "But I was afraid of what they might do to me. I'm a coward, you know. I've always been afraid of things—I don't know why. But I tried not to tell any lies. I didn't think then—what you said just now—that to tell only half the truth is a form of lying. Perhaps—do you think—I ought to tell Jim?"

"Yes, I think you ought. I think he deserves that you should not keep anything from him. Why did you not tell him before? Were you afraid you would lose his love?"

"No. I don't think anything I could do would make him love me less—he's like that. It was for Luke's sake I did not tell. He would have asked how I had come to hate Luke so much. I did not want him to know what Luke had done to Midge. You see, I had loved Luke and—you'll think this odd—after he was dead I loved him again."

"Yes, I can understand that. Death has a way of wiping out hatred. And it does more than that: it increases understanding. It's queer, but after people are dead you find that you understand them better. There's a poem that says, 'What the dead have no speech for, when living, they can tell you, being dead.' Perhaps that's true. I don't know. But I think you'll find, when you tell Malony what Luke did to Midge, that he won't hate him for it. He'll understand quite well that he did not understand what he was doing.... Annie-Laurie, why haven't you remarried Malony and had another child?"

She knew, but she wanted Annie-Laurie to tell her, and Annie-Laurie told her.

"I promised Luke I wouldn't. Once, when he was very ill one night and thought he might die, he made me promise. I tried not to, and then I had to, just to keep him quiet. After he was dead because of—what I'd done—I felt I had to keep that promise. It was the only reparation I could make."

"That was a promise for which Luke had no right to ask, and you have no right to keep."

"I have to keep my word," said Annie-Laurie stubbornly. "You were talking only a little while ago about the importance of truth."

"It's difficult," said Nadine gently. "In my own life I've found decisions about truth almost the hardest of all to make. When to speak out and when to hold one's peace. Whether it is best to hurt someone with the truth or make them happy with a lie. It's dreadfully difficult. Generally I think it's a question of charity. Those who are leaving the world have no right to impose their will upon those they leave behind them; that's a sort of seeking after power that's deadly selfish. And no one has the right to seek ease of conscience at the expense of another's happiness; that's selfish, too." Nadine pushed her fingers up into her hair with a despairing gesture. She was no good at this sort of thing. She hated doing it. Hilary ought to have been doing it. Mean of him to have put it on her. But love for Annie-

Laurie drove her on. "Even though you are together, yet you can see from Malony's face that he's a most unhappy man. He wants proper married life—children and a home. You've no right, just because keeping your promise to Luke eases your misery of remorse to keep Malony on the rack."

"You see," said Annie-Laurie slowly, "it's Luke I really love."

Nadine looked at her. So that was the likeness between them. Annie-Laurie couldn't let go of Luke, any more than she had been able to let go of David. She had gone with Malony, even as Nadine had gone with George, but not with the single mind.

"Let your love die," she said sharply, almost savagely. "Cut it right out, like a cancer. Cut the whole past right out. Try your hardest to forget it. People with divided allegiance are crazily unhappy, and make others unhappy. Let it be Malony, and Malony only, with what he stands for, now and until the end."

Annie-Laurie wrung her hands in an unconscious gesture of wretchedness.

"It would be like killing Luke over again."

"Nonsense! That's sheer sentimentality. When I said, 'Let your love die,' I meant die out of your conscious mind, out of the part of you that has to deal with daily living here and now. It will live on in the innermost part of you, of course. Everything we've had and been does that. Perhaps in some way we find it all again after this life. I don't know. I only know that here and now, today, the happiness of those we are with is what matters. I've no right to talk, Annie-Laurie. I haven't practised what I preach. But I'll try—if you will."

Annie-Laurie said nothing, and Nadine didn't look at her. She leaned back against a rock behind her and shut her eyes. She was about at the end of her tether. She'd probably made a complete mess of everything. She felt just about savage with Hilary. He should have done the job himself.

There was a trampling in the wood, and the sound of a boy's voice calling, "Cooee!"

"Tommy come to find you," said Annie-Laurie.

Nadine opened her eyes, wondering for how long they'd sat here in silence. Annie-Laurie, very white, but looking oddly peaceful, was standing up holding the basket of greenstuff. Nadine, getting to her feet, saw her looking about her as though seeing for the first time this place where they had been sitting. The small patch of turf, pungent with thymy things, had been soft to sit upon between the boulders of grey rock, and well protected by the bog-myrtle bushes. Dividing it, the small clear brown stream ran merrily over the polished stones, to lose itself in the iris leaves that fringed the river, a sheet of silver under the sun. Annie-Laurie looked steadily about her, for this for her was the heart of the wood, and then led the way upstream. Nadine, following her, knew without a word spoken that all would soon be well with her.

They reached the clearing at the same time as George, Ben and Tommy.

"We've been anxious, Nadine," said George, his worried face relaxing at the sight of her.

"Long past lunch-time, Mother," explained Ben.

"With apple dumplings getting tougher and tougher in the oven, Mother," said Tommy reproachfully; but his eyes sparkled, and in two bounds he was with her and subjecting her to one of his bear hugs. Though bruised she gloried in his strength for a moment, then, feeling the bruises more than the glory, held him away from her and gently touched his cheek with her finger. "Forgive us, darling. We haven't got our watches, and we sat down and talked, and the sun was nice and hot and we forgot about lunch. But I've got your water-cress. Look!"

"Jolly decent of you, Mother," said Tommy, surveying the basket, and then subjecting her to another hug.

Ben also surveyed the basket, and looked at his mother with laughing eyes.

"That's not water-cress, Mother, it's water-parsnip, and not edible. Sometimes it's called fool's-cress, because—well"—he grinned—"people get mixed up between the two sometimes."

Tommy roared with laughter.

"Just as decent of you, Mother, all the same."

CHAPTER

16

– 1 –

SALLY ALSO WAS RETURNING to the Herb of Grace, speeding home in the train after her few days' shopping in London, and she, like Caroline, had a suitcase bursting with presents for everybody. She had spent many hours choosing the presents, and they were very exquisite and very expensive, and as well suited to their recipients as Sally's loving understanding could make them; which was very suitable indeed. For Sally was not one of those introverts who buy for others the presents they would like to have themselves, she was an extrovert who left herself out of it completely and whose knowledge of the likes and dislikes of others was profounder than she knew. She hadn't at all enjoyed buying the book of anatomical diagrams for Tommy, because, surfeited with the nude as the relatives of artists tend to be, the human form unclothed—especially unclothed right down to the skeleton—revolted her, but she had both studied it, to make sure it was really as good of its kind as it could be, and bought it at a most exorbitant price. And the bottle of scent for Auntie Rose wasn't her own taste at all, stunning the nose as it did in exactly the same sort of way as Auntie Rose's brilliant satin blouses stunned the eye, nor the pale pink notepaper with golden initials on it for Caroline. But there were a few things that, besides being well-suited to the friends for whom she bought them, were her own taste, too; noticeably the lovely sailing-ship in a bottle for Ben, and two little Rockingham china lambs for Annie-Laurie. Hilary Eliot, last time he had come over to the Herb of Grace, had sat next

283

to her at tea and had said casually, "You and Annie-Laurie ought to have a lot in common. Did you know she had been a shepherdess, too?" And then in a low gentle voice, "Do make friends with Annie-Laurie."

And she had answered, with one of her straight, clear looks, "Yes, I will." But that had been the day before she went away, and she hadn't had a chance yet. But when she got home she would summon up her courage and try again, in spite of the frustration of her first effort, for Hilary had looked at her as though he had thought that in some way he thought her friendship was necessary to Annie-Laurie. She couldn't see what use it could be, when Annie-Laurie didn't want it; but perhaps if she gave her the lambs she would want it. That happened sometimes when one gave a gift; if it was a lucky gift, one that touched the heart to acceptance, one got gathered in along with it, like the tail of the kite with the kite, and there you were.

She had little hope that David would gather her in with her gift to him. She felt that his gift was probably a failure. She had not known what to give him. She had gone into shop after shop and walked round and round in circles for what had seemed like hour after hour, but nothing she looked at had commended itself to her as a suitable gift for a woman to give a man she loved when the man didn't love her. The weary circling of her body had seemed to echo the weary circling of her thoughts in these days. That afternoon when they discovered the frescoes he had seemed to come suddenly most gloriously close to her. A wild hope had sprung up in her, and had burned brightly for a week or so, while they toiled together at the cleaning of the walls. Then, as the time passed and nothing happened, and David got more and more absorbed in the Chapel, seeming to find in the restoration of its beauty the stimulus and comfort that he had before found in his friendship with her, the hope died, and bitter shame took its place. Her own arrogance appalled her. Who and what did she think she was, that she should expect this famous and accomplished man to love her? She was much younger than he was, she had neither gift nor beauty to match his. And yet, trying to see things as they were, as was her habit, aware that excessive shame was just as distorting to the judgment as excessive arrogance, she knew that she ought to be his wife. That pang of recognition with which she had looked at her father's drawing of him had been like a push in the back, saying, "There you are, that's what you were made for, hand yourself over and be quick about it." But you couldn't hand yourself over if you weren't taken. And at this point her thoughts would come up against Hamlet's words, "The readiness is all," and cling to them as to a rock. That put it in a nutshell. That was the only possible attitude to life and death, as well as to love. You had to be ready to be used or not used, picked up or cast aside, and it didn't really matter which it was provided you yourself were pliant to fate like a reed to the wind.

Then she would understand that, though she had recognized David as her mate, it would not really matter if he did not recognize her as his. It was one of the glorious things about life, that for the pliant there was never really any lasting emptiness. They said that even into the emptiness of physical blindness there crept eventually new awareness and new powers. Though David never took her to the place in his life that was rightfully hers, something else would eventually fill that emptiness—some extension of the power of his art or some other love. And for herself, if she could manage to welcome sorrow as readily as joy, it would shape her as deftly as joy could have done to whatever beauty of being it was within her power to reach.... But at this point her reasonableness would give way beneath her, and she would find herself back where she started from; shamed and miserable, and not knowing what on earth to get David for Christmas.... And it was at this point, this very morning before she caught her train, that, in a mood of complete hopelessness, she picked up a bit of Venetian glass from a counter, meekly paid the huge price demanded, and stowed the parcel away in her bag. She had not opened it since. It was in the suitcase with her other presents. She did not even remember very clearly what it was—some sort of a cup, the handle formed by the curved body of some animal or other, crystal, blue and green, like clear water. She thought it was pretty. Venetian glass almost always was.

She was very tired and her head was aching—a most unaccustomed state of affairs with her. Never mind. She was going back to that bit of Hampshire between the river and the sea that was now to her the most beloved spot on earth; that was home. She supposed it wasn't really home, but it felt like it. She knew she would never love any houses as she loved the Herb of Grace and Damerosehay. Especially Damerosehay, the House of the Perfect Eaves. She had gone there a lot lately to see Lucilla, and the more she went the more she loved Lucilla and the house. Every time she left them she felt as though she were tearing herself up by the roots. She had taken her father to see Lucilla and, as Nadine had foreseen long ago, she liked him. And he liked her. And his liking seemed to bind her even more firmly to the place that was David's home. That was why she loved it so much, of course, and Lucilla so much. They were David's. They had made him. She had given herself so utterly to this love of hers that it permeated every part of her being, and nothing that was not connected with David seemed to have any value for her any more.... How on earth was she going to get through the rest of her life if.... She pulled herself up abruptly and groped after Hamlet, but she couldn't seem to get hold of him; she was too tired.... She shivered, though it wasn't a cold day, and pulled her long, soft brown fur coat more closely about her. She pulled off her hat, lay back in her corner seat and shut her eyes. Though her head was aching too much for her to reason with herself, she could think of nice things—the Cumberland hills, the lambs, her Nannie, who had taught her this trick of detachment. "When you're sick or sorry, child," she had said, "think of other things as much as you are able. It's just practice. Start young and you'll get the trick of it." And most astonishingly, after a little while of going back to childhood and remembering Nannie in her blue print dress, with her white apron on and her sleeves rolled up, turning on the bath-water and humming a little song as she did it, she fell asleep.

– 2 –

Lucilla, meanwhile, was giving her favourite grandson a piece of her mind. Margaret was out, and they were having an early tea together in the Damerosehay drawing-room; early because John Adair's car was out of order. George had taken the boys to the local meet in his, and an SOS from the Herb of Grace had informed David that his car was Sally's only hope of getting home that night. Lucilla, when really roused, could give those she loved a piece of her mind in such a manner that their very souls squirmed within them. Those she did not love were never treated to these spiritual flayings; for, after all, as she was wont to say when making it up afterwards, it is only when you love people very much that you care really desperately how they behave. For Lucilla was not one of those who are blind to the faults of those they love. Quite the contrary. The more she cared for people, the more did she see their faults and labour for their removal with the perseverance of someone with a piece of emery paper rubbing away at the rust on a bright sword.

She sat now extremely upright in her chair by the fire, one hand holding a delicate fan between herself and the blaze, the other holding the arm of her chair for support; for, though she gave no sign of weakness in voice or demeanour, she really found these deliverings of pieces of her mind as much of an ordeal as did the recipient of them. The Bastard lay at her feet, his chin on her shoe. Pooh-Bah lay on the hearth, his chin on his extended paws. Though lying as still as if carved out of stone, neither dog slept, and their eyes gleamed brightly. They knew David was getting it. They were, so to speak, standing by to see fair play. Lucilla's cup of tea was untouched, and she ate nothing. David, on the contrary, was going on steadily with his tea. Upon these occasions he always employed himself if he could. It kept up his morale.

"You must do one thing or the other, David," said Lucilla.

"You must either ask Sally to be your wife, or you must take yourself off out of her way. You must know that you are an extremely attractive man, you must know that she loves you, and to be perpetually with her as you are, perpetually battening upon her youth and strength and draining her sympathy, and giving nothing whatever in return, is so cowardly and so selfish that I cannot reconcile the man that you are now with the man I have hitherto known. I do not know what has come over you, David; I simply do not know."

"Grandmother, why should you think that Sally loves me? Has she told you so?"

"Don't be ridiculous, David! Of course not. She'd die sooner than tell me, or anyone. She has a fine reticence; never would that girl willingly allow a trouble of her own to make things uncomfortable for other people. But, though I am an old woman, I thank God that I still retain the use of my eyesight and my mental faculties. The young— and Sally is very young—are never as skilful at hiding what is happening to them as they think they are. Now, don't prevaricate, David. Can you sit there and tell me that you do not know that Sally loves you?"

David put down his teacup and faced her squarely.

"No, Grandmother, I don't sit here and tell you anything of the sort. I didn't know for some while, and then—it was the day we found the frescoes—I suddenly did know. But I knew, too, that not to be loved in return would do her no harm. She's too fine a creature to let frustration embitter her."

"Really, David," said Lucilla, with powerful indignation, "you are an extremely hard man. I do not know when I have heard a more cynical or arrogant remark. Is it your habit, nowadays, to go through life inflicting pain on others and then rejoicing in the excellent effect it will have upon their characters? Has this dreadful war made a sadist of you?"

She'd got him there. He went white, and could not answer. All through those years that had been one of the questions that had haunted him.... Shall I get used to this killing? Shall I get accustomed to inflicting agony? Shall I, at last, think nothing of it?... But though she was as deeply wounded by the blow she had dealt him as he was, she went inexorably on.

"How you can not want to marry Sally I am unable to understand!"

"I do want to marry her, Grandmother. With all my heart and soul I want to marry her."

Lucilla's icy self-command suddenly crumpled. Her fan fell on the floor, and both her hands came out to him in a touchingly child-like gesture of pleading.

"Then, David, my darling, why in the name of common-sense and love and mercy can't you?—David, mind what you're doing with that wretched trolley!"

David had now abandoned the attempt to eat any more tea, and had pushed the trolley impatiently aside. It rucked up a rug and shunted against a little table with books upon it. The table went over, and the books.

"O.K.," said David callously. "Nothing to smash."

He could be at times, as Lucilla had said, a hard man.

"I dislike American colloquialisms about as much as I dislike trolleys," said Lucilla. "But neither as much as I dislike criminal stupidity."

"Grandmother, is it criminal stupidity to look at this from the viewpoint of Sally's eventual happiness? Can I make her happy? Much older than she is. Not particularly healthy. In a rotten state of nerves. Worst of all, not really in love with her. Have I any hope of making her happy? I'm too scared to try. I've lost my nerve for—nearly everything."

"How can you say you're not in love with her when you want, so you say, with all your heart and soul to marry her?"

"I don't feel about her as I have, in the past, about—other women."

"One woman," corrected Lucilla. "Nadine. David, do you still feel yourself bound in spirit to Nadine?"

"No!" said David softly, yet with a sort of violence. "She's—pretty effectually—cut me right out—"

Lucilla, as she paid a startled silent tribute to her daughter-in-law, saw light. So Nadine had done it, completely and wholeheartedly, at last. But she'd done it too suddenly, as all things that are desperately hard to do are done as a general rule too suddenly. David, though wanting release, had nevertheless been stunned by its suddenness, perhaps its apparent brutality, that had not been really brutality at all, but just the quick slash of the surgeon's knife. It had also perhaps humiliated him. He was proud. He had wanted to be cast aside, and yet, when given what he wanted, he had been insulted. How typical of poor human nature! She smiled at him with tenderness. Naturally he needed time to recover his balance.

"Darling," she said in sudden penitence, "I don't think it was quite fair of me to say that you battened upon Sally and drained her. I'm sure you did not mean to do that."

"No, I did not mean to do it; but I see now that I did it," said David. "I was like a leech at that time; a leech with you, too. But lately I've been careful. The frescoes helped. Since the day I told you of Sally, she and I have scarcely been alone together; we've been working all the time on the walls with her father and Ben. She's been more interested than any of us. She's not given me a thought."

"Really?" said Lucilla dryly.

But she still smiled at him, and David realized that the worst of her displeasure was past. Very soon, now, she would melt altogether, and later still she would be overwhelmed with misery at the thought of her own anger, and her misery would be as devastating for them both as her anger had been. But she had not reached that point yet.

"We must get this clear, David," she said, "You think you do not love Sally because you do not feel for her the passion you felt for Nadine. You'll never feel that again. Nature knows what she's doing, and she does not allow us to be torn by passions we've not the strength for. You're too old and tired for that sort of thing."

"There you've put it in a nutshell, Grandmother. Sally isn't. She's young and ardent."

"Not in the way you mean. Don't you know anything about women? Don't you know the difference between a woman like Nadine and a woman like Sally? Nadine—she can't help it, poor dear—was born a hungry, unsatisfied woman. Her perpetual search after perfection is a lovely thing in her; because of it her home and her person will never be less than exquisite; but it makes all the normal relationships disappoint her by their imperfection, so that she looks beyond them for happiness. At least, she did until now. I think that perhaps, just lately, a glimmering of sense has been vouchsafed to her. Sally—and she couldn't help it either—was born the other way round. She does not demand gifts of life, she just loves it for itself, and her humility makes her feel that what she is given is always far too much. She'll feel exactly the same about you as she does about life. You won't disappoint her."

"I'd give my right hand to be sure of that," said David miserably.

"There's no need to do anything so dramatic, dear," said Lucilla dryly. "All you've got to do is to rely on my judgment."

"Grandmother," said David, smiling, "I believe you think that if the whole world relied on your judgement the millennium would come."

"So it would," said Lucilla calmly. "I'm not eighty-five for nothing. This modern craze for putting the young in positions of authority—headmasters in their thirties, bishops without a grey hair on their heads, generals who scarcely need to use a razor—ever since it took hold the world's gone steadily downhill.... But we're wandering from the point, dear.... To return to Sally. She's a born mother. You want children, don't you?"

The suddenness of this question startled him so much that he answered with equal suddenness, "With my heart and body—far more desperately than I can tell you. With my mind—no. What sort of world is this to bring them into? That's another consideration that's holding me back."

"A very cowardly consideration, dear. A mere shirking of responsibility. It's a heavy responsibility, of course, a double one—responsibility for the children themselves and responsibility for the world they must live in. But I know of no better incentive for the building of a decent world than the possession of children who must live in the world you've built."

"You talk, Grandmother," said David wickedly, "as though you thought the building of the new world was the responsibility of the young; or the moderately young."

"Of course. So it is."

"But you've just said that only the old—"

But Lucilla was not to be caught out.

"Not a word did I say about the young sitting down and doing nothing. They must build, of course, but relying upon the judgment of the old."

"I see."

"I only wish you did, David," sighed Lucilla.

"Grandmother, I should feel so utterly ashamed; taking so much from Sally and giving her so little."

"Do you no harm to feel ashamed. Do you a world of good. As I've told you before, you're too proud."

"And then my rotten health. I'm afraid she won't have an easy time with me."

"I don't suppose she will. I haven't exactly had an easy time with you myself. Yet the glory and joy of my life has been to be your grandmother."

He was kneeling beside her, hugging her as he had been used to do as a small boy. Wave after wave of penitent misery swept over her. What a brute she had been to him. What a brute!

"Did I lose my temper, David? Oh, my darling, forgive me! Please forgive me!"

"Nothing to forgive," said David. "I always enjoy your scoldings. And they always clear the air. A regular catharsis, they are. What I don't enjoy is your self-reproach afterwards."

"But, my darling, I said the most dreadful things to you. I'd no right. I didn't mean any of them."

"Then am I not to rely on your judgment?"

She pushed him away from her, her penitence swept away by a sudden return of irritation, and looked at the clock.

"Yes, dear, of course. Look at the time! Kneeling on the floor there asking silly questions! Weren't you to meet dear Sally? And look at the time!"

David jumped up.

"Plenty of time if I step on the gas.... Look at the state the room is in! We might have been having a tornado in here, instead of just a domestic crisis."

"Leave it, dear. Margaret can see to it. It's all the fault of her wretched trolley. Hurry, David."

David hurried. He was just opening the front door when he found Lucilla beside him.

"You know what a child she is for giving presents. Or perhaps you don't know. I do. Worse than Caroline. She'll have Christmas presents for everybody. You haven't got a thing yet, I know. You always leave everything till the last moment—"

She held out her hand. On the palm lay the glorious emerald ring, her greatest treasure, that she had worn all her life. He took it, and kissed the palm.

"Grandmother, you're the gracious star. You've put apparel on it."

"I don't know what you're talking about, dear. But believe me, David, what you are doing is right and fitting. Give yourself to it, and you'll soon know."

He was gone, and she shut the door behind him. Turning round, she found that the two old dogs had followed her out into the hall. Their eyes were very bright and their tails were wagging.

– 3 –

The train stopped with a jolt, and Sally woke up. Radford! She'd nearly got carried past. Her head was still aching, and she felt half-stupefied with sleep and fatigue. She grabbed her two suitcases off the rack and half fell out of the carriage, leaving her hat and gloves and handbag behind her. The cases were dreadfully heavy, and to her fatigue the air felt icy. She set them down in front of her and fastened up her fur coat, that had come undone in the train, while her eyes swept anxiously up and down the platform. Where was Daddy? He'd promised to meet her. She wanted him dreadfully; as badly as Caroline had wanted George a week ago. But he wasn't there. He hadn't come. No one was there whom she knew. And Nannie, about whom she had been dreaming so happily three minutes ago, was dead. Sally, the grown-up and courageous, was suddenly all to pieces like a five-year-old. Her throat swelled with the tears she would not shed, and she stood quite still, looking piteously about her, not knowing what to do, her curly head rumpled, her bare hands holding her coat closely about her throat against the cold.

David, arriving late in spite of having driven to the public danger all the way from Damerosehay, and striding down the platform also to the public danger, saw her before she saw him. He had never seen her look like that before—a piteous, frightened little girl. Something seemed suddenly to break in him, some hard shell of self-pity that had formed itself about his long misery, keeping it in, hindering its dispersal. In his thoughts of them both it had always been he who suffered, he who took, and she, always so happy and strong, who must eternally give. Now suddenly he saw that it wouldn't be always like that. Even the strongest and happiest had their times of weakness, and turned to those they usually supported for support; and got it. He was suddenly gloriously elated, released, glowing with relief and delight. Queer paradox! Happy because the beloved suffered.

"Sally!" he called, striding towards her. "Sally!"

She looked round, her white face going suddenly pink with delight, She took a step towards him, and fell over one of the suitcases. He caught her arm, but the suitcase fell smack upon the platform.

"Sally, what is it?" he demanded. "Are you all right?"

"I'm all right," she laughed. "I'm tired, I think. And I fell asleep in the train, and only just woke up in time to get out, and—where's my hat?"

"Not present," said David. "Nothing here but Sally and two suitcases."

"It's gone on," said Sally, eyeing the departing train. "My gloves too. And my handbag. Everything in it. Ration book and ticket and all."

"It doesn't matter," said David, picking up the two cases. "Nothing matters, now you're back. I'll ring up about your bag when we get home. Are you properly awake now? I haven't a hand left to hold you up with."

"I'm awake," she said, and followed him down the platform.

But, looking back at her, he saw that she had gone white again, and was blinking as though the lamplight hurt her eyes. With her ruffled head, she looked less like the young lion to which he was accustomed to liken her than a downy owl woken up too soon. These comparisons, he thought tenderly, were scarcely suitable in the circumstances. He ought to be likening her to some flower. But she wasn't flower-like, his dear young love. Even half-dead with fatigue, she was too vital and too loving to be likened to a flower.

At the barrier he dealt in a masterly manner with the ticket collector, defrauded of Sally's ticket, and then tucked her up in a rug in his car.

"Daddie?" she asked anxiously.

"He's all right. But the car's conked out. The magneto. Lucky for me. I've shoved your suitcases in the back."

"The case I kicked over has my Christmas presents in it," said Sally sadly, as they slid down the street. "Some of them smashable. I wish I wasn't such a clumsy idiot!"

David stopped beneath a lamp-post even as George had done with Caroline earlier in the month. The Eliot men were rather good at knowing what was expected of them.

"Would you like to open it and make sure everything's all right?"

"Yes, please, David. The blue one."

He lifted it over and put it on her lap and she opened it.

"I have one of those ships in a glass bottle for Ben," she said, but he noticed that her fingers went quickly to quite a small package thickly wrapped in tissue paper, and felt it anxiously. She gave a cry of distress.

"Smashed?" asked David sympathetically.

"Yes," she said.

"Not Ben's bottle? It looks too small for that."

"No—it's—yours."

She was far too tired to hide her distress or her love or anything whatever. David cast a brief mental glance of sheer astonishment back at the man who a short while ago had doubted if he loved Sally enough to ask her to marry him, and then gently took the parcel out of her hands and unwrapped it. A few fragments of exquisite glass fell apart on the paper, like dropped lily petals, but the curved handle of blue-green was unbroken. It was a lovely little lion, the lion of Venice.

"Sally!" cried David. "A lion. A perfect little lion. Look, he's not hurt at all. Sally, darling, it's yourself you've given me. Sally!... Here, let's get out of this!"

He shut the suitcase and put it behind, wrapped up his lion and stowed it in the little recess on the switchboard, and raced them out of Radford. Out in the country he stopped the car and hugged her.

"Sally, could you marry me? I've wanted you for a long time now. Please, Sally. Not fit to black your shoes. But please, Sally."

Sally saw no necessity for answering. Anyway, she couldn't. She was crying with the utmost joy and luxuriance, nestled against him like a five-year-old. Ten minutes later they drove on again, laughing and talking softly. With the resilience of youth and strength, Sally had shed her fatigue, her headache and her pathos, as though they had never been. She was her usual warm, glowing, sturdy self; though not quite her usual self, David noted; the last few minutes had brought a new enrichment, a sparkling light upon her, such as comes when a parched garden has been made new with rain, but the rain has passed.

"Sally, forgive me," he pleaded.

"What for?" asked Sally.

"For a great many things."

"I don't know what they are," said Sally.

And indeed she did not know. She would never know when she needed to forgive him, because whatever he did it would always seem right to her because he did it. He thought to himself, with a sudden quirk of humour, that it was as well for his immortal soul that Lucilla's devotion was not of this type.

"Why are you smiling, David?"

"I was thinking of Grandmother."

"David!" whispered Sally. "Let's not go back to the Herb of Grace! Let's go home!"

"Home?"

"To Damerosehay. To Grandmother. I've got my night things in my bag. I'd like to spend the night at home. Daddy won't mind. We can ring him up."

"Bless you," said David, and swung off down the rutted lane that led to the road through the marshes, the road by which all the Eliots always returned to their home.

As they turned the corner between the two cornfields, the strange wild one in the marsh to their right and the cultivated one to their left, the sea-wind met them. The sea was a distant line of silver under the rising moon, and the stars were already in the sky. It was a place of memories for David.... Here, once, he had met Nadine, returning home.... He greeted her, in his thoughts, and thanked her, and then bent his whole strength to make this home-coming one of great happiness for the girl beside him.

"I tell you what, Sally," he said gaily. "Let's get solemnly engaged in the oak-wood. It ought, really, to be in Knyghtwood—the place where we met each other and you thought of Pisanello's picture. But I love the old oak-wood."

"I do, too," said Sally. "I always feel as though it were part of

Knyghtwood. I suppose all woods everywhere are really just different bits of the one wood, pushing up through the earth like the different bits of the sky that shine through the clouds are the same sky. And the oak-wood is your special bit of wood, the heart of it for you. David, it's lovely tonight! Look at the old castle, like a strong old animal, crouching down there, guarding the marshes, and the Island all ebony and silver."

"Peaceful tonight," said David. "It can be wildly stormy sometimes you know. Not sheltered, like the Herb of Grace. Will you mind that?"

"No. Damerosehay has such strong walls. And there's the oak-wood between us and the sea."

They were in the oak-wood. The old twisted trees gathered them in as they had gathered so many Eliots returning home; as they would gather these two, and their children, for years to come. The car glided silently over the moss-grown drive, then stopped.

"Now then, Mrs. Eliot, hold out your hand, please."

Sally held it out, and he slipped Lucilla's ring upon it. Sally was speechless. They kissed each other lightly, gently, without passion, but they kept nothing back. David, though sadness for the last time throbbed in him somewhere, knew it was all right.

CHAPTER

17

– 1 –

JILL AND THE TWINS had made themselves responsible for the holly for the Christmas decorations, and a few days before Christmas, armed with a huge basket, with Mary in attendance, they entered Knyghtwood punctually at two o'clock. The weather was still astonishingly mild. Now and then sudden storms of wind and rain swept in from the sea, but they passed again, and the sun shone and the sky was blue, and the birds were surprised into trying out a phrase or two of their spring song. It was, as always, enchanting in Knyghtwood.

"But there must be no lingering," said Jill firmly. "From what you say, we've a long way to go, and you must be back to your teas. If you think we'll find the best holly in this far place you know of we'll go straight there, and not stop to pick anything on the way. Then if there's nothing in this place of yours we'll pick the holly in the wood on our way back. What's here is not so bad."

The twins looked with contempt upon the holly-trees they were passing. It wasn't a good year for holly, and the berries were rather few and far between.

"There's lots of berries in the Place Beyond," said José.

"You can't know for certain, ducks," said Jill. "You've only been there the once, so you say, with Miss Adair, and that was a long time ago."

"We didn't go with Sally," corrected Jerry. "José and me and Mary went alone to our place. Sally stayed behind in her place."

"Her place?" queried Jill.

"She saw David there," said José. "She had candle eyes after she'd been in her place with David, and Mummie and Annie-Laurie had candle eyes when they came back from the wood with the water-cress that wasn't."

The sharpness of them, thought Jill. Not a thing could you keep from them.

"Will there be candles lit again in the wood, as it's nearly Christmas?" asked Jerry.

"No, dear," said Jill. "There are never candles in the wood. There are lighted candles in Christmas-trees, and in people's eyes when they're happy, but not in woods."

"There were the first day we came. We saw them when we went away."

"The sunset behind the trees, perhaps," said Jill. "Grand sunset it was that evening, I remember. I passed the remark to Auntie Rose at the time. Haven't I a place of my own in this wood?"

"Near ours," said José, and slipped her hand into Jill's.

Jill held the small hand firmly. A few weeks ago José would not, gratuitously, have made that small gesture of love. For months now, ceaselessly, had Jill been giving all that she had and was to these hard-hearted young scallywags, and now, at last, they were throwing to her now and then the first few flowers of their spring. "There's the owl," said Jerry.

Jill looked up, and saw the beloved creamy form blundering along through the trees, in front of them; yet he only seemed to be blundering; he never bumped into anything.

"Now what's he doing, out and about at this time of day?" she wondered. "It's mostly only morning and night we see him. He must be staying up late for a Christmas party."

"Rat and Mole are going, too," said José.

And, sure enough, the owl kept flying on just ahead of them, as though they all had an appointment in the same place.

"The Person with the Horns will be going," said Jerry. "And perhaps the Person with the Pipes—though I'm not sure."

"No, not him," said José. "He's in bed for the rest of the winter. Like the squirrels."

"Well the rabbits, anyway," said Jerry, "and the field-mice and the birds and the toads and the frogs. And the badger."

Jill paid little attention to this. The twins had many fantastic creatures as companions of their daily life, and she did not even try to keep track of the invisible persons who had nursery tea with them, went out for walks with them, splashed about in the bath with them and slept under their beds. Occasionally these persons were troublesome. The one with the pipes, for instance, thought that on a fine day lessons were sheer waste of time, and when the twins rebelled against the processes of education, he would lend them his moral support to an extent that made their yells and kickings far harder to subdue than if he'd kept out of it.... Jill was glad to hear he was now in bed.... Rat and Mole, too, were extraordinarily troublesome. They wouldn't eat milk pudding. And as, in some way that Jill didn't attempt to understand, their spiritual union with Jerry and José was very close indeed, when they were present the twins wouldn't eat it either. But the Person with the Horns exercised an influence that was entirely good; and for this reason, though unfortunately he put in an appearance less frequently than the other persons, he was more real to Jill than the others. Also, of course, there were already two portraits of him in the house—Ben's in the drawing-room and the one on the Chapel wall—and the little carving in the alcove. The twins had never told Jill that the Person with the Horns and the white deer were the same, but Jill had no doubt of it.

"There go the rabbits and the birds," said José. "Look!"

Jill looked, and saw the white scuts of two rabbits darting along just ahead of them. It was true that the birds seemed flying about a good deal, and mostly in the same direction.

They very soon passed the oak-tree that was Nadine's place; it wasn't very deep in. And they crossed over the first little bridge to Ben's Brockis Island, and the second little bridge to the deeper bit of the wood beyond. And they came to the stream that was Sally's place, with the break in the bog-myrtle bushes to the left that led to Annie-Laurie's place; and then they were in a part of the wood where none of the others had ever yet been. Even Jill, though she had run about Knyghtwood often as a little girl, had not been as far as this for many years, and she looked about her with the interest of a traveller in a strange country.

Once the stream was left behind, the character of the wood changed. It became deeper and more mysterious. There were no more birches, wild crab-apples and hawthorns. The oak-trees still persisted, but they were much larger, and among them were those splendid knights of the forest, the armoured beeches. The hollies, old as the conquest, grew to a great height here, they had more berries on them and their polished leaves sparkled with reflected light. The ground was thick with akermast. Here in this deeper part of the wood there were none of the fragile winter flowers that had so delighted Nadine; but the splendid lichens, from which in old days the country people had been used to make their medicines, grew abundantly, and purple light gathered about the oaks. There still seemed an unusual number of animals and birds about, and they still seemed to be going in the same direction. A glorious flash of colour suddenly sped by them.

"A yaffingale!" cried Jill in delight.

The woodpecker had flown between two giant beeches, that leaned together to form an archway. Jill and the children followed. Within the archway the character of the wood seemed once more to change very slightly. The trees grew much closer together, and it was darker, and held a greater stillness. Jill, perhaps, might have felt a little uneasy lest they lose their way, only she found now that they were following a path through the wood. She did not know where the path had begun, or how they had come to find themselves upon it, but here it was—a mere thread of a path, but easy to follow.

"I know now," she said suddenly to the twins and Mary, who were running on ahead of her. "I came this way once when I was a little thing. It leads to the old Buckpen, where they used to feed the deer in the winter-time. Long ago, that was. There aren't any deer now."

A little later she was not so sure. They had come to a brilliant holly-bush beside the path, with opposite it a clump of ferns growing beside a mossy rock, and stooping to tie up her shoelace, she fancied she saw dainty hoof-prints upon the path. Country-bred girl that she was, they were not prints she was familiar with. She bent to examine them, her heart beating a little. They were so light, so exquisite, and the moisture that had soaked into them from the ground caught the light with so silvery a gleam, that they might have been flowers lying there. They had a joyous look. Jill felt quite sure that the creature who had made them had not been walking sedately, but leaping eagerly. Yet how very light he must have been, to make these fragile prints! She stood still looking at them, trying to recapture that long ago day of her childhood when she had followed this path to the

Buckpen. She remembered that she had found it, but oddly enough she couldn't remember what had happened to her there. At least, nothing that she could put into words. It hadn't been the sort of thing that happened in other places, and its utter unlikeness had made comparison impossible, and so the words used to describe other experiences weren't any use to describe this one. There was a dazzle of light in her eyes from those bright prints on the ground, and she closed them.

Reaching back to that day, she could not visualize, but she could feel. It was a glow of warmth that she felt, like a drench of sunshine, only possessing not her body only, but her whole being, and holding the same annihilation of time and distance that is the miracle of light. All things were present with her then, all things and persons that knowingly she possessed in love, and all to which her awareness reached out in love but of which her finite mind could make no symbol. She had it all in the glow and the light, in the tiny fraction of time between the closing of her eyes and the opening of them again and the lifting of her head in renewed purpose. The renewal brought no change in her outlook, no fresh direction to her life, merely a strengthening of all that she had and was. She would not, afterwards, remember much of this moment; though she would remember till she died the brilliant holly-tree beside the path and the clump of ferns and the mossy rock.

She looked about her. The hoof-prints were there no longer. She was not surprised. She knew there had been no deer in Knyghtwood for very many years. Remembering her childhood, coming near the Buckpen again after so long, it was natural she should have been fanciful just for the moment. The twins and Mary had also disappeared. She was not surprised at this either, nor disturbed. They'd gone to the Buckpen. They'd been there before, they said, and knew the way. She'd not pursue them into a place that she felt belonged only to children. She'd wait for them here, and rob that holly-bush for the Herb of Grace. She'd never seen such holly, glowing here like fire in the heart of the wood.

– 2 –

José and Jerry and Mary ran eagerly on along the path. Last time they had come to the Buckpen it had been autumn, but now it was nearly Christmas. It would be different today. Not that they could really remember what it had been like before, apart from the light and the warmth and the creatures; but it would be bound to be different now. Everything was different at Christmas.

Upon each side of them the ground rose steeply, so that they ran along the narrow path between the walls of gnarled beech roots and great clumps of fern. A rabbit lolloped ahead of them and a jay darted past. The path sloped downhill now, as though coming to a hollow in the wood, what Jill called "a bottom." Then it took a sharp turn to the right, and ended abruptly against a great rampart of holly that completely filled the space between the banks. The rabbit, however, was not discouraged; they saw its white scut disappearing beneath the holly. And they were not discouraged either. They had got through before, they remembered now, led by a blackbird, and though they had got their clothes in a great mess, Jill had not scolded. She never scolded about torn and dirty garments. She knew them to be inevitable if one was ever to do anything worth doing. They went flat on their fronts, and Jerry first, followed by José, followed by Mary, they wriggled their way along the small tunnel through the holly that had been made by the passage of many creatures going in and out between the Buckpen and the wood. It was extremely prickly, damp, dark and uncomfortable, but they took no notice of that.

"Scrape, scrabble and scrooge, Rat," encouraged Mole in the van, and Rat behind him scraped and scrabbled and scrooged.

"How does the Person with the Horns get in?" she wondered aloud, as they paused to get their breath and remove prickles out of themselves. "He couldn't get through here."

"Jumps over the top," said Jerry, "He's a Fairy Person. He can jump as high as the moon."

"Hundreds of years ago, when all the deer came here to be fed, did they all jump over the top?"

"No," said Jerry. "There were breaks in the holly hedge then. It's grown all round since. Come on."

They went on again, wriggling downhill all the time, and suddenly they were there. They rolled down a grassy bank, just as they had done before, sat up and opened their eyes.

As Jerry had guessed, in the last hundred years a great rampart of holly and yew had grown all round the Buckpen, keeping it inviolate, so that the feet of men never trod it now. A few of the older country people, or a few of the younger who, like Jill, had found their way into it as children, knew vaguely that it existed somewhere in Knyghtwood, but that was all. It was now the possession of the creatures only. Once the foresters had fed them here in the winter, but not now. Yet it appeared that in this place they were still cared for. No cold winds could penetrate to this sheltered hollow; there were berries in abundance for the wild things, grass and water. Traps were never set here, and men with their guns never came near with their terror.

A grown-up coming to this place would have seen a beautiful green lawn in the midst of the wood—one of those lawns for which this bit of country was famous, with a stream running through it, and built upon its banks the ruins of an old stone building that might have been a chapel in the woods, or a hermitage used by the monks from the Abbey, and later still perhaps a shelter used by the foresters when they came to feed the deer. Three of the walls still stood, with narrow lancet windows in them, but the fourth wall and the roof were gone. Yet it still made an adequate shelter, for the giant yews growing round it stretched their branches to meet each other, and woven together made a thick green roof, and blazing hollies stood upon either side of the entrance. Roots of primrose and violet and foxglove in the grass, tall iris swords by the stream, thickets of bramble here and there, clumps of hawthorn and the long, thorny branches of wild rose, showed what a bower of flowers must be here in spring and summer. The stream, where it widened out into pools, would itself be emblazoned with colour, carrying upon its breast floating islands of flowers—buckbean and water pimpernel and bur-reed. Though it was December, there was no lack of colour in the Buckpen because of the birds, robins and tits, bullfinches, jays, yellow-hammers, a couple of kingfishers and the yaffingale. The white owl was here, too, sitting motionless and beautiful upon a branch of the yew that stretched like a lintel over the front of the stone building by the stream. All the birds from Knyghtwood seemed to have gathered here this afternoon, and their glancing wings made a web of colour in the clear air. So golden was the air, so bright and warm, that it was as though amber wine brimmed the Buckpen like a cup.

The animals were not so much in evidence as the birds, but small stirrings in the grass, a glimmer of bright eyes peeping from the bushes, the outline of small furred bodies seen and then not seen, told of their presence. They were here in their numbers, and they were evidently not afraid, for they did not scamper away from the children. That was the wonder of the Buckpen: nothing here seemed afraid; some strong influence, lasting through the centuries, had made of this place a sanctuary, so that the creatures did not prey upon each other here. And more than that, at Christmas time this seemed a place where they not only did not hurt each other, but came for healing after they had been hurt. A rabbit hopped past the children on three legs, holding up a fourth that had been injured, and disappeared inside the little ruined building where the owl sat. And a little later a bird with a hurt wing flew after him with ungainly flight. And he was followed by a badger—yes, actually, a real stripy badger. And the children saw other little creatures darting through the grass and going in with their hurts.

"Did we go in, too, when we were here before?" Jerry asked José, looking at the ruined building where the owl sat.

"I don't 'member," said José, puzzled.

"Let's go now," said Jerry.

But for a little while they stood still, hand in hand, just looking, awed and shy. The sun was setting now, and the glory dazzled them.

"Is there a light inside?" whispered José, rubbing her eyes.

"Yes," whispered Jerry. "There's someone there."

They looked at each other enquiringly.

"We haven't anything the matter with us," said José.

"Specs we have, that we don't know about," said Jerry hopefully. "People have things the matter with their hearts and fall down, and don't know about it until they wake up dead."

The sunset deepened all about them. The sky above, feathered and delicately tinted with small clouds of saffron and rose-pink, bent over them like the arched wings of a bird, and in the stream below, in every polished leaf and blade of grass, the glory was reflected. The birds of earth, beneath the great brooding wings, were singing softly, the radiance of their feathers deepening in the golden light. There was a fragrance in the air, as though the fires of sunset drew from the heart of things a distillation of worship, and behind the clear bird voices, within the great silence, a rhythm, like heart-beats felt but not heard. The berries on the holly-bushes that stood one on each side of the ruined chapel glowed like a thousand lamps, and within the light shone more and more brightly, and made a gold path from the door to the children's feet.

Hand in hand they trod the bright path through the warm and golden air, and came to the ruined chapel, and hand in hand they went inside.

– 3 –

When she had filled her basket with holly, Jill sat down on the rock and waited happily for the twins. She did not find the waiting irksome, for she had been born one of those fortunate people who are never in a hurry and never restless. She had never felt restless in her life. In all that she did, in all that she saw, she was aware of a deep, upspringing wonder, as though she did it or saw it for the first time. Blessed with a mind neither retrospective nor anxious, the past and the future did not pull her two ways with remorse and dread, and the lovely freshness of each new-made moment was apparent to her focused vision. As she sat on the rock she was not consciously thinking any more of the mystery of that moment when she had thought she saw the shining hoof-prints on the path; she was watching a nuthatch running like a little mouse up the trunk of the tree opposite her, listening for the tap of its beak, feasting her eyes upon the glow of the holly berries above; yet because of it she saw a little more deeply into the beauty of bird and berry, heard a music in the tappings that she would not have heard before. And so it would be for the rest of her life.

The music of the nuthatch was lost in the music of small feet running, and the twins and Mary were with her again; incredibly dirty, leaves in their hair, mud on their faces and their reefer coats, but with very pink cheeks and candle-eyes. Jerry was carrying a great branch of holly, whose berries were so bright and lovely that even those in Jill's basket looked a little dim in comparison, and José clutched (wonderful for December) a tiny bunch of wild white violets.

"They were growing inside," she said.

Jill did not ask inside where—she did not, like Sally, question them as to where they had been or what they had seen. She knew how worrying, even how agonizing sometimes, the questions of grown-ups can be to children, whose capacity for experience so far outstrips their capacity for talking about it; and in after life it's the other way round, thought Jill—adult and educated folks seemed to experience so little of any consequence, and yet to say such a vast and wearisome amount about it. Besides, she thought, questions are intrusive, in any case. What people did not tell you about themselves was none of your business.

"Come along now, my ducks," was all she said. "We must hurry if we're to get home before it's dark."

But they astonished her. Before she had time to get up from her rock, José had flung herself into her arms. Jerry didn't commit himself that far, but he butted his head against her shoulder, and then stood smiling at her out of his candle-eyes. Mary meanwhile leaped from the rock to her shoulder, and draped herself there like a dirty white feather boa, licking her ear. Jill, her arms full of José, smiled at by Jerry, licked by Mary, felt herself as though wrapped round in warmth and light; it might have been a cloak of fire that she wore, only she was neither burned nor blinded; she had not felt this way since Alf had held her in his arms and loved her. These three, also, were loving her.

The astonishing demonstration of affection ended as abruptly as it had begun. Jerry, suddenly recalling crumpets for tea, headed immediately for home, holding his blazing branch of holly aloft like a torch; and Mary dived off Jill's shoulder and bustled after him; but José, though she scrambled off Jill's lap, still kept close.

"For you," she said, holding up the bunch of violets.

"For Mummy," prompted Jill.

"No," said José. "For you."

"For Mummy," insisted Jill. "I've had you all the afternoon. Mummy hasn't. Let Mummy have the violets."

José scowled, then capitulated, for when they were out for a walk she was used to Jill finding pretty things for her to take back to Mummy. Then suddenly she smiled and ran along the path after Jerry, holding her violets very carefully. This time she had picked them herself for somebody. The sensation was quite novel, and most extraordinary, yet pleasing, and lent wings to her feet. Jill, contented, followed after.

At the door of the Herb of Grace they paused and looked back. It was nearly dark now, with the stars pricking through. The last fires of sunset were still flaming low in the west, and a thousand candles had been lit upon the trees that stretched their shade deep beyond deep in the dark wood.

CHAPTER

18

– 1 –

$\mathcal{E}$VERY GROWN-UP AT THE HERB OF GRACE and at Damerosehay was determined that this should be the children's Christmas—such a Christmas as they had not known before in their unsettled young lives. They themselves looked forward to it with a certain amount of dread.... The state of the world and their own fatigue combined to make them feel that a condition of mind humble and prayerful, meals requiring the minimum of preparation and recreation consisting of nothing more strenuous than dozing in an armchair with a detective story, were their idea of a suitable Christmas in the circumstances.... But that would not do for the children, and they girded themselves with heroism for the fray. And, as it turned out, not in vain, for when the time came it was for all of them—the grown-ups as well as the children—a day of sheer delight, one of those magical times that are not forgotten while life lasts, when it seems as though nothing can go wrong; as though human imperfection were aided and sustained by something outside itself, and just for once allowed to bring to perfection everything that it attempted. John Adair, looking back afterwards, remembered that from the very beginning he had been aware of the pulse of creative joy beating in the house. So great was its strength that he should not have been taken by surprise when it broke right through the crust of things and took them all in charge.

Yet he was surprised, for during the week before Christmas, in common with the rest of the grown-ups, his emotional state had been one chiefly of profound exasperation. As if the preparation of festival meals with not enough sugar, less butter, and no suet at all, the decoration of a large Christmas-tree when you couldn't buy so much as a silver star or a strip of tinsel, the purchasing of Christmas presents when you hadn't a single coupon left and all the books you ordered were out of print, were not enough to try the temper, Ben had decreed that there must be a dramatic entertainment; and not only an entertainment, but a carol service in the Chapel to inaugurate it properly as a chapel, and not a store-room.

"Must we have both?" Nadine had asked patiently, trying hard to keep the weariness out of her voice, as she and George, David, Sally and Ben sat round the fire at tea one day, a few days before the twins' visit to the Buckpen. "Wouldn't the carols be enough without the entertainment?"

"But we said when we first came that we'd have a play at Christmas," Ben reminded her. "Don't you remember? They always did in the old inns. The actors used the gallery, and the audience sat in the yard below."

"If you want to sit us all out in the stable yard in midwinter, and prance about on that outdoor gallery of Malony's, just say the word, old boy, and I'll order a large hearse for the lot of us and have done with it," said George resignedly.

"No, we'll do that in the summer," said Ben. "This time we'll act in here, in the hall. We'll have the stage at the foot of the stairs, and use the stairs for exits and entrances. Part of the show we'll stage actually on the stairs, where they branch in front of the alcove. It'll be awfully effective. You and Father needn't have anything to do with it, Mother. Tommy and I and Caroline and the twins will do it all. At least, Sally will coach us in the carols; won't you, Sally? You're awfully musical. And of course David must do something spectacular. And you, Sir," he said shyly and sweetly to John Adair, "you'll help me make the costumes, won't you?"

Only Sally showed enthusiasm for the task assigned. John Adair growled tragically, yet with a gleam of interest in his eye, for, exasperating though it would be to have to set aside his work for a week and play the fool with bits of coloured paper and what not, yet it would interest him to see what ideas his pupil Ben had on the subject of costume design. But David groaned with no gleam in the eye, for he had to the full the professional actor's hatred of getting mixed up in amateur efforts.

"What were you thinking of doing, old boy?" he asked gloomily, "It will be darned awkward getting about on those stairs. There's no space."

"We can do the getting about parts on the stage below. First we'll have a dramatization of 'The Wind in the Willows' that I've planned out. Rat and Mole and so on. That'll be just us five, so you needn't bother with it. And after that you and Sally can do the balcony scene from *Romeo and Juliet*—"

"*What?*" interrupted David in horror.

Sally, who had glowed with delight at the thought of the carols, now went pale with dismay.

"Oh, I couldn't, Ben; I just couldn't!"

"Why ever not?" demanded Ben.

"The size of me!" cried Sally. "And I can't act, either. And with David—"

"Won't you like acting with David?" asked Ben in surprise. "You're engaged to him, aren't you?"

"That's why!" groaned poor Sally.

"Leaning over a balcony, no one will notice your size," said Ben inexorably. "We'll rig up the balcony across the stairs, in front of the alcove, with a lamp burning behind your head in the alcove, making your hair all golden. It'll look grand. I've thought it all out."

John Adair was chuckling into his beard.

"It just can't be done, old chap," said David firmly. "I'm having a rest cure."

"You've had it," said Ben heartlessly. "And by this time you ought to be able to play Romeo in your sleep."

"No hope, you two," said John Adair. "Haven't you discovered, yet, that what Ben ordains sooner or later comes to pass? Always, throughout life, Ben will get his own way. It's not selfishness, mind you, but his perfectly accurate conviction that his way is the right way. In this respect his Grandmother lives again in him. When a man has a strong will, backed by the conviction that he is right, he turns into just a common dictator, but when his will and his conviction are backed by the fact that owing to some felicity of vision he *is* right, the chances are that he may become a great man. Time will show whether Ben—"

But Ben was not attending.

"Mother, you know that old fur coat of yours—the stripy one—it would do nicely for Badger, wouldn't it? And Grandmother has an old sealskin coat that would do for Rat. You'll help with the costumes, too, won't you, Mother? You're so awfully good at dressmaking." Nadine, who had been clinging as to a lifeline to Ben's statement that she and George need have nothing to do with this affair, let go of the lifeline. "And Father will manage the lighting, won't you, Father?"

"Malony's better at that kind of thing than I am," suggested George weakly.

"I know, but Malony and Annie-Laurie will be taking part in the show."

"Good heavens!" said David. "What are they going to do?"

"Some sort of turn on their own. They've just got to be in it. They're troubadours."

"You've asked them?"

"No. I thought you could."

"Not on your life!" said David violently.

"Then Sally will," said Ben placidly. "They won't like to refuse Sally when she's just got engaged."

"No, Ben!" implored Sally.

Ben waved this refusal aside for the moment and returned to the subject of her clothes.

"You'll wear the Botticelli thing, won't you? You know, the blue-green thing—"

"Oh, Ben—" pleaded poor Sally.

David stretched a hand under the tea-table and gripped hers. He loved in her this sensitive shrinking from making a show of her love. During these last days, since they had taken the plunge, each response of hers to all the new situations created by their coming together had seemed to him lovely and right. Always she rang true. With each new day he fell more deeply in love, and became not only more sure of her, but more sure of himself. He would be able to make her happy. Grandmother had been quite right.

"'But lo, a light in yonder window breaks. It is the east and Juliet is the sun,'" he declaimed, smiling at Ben in capitulation, his hand gripping Sally's tighter.

His meaning came to her. Because of her, there was a new morning, a re-birth in his life. She was so happy she hardly knew how to bear it. She smiled at Ben, too.

"All right, Ben."

Nadine did not miss the tone in David's voice, the light in Sally's face. But she had taken the plunge, too, and she smiled at them, and because of them, with all her heart. And dear old George was looking at her with profound and loving commiseration, because of this darned entertainment. And John Adair with profound and loving admiration; because she had smiled. The love of these two older men was suddenly very precious to her.

"If we're all in this, even your poor old parents, it beats me where the audience is coming from," said George to Ben.

"Grandmother, Aunt Margaret, Uncle Hilary, Jill, Auntie Rose, and all the people round here who have been nice to us," said Ben. "What are you all groaning about? This is an inn, isn't it? If we aren't hospitable this first Christmas, then we don't deserve to live here."

"But they'll expect to be fed!" gasped Nadine in horror.

"Oh, not much, Mother. Just a few sandwiches and drinks and things. It's wonderful what Auntie Rose can rake out from under her nephew's counter if Tommy wheedles her."

And so it went on, like a snowball rolling. The exhausted elders would have died of the orgy of preparation had they not been sustained by the laughter of Tommy and Ben, Caroline, Jerry and José, ringing through the house from dawn to dusk.

– 2 –

One evening, after tea, Sally took a box tied with scarlet ribbon out of her drawer, slipped on her fur coat and went across the stable yard and up the steps to the flat above. She had chosen a moment when she knew that Annie-Laurie was alone there. She knocked at the door, and then stood waiting, decidedly scared. She understood Annie-Laurie better now, for David had told her something of her history; but she had no idea how Annie-Laurie would take this intrusion. She had no idea what she was going to say or do. She was just obeying Hilary and Ben—those two gentle Eliots whose gentleness did not seem to prevent them getting their own way with typical Eliot success.

The door opened, and Annie-Laurie and the cat Smith stood upon the threshold, with behind them the pretty lamp-lit room, a fire burning on the hearth. Annie-Laurie wore a flowered overall, and the smell of ironing made Sally wrinkle her nose appreciatively.

"Could I come in a moment, Annie-Laurie?" she asked shyly. "Or are you too busy?"

From force of habit Annie-Laurie had stiffened defensively at the sight of an uninvited visitor violating the sanctuary of her home, then she relaxed and smiled.

"Please come in," she said. "I've just finished. Won't you take your coat off?"

Sally hated herself for putting on her fur coat, as she saw Annie-Laurie's hand unconsciously caressing the lovely fur as she laid it over a chair. It had been lying in the hall, and she had just picked it up as the first wrap that came to hand. But it looked like flaunting her detestable opulence in front of Annie-Laurie. She felt, with shrinking, the firelight flashing on her emerald ring, lighting up her vulgarly bright hair, stressing those so commonly robust curves of her strong and healthy body. Beside Annie-Laurie's fragility she felt like an overblown dahlia towering over a snowdrop. She had everything. Even David now. There was not a single thing, now, that she had not got. When Annie-Laurie turned round to her again, her cheeks were hot with shame and her eyes as beseeching as those of a child caught stealing jam from a cupboard. And she stood as a child stands, straight and shy, holding the white box between her hands, wanting to give it, but not knowing how. Annie-Laurie's painful jealousy was suddenly eased. Really, she'd never been as shy as this, not even in her greenest years. It was she, so she discovered, who must take charge of this interview and put her guest at her ease.

"Do you like my room?" she asked. "Mrs. Eliot gave me the lovely bits of old furniture, and I made the curtains and cushions."

Sally looked about her with admiration.

"It's lovely, Annie-Laurie. You've arranged it all so well, I'll never be the homemaker that you are."

"Yes, you will," laughed Annie-Laurie. "I haven't congratulated you, have I? I'm so glad for you."

The words came out with a little difficulty, yet, as she said them, she found to her intense relief that she meant them. A large part of her past mental misery had been caused by the intense bitterness that, against all her desire, had choked her natural friendliness. It was queer, she thought, how the thing that she had done, unknown to a soul, had seemed to lie in her like an ugly rock in the centre of a stream, gathering to itself all other sins and failings, so that they piled up around it, damming the natural flow of her being. Now, everything confessed to Nadine and Malony, the thing seemed to have gone, and her reactions were natural again—almost.

Sally sat down in one of the two chairs before the fire, the white box still held between her hands.

"I'm glad for myself," she said simply. "I didn't know one could be so happy. Yet I'm scared of not being equal to it. Letting David down. You know what I mean. Though Damerosehay will be our real home, we'll have a flat in town for the working times, and I'll have to be a good hostess—and—that sort of thing."

"You'll manage," Annie-Laurie assured her, and sitting now in the other chair, she leaned back and laughed softly, luxuriating in the glorious, unchecked friendliness that was flowing now between the two of them. Not for years had she sat like this with another girl in the firelight and talked over the dear trivialities that make up the warmth of life. She could feel them all there waiting to be talked about; furniture, saucepans, trousseaux and the rest. "You'll have a big wedding? A white one?"

"Oh no," cried Sally in horror. "As quiet as we can have it. In Uncle Hilary's church, with him to marry us. And not white. I'd look bigger than ever in white."

"Blue?" asked Annie-Laurie.

"David says golden-brown—lion colour. He says I look like a lion; a nice one. And Ben told me this morning that I reminded him of Mowgli's wolf. I don't think it's very flattering of them, do you?"

"I know what they mean," smiled Annie-Laurie. "You'll have to have a hat of some sort, of course—not just a handkerchief tied over your head, like you usually have."

The talk flowed on quietly and happily for a little while, about nothing at all, and Sally was not shy and ashamed any more; but she still seemed unable to approach the matter of the box in her lap. As always when she gave presents, she was seized by a host of misgivings: that she had chosen the wrong thing; that it wasn't as nice as she had thought it was; that there would be a break or flaw somewhere; that perhaps its value would seem too little and her friend be hurt by her lack of generosity; that perhaps it would seem too much and make her look like that detestable thing, a patroness; that present-giving was really only a form of self-indulgence and perhaps it was best not to indulge in it at all. Annie-Laurie, seeing all this in Sally's naïvely revealing face (really, she thought, she was as transparent as a child, and David Eliot would have his work cut out defending her from exploitation), was obliged to come to the rescue.

"What's in that box?" she asked, with a touch of mischief that took Sally completely by surprise; and no wonder, for all the swift changes of mood, the lightness and the humour which had once made Annie-Laurie so fine an actress had been extinguished in her for a long time, and never seen by those who had known her only at the Herb of Grace.

The swift happy question was suddenly in keeping with the red ribbon round the box, the Arcadian lambs inside. With a sigh of relief Sally leaned forward and put the box on Annie-Laurie's lap.

"It's for you. For Christmas. It's two little Rockingham lambs. You see, Uncle Hilary told me that you used to look after the sheep in your mountains. And I worked with the sheep, too, in Cumberland, during the war."

Annie-Laurie, smiling and murmuring her thanks, was savouring the pleasure of undoing the red ribbons, lifting the lid of the box, carefully unwrapping the lambs from their cotton wool. She adored pretty things, but until this moment she had forgotten that she did. With a cry of delight she held the lambs in her hands. They were snow-white, and they had blue ribbons and bells round their necks, and they carried Annie-Laurie straight back to her happy childhood.

"Sally, they're perfect!" she cried. "Bells! I used to tie bells round the lambs' necks at home. It used to make the old shepherd furious. But he couldn't swear at me as he wanted to because he'd given me the bells. Very old Morris-dancers' bells." She looked up at the bright bunch hanging from the beam. "There they are."

"I thought of your bells when I saw the lambs," said Sally happily. "Are those the ones that you wore for your Christmas Tree dance that David told me about?"

"Yes, those are the ones."

"Annie-Laurie," cried Sally, with impulsive eagerness. "I wish you and Malony would come back on the stage again. It would be lovely to have you in London. We'd be friends and help each other."

Annie-Laurie had felt her reactions to be normal again... almost... not quite. Suddenly the old terror gripped her again—that fear of the shame, the whispering voices behind her back.

"No, Sally, I couldn't! Not possibly. I can never go back, Sally. Never!"

Sally's cheeks went crimson with shame at her blunder.

"I'm so sorry, Annie-Laurie. Please forgive me. I'm about the most blundering fool who ever lived."

Annie-Laurie mastered herself quickly, stood up and put the lambs on the mantelpiece.

"No, you're not. You say straight out what's in your mind, and I like that in you. I know I ought to go back, for Jim's sake—but I can't." She sat down again. "Tell me about Damerosehay. I've not been there."

They fought their way back to the warm trivialities, and were at ease again until the clock struck six.

"Those carols!" cried Sally. "We were to have a carol practice at six. You're coming? Without your voice we're just no good at all."

"We're no good with it," said Annie-Laurie gloomily. Then she brightened. "They always say depressing rehearsals make a good performance you know. If things go too well in rehearsal you crash on the night."

"If only all these outside people were not coming!" sighed Sally, struggling into her fur coat. "Ben keeps thinking of more and more he'd like to come—and Juliet in the balcony scene gets worse and worse."

"Poor Juliet!" laughed Annie-Laurie. "How is the children's animal thing going?"

"Ben said it's dreadful," said Sally. "They're trying to do a telescoped version of 'The Wind in the Willows,' and it won't telescope."

Annie-Laurie had moved to put out the lamp, and while she did it Sally looked up at the bunch of bells over her head gathering her courage to obey Ben's command and ask for the help of the troubadours. She could not have done it but for her father's remark, "Ben's perfectly accurate conviction that his way is right."

"Annie-Laurie! Do your Christmas Tree dance for us, you and Malony! Just at the end. On the stage at the foot of the stairs. It would be lovely, and just right. If everything else is a mess, there will be that one perfect thing. Annie-Laurie, you must!"

She had put her arms impulsively round Annie-Laurie, and could not see her face, but she felt the stiffening of her body. But this time she did not apologize. Ben was always right, and her own instinct, too, told her to hold tight and go on.

"Yes, Annie-Laurie. Please. You owe it to the Herb of Grace."

As a rule Annie-Laurie disliked endearments, but there was no suggestion of an endearment about the embrace of Sally Adair. The strength of her arms, the whole-heartedness of her hug, were more like some act of nature, like a great breath of spring wind that nearly takes you off your feet, or a sudden burst of sunshine through the clouds. Sally's embrace was given rarely, but when it was given it definitely altered things. Annie-Laurie felt warm and safe in her arms, even as she had felt when she first came to the Herb of Grace. "You owe it to the Herb of Grace." It was true. She did. She withdrew herself gently and reached for her coat hanging on the peg beside the door.

"Very well," she said. "I'll do it."

Together they went out into the moonlight and down the steps to the yard. Each of them knew now that they were necessary to each other, and would be friends until the end of their lives.

– 3 –

Ben's dramatization of "The Wind in the Willows" continued to be no good at all. His designs for the costumes were admirable, and they were superbly made by himself, Nadine and John Adair, and he was full of bright ideas. But they were too bright. His cast—Tommy, Caroline and the twins—were incapable of carrying them out. Tommy and Caroline could learn their parts, but they were without dramatic ability. Jerry and José had plenty of dramatic ability—too much, in fact—but were of too tender years to commit their lines to memory. Or else they wouldn't. Patiently Ben repeated the short, simple sentences to them; but when asked to say them after him, they merely replied with the two words. "Hot Sausage." No one knew what they meant, but the fact had to be faced that they had decided to be not only unco-operative, but definitely obstructive. Ben finally, just two days before Christmas, fell a victim to despair, and David was called upon in his professional capacity to give advice. John Adair came with him, and stood leaning against the mantelpiece in the hall, chuckling into his beard, intrigued to see how the famous actor would deal with the situation, and finding him, as he expected, nervous.

"Scrap it," was David's advice to Ben. "Much too difficult, old boy. You've aimed too high. Cut your losses and start again. Why not turn the speechlessness of these darned twins to good use and have mime?"

The drooping spirits of Ben, Tommy and Caroline rose a little.

The twins, who were seals this morning, stopped slithering round and round the hall floor on their fronts and lay still to listen, with lazily flapping fins. David looked at them. Gently the fins rose and fell, now and then a tail waved, or a nose was lifted to sniff the air. They were lying in the ripples with the hot sun on their backs. For a queer flashing moment he saw the gleam of the water and felt the sun; it gave him quite a shock. Then he saw the light. No good trying to control genius with whip and rein. It must take its own way. He addressed them.

"Jerry and José!"

"Hot sausage," said Jerry.

"Hot sausage," said José.

"Stow that," he said sternly. "Life is real, life is earnest, especially in such a terrible crisis as has now arisen. If you don't want to do the nice play that Ben has written for you, what *do* you want to do?"

"Hot sausage," said Jerry.

"In the little house," said José.

"What little house?" asked David.

"In the Place Beyond," said Jerry. "The man gave them hot sausage."

"And bandaged them," said José.

Memory stirred in David.

"The Place Beyond. That's where you went that day in the autumn when Sally lost you and I drove you home in my car. It's in Knyghtwood, isn't it?"

"Yes," said Jerry. "But Beyond."

"Beyond what?" asked John Adair.

"Where the rest of you go."

"What was the man like?" demanded Ben.

"Big," said Jerry. His eyes went to John Adair and fastened on his beard. "A beaver. And he laughed. He had a dressing-gown on."

"How do you know it was hot sausage he gave them?" asked Tommy, always interested in food.

"It was good," said José. "They liked it."

"The term hot sausage is used symbolically?" suggested John Adair. "Another would perhaps have described the nourishment provided by this unknown personage as honey dew and the milk of Paradise. It's all a question of digestion. Coleridge's was weak, I believe. He would have turned nauseated from the thought of hot sausage.

It was the unsubstantiality of honey-dew (what is it, by the way?) that doubtless appealed to him. And milk of Paradise sounds pre-digested."

The children never listened very much to Old Beaver when he rambled on.

"Who were the blokes the man gave the sausage to?" asked Tommy.

"They weren't blokes," said Jerry.

"Animals?" asked Ben eagerly.

"Some of them," said José.

"And birds?" asked Caroline, with shining eyes.

"Yes," said Jerry.

"And he bandaged their hurt paws and mended their broken wings?" asked Ben.

"Yes."

"Was his beard brown, and had his dressing-gown a dark hood that he wore over his head?"

"Yes."

"Was he like the man in the picture I painted?"

"Yes."

Ben was almost panting with eagerness.

"The man who painted the Chapel walls and carved these posts and the little white deer in the alcove, and was Mine Host of the Herb of Grace? And you saw him out there in the wood?"

"Yes."

"Had he the white deer with him?"

"Yes. The Person with the Horns."

"They're saying yes like a parrot," said David. "You're getting them rattled."

"We never get them rattled." said Tommy, "It's they who get us rattled. They've made it all up, of course. They've got it from that yarn of Auntie Rose's."

"What yarn?" asked David.

"Oh, some yarn Auntie Rose's Fred's great-grannie told him when he was a boy. Ben will remember."

"A monk from the Abbey," said Ben, quickly and softly, "loved birds and beasts. He built a chapel in the woods and fed them there and looked after them when they were sick. That's a legend that must have been handed down for generations. Fred's great-grannie, perhaps, heard it from her great-grannie. Auntie Rose told it to us. If she hadn't, perhaps it would have been lost."

"Well, we'll see that it isn't," said David. "We'll drive it home. Did Auntie Rose's Fred, by any chance, identify our chap here with the monk of the woods?"

"Yes. He told Auntie Rose that only a chap who loved birds and beasts could have carved those pillars and the white deer. Fred must have got to know the man from living in the house, like we have. Fred was keen on the creatures, too. Auntie Rose said he never shot anything."

"You don't either," said Caroline. "Not like Tommy."

"The dynasty goes on," said John Adair. "And a man's sons are not always those of his own flesh."

"What had better go on," said David, "is the rehearsal." But for a moment his eyes met those of John Adair; he had lost his own father in his boyhood, but in these last few weeks the loss had been made good. "I can see the thing shaping. We'll have a stage shaped like an L, taking in the stairs and the drawing-room door as entrances, with the Christmas-tree at the angle of it. Write out the legend, Ben—in blank verse, if you like and then you can sit under the tree, as Badger, and read it. The stage will be Knyghtwood. The stairs will lead up to the Place Beyond, where the alcove is. Our monk will be there, with the white deer in the alcove behind him. The creatures will come in through the drawing-room door and go up the stairs, and he'll deal out hot sausage. The twins will show us how it should be done. Mr. Adair will be the monk."

"Not on your life," said John Adair.

And the twins agreed with him.

"His beard's all wrong!" they yelled in outrage.

"Thank heavens he's got a beard," said David, "and don't cavil as to its colour. Now we'll have to work like hell. Only two days. Where's Ben?"

Ben had already slipped away into the drawing-room to write out the legend in his best blank verse.

CHAPTER

19

– 1 –

THROUGH THE BLUE DUSK of a perfect Christmas Day the guests drove to the Herb of Grace. The gate had been left open for them, and the oak-trees seemed to bend over them in a friendly sort of way as they bumped their way along the lane. The headlights of their cars showed a few sparse flowers on the gorse-bushes—the English gorse that keeps a few golden blossoms all the winter through, even beneath a coverlet of snow. But there was no snow tonight, though it had turned frosty. The sky was cloudless, and the few stars that had appeared shone very brightly, giving promise of a blaze of glory to come. At the turn of the lane they heard the owl hooting in Knyghtwood, but the ghostly trees upon either side made no sound, for it was a windless night. The lanterns had been lit and placed upon the walls, and down at the bottom of the lane they could see the glint of them upon the water. Light streamed from the Herb of Grace, from every window and from the open front door, and the very jubilation of that light had something to say of the utter happiness of the day that had been spent within. To most of the occupants of the cars the world seemed a dark enough place, but at the sight of that light their heavy hearts lifted a little. There were still children in the world, and while there were children, men and women would not abandon the struggle to make safe homes to put them in, and while they so struggled there was hope.

As they went up the steps to the green gate, and along the garden path to the front door, those men and women were typified for them by George and Nadine, standing at the door to welcome them, with their children behind them. And within were Lucilla, Hilary, Margaret, John Adair, Sally and David—men and women whose worth was a good thing to feel about one on Christmas Day. But it was the children who mattered. It was the children who were the point of it all.

As they were divested of their wraps they exclaimed in delight at the appearance of the wide old hall, with the yule log blazing on the hearth and the holly-wreathed lights burning in their candle-sconces all round the walls. Their seats had been arranged diagonally across the hall to face the L-shaped stage, with its exits to stairs and drawing-room. At its angle stood the glorious Christmas-tree, bright with lighted candles. In the end, as it represented Knyghtwood, it had been decided to give it no decoration except the candles that burned in the wood at sunset. And it needed no other, for the candles shone so gloriously that looking at them the Eliots almost forgot the awful job they had had getting them all fixed upright. The stage was covered in green cloth and Knyghtwood holly, and holly concealed the footlights. The old carved posts to the left of the front door were lightly wreathed with ivy, and looked like trees growing.

George and John Adair and David handed round cocktails (Sally and the children having mysteriously disappeared), and as they made them last as long as possible, the guests became conscious of a delightful jovial glow of hospitable warmth wrapping them round; which most of them put down to the potency of the admirably mixed cocktails, though just a few noticed the formation of the stairs, and were reminded of a great dark figure with arms held out in welcome. They all noticed the alcove where the stairs branched, and the strange little carved figure within it, so cleverly lit by a concealed light, so that it shone like a lamp. They became increasingly aware of that shining image. They did not know what it was, but it drew and held them.

Until their attention was captured by a thread of music reaching out to them, pulling at them. Somewhere in the depths of the old house young voices were singing the Adeste Fideles.

"Will you come this way?" said Nadine, and she led them through the hall to the kitchen, garlanded with greenery, and up the turret stairs to the Chapel.

They had heard of the discovery of the frescoes, and they caught their breath in amazement. The candles had been lighted in the branched candlesticks on the altar, and the pots filled with holly and fir, and above them rose the strange figure of the great white deer with the crucifix in his antlers, dominating the Chapel as the little carved figure below dominated the hall. They sat on the benches and looked about them with delight at the trees and flowers, the birds and beasts, and the young knight riding through the wood, while behind them Sally and Annie-Laurie, Malony, Jill and the children, standing in a row one on each side of the door, finished the Adeste Fideles and embarked upon the First Nowell with a perfection of tone and rhythm which they had not dared to hope for during the preceding awful week. It was, as Annie-Laurie had prophesied, all right on the night, and the glorious conviction lent such wings to their voices that the tentative efforts of the guests were soon caught up and lifted into a volume of sound so satisfactory that Sally, followed by David, was able to leave them and slip away.

When she had gone, Annie-Laurie led the singing, her sweet, clear voice rising in carol after carol. They were all so absorbed, singing in that lovely glowing place, that only Malony looked at Annie-Laurie. And he could not take his eyes from her face as she stood there singing, sword-straight, her hands behind her back, her eyes quiet and happy. Just so, with that perfection of simplicity, had she sung in the old days. His heart pounded with joy. She was coming round, his girl. At last she was coming round. This place, this blessed place, had healed her. He could no longer sing, so much too large had his throat become for his too-tight collar. He loosened it impatiently with his forefinger and croaked like a raven. Annie-Laurie heard him and looked round, her eyes lighting up with tender amusement. It was a sweet look that she gave him, over the heads of the twins—the kind of look she had given him when Midge was a little thing. That good old bloke the Reverend Hilary had been right. He had said it would all come out in the wash (or words to that effect), and it had. His eyes holding Annie-Laurie's, he suddenly found his voice again, and bellowed of the holly and the ivy as loudly as any of them. That was the last carol. When it was over Annie-Laurie opened the door, and they went down-stairs to laugh and talk in the kitchen, and be told about the frescoes, and eat home-made fudge, until a bell rang and Nadine led them back into the hall.

– 2 –

What next, they wondered, settling into their seats while the lights round the walls were put out and the hidden footlights shone in their place. These Eliots were extraordinarily good at throwing a party. What next? There was a moment of thrilled expectation, and then the drawing-room door opened and Romeo in his silver-grey doublet and hose, a short orange cloak over one shoulder, the light gleaming on his silvery fair head, came through on to the stage. There was a gasp, and then silence. It was difficult to believe their good fortune. They were to see one of the most famous actors of their generation playing his most famous part, and they were not to pay a penny for the privilege. Just one whisper broke the silence. It came from an old gentleman in the front row.

"Fifteen shillings, at least, a seat in the stalls costs you nowadays," he whispered delightedly behind a horny hand to his daughter.

"Ssh!" said his daughter severely.

But he had expressed the feelings of them all.

"He jests at scars that never felt a wound.
But soft! what light through yonder window breaks?
It is the east and Juliet is the sun."

The familiar words floated out into the room like music. The incomparable beauty of the golden voice, the silvery figure, gripped their hearts. All David's family, with the exception of Lucilla, as always when they saw him on the stage suffered from sudden shock. Was this David, often so edgy, so difficult, often (though of course they loved him) such a sore trial to them? The perfect co-ordination of voice and movement, that complete absorption of the artist in his art that gave to it a depth that suggested stillness even while he spoke and moved, the grace and beauty so quietly and unself-consciously worn, the exciting sense of power held back—those marks of a great actor gave an illusion of perfection that lifted this figure above all human frailty. Impossible to reconcile this David with the other. Then, abruptly, they didn't try. This was Romeo, not David. The two had nothing to do with each other.

But Lucilla was the exception. She sat between Nadine and George in the back row to which the family had been relegated to keep the heat of the fire off the guests. Though she was unaware of it, she looked beautiful in her old but well-cut, full-skirted black velvet dress. Draughts were inimical to her, and because of them she had a black lace scarf draped over her white hair and round her shoulders. She sat very upright, her blue eyes fixed on the man on the stage, and her hands were folded quietly in her lap. She saw no discrepancy between David her grandson and David the actor, because for her the transformation of the one into the other was not a sudden thing, beginning with David and ending with Romeo, but a process that began much farther back than that and stretched much farther on; it began in her own being, and reached on through the beings of unborn children for she could not know how long. Her body had only partly helped to make the body of the man on the stage, but she knew that it was her spirit alone which had created his genius. David's father had been her very special child, spiritually the child of great love and sacrifice. Because of her anguish of self-denial, Maurice had been born. David's beauty was Maurice's, but his genius was the flowering of her anguish and the resurrection of her death. She knew now, at the end of her life, that that was always the way of it. "Except a grain of wheat fall into the ground and die…" The genius would flower again, perhaps, in one of his children or grandchildren, and in that child's child, and so it would go on; but it would have been lit from the same spark. She felt no pride, only a humble thankfulness that she had died that death. There was no discrepancy anywhere. It was natural that the lamp should be a frail earthen thing in comparison to the light within, for it had not created it, and only held it for a short moment…. As the alcove up there held the shining figure of the white deer, as this house held a spirit of whose strength she was deeply aware this Christmas night, and to whom she offered salutation.

"Romeo… take all myself."

With a sigh Lucilla relaxed and looked up to the balcony from which the warm, deep voice floated. Sally was doing well, dear child; but she was not hoodwinking her audience into forgetfulness of her personality. She was not Juliet, but merely Sally Adair playing Juliet to the best of her ability in the circumstances. But she looked very lovely. A piece of scarlet brocade stretched across the stairs was her balcony, the illumined alcove was her window. Her peacock-blue gown made a wonderful splash of colour, and the light behind her set her hair on fire. David had taught her to speak her part very prettily, and Lucilla could feel that all shrinking and fear had left her once she was well launched, leaving her utterly glad to be his foil.

"For stony limits cannot hold love out,
And what love can do that dares love attempt."

Is it well with the child? That eternal question that goes with the begetter of life through every moment of every day and every night was very alive in Lucilla this evening. All was well with her grandchildren, David and Sally. She thanked God for it, and remembered the son and daughter upon either side of her. She put out her hand impulsively and took George's. He turned and smiled at her, and she saw the new happiness in his eyes. All that he had to give he had given Nadine long ago, all that love could do to make her happy he had done. Had she let him in at last? For the first time since Romeo had stepped on the stage to make love to the young Juliet, she dared to look at the woman beside her. On and off through the evening she had been haunted by those earlier words of Romeo that had not been spoken tonight.

"Did my heart love till now? Foreswear it, sight!
For I ne'er saw true beauty till this night."

Nadine met her look with a steady, smiling glance. Her face looked worn in the light of the fire, but peaceful as Lucilla had never seen it, and Lucilla knew that on this Christmas Day she had, at long last, let George in. With these, too, also, all was well at last.

Hilary was beyond Nadine; he was a happy man. And Margaret on the other side of George looked tired but happy; and when they were settled in Lavender Cottage, Lucilla hoped she wouldn't even look tired. And her five young grandchildren, George's children— she looked about for them, but could not see them: bless them, they must be getting ready for some little entertainment of their own— they were all right. She had never been so happy about her dear Ben as she was now. He had grown steadily stronger this winter, and he had lost that nervous hesitancy that had so troubled her. He had a new confidence, a new certainty, which she believed he owed to that good man (where was he, by the way?), John Adair, her Sally's father. Sally! She was a little afraid to examine too particularly the elements of her quite extraordinary love for Sally. She loved her for herself, of course, but there was also in her love an element of quite selfish gratitude. Damerosehay, her beloved home, and David her dearest and her best, had nevertheless become a bit too much for her just lately. She was glad now to keep just her deep love for them, but to transfer the responsibility to Sally. She was equal to it. Her voice came floating down to Lucilla, assuring her of that.

> "And yet I wish but for the thing I have:
> My bounty is as boundless as the sea,
> My love as deep; the more I give to thee
> The more I have, for both are infinite."

Lucilla shut her eyes in unspeakable thankfulness. It seemed to her that she hardly had a thing left to wish for. The lovely rhythm of voice answering voice flowed on like music, but the words singing in her mind came from another play of her beloved Shakespeare. "If it were now to die, 'twere now to be most happy; for my soul hath her content so absolute—"

It was nearly over. The girl's voice, and the man's answering, for the last time.

> "Good-night, good-night! Parting is such sweet sorrow
> That I shall say good-night till it be morrow....
>
> "Sleep dwell upon thine eyes, peace in thy breast!
> Would I were sleep and peace, so sweet to rest!"

— 3 —

Ben had opened the drawing-room door noiselessly from within, and Romeo had stepped into the wedge of darkness. Juliet had gone away up the stairs, and the balcony was empty. There was a moment's sense of almost intolerable loss, and then the lights were lit and everyone was laughing and talking, and congratulating Lucilla upon the brilliance of her family, and the home-made fudge was going round again.

"Are you getting tired, Mother?" Nadine asked Lucilla.

"Only nicely tired," said Lucilla. "I doubt if I've ever felt so happy in all my life." She reached out a hand and laid it on her daughter-in-law's knee. "Nadine, my darling, you have done everything I wanted you to do, and you are my very dear child."

"I'm glad you're pleased with me, Mother," said Nadine, meekly, but with a flash of slightly sarcastic humour.

George, concerned that Lucilla should be even nicely tired, was shoving an exceedingly hard velvet cushion down her back.

"It's the children's show now," he said, "and then it's the turn of the domestic staff, and then I think that's the lot."

"Mother!" cried Margaret in distress, "you haven't got your foot-stool, and the draught under the front door is wicked. Hilary! Did you leave Mother's footstool in the car?"

"Don't *fuss*, dear," implored Lucilla. "Stay where you are Hilary. The lights are being put out again."

They went out, and Nadine adroitly removed the hard velvet cushion from behind Lucilla's back and slipped it beneath her feet.

"My very dear child," repeated Lucilla.

The drawing-room door opened again, and a slim young stripling in striped tights and a striped cloak came through wearing a realistic badger's mask that hid his face. But his grace and lightness of movement, like David's, but without the assurance of David's training, proclaimed him Ben, even before he lifted the badger's snout back over his head like a hood and showed his brown face. He had his Pan-pipe in one hand, and a long white scroll in the other, and he bowed to them very courteously before he sat down at the foot of the Christmas-tree and began to read from his long scroll. Lucilla's heart swelled with pride. There was not a trace of nervousness about him, and his voice was clear and perfectly modulated as he began to read the Knyghtwood legend in simple lovely verse that she knew he had written himself. She glanced at her son and daughter-in-law. They had, she considered, never fully appreciated their first-born, never fully realized his quality, that was perhaps the flowering of his mother's first and only willing yielding to her husband's love. She noticed with satisfaction that Nadine's head was almost arrogantly lifted and there was a faint tender smile on her lips. That's all right, thought Lucilla; as the years go on she'll take in him the same sort of delight that once she took in David. George's mouth had fallen open, and he was passing one hand in a bewildered sort of way over his thick grey hair. (How much better he was looking, by the way. Upon him, as well as Ben, the Herb of Grace had seemed to work a miracle of healing.) It's jolted him, dear old boy, thought Lucilla; do him good. Hilary, she noted, was smiling at her with an echo of her own delight. He had taught Ben, once, and had always been aware of his quality.

Ben's story began with the founding of the great Abbey beyond the river by King John as an act of reparation for his sins, and told how for forty-five years the monks laboured at its building, until at last the glorious place was finished and they could take up their work of prayer and labour, carried on until Henry VIII of detested memory drove them away. But before that evil day came there lived at the monastery a lay-brother, a fine artist and craftsman, a man of jovial disposition, bountiful and warm-hearted and overflowing with good-will to all God's creatures. As was only fitting for a man of such gifts, he was appointed by the Father Abbot as host of the Pilgrim Inn, Maison Dieu, where pilgrims visiting the Abbey were lodged and entertained; this same inn where they were gathered now. A great host was this Brother, with a huge welcome for all who came, and safely and warmly did he lodge them here, and tender was his care of them. The fare was frugal, perhaps, for such was the Brother's love for all living things that he would permit no snaring of the wild creatures to satisfy the greed of man; but there would be bread in plenty, made from the corn that the monks grew in their wide fields, and wine from their vineyards, and milk and butter and cream from the dairies. The pallets would be hard, and the furniture of the simplest; but in cold weather there would be a roaring fire on the hearth of the great hall, and their eyes would feast upon beauty wherever they looked, for the frescoes and carvings of their artist-host were lovelier than any tapestries and silken hangings. And great was this man also in wisdom and counsel, and skilled in the care of sick bodies as well as sick minds and souls and those who became members of his flock for only a short while under this roof would not forget him while they lived. But it was not enough for this Brother that he should spend himself upon human creatures only. The animals and birds also were God's sons, and for them also he built a Maison Dieu within the woods. Here in the cold winters he would feed them—the deer and the rabbits, the badgers, the foxes and the birds. Such was his power over them that they were always at peace with each other within the sanctuary that he had made for them, and they were so tame that when they had hurt themselves they would come to him that he might tend their injuries. There was one animal in particular who was his special friend—a great white deer who was always with him in the woods, and was of such incomparable beauty that there were those who thought him not quite a creature of this earth. Of the death of this man there was no record, nor of the death of the deer. The body of the one, perhaps, lay within the Abbey garth, and the body of the other, if he was really a creature of this earth, within the woods. But their spirits lived on. Still, in this house, was welcome and safety and healing for mind and body. Still, in the woods, the creatures found sanctuary. Still, both here and there, came sometimes a half-seen vision of great beauty to gladden the mind of a man and the heart of a child.

No one quite knew at what point in the earlier part of Ben's narrative they became aware of the figure who stood at the branching of the stairs, a bearded burly figure clothed in the rough habit of a Cistercian monk. His arms were held wide in welcome, and his hooded head was thrown into relief by the illumined figure of the white deer in the alcove behind him. First one and then another saw him, and when their awed attention had been entirely captured, Ben paused for a moment in his reading, glanced at the front door, which mysteriously opened at this point, and then with his eyes followed the progress of unseen pilgrims across the hall and up the stairs to their host. It was so cleverly done that those pilgrims were as real to the audience as though they had been actors of flesh and blood. They could hear their footfall and their voices, and see how their feet trod eagerly the worn, bent bow of each stair. The door softly closed, and Ben began reading again of how the animals, too, had had their sanctuary, and the drawing-room door opened and two little animals ran through—a water-rat and a mole, soft and furry, with brown bright eyes peeping through the masks that covered their faces. They ran upon all fours, but Mole held up his left hind foot because he had hurt it, and Rat kept stopping and holding a paw pathetically to one eye, which seemed to have something in it. They ran up the stairs to the Brother, and he held out his arms to them, and bound up Mole's paw and removed the obstruction from Rat's eye. A magnificent but extremely wicked-looking fox was the next animal, whom one gathered from his size to be Tommy. Half-way across the stage he paused and groaned, holding a stomach obviously a good deal too full of stolen goose. Everyone was laughing now, and their amusement was echoed by the big man above. His laughter rolled down to meet poor Fox, who hung his head comically, and then lolloped up the stairs to lap a healing dose from a big brown bowl. He was followed by a sweet-faced rabbit with a torn ear, who must be Caroline, fol-

lowed by Mary and the cat Smith. They were attached to the person
of the rabbit by green ribbons, as a precautionary measure but the
spirit of the thing seemed to have entered into them, for it was they
who pulled Rabbit, not Rabbit them, up the stairs to the Brother.
Their entrance was the sign for Ben to finish his narrative, pick up
his pipe, play a sweet air, and begin to sing the song that Annie-
Laurie had written for the occasion, the other animals joining in
with their clear, high voices, to the rumbling accompaniment of the
Brother's deep bass.

"Sing hey for the moon and the starry sky,
 The river, the wood and the sea,
For the fish and birds and animals all,
 And the grass so green on the lea.
But most of all for the fair Christmas rose
 And the lights on the candied tree.

"Sing hey for the chimney and roof-tree wide,
 Sing hey for the walls and the floor,
For the warmth of fire on the glowing hearth
 And the welcoming open door.
But most of all for the peace and goodwill
 And the joy at our deep heart's core.

"Sing hey for the men, the hosts of this house,
 Sing hey for the first and the last.
Sing hey for the guests who have gathered here,
 Both tonight and in pages past.
And sing hey for the love between host and guest
 That will hold them for ever fast.

"Sing hey for the God who fashioned for us
 This bountiful splendour of earth,
Sing hey for courage and wisdom and love,
 For beauty and healing and mirth.
But most for the Child Who on Christmas Day
 Took upon Him our human birth."

During the last verse a chiming of bells was heard, and the children came trooping down the stairs, singing the first verse again.
When they reached the stage they divided, and a fairy-like figure in
silver and green floated out from among them. It was Annie-Laurie

in a wide ballet dress of frosted fir-dark green. Her bells were round
her waist, and she had a wreath of Christmas roses on her hair. Malony as Father Christmas came through the drawing-room door at
the same moment, while David unseen in the drawing-room played
the air of their dance upon the piano, and the children, gathered
round the real Christmas-tree, hummed it very softly. The genius of
Annie-Laurie was, as David had said, unforgettable. The comic antics
of Father Christmas, the children in the animal costumes, the bril-
liantly lighted tree, made a bizarre background against which her
delicate loveliness drifted like thistledown against the bright colours
of a summer day. And it was the thistledown that captured the attention and held it as though with a spell. Hilary, watching her with an
intensity that missed nothing, thought that most touchingly in her
dancing did Annie-Laurie express her own personality; her essential
childlikeness, her truth and tenderness, even her fear. She was like a
child in her unself-consciousness and absolute absorption in what
she was doing, and her simple movements had a clean perfection
that was like light. The softly chiming little bells, the half-smile on
her lips, the arms held out now and then in welcome to the Christmas-tree, peopled the shadows with unseen children. And now and
then she would pirouette lightly to one side, as though a puff of
rough wind had caught the thistledown and scared it; and then she
would hold out her hand to Father Christmas, and he would swing
her back to the centre of the stage again. Like a flame aspiring, David
had said. Hilary thought it a perfect simile. She was like one of the
flames on the tree behind her, as light and delicate, as fragile, and
with the same power of lifting one for the moment out of the mud.
Hilary always found it impossible to look at a candle-flame and
remain gloomy. The shape of it, like tapering hands held palm to
palm in faithful prayer, the wavering yet hopeful fight against the
darkness, its tiny, loving glow of warmth. It was no wonder that
Mother Church, all down the ages, had had such a passion for lighting candles. Go on, Annie-Laurie! he cried out to her wordlessly.
Don't stop! Don't stop! But she had stopped. With a final tinkling of
fairy bells the thistledown had drifted down to rest. And—now she
was holding out her hands to the invisible fire and singing the bell
song, the children accompanying her very softly. Then, singing still
more softly, they trooped noiselessly away, led by Father Christmas,
and only Annie-Laurie was left, singing the last verse alone, with the

Brother still up there on the stairs. To the music of her own bells she drifted once more round the stage and then up the stairs towards him, and bending towards her he gathered her in as though she were the spirit of all delight. Then the lamp that illumined the alcove went out, and only the Christmas-tree was still shining.

– 4 –

The stand-up supper in the kitchen that now followed was uproarious, by reason of relaxed tension.... For Annie-Laurie's genius had swung them rather high, and they returned to earth with a bang.... Also the supper—the result of a genius in Nadine and Auntie Rose no less of its kind, and the vigorous rakings of Auntie Rose beneath the counter of her nephew the grocer—was almost pre-war. The guests ate and drank, waited upon by the actors, still in their costumes, until some lingering sense of decency bade them forbear, and even then they were reluctant to go home. Not for years, they said, had they been to such a splendid party; and some of them added softly, and with perfect truth, that not for years had they felt so welcomed, so happy and so hopeful; or so safe. It was not only the family, it was the house. There was something about the house....

But they had to go home. Pilgrimages, these days, were unfortunately not the leisured affairs they had been in the old days; they were over tragically soon. One by one they said their reluctant good-byes, went out into the night and drove away slowly, looking back at the lights still streaming from door and windows.

The family and household were left to sit for a little round the fire, devouring the food and drink that was left, and congratulating themselves upon the glorious success of their evening.

"It was worth it," said Nadine, sitting with Mary on her lap, exhausted yet happy. "I'm glad we did it, George."

And she yawned and leaned shamelessly against him, one of her hands in his, the other resting on Ben's shoulder, where he sat on the floor leaning against her knees.

"Taking it by and large, I'm glad we came to the Herb of Grace," said Tommy thickly, through the very last sausage roll, that he was sharing with the cat Smith.

"Everything," murmured Caroline, divested now of her rabbit's mask and curled up sleepily against George's other shoulder, "has turned out just perfect."

"Yes, darling, it has," said Lucilla, her hand in Sally's. "And I'll take a glass of sherry before I go home."

"Mother!" expostulated Margaret, propped against Hilary. "That's your second tonight. You'll have indigestion."

"Since when has sherry given me indigestion?" demanded Lucilla indignantly. "Don't fuss, darling. Up to the top, David."

There was now exactly half an inch of sherry left in the decanter, and David bestowed it upon Annie-Laurie, where she and Malony sat together on the settle by the fire, his hand in hers, Jill and Auntie Rose on the other settle, each with a twin asleep in her arms. It was a queer thing, but an extraordinary lack of reserve seemed to have fallen upon them all. Looking round, he perceived that he, Tommy and the cat Smith, were the only ones who weren't propped against somebody, or holding somebody's hand; Tommy and Smith because of their absorption in food, and he because both sides of Sally had already been appropriated by her father and Lucilla. He sat down on the other side of Annie-Laurie and took her hand gently.

"What about it?" he murmured. "Didn't it come back?"

She looked at him enquiringly.

"The love of it," said David softly. "It came back to me. A little while ago I felt I never wanted to be behind the footlights again. Tonight I knew it was the only place where I ever really do want to be; apart from in my home with Sally. We belong there, you and I and Malony." He still held her hand, and the firm clasp of it, like the clasp of Sally's arms the other day, told her what a steady strength the friendship of these two would be if she liked to trust to it in the days to come. Beyond her David could feel Malony's passionate encouragement. "Shall we go back, the three of us?"

"Yes," said Annie-Laurie.

Malony let out a deep sigh of relief and helped himself to the last mincepie.

The clock struck a very late hour.

"Those children should be in bed," said Lucilla, regarding the twins. "And so should I. I've finished my sherry. My dears, this has been a very perfect Christmas Day. A sort of heavenly day. A gift to us, I think. Whatever happens to us all we'll never forget it. Hilary, dear, where did you put my coat? Sally, darling, you're coming back for the night, aren't you? Nadine, my dear, good night. This is a wonderful home, this Herb of Grace, and to be the mistress of it will be the crown and glory of your life, I shouldn't wonder. Good night, George, my dear boy. It's very sweet of you, Margaret dear, to be winding me up in this nice scarf, but it's not mine. Good night, my darling Ben. Good night, Tommy. Good night, Caroline. Jill, what a blessing you are! And you too, Auntie Rose. Annie-Laurie, I'm glad I've lived to see you dance.... Good night.... Good night...."

She talked on at random as the Damerosehay party got under way, trying to ease for them all the hard parting from this perfect day.... Good night, good night, parting is such sweet sorrow.... She kissed the flushed, happy faces of her younger grandchildren, and went out into the night with the two elder ones, David and Sally, one on each side of her to help her down the steps. Sighing with thankfulness, she was tucked up in the back of David's car, with her faithful Hilary and Margaret one on each side of her, and David and Sally in front, where she could gloat upon the sight of them there.

Yet as they drove away under the Christmas stars it was of the two old houses that she was thinking, Damerosehay and the Herb of Grace. Their village helper and her daughter were spending the evening at Damerosehay, to look after Pooh-Bah and the Bastard. When they got home they would find the drawing-room fire burning brightly and the lamps lit with the two old dogs dozing on the hearth. The house would welcome them and gather them in, and when they had talked a little in front of the fire they would go to bed, and, the spell of this happy day still upon them, sleep deeply and happily, wrapped in its peace. And in the Herb of Grace, too, the lights would go out one by one in the windows, and the sleepers would be at rest. But the houses would not sleep. Lucilla fancied that they would greet each other across the quiet fields and through the night. Each had its long and living history, sap rising in the wood of the old tree to nourish the new branches. And tomorrow would be a new day, and a hard one. But the sap rose from inexhaustible depths, and the spring would come again.

Also By Elizabeth Goudge

The Bird in the Tree
*Book 1 * The Eliot Heritage*

In her fierce devotion to the Eliot clan, Lucilla Eliot had worked to make Damerosehay, her home on the Hampshire coast, a beautiful refuge, capable of withstanding any threat to family happiness. Now her lifetimes's labor was about to be destroyed by her favorite grandson, David, in love with the estranged wife of another man. Would he sacrifice his love to preserve his family's integrity? **$10.99**

The Heart of the Family
*Book 3 * The Eliot Heritage*

Here is the culmination of the story of the remarkable Eliot family, spanning four generations: Lucilla, David, Sally, Nadine, George, Ben and Meg. Their lives are intricately woven together in a tale of startling beauty and immense depth. **$10.99**

The Dean's Watch

An English town in the mid-nineteenth century forms the background for the warm and gentle story of Isaac Peabody, an obscure clockmaker, and of Adam Ayscough, the brilliant dean of the cathedral. The strange, healing force of unselfish love is revealed with its power to alter and redeem the lives of all whom it touches. **$10.99**